STRICTLY BUSINESS

Star waited until the video and still photographers were finished, and all the evidence had been tagged. The heat of the morning had released the smell of death. She put a Vicks Inhaler to her nose and breathed deeply, pulled on her latex gloves, and opened the passenger door of the Mercedes. She crawled in on one knee, avoiding a dried puddle of blood near the corpse's head.

Then she backed out of the car. "Morning, Mitchell. This one's pretty bad," Star said, pointing to the woman's raised and spread legs. "I think she's been raped."

"Women's intuition?" Mitch asked.

"No, her underwear's missing. This was a profiling sister. She obviously had the bucks and the job. You don't go to work carrying a snakeskin bag, wearing Maud Frizon shoes with no panties or stockings. He took them with him—the warped son of a bitch."

DO NOT GO
Gently

JUDITH SMITH-LEVIN

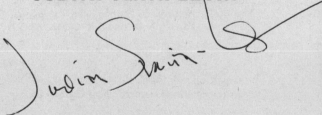

HarperPaperbacks
A Division of HarperCollinsPublishers

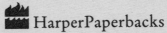 HarperPaperbacks
A Division of HarperCollins*Publishers*
10 East 53rd Street, New York, N.Y. 10022-5299

This is a work of fiction. The characters, incidents, and dialogues
are products of the author's imagination and are not to be
construed as real. Any resemblance to actual events or persons,
living or dead, is entirely coincidental.

ISBN: 0-06-101109-6

HarperCollins®, ®, and HarperPaperbacks™
are trademarks of HarperCollins*Publishers* Inc.

Cover illustration: Cathy Saksa

First printing: October 1996

Printed in the United States of America

Visit HarperPaperbacks on the World Wide Web at
http://www.harpercollins.com/paperbacks

❖ 10 9 8 7 6 5 4 3 2 1

When I was twelve years old,
I told her I wanted to be a writer.
She advised me to learn to type.
In loving memory of my mother,
Jessie Mae Smith

ACKNOWLEDGMENTS

The road to the printed page was a long and hard one. There were so many on this journey who provided encouragement, laughter, and lots of love. Starting when he was five years old, my son Jason and I crisscrossed the country on our quest for a good life. And so, I want to thank all of those who gave so much along the way.

From the beginning, they encouraged my teenage prose, and provided this only child with sisters that are closer than blood, because we chose each other.

Darlene Spencer-Peterson, Warrine Martin Pace-Tidwell, and Gloria Noble-Carter.

Thirty-six years a family and counting.

The Kids: Ian Spencer, Rashaan Peterson, Shavon Carter, and Sherman V. and Bontesha (Bonnie) Tidwell.

Toni Lopopolo, (aka "Sweetie-Darling") my agent and friend, who pulled me through the "I can't do this." And who knows as many lines from classic movies as I do.

Maureen O'Neal, my first editor at HarperPaperbacks, who also became my friend.

Carolyn Marino, my current editor, whose patience, style, and skill are much appreciated.

Patricia Currie Gatti, goddess of the computer-challenged, and the fastest fax retriever in the east.

CHICAGO, ILLINOIS

My aunts, Dolores Rivers, Eva Thornton-Edwards, and Elizabeth Bassett.

My favorite cousin, Dolores Rivers.

My first mentor and editor, Alberta Myers.

Also, Barbara Ruth Davis, entrepreneur, self-made businesswoman, my friend for nearly thirty years, and the best teller of jokes I know.

And Dick Biondi - Yesterday, today, and forever.

WORCESTER, MASSACHUSETTS

Charna and Howard Lewis, Charles S. Blinderman, Ph.D., Phyllis and Anthony Hodgekinson, James Wallace, Esq., James Barnhill, Esq., and Glenna Del Signore.

WORCESTER POLICE DEPARTMENT

Richard Daly, my first C.O., who provided me with never-ending support, humor, and the wellspring of his knowledge and experience.

Sam Bracey and Earl Brown. From the Academy to the street, we circled the wagons around one another, and Loman Rutherford, fellow pioneer, who saved my life.

James Sullivan, and Harold Skarin, who were responsible for my becoming the first female police officer in the city's history.

Partners and friends, Steve Del Rosso, Gerry Perna, Tommy Corsac, Tommy Belezarian, Eddie Gardella, Bobby Lombardi, Ronnie Almstrom, and James Paradis.

Carol Chaput, whose matron's office sometimes provided pause from the madness on the street, and laughter to cope with it all.

LOS ANGELES, CALIFORNIA

Etta Vee and Gip Traylor, Tom Costa, Charles Cochran, Retha Watts, Dorothy Allen, Dorcas Shaktman, and Marillyn Holmes, whose generosity of spirit, brought a dream into reality.

TWENTIETH CENTURY FOX FILM CORPORATION

Erma Hunter, Linda Doty, Stan Hayes, Reve Mason, Randall Barton, Dolores Arabella Chavers, Chip Oliver, Mark and "Shugee" Willis, Kelly and Norma Miller, Diane Wickes, Ted Hollis, and The Cardellio family—Mark, Joe, and Emily.

Rosemary Chiaverini, who opened the door to M*A*S*H* and the 4077th.

Denise O'Donnell, my ace partner in crime.

Maryann Johnson, my suitcase-totin', plane-hoppin', cake-bakin' sisterfriend.

Willette Klausner, from Universal Pictures, who saw the promise early on and nurtured it.

Alan Alda, for his graciousness, encouragement, and support.

CARMEL, AND THE MONTEREY CALIFORNIA PENINSULA

Bill and Alice Kling, Maxine Jennings, Helen East, Glenda Finn, Edgar and Harriet Daniels, Edward and Linda Crankshaw, Dot Harris, John Thompson, Art and Jean Lewis, Hunter Finnell, George and Judy Baird, Sandra Humes, John and Chris Nunemaker, Marly Davis, Diana Hardy, Francine Mandeville, Russell and Bree Tripp, Geza and Cynthia, Patty Stephenson, The Hon. Don Jordan, Mayor of Seaside, Narayan Thadani, Mary McRory, Barbara Carballo, Barbara Cooney, Nancy Bertossa, Gina Aiken, Jackie Mathis-Craghead, Fred Harris, Nadine Rosillo, Jackie Morganfield, Linda Deutch, Michael Stamp, Esq., Sharon Patterson, Burt Valdes, David Henderson, Marcellus Moore, Mebby Van Ostran, Carol Minot, Sherry Whigham, Nadine Rosillo, and Willie Campbell.

Seaside City Hall: Wanda, Joyce, Janet, Rick, Cecil, Romeo and Mary.

The Seaside Library: Susan, Pat, LaVerne, Teddy, and Michael.

The Literacy Volunteers: Karen, Betty, and Donna.

The Sun Street Ladies: Kathy, Terry, and Betty.

The Carmel Library: Marcia and Dee.

The "Two Bobs," Carmel's premiere mystery writers: Robert Irvine, and Edgar Award Winner Robert Campbell. Thanks guys for the book signings and the support.

Chuck - Charles Richardson, "The Chief." Here's your 50 percent, along with 100 percent of my love.

Tony Gambale - For laughter, lessons, and lifetimes, shared.

Katy Curry, and Rosine Culcasi, for the food and the fun.

Angie Frausto-Parrish, for the use of the pool, and lots of laughs.

Patricia Emery-Del Vecchio, veteran of "casa cruising," marathon laundry weekends, Pat Riley sightings, and long drive rock and roll sing-a-longs.

Bill Bates—Frick and Frack. There aren't enough ways to say thank you. I am forever grateful.

Dr. John Hain, Forensic Pathologist, Monterey County. For the many long and gruesome conversations, complete with photos.

Mother Francisca, of the Carmelite Monastery. For her prayers and for always knowing when I need to hear the truth.

Lois Carwin, for sharing her mother's homemade pickles, an unbelievably great recipe for escalloped grits, and my passion for *The X-Files*.

The Women Warriors: Kaye Baker, Elaine Cass, Esq., and especially, Arlene Soto, for going the distance and staying strong. We stood on the front line together, suffered the greatest loss, and still we won the war.

Linda Harris, for the shared love of cats, and the many tapings. My Carmel sisterfriend, Sharon Johnson, for the "blessing" on each submission.

Arleen Crosby, for making me and mine, feel like family. Your "White Christmas" is surely coming.

Wild Willie, Cleanhead, aka Iggy, thanks for the "sammaches."

"D+" Daniels, for the countless readings and ratings.

"Mr. Ed." for the moves, the favors, and especially the faith.

Fay Lim-Baker, my Seaside to Seattle bud, who makes tripsto the airport, and gets me to hop the ferry for mega-eating and mini-shopping.

THE RYAN RANCH CREW

Mary Waldorf, Melinda Manlin, Sandra Castro, Neli Moody, Anne Cathey, Howard Kutcher, Virida Harbridge-

Sarmento, Don Johnson, Martha Laurence, Linda Ferrari, Robin Upton, Glenda Ransom, Ahlan Roberson, Ashley Streetman, Linda Lin, Cindy Schwartz, Paul Calcatera, John Pollock, Sandy Sandstrum, Marliese Aiken, and Chase Weaver.

And finally, my extraordinary son, Jason William Levin, who learned at an early age to make melted cheese sandwiches in a toaster oven and to play quietly, because mom was writing. My little curly-haired boy has grown into an exceptional man. A talented, accomplished and gifted musician, who is beautiful, inside and out. He makes me proud to be his mother, and his friend.

And AnnaLisa Boyd-Levin, who had the good sense to marry him and become my daughter in every sense of the word.

TYGFMBTNLAEIPA

Judith Smith-Levin
Bainbridge Island, Washington

AUTHOR'S NOTE

The city of Brookport and the county of Mercer, Massachusetts, exist solely in imagination.

The residents of the city, its locations, and events are all fictitious.

The depiction of police procedures are based on fact. Any resemblance to persons living or dead is purely coincidental.

JSL

PROLOGUE

The first shot entered her left cheek and exited just below the right side of her chin. It felt as if she'd been stung by a bee. Her head turned slightly to the right and she put her hand to her face. At that moment, her tongue and teeth exploded, filling her mouth with blood.

The second shot entered her left hand, shattering the bones. The bullet traveled straight through to the right side of her cheek and rocketed out, taking with it an inch and a half of flesh, which disintegrated as the steel burrowed itself two inches into the oak tree she'd climbed as a child.

Her ankles caved in toward one another. She was buckling.

Her eyes were watering. Was she crying?

In her right hand she held a plate filled with Nadine Johnson's barbecued chicken and knockout potato salad.

She'd taken a breast and a thigh. That was just for starters.

She planned on being greedy. She loved Nadine Johnson's chicken. She had been raised on it. "Miss Nadine" had been her mama's best friend, and when her mother died, Nadine had become a second mother to her. She grew up savoring that flavor.

Nadine had called her the night before last to tell her that she was giving an engagement party for her and Darnell. She asked Nadine to please make her chicken. The older woman laughed and said she was going to make enough chicken to feed a small country. And that's exactly what she did. When they arrived, the smell of that chicken reached into the open car window and grabbed her. She told Darnell she could smell Nadine's special sauce a block before they reached the house.

The sight of the smoke rising from the grill and the mounds of spicy chicken resting on the big white platters on Nadine's picnic table had made her heart glad. All that work for her, and now she was spoiling it, falling like this.

She knew she looked drunk, but she hadn't even had a beer, even though it was such a hot day. She'd only had a couple of big glasses of lemonade. Her body sagged toward the lawn. She stretched her arm out farther, trying to keep Nadine's voodoo sauce off her new white dress.

This couldn't be happening. She tried to raise her head, but couldn't. Out of the corner of her blurring eyes she saw Darnell running toward her.

Poor baby, she thought. Was he screaming?

She couldn't hear him. There was a terrible rushing sound in her ears. He looked so upset. She didn't mean to embarrass him, she was falling as gracefully as she could.

She didn't know that her body was spinning, drilling down toward the ground like an out-of-control child's toy. She tried to look down, to see how far she was falling, to gauge how hard she would land. Her eyes traveled downward, one at a time. She couldn't control them.

As she spiraled, her back spun into the shooter's gun sight.

The third shot sliced through the base of her skull, severing her spinal cord and racing up, tunneling through her brain, shattering bone and exiting from the top of her head.

A geyser of blood, bone, and brain tissue sprayed across the top of her dress and out behind her onto the garage and the lawn.

She hit the ground, hard. The plate of food went flying.

What's happening? She tried to speak, but the words drowned in the blood in her mouth.

Her shattered head filled with the smell of cake baking.

She heard her mother calling. It was her birthday, and she was five years old. Her mother was baking chocolate cake, her favorite. She was a big girl now, and she must be very careful so she wouldn't get any chocolate on her new snow-white dress. Mama had made it especially for her.

Darnell was on his knees, leaning over her. He was screaming, crying, calling her name again and again. She wished she could say something, tell him she was all right, but her face didn't seem connected. She knew she was moving her mouth, but she couldn't feel it.

Through the pounding in her chest and the roaring in her ears, her hearing returned. Voices screamed. Above the din she heard Nadine's deep whiskey contralto wailing, shouting, calling on Jesus. Somebody was sick. She heard retching. She wished she could help, but she was tired, so very tired.

Suddenly, she felt cold, her arms and legs freezing. Hands touched her, and where they lay, she momentarily felt warmth, but it was fading. Her body was shaking, trembling from the cold. All she wanted to do was to close her eyes and rest.

If she could just sleep for a little while, everything would be all right.

1

There were two things Homicide Detective Lieutenant Starletta Duvall could count on. One, on the hottest day of the year, the air-conditioning in the station house would break down, and maintenance would drag out one of its antique fans. And two, Detective Leo Darcy would wear his Hawaiian shirt.

Darcy and his wife Thelma had taken a trip to Honolulu about three years ago, and Leo had searched the islands until he found the most repulsive shirt ever to grace a tourist-trap store. This shirt would have made Tom Selleck look like a goon.

It was bright orange, with something that looked like fish eyes floating in glue emblazoned all over it. On any patch that was orb-free, there was a grotesque tree or a weird-looking fruit of some kind. Darcy had unerring intuition as to when he should wear it. Always on a day when a crayon would melt in your hand, Darcy wore his shirt. Today he'd paired it with icky green pants that hung just below his belly and bunched around his once-white canvas moccasins.

Leo Darcy weighed about two hundred pounds and stood, maybe on a good day, five-foot-seven. He had planted himself in the center of the squad room, reading a computer printout while stuffing purple squares of bubble gum into his mouth.

Star ran her hand over her damp forehead and down the back of her neck. She swiveled lazily in her chair, watching Leo chew with his mouth open. All she wanted was for the day to be over. It had been a fairly quiet one. The worst case had been a stabbing, two winos fighting over a fan in a flophouse. She gave the call to Gambale and Mason. For once, she was doing what a lieutenant was supposed to do. Supervising. She looked at the clock. A couple of hours more and she was home free.

She closed her eyes, picturing herself in the shower, almost feeling the cool water beating down on her. Some Jr. Walker on the box, a little "Shotgun" and some "Roadrunner" and she would be good as new. God bless Motown! She was thinking about dragging her best friend, Vee, down to the Cadillac Grille, the newest dance club in town.

She looked at her watch. Vee should still be at her desk. She picked up the phone and dialed.

"Good afternoon, Michaels, Soto and Associates."

"And just who are you associating with?"

"Hey, girl," Vee said.

"Hey, what's doin' for you after work?"

"Nothing much."

Star could hear the faint clicking of computer keys. She pictured Vee cradling the phone to her ear. She leaned back in her chair.

"Let's go dancing, at the Caddy."

Vee's laughter poured from the phone. "The Cadillac Grille? Did somebody hit you in the head? You must be delirious."

"C'mon, you know it's fun."

"Fun!" Star could see Vee shaking her head. "It's the gold tooth, polyester capital of the world, okay? It's where old leisure suits go to die."

Star smiled. "It's not that bad."

"What?" Vee's voice rose an octave. "The last time we was in there, this guy asked me to dance, and the man had so much gold in his mouth and polyester in his suit, I thought if anybody rubbed against him, he'd go up in flames! Molten gold everywhere, it woulda been like that scene in *The Ten Commandments,* you know, where they melted down the gold to make the calf. This man could have made a whole herd just from his front teeth alone. Lord knows what was in the back, probably a couple of diamonds or something."

Star doubled over laughing. She knew she was being watched, but she couldn't help it.

"Vee . . . "

"Uh-uh, don't Vee me, honey. You know I love you, you been my friend my whole life, but puh-leese, let's go somewhere else."

"Verenita Spencer-Martin, are you telling me you don't want to be around yo' peoples?"

"Don't start."

"It's ladies' night. They lay out that fine, tasty buffet about eight, and it's free."

"I know that."

"And you know nobody makes hot wings and ribs like Mose, and he's cooking tonight."

"Star . . . "

"He likes you, he always gives you the best pieces."

"Uh-huh," Vee said. "Have you looked at his mouth? Mose looks like Fort Knox on a sunny day. Why can't we just go someplace else?"

"Because they play my jams, you know, Marvin, Smokey, the Temps, all that."

"Girl you need to get with the times, even Berry Gordy done left Motown!"

"Please," Star said through her grin, "please, please, please?"

"Okay, James Brown, but you owe me, big-time."

"Deal. I'll help you clean out your basement, since you're always complaining about it."

"I'll believe that when I see your big feet on my floor, with a broom in your hand." Star heard Vee go back to typing. "Pick me up."

"About seven-thirty?" Star asked.

"Fine, I'll be ready, and listen, if one gold tooth flashes my way, I'm outta there, hear me?"

"I hear you. I will personally check the mouth of any man who tries to talk to you."

"Thank you."

"Say hi to that fine partner of yours. In fact, bring him along."

"He's got a gold tooth with a ruby in it," Star said. "He just got it today."

"For him I'll make an exception," Vee said. "Later." She hung up the phone.

Star, still grinning, put the receiver back in the cradle and leaned back, looking out of the window.

Good old Vee. She knew she could count on her. They had been Lucy and Ethel all their lives, always there for each another, since they were in diapers.

More sweat rolled down her cheek. She wiped it off with the back of her hand. Sweat was just exactly what she needed, but not here—out on the dance floor.

She needed to go out and shake her butt till the water ran off her and her shirt stuck to her back.

Music and dance were her salvation. Once while she was in high school, it had taken her almost twenty minutes to fix her long hair after her first serious dance class. That night, she talked with her father about getting it cut. He hadn't wanted her to do it, but he knew his daughter; the hair was interfering with her dancing, so it had to go.

The next day, she came home from the hairdresser's with what her father described as "not enough hair to cover a tick."

He called her "Beany" for a few days, but he got over it. The memory made her smile. He'd always told her to make her own decisions and deal with the consequences, and she did, knowing he was in her corner, even if he did laugh every time he looked at her.

She still wore her hair that way. It made her life easier, no fuss, no muss. Wash it, blow it dry, and hit the bricks. That haircut allowed her to sweat and get as funky as she wanted, and never have to worry about her hair "going back."

Vee always said she had "good" hair anyway, the kind that "didn't get kinky in the clinches."

Well tonight was a definite nappy-headed, shake-your-booty night, she said to herself. She really needed to cut loose, and sometimes the dance floor was better than sex, and a lot less aggravating. When she was done, she could go home, shower, and collapse in bed, just as tired as she would be from any all-nighter, and in the morning she didn't have to listen to it in her bathroom.

After ten years in Homicide, she was thundering toward burnout. One more hot day with Leo's shirt and she was going to run screaming through the squad room. She turned in her chair, facing him again.

He was reading to himself, his lips moving. The waves of hot air in the room gave his face a bad sci-fi movie effect, making his Saint Bernard features pulse with a life of their own. His face appeared to be struggling to keep from letting go and mercifully slipping down and covering that hideous shirt.

On his hip, his gun stood out, forming an additional lump, which for some reason she found hilarious. Her mind instantly formed a picture of Leo drawing his gun, shifting his fat, and chewing gum all at the same time. She snorted a laugh and he looked at her. Star spun the chair toward the window, to keep from laughing in his face.

Outside, you could actually see the heat rising from the pavement. Her father's face flashed across her mind.

When she was a little girl, on hot days like this he would take her to the park, where it was green and cool. They would walk, and end up sitting by the pond, under the oak trees in the shade, feeding the ducks and talking for hours.

Her father was the smartest man she ever knew, and the only one she ever completely trusted. Her mother used to say she was Daddy's girl from the beginning.

She looked so much like him that the old folks said he "spit" her out. They shared the same pale brown, gold-flecked eyes and lazy smile. She took her height from him as well, standing six feet tall, with long, strong legs and her father's deep, throaty laugh. Sometimes, when she looked in the mirror, she saw him looking back.

Her mother died when she was twelve, and her father raised her. Even now, after all these years, his death was as fresh in her mind as if it happened yesterday, instead of when she was nineteen years old. It had been so stupid, so senseless, all because he was a good cop.

This is definitely a park day, Pop, she said to herself, remembering their talks, how they rambled from subject to subject. He was a patient man, and he always had the answers to all of her questions. More important, he encouraged her to ask, to never take things as they seemed, and above all, never feel stupid about speaking up and asking for information when she wanted to know something.

A smile crossed her lips. Her dad had been her champion, her best friend, and co-conspirator in ruining their dinner appetites on those lazy, hot days by stuffing themselves with countless little white pleated paper cups of orange and lime sherbet.

Her mother hated "park days."

A charcoal-colored young man on a skateboard glided into view, bringing her back to reality. He wore a neon-green baseball cap turned backward on his head, with the bill facing his bony shoulders. His long, thin arms waved around like he was riding the biggest wave off the Kona coast. A white tank top and bright red baggies hung on his skinny frame. His feet sported a pair of expensive, NBA-endorsed Nike basketball shoes.

"Look at this little cutie," she muttered. "Where'd you get them shoes, youngblood?" She watched the boy swaying her way.

He was no older than sixteen, with a long face, and a smile to rival Magic Johnson's.

"Mmmmph, with a little more meat and a few more years on you, little brother, you could be a heartbreaker. I sure hope you last long enough."

The boy sped closer. Star watched him. Their eyes met. His grin got wider.

Lord, he's a pretty child, she thought. Just the kind of young man she found herself looking at in pools of blood, at least every other week. "I sure hope I don't come up on you sometime, little brother, 'cause you got on the wrong color, or 'cause somebody wants your kicks."

He looked at her sitting by the window.

He dipped with his knees and angled the board nearer the building. Her pale brown eyes followed his gliding moves, scopin' him out.

He grinned at her. She smiled back. He made a kissing motion. Star winked.

The boy glided down the pavement, the wheels under his board clattering loudly.

Star watched him until he was out of sight, wondering what he'd think if he knew she was the "5-0." She laughed to herself, and looked down at her watch. Sweat glistened on her wrist.

Darcy was unwrapping another piece of bubble gum when Star's luck ran out. She picked up the receiver on the first ring.

"Homicide, Lieutenant Duvall." She grabbed a pen and began writing on the pad in front of her. When she finished, Leo Darcy was standing at her desk.

"What you got, Star?"

"A shooting at a barbecue."

Darcy pulled a small, battered notebook from his breast pocket. "Where?"

"Chelford Park, 6021 Blackstone Boulevard."

"Soon as I get Rescovich outta the can, we're there," he said, moving quickly toward the squad room double doors.

"Uniforms are on the scene and the meat wagon's on the way," Star called out to him. "Paresi and I will be right behind you."

She looked around the room. "Where is Paresi?"

Darcy hollered over his shoulder. "He went upstairs to get a drink. He'll be right back."

As if on cue, Starletta's partner appeared in the doorway. Homicide Detective Sergeant Dominic Paresi was a shade over six feet two inches tall, with thick black hair and azure blue eyes.

His profile was as classically Italian as Michelangelo's David. Women loved him, and he knew it. Being the youngest and the only male in a large Sicilian family of five doting sisters, Dominic Paresi loved women. He had learned from an early age to both respect them *and* wrap them around his little finger.

Paresi sidestepped out of Darcy's lumbering way. "Who set fire to him?"

"We got a shooting at a barbecue." Star picked up her purse.

"Where?" Dominic handed her one of the two large, icy cups of cola he was carrying.

"Chelford Park on the Blackstone Boulevard side, 6021." She took a long drink. "Bless you, Dominic, you must have been reading my mind."

He smiled at her. "Don't I always know what you want?"

"Yeah, right." She smiled back. "Thanks anyway."

"Don't thank me, honey buns." Paresi reached up to the attendance board and moved the markers by their names to the out position. "These were free, compliments of the new counterman at the roach motel."

"What?"

"The new guy upstairs."

"What new guy?" she asked as they walked toward the door.

"The one with the eyes, you know, each eyeball is looking in a different direction. He told me to tell you that he's available."

Star laughed. "Gee, how lucky can I get?"

Paresi laughed with her. "I swear, I'm not making this up. His name's Elvis, and he told me, I'm quoting here, he wants to love you tender!"

She laughed again. "Tell him I'm married to you. That should cool him off." They headed for the stairs.

"Not a chance. I like free sodas. He's got the keys to the kingdom up there. Dig it, there's not one machine that he can't open. Play this right, and we never have to cough up exact change again. Think of it. Free everything! What say we stop by on the way out, so you can thank him personally."

"I'll send him a card," she said.

He crouched in the shade of a wall on the roof, watching them running all over the place like a bunch of black ants. It looked like one of those old silent movies where everything was sped up, moving faster than real life. They were screaming, yelling, running all around. Over in the corner, near the side of the house, one of the black bastards was puking.

"Wimp son of a bitch," he said. He took another look at the woman on the lawn. "Nice work!" It was artistic, he thought to himself, and laughed. The way she was sprawled out, her black skin, the white dress, the green grass and all that red sprayed over the white wall of the garage behind her. There was definitely beauty in it. He wiped his mouth; the sight turned him on. He'd had the biggest fly-busting hard-on since the first bullet ripped through her cheek.

He stood up, moving back into the shadows. For a second he pressed his throbbing crotch against the cool wall. He felt as if he was going to explode, but the feeling was passing. Quickly, he reached into the brown canvas bag at his feet and pulled out his Minolta. He aimed, adjusted the telephoto lens, and rolled off a series of snaps.

He stopped, again pressing his body to the wall. Sweat rolled from his forehead into his eyes. Lust was overtaking him. For a moment he thought he would come, right there, without even touching himself. The sound of sirens in the distance snapped that thought out of him.

He swiftly shoved his M–1 rifle back into the canvas case. He placed the camera and the lens into another canvas bag and quickly checked the ground, making sure he'd left no spent shells or other clues. Satisfied, he sprinted for the open door that led to the stairs and down and out of the building.

2

Star took a deep breath before opening the car door. She'd never gotten used to it. The fragility of humans. It was literally here today, gone tomorrow.

Paresi stood on the curb. "I got a feeling we're in for strawberry jam in the sun."

"What a poetic way of putting it," she said.

Paresi's gallows humor always calmed her, even though she didn't let him know it. Her sarcastic responses made him smile. It was a scene of nonchalance in the face of horror that they constantly played with each other. The worse the scene, the funnier they got. It kept them both from screaming sometimes.

Neighbors lined the driveway, craning their necks, trying to move up the asphalt for a look behind the house. They shouted questions as the detectives walked the gauntlet.

Star clipped her gold shield to her belt as she walked. A skinny, light-skinned woman with dyed blond hair pointed to her and elbowed her friend.

"Hey, she'll tell us what's happenin'." The woman fell into step with Star. "What's going on back there, sistuh?"

Star turned, raising her hand. "I'm sorry, ma'am, you'll have to stay back, please."

The woman regarded her with cold eyes. "Who you think you talkin' to, you seditty bitch!" She curled her lip. "You the only raisin I see in all this milk, least you could do is help out your own."

Star stopped, facing the woman. "That's exactly what I'm doing, because one of *our* own is lying back there, shot down like a dog, and it's my job to find out why. If I let you go back there, I might as well let everybody out here back there. Let them stomp on clues, pick up souvenirs, just mess up the whole scene and in general keep me from finding out who killed her, so why don't you just tell me, how much help you gonna be back there, gawking and most likely puking, sis-tuh?"

The woman stepped back, embarrassed, her face red. Paresi looked over his shoulder and signaled a uniformed officer.

"Get these people out of here."

"Yes sir." The officer started herding the crowd back toward the sidewalk.

"Don't you get tired of that?" Paresi said as they neared the back of the house.

"Like you wouldn't believe." She looked at him. "I feel like Rodney Dangerfield. Respect is really absent on this job. I guess she thinks I'm here because Affirmative Action said I'm supposed to be here. Never mind my busting my ass for fif-teen years, dealing with shit she can't even imagine. I'm sup-posed to say, 'Yeah, y'all c'mon back, cause we's homies.'"

"Take it easy, take it easy, it's just a natural thing with folks, when they see one of their own, they think they can get some inside stuff."

"I guess, but today I'm too hot and too tired for it. Besides, why do people want to see this? What's wrong with the world? They do live shows from emergency rooms, and peo-ple tune in. We get *paid* to look at this shit, and it bothers me. What would make a rational human being want to look at another poor soul who's been crushed, stabbed, bludgeoned, shot, strangled or God knows what, and think of it as enter-tainment? Why would anybody want to see that?"

"Makes 'em feel lucky," Paresi said.

"Yeah? What's next, autopsies and embalming in living color during the dinner hour?"

A young girl with blue-black skin and a headful of braids, each one sporting a different-colored, plastic bow-shaped bar-rette, raced up the driveway and darted between the detectives.

Star grabbed her arm. The child sucked on a popsicle, twisting her body, trying to run behind the house. Star held her tight.

"Hey . . . *hey!*"

The little girl looked up at her. "Is a dead lady back there?" she asked, her eyes as big as chocolate drops. She wasn't any older than Vee's daughter.

"Go home, sweetie. There's nothing back there for you to see."

"I wanna see the dead lady." The little girl's lips were purple from the grape popsicle.

"Go home." Star turned the child firmly around. "Go on, or my partner's going to take you to jail."

The little girl looked up at Paresi. He lowered his mirrored sunglasses and glared at her over the frames.

"Go home, kid, before I send you to sleep with the fishes."

He said in his best *Godfather* accent.

The little girl giggled and ran back toward the street.

"Thanks, Vito," Star said.

"Anytime," he whispered, still in character.

When they turned the corner of the house and entered the backyard, Star's stomach tightened. The woman lay sprawled on the grass, her legs spread and knees bent. One white sandal was halfway off her foot.

The guests were quiet now. Muffled sobs could be heard here and there, but for the most part it was like stepping into a bad dream.

Paresi stared down at the body. He took off his shades and ran a hand over his face. "*Marrone!* Her brains are everywhere, even in the driveway."

Star looked away.

Jack Rescovich approached her, carrying a set of plastic tongs and a small transparent bag filled with gray, glutinous material.

"Jack," she said.

Rescovich was a chunky, block-shaped man with a face like chewed gum. Giant perspiration stains ringed the underarms of his short-sleeve yellow shirt; wet patches showed through the latex gloves he wore. He looked at her through his cheap sunglasses and grinned.

Her insides shuddered. He reminded her of a cartoon wolf. He was one of those guys who definitely believed "the myth." He'd been leering at her for the three years he'd been in Homicide, and she detested it. He licked his thick lips and smiled wider.

"Got some brain tissue here, Lieutenant." He turned and pointed. "I found it over there, where the marker is, by the tree . . . musta shot out twenty feet."

"Swell," she said, walking away from him.

Rescovich watched her talking to Paresi, wondering if the two of them were doing the horizontal mambo. The vote in the unit was split, fifty-fifty.

Jack sucked his teeth. "These broads are always yapping about how they want to be treated equal to men, but they still play games . . . fucking lieutenant, decorated veteran of the squad, yadda yadda . . . all that shit don't mean diddly," he muttered. "She's still just a hot spade broad that likes showing it off."

He spat on the grass at his feet, his eyes on Star. Look at this, the hottest fucking day of the year, and she's got all her back and shoulders out.

Everything on view like a fucking smorgasbord, and I'm supposed to think of her as my "superior officer," keep my mind on the job. Get fucking real, this bitch is asking for it, and one of these days I'm gonna go for it, show her what a real man is, and it ain't that fucking guinea.

Star turned and looked at him for a moment, as if she could hear his thoughts. His mouth went dry. He swallowed twice, trying to work up some moisture.

She turned away, back to Paresi.

"You okay, pard?" Paresi asked. "You don't look so hot."

"I'm fine, it's just Rescovich standing over there talking to himself. He gives me the willies."

Paresi glanced over his shoulder. "He gives his mother the willies."

Star walked back to the body and waited for the photographers to snap and videotape the scene. When they were done, she knelt beside the corpse, pulling a pair of surgical gloves from her bag and putting them on. She leaned in as closely as she could, avoiding the lifeless eyes that appeared to be searching her face. A slight odor rose from the body.

She studied what was left of the woman's head. A glittering jewel still firmly attached to the only remaining ear caused her to let out a low, soft whistle.

"That's a real diamond," she said, pointing to the dead woman's hand. "This too."

Paresi squatted beside her. "Quite a rock."

"Yep, about three karats, I'd say." Star touched the bloodied cloth of the woman's dress. "Real linen. Looks like she had some coins and she was about to get married." They stood. "She had it going on, that's for sure."

Paresi walked around the body, looking out over the rooftops. "I can't figure this one. I mean, it's a good neighborhood, the streets roll up at nine o'clock, nothing. So why would a woman get taken out in broad daylight at a barbecue?"

"Damned if I know." Star shaded her eyes. "From the position of the body, I say the shooter hit from a high window or a rooftop, over there." She pointed. "North. What do you think?"

Paresi nodded in agreement. "The roof gets my vote. This is a family neighborhood, no shooters banging away in the attic."

"Maybe," she said. "Unless it's a neighborhood thing . . . family vendetta, or something like that."

"Nah, I don't think she even lived in the neighborhood. Word is this was an engagement party for her and her boyfriend."

Star circled the body again. "Well, somebody is pissed. They practically took her head off."

"Yeah. But this ain't gang territory. It's a clean neighborhood."

"Let's find out. Get some uniforms out door-to-door and searching the rooftops. I want them to hit any building three stories or more, in that area, and fan them out in a four block radius on all sides."

"We're already on it, Lieutenant," Darcy said from behind her. "Brenner and his guys are on the doors, and Cannon and Robbins have their guys on the roofs."

"Good. Thanks, Leo," Star replied.

"Uh, Lieutenant?"

She turned to find a very shaky uniformed rookie facing her. His face was as green as the grass where the body lay. "What is it, Gary?"

Gary Kilborn swallowed three times before he was able to speak. "Uh, I was gonna . . . uh, tape and chalk the area, and I wanted to, uh . . . I wanted to know if you want me to chalk the, uh . . . garage and driveway . . . uh, the spray . . . you know, where all the pieces went." He gulped air.

Star knew the look. "If you're going to be sick, Gary, please do it out of my sight. When you're finished, get Rhodes to tape and chalk, while you watch."

Kilborn glanced again at the corpse and turned a lethal shade of white. His red hair and mustache made it look like portions of his face were on fire.

"Yes, ma'am." He choked and ran from the scene, disappearing behind the garage.

"Rookies," Star said.

"C'mon, tough guy, you were the new kid on the block once." Paresi nudged her with his shoulder. "You wanna talk to the boyfriend, or do you want me to do it?"

Star looked at the long-legged, brown-skinned man who sat sobbing on the back porch steps. He wept loudly into a dish towel, while a large, cinnamon-colored woman held him in her arms, gently rocking him back and forth.

"I'll take him."

"Right." Paresi headed for the coroner's crew.

Star crossed the lawn to the stairs and sat down next to the weeping man. His wails tore at her heart. She'd have to be patient. It would be a while before he would be able to talk to her, and she knew the first thing he'd say would be, "Why?" What could she say? She was the one with the shiny gold shield, she was supposed to have the answers.

What could she tell him? An hour ago they had been a young couple, happy, in love, and now he was alone, because his woman was lying in the grass with half her head gone.

The man wept loudly.

She looked away, wishing she was somewhere else. She'd have to call Vee. No booty shaking at the Caddy tonight.

Across the lawn, Dr. Mitchell Grant was walking up the driveway. His head turned slightly as he sighted the blood and brain tissue.

Mitchell Grant was a very tall man, who walked as if he owned the world and everything in it. A kind of unhurried, predatory step that made women stop in their tracks to watch him. He was Mercer County, Massachusetts, Chief Medical Examiner, and one of about five hundred forensic pathologists in the entire country.

His celebrity was national; he'd been called in to work on high-profile cases in other states, as well as in the Commonwealth. He'd also been written up in *Time* and *Newsweek* and interviewed on national television. Even so, he was a team player who believed in a hands-on approach to his profession.

He had a staff of pathologists working under him, but preferred taking on as many regular cases as possible. Usually men of his caliber handled only the glamour jobs, the VIPs, celebrities, and big murder cases, but Grant liked getting in the trenches. Star admired that.

She watched him standing with Paresi, over the body. The suit he was wearing cost enough to feed an entire inner city family for about a year. She chastised herself for thinking that. Grant was one of the good guys. He couldn't help it if he came from old Boston Back Bay money. In spite of his wealth and cool elegance, he was still one of the gang, and he was positively stunning to look at. And you couldn't help but look, first at his height, and then at his face. The guy was beautiful.

The first time she saw him, she was a cadet in the Academy. He took her breath away. He had the most perfect face she'd ever seen. Deep-set, sea-green eyes, high cheekbones, a beautiful aristocratic nose, and lips that made you want to go to church. When he smiled, he showed perfect, straight white teeth. She knew that smile was natural and not the result of braces and orthodontics. She doubted the man had ever had an ugly or awkward day in his life.

He reminded her of Robert Redford, except there was a hint of danger about Mitchell Grant, especially in his eyes. Something in him always put her on alert. He looked like the kind of man who could make a woman lose control, and that made him scary.

He was, as far as she could see, unflappable. Never a five o'clock shadow, a raised voice, or a rumpled suit. Just once she wanted to see him sweat.

From what she'd heard about him, he did a lot of that, but to her, he just didn't fit the stories. Maybe they were true and maybe they weren't. Cops gossiped more than little old ladies. They called him the "Annihilator" and said he was a destroyer of women. Nearly every cop she knew had a story about Mitchell Grant's libido. They said nothing with breasts was safe around him.

He had always treated her with respect. Over the years they worked together, his attitude toward her had always been professional. Oh, he was friendly, and very funny, something that no doubt helped him deal with the misery in his profession.

They laughed a lot. He'd known her dad, who had always spoken highly of him. Maybe that's why she didn't believe all the talk. Besides, he'd never made a pass at her.

Star looked around the yard at the cops in uniform and out. Most of these guys couldn't say that, she thought to herself, so she didn't put too much stock in the station grapevine.

Grant circled the body as she watched him. It was one of

the hottest days of the year, and everybody was sweating waterfalls, but he was totally cool. Didn't he ever lose it?

Next to her, the weeping man sighed. She faced him. "I'm Lieutenant Duvall," she said. "I know this is a terrible time, but I have to talk to you."

The man wiped his eyes and tried to speak. His mouth trembled and tears ran down his face.

Star took his hand. "I'm so sorry," she said softly and truthfully.

He grabbed her hand tightly. The heavyset woman who had been holding him rubbed his back tenderly. "His name is Darnell . . . Darnell Pope," she said, her voice husky with tears.

Star nodded. "Thank you." She looked deeply into the man's eyes. "Darnell, I know this is hard, but I have to ask you some questions."

He nodded, and swallowed a sob. "I know, the sooner you get your answers, the sooner you catch the bastard what killed her."

Star stood up, still holding his hand, bringing him with her. "That's right, that's right."

The heavy woman opened the back door and they followed her inside.

Across the lawn, Paresi and Mitchell Grant stood patiently as the forensic team measured the distance of tissue and blood from the corpse. When they finished, the two men moved closer to the body. Paresi shoved his hands in his pockets. "So whaddya think, Doc?"

Grant pulled a pair of latex gloves from his inside breast pocket and slipped them on. He squatted beside the body and inserted his forefinger into a portion of the wound. A piece of skull came loose and brain tissue leaked over his finger.

"I think it's a goddamn waste and a shame. That's what I think." He straightened and walked around the body, looking at her from another angle.

Paresi moved next to him, trying to see through his eyes. "We think the shooter hit from that direction." He pointed toward the buildings across the street.

Grant peeled off the gloves and handed them to an aide who had appeared out of nowhere. "I agree, but I'll know more once I get inside."

"What time will that be?" Paresi asked.

"Don't know, I'll call." He clapped Paresi on the back and walked away to talk with members of his team.

Paresi watched him, taking in the fit of the doctor's cream-colored Armani suit and his precision-cut hair.

Mitchell Grant was a hard guy to figure. Rich, classy, yet he was a locker room legend. In the world of hounds, a dog was a dog, but this guy was the Hound of the Baskervilles. It was no secret that Grant had made his way through most of the women on the city payroll. Doctors, lawyers, secretaries, clerks. Hell, there may have even been a cleaning lady or two. Word was, the guy was insatiable.

Paresi's personal favorite among the legends that circulated through the department was one about Grant boffing a nursing student in the morgue; just shoved a stiff off the table and let it rip.

You had to hand it to a dude who could raise the flag in that place. Especially one as old as Grant. Paresi guessed he was at least fifty, though he didn't look it, even up close. Maybe, Paresi thought, if he kept working out and popping megavitamins, he'd be like that at fifty . . . hell, seventy-five, he was Italian!

3

What a day he'd had. The memory of the black woman made him smile. He stripped off his shirt, a goofy grin on his face.

In the kitchen, his wife was making a cold supper, which meant baloney sandwiches on white bread. He didn't want any.

This night called for a celebration. He was going to shower, change and head out. He'd already set the VCR to catch the news, tonight was going to be party night. Later, after the lump he was married to was in bed, he would develop the pictures he'd taken.

She called him again, asking if he wanted mustard or mayo on his sandwich. She'd made the same goddamned cold supper for the last eight years on every bleeding hot day. Wouldn't you think by now the cow would remember that he hated mayonnaise? She was bellowing at him. Fuck her! He wouldn't answer. Couldn't a man have privacy, even in his own friggin' bathroom?

He stepped out of his pants and undershorts, leaving them in a heap on the tile floor. Standing close to the full-length mirror, he examined himself. Not bad for a guy crowding forty. Lean, no flab, nearly six feet, he was a fucking Adonis.

"Very hot!" he whispered to his reflection. He moved in closer, studying his face. His slate-gray eyes stared back at him. His boss had been after him to get a haircut; he'd been wearing his long, black hair in a ponytail since 1970. The boss was breaking his balls, so he did it. He hadn't wanted to, but now he was glad. The shorter cut set off his high cheekbones and full lips.

Some of the girls at work said he looked like a model, but

unlike the glamour boys in most of the fashion magazines, he was no faggot. Women were always hitting on him, and he usually hit back. The first day he'd come to work with his new look, one of the girls upstairs had just about come looking at him. He could smell her; fucking, brainless cunt.

He stepped back, turning around, looking over his shoulder at his muscular, tight behind. He slapped his own flesh, the sting giving him pleasure. Women loved his ass. He was always getting pinched in the bars he frequented. He faced the mirror again, smiling at his reflection, loving the look of his own body.

He reached down, eyes on his mirror twin, and squeezed his prime feature. He lifted the weight in his hand and smiled.

He stroked himself, watching it grow in the mirror.

"You coulda been a star in the porns, my boy," he whispered. "You coulda been big!" The joke made him laugh.

He closed his eyes and again saw the woman. Heat crawled down his arm and settled into his stroking hand. He pumped himself, the memory of the afternoon fueling him. He moaned, his body jackknifing. Panting, he lay his head against the mirror, waiting for the pounding to stop, listening to his heart slowing down to a normal rhythm.

Once again his wife's voice invaded his sanctuary. He turned his head, pressing a sweaty cheek against the mirror. He couldn't speak, not yet. He wanted to tell her to shut the fuck up, but later . . . later.

When he could breathe, he picked up a towel and wiped the glass. He tossed the towel on the floor with his clothes and stepped into the shower. He turned the water on full blast and leaned into the cold, stinging spray. His body trembled with aftershocks of pleasure as the water beat down on him. With his eyes closed, he sank to the shower floor, letting the icy water rain down on him. God, he felt good.

Mitchell Grant sat in his office, long after his day was officially finished, turning a diamond ring and earring over and over in his long fingers. He had personally removed the jewelry from the woman's body to be certain it was returned to her family. He put the pieces into a brown evidence envelope, sealed it, got up and put it in his safe.

After he'd locked the safe door, he again glanced through the file marked CHARLOTTE WILSON. It looked routine. He could have turned it over to somebody else, but long ago he had learned to listen to his gut, and his gut told him to take this one.

He'd been a pathologist for nearly twenty-five years, going back to study forensic pathology some eighteen years ago.

His former wife, Carole Ann, had thrown fits about his returning into training at his age. What did she care about how he felt? All she wanted was to spend his money and look good at the country club. Their marriage had been a joke. By the time it was over, he hadn't slept with her in so long, he couldn't even remember what she felt like.

Truthfully, sex had always been a problem with them, even when they were dating. She never let him touch her, and it just about killed him. She told him she was afraid if she got pregnant, he'd leave her. She said she needed that ring to be "secure." He agreed to marriage, just because he couldn't look at her without wanting her.

What a dope, he thought. He'd been intrigued with her cool, icy, Grace Kelly–like beauty. They met at a campus mixer, and he was immediately obsessed with the idea of having her.

She knew what he wanted, and she knew he was one of the richest guys on campus. She had sat at all those stupid basketball games, cheering him, and she'd put up with his hands all over her afterward, because she wanted his money. In spite of her aloof looks, Carole Ann's parents were dirt poor. She was in school on a scholarship, and finding a rich husband was more important than any of her classes.

Landing the best-looking guy on campus was a major feather in her cap. After they were married, she shut him out totally.

But he was married, and in his family, it meant for life. He knew his father played around. His mother knew it too, but she pretended all was perfect in their marriage. When his parents celebrated their thirtieth wedding anniversary, he begged off, saying he was too sick to attend. Carole Ann went, and he spent the evening at a motel with a nurse named Angie. The memory still made him smile.

He'd been amazed when Carole Ann got pregnant. As near as he could figure, their daughter was conceived on a night when Carole Ann had been celebrating with her tennis group. They had won some tournament at the club, and she'd come home slightly looped. For some reason, the sight of her with her hair in a ponytail, all giggly and flushed, turned him on, so he pounced. He touched her so infrequently, they both forgot about birth control.

She had been happy, though, when she found out she was expecting. It was time they had a child, she said. People were talking.

His daughter had been the only thing good to come out of that union. She was always proud of him, telling her friends that her daddy was a doctor like Quincy on TV.

He never regretted his choice to go back into training. He loved his profession, and forensic pathology put him on a path he found endlessly fascinating.

Forensic pathologists were a special breed: medical detectives whose clients were the dead. The whole concept of using the body for clues, having the dead point the finger at their killers, totally intrigued him. He liked his Quincy reputation, but Jack Klugman made it look easy, wrapping up all the loose ends and solving the case in an hour. Sometimes it took years.

He placed the Charlotte Wilson file on the center of his desk, taking a moment to straighten it, making certain it was dead center. He liked order. It made his life hum—at least here, in the office. His personal life was a different story. When he divorced Carole Ann, he became like some wild thing freed from a cage.

After enduring that dead marriage for its entire eighteen-year span, he went a little crazy, going after young flesh with a vengeance. No more hiding it, no more being discreet. He was out there, taking all comers, and they came in swarms.

They flocked to him, followed him, threw themselves at him, and made him feel like a god, or, more realistically, a rock star. His profession really turned them on. Nothing like death to make people want to celebrate life. They were always there, warm and willing.

After a time, it became an ego thing as well. The gray streaks in his hair mixing with the blond, the lines around his mouth and eyes growing deeper, only seemed to turn them on more. It was a kick, bedding and satisfying girls his daughter's age. But lately it was getting old. He wanted something more. Something and someone stable.

Starletta Duvall. She caught his eye in the Academy. That dark blue serge uniform couldn't hide the fact that she was a beauty. He'd been intrigued from the beginning.

He watched her during his lectures and even in their sessions at the morgue. She was her father's daughter, all right; she had his guts. She never flinched and she never looked away, no matter how horrible the cadaver on the table.

He smiled, recalling a time during her first weeks in the Academy. The class had returned from lunch, and Star found a plain manila folder on her desk. She opened it. Being the only woman in this group of cadets, she had suffered more than a few "indignities." Some of the men seemed determined to break her, even more so than other female cadets he could remember.

For some, her very appearance was a threat. On top of that, she showed courage in facing them on a daily basis, more than most of them would have in her position. It wasn't until after graduation that her classmates found out she was the daughter of a decorated police officer who had died in the line of duty.

The day she opened the folder on her desk, they were all waiting, some smirking, some grinning outright. It held pictures of a group of bombing victims from a radical fringe group in the sixties.

The photos were gruesome, showing body parts, severed heads and limbs. Some had close-ups of brain tissue and entrails splattered on walls. There was one particularly horrible shot of a nude male torso embedded in one of the walls, in glorious color.

He hadn't known what the cadets were planning, and he was sorry for her. He needn't have worried. She looked at each and every photo. Finally, she spoke, saying how amazing it was that the human body could be destroyed like that.

It took all the control he had not to laugh out loud at the disappointed faces in the class. Instead, he went to her desk and looked over her shoulder, checking the pictures and explaining to her just how this amount of damage was possible. That day, she earned her stripes in his book.

Len Duvall would have been proud. She carried his name with nothing but class. From the beat to the gold shield, she was a complete professional. He liked and respected her.

He had liked her dad too. Mitch recalled aiding in his autopsy. He'd been an Assistant Medical Examiner then, and it was the first time he allowed himself to feel anything for the victim on the table. During the postmortem, he found his eyes wet with tears more than once at the stupid way the man had died.

Later, after she'd been on the job a while, he'd wanted to ask Star out. But he was trapped in that fake marriage, and he knew she wouldn't date a married man. When he was finally free, his rep got in the way. Whenever he talked to her longer than five minutes, he could see the wheels turning in people's minds. He didn't want her name on the grapevine; besides, she'd never shown an interest in him. Maybe, he thought, she wasn't into white men.

Still, he knew that one day he was going to get up the guts and ask her out. All she could say was no. He straightened the file again and picked up the phone. She answered on the first ring.

"Homicide, Lieutenant Duvall."

"I was hoping you'd still be there." He looked at his Rolex watch. "It's pretty late."

"Dr. Grant?"

"Yes."

"Yeah, we're still here. Paresi and I are just about to order Chinese. It looks like we'll be here a few more hours. What can I do for you?"

"I just wanted to tell you the autopsy is tomorrow morning at eight. Will you two be coming?"

"Sure, we'll be there."

A thread of silence hung between them. He wanted her to keep talking. He leaned back in his chair, cradling the receiver with his shoulder. "How's the investigation going? Anything turn up?"

"A thirty-caliber bullet, dug out of a tree, that's it. The rooftops were clean, and of course the entire neighborhood is blind."

"Tomorrow's another day," he said.

"We're hoping. You know how optimistic cops are!"

They laughed together.

"It'll get better."

"I hope so, " she said. "Thanks for the pep talk."

Another silence, he couldn't think of anything to say. Finally, he managed, "Good night, Lieutenant."

"Good night, see you in the morning."

Mitch hung up the phone and sat for a moment with his hand resting on the receiver. He had to struggle against calling back and inviting himself to the squad room for Chinese take-out. He wanted to see her again. Standing up, he pulled his jacket on. A lock of his thick hair fell over his forehead. He ran his fingers through it, pushing it back. He was turning out the lights when his secretary, Lorraine, walked into the outer office.

"Hi, Mitch." She waved at him through his open door and grinned in her best southern belle style.

He picked up his briefcase and walked toward her, closing his door behind him. "Hi. What are you doing back here?"

"I was on my way home from the gym, and I saw your lights were on. I thought I'd come in and see if you needed any help."

He couldn't believe he'd once found that magnolia and honeysuckle accent charming. She stood there, wearing a bright green, low-cut spandex leotard and a pair of tight, white shorts. Secretarial help wasn't what she was offering.

Mitch smiled. "I appreciate it, but I was just closing up, on my way home."

"Great!" Lorraine's smile widened. She fluffed her blond mane. "I haven't had dinner. Why don't we get a bite together?"

He remembered the last time they "dined" together. It was tempting, but she was a clinger. Lorraine had come into the office the next day with flowers for him and wedding bells in her eyes. Uh-uh, he didn't need that.

"Not tonight, Lorraine. I'm really beat. I'm just going to stop at the deli and pick up a sandwich."

Lorraine's smiled wavered. "That sounds great. Why don't I just tag along, keep you company?"

"Not tonight . . . bye!" Abruptly, he walked out of the office.

Star hung up the phone. Paresi sat grinning at her across the desk.

"Why am I seeing all your dental work?" she asked, with a raised eyebrow.

"That was Mitch, right?"

"Yeah, so?"

"Did he ask you out?"

She stared at him, her eyes wide with surprise. "Get outta here, of course not. He just called with the time for the post tomorrow."

Paresi laughed, a low, dirty chuckle.

"Stop that!" Star felt the flush in her face. "I'm not his type."

"You got a pulse?"

"Only on Tuesdays." She grabbed the menu from his hands.

"Let's get to the good stuff."

"I'll bet that's just what Mitch is thinking."

Star put the menu down on her desk. "I've known him since I was a rookie. He's not interested in me and I'm not interested in him."

"Smart," Paresi said. "I wouldn't want you in the club."

"What club?"

Grinning, he looked her in the eyes. "The Mitchell Grant Fucked-and-Dumped Club."

Star shook her head. "I don't believe that crap for a minute. He's never come on to me."

"He's biding his time. The guy's a master."

Star shrugged. "Well, if you're right, and it's true, you got nothing to worry about. I'm not a joiner, I don't do crowds. I'm the whole show, or no show. Now, do you want to order or not?"

4

The next morning at 7:55 A.M., Star and Paresi entered the squat gray building that housed the Medical Examiner's office and the morgue. They passed through the reception area and down a hallway to Mitchell Grant's outer office. His secretary, Lorraine, looked up when they entered, her permanent, artificial smile in place.

"Good morning, officers," she said cheerfully. "Go right on in, he's expecting you."

"Thanks." Star hated the woman's syrupy southern accent. It always made her feel as if the bloodhounds were on her trail.

"You're welcome." Lorraine watched Star walk ahead of Paresi. She smiled until the two officers disappeared through the door.

Dr. Grant was waiting for them. He sat at his desk, dressed in blue scrubs, a tuft of dark blond chest hair showing beneath the V-neck cut of the shirt.

"Morning," he said.

'Good morning," they answered in unison.

"Looks like another hot day," he said.

"Yep," Paresi agreed.

When Star sat on the couch, her dress rode a little high for a moment and both men took notice. She pulled the bright red fabric down, covering an expanse of bare thigh. Mitch noted that her toenails, peeking from the straps of red sandals, were painted the exact shade of her dress. Paresi caught his eye and they smiled at each other.

Mitch gestured at the small refrigerator in the corner.

"There's fresh orange, pineapple, and grapefruit juice, if you want it, and there's coffee and rolls on the table."

Star looked at the pastries neatly arranged on the coffee table. "Never before an autopsy, thank you."

Paresi reached for a pecan-covered Danish. "A few cold cuts never stopped me. I haven't had breakfast." He poured himself a cup of coffee and bit into the pastry. "Mmmmm, cherries, nice surprise!" He held the roll out to Star. "Wanna bite?"

"No thanks." She looked at Mitch. "This is a hell of a way to start the day."

"We're starting it a lot better than Charlotte Wilson." He walked across the office and opened his safe, pulling out the brown evidence envelope. He handed it to Star. "Here's her jewelry."

She opened the envelope and emptied the contents into her palm. The diamonds sparkled against her skin. "These are beautiful."

Mitch watched her hold the ring up to the light, her pale brown eyes reflecting the sparkle. "Beautiful," she said again.

"Very," he agreed.

The intercom buzzed. Lorraine's voice filled the room. "They're ready for you in autopsy room A, Doctor."

"Thanks, Lorraine." Mitch turned to them. "Time to rock and roll."

Paresi stuffed the last of the Danish into his mouth as they walked out of the room.

5

His day had gotten off to a rotten start. He'd boffed his wife twice, just before dawn, and true to her fashion, she just lay there both times, like a dead whale. Sometimes he wondered how he got it up for her. It was a good thing he had a great imagination and a lot of memories.

Now, as if his day hadn't started badly enough, he was late for work and stuck behind some old man doing about two miles an hour on a nonpassable road. As he crept along behind the old fart, his thoughts went back to the day before. The image of the woman set him throbbing again. Sometimes, he wondered why he stayed married to the pig; she couldn't even take care of a morning hard-on. He drove with one hand for a while, enjoying the feel of himself until he could slide past the geezer.

By the time he got to work, his boss was in a meeting. He was able to sneak into the locker room, get his book, and get out on the floor without anybody noticing.

He straightened his lucky red tie and walked the aisles. He actually liked this place. The miles of television sets, stereos, CD players, computers, even household appliances—it was really something. Electric City was the biggest store of its kind around. Everything electronic was here.

He was a good salesman, and he liked getting first pick of top-of-the-line merchandise. Lately, he'd been looking at video camera equipment, but he didn't think he was ready for tape yet. Besides, there was something poetic about the still camera. But one day . . . who knows?

He looked across the vast showroom, spotting Dennis Glover watching him.

"What are you looking at, you geeky bastard!" he muttered through a dazzling grin.

Glover's lips curled in a rictus that was supposed to pass as a smile. Then he turned away, busying himself with straightening the price labels on a shelf of video recorders.

He sneered at Glover. "Pasty bastard, you won't say anything." He snorted a laugh. "If you do, I'll stomp your ass into infinity."

Still laughing, he strolled toward the refrigerator section. A thin, brown-haired woman with dark circles under her eyes was walking down the aisle, opening the doors of each refrigerator, peering inside and muttering. A kid, about four years old, trailed her, whining in a high-pitched voice. The little boy had what looked like chocolate on his face . . . at least he hoped it was chocolate. He straightened his tie and approached them.

6

Dom Paresi shoved a stick of Doublemint gum into his mouth when Mitch removed the woman's liver. The organ separated with a wet, gushy sound. Paresi chewed harder. This wasn't the part of an autopsy that gave him nightmares. It was when they opened the skull and removed the brain. The sound of the saw, the whine, was a hundred times worse than a dental drill. The fine mist of bone flying, that was the worst. Maybe he wouldn't have to go through that today. Most of the woman's head was in a stainless steel basin on the small parts dissection table to Mitch's right.

Star watched intently as Mitch handed the dripping organ to an assistant, who placed it on a scale suspended over the table. The scales always reminded her of the ones in the produce section of the supermarket.

Mitch spoke into the tiny microphone attached to the front of his scrubs, giving the particulars as he examined each organ he removed. A recorder taped the details for later transcription. Nobody in the autopsy room was prepared for his finding as he examined Charlotte Wilson's female organs. She was about twelve weeks pregnant.

Star heard a gasp, and was shocked to find it had come from her.

"Are you okay, Lieutenant?" Mitch asked. His green eyes showed concern through the Plexiglas eye safety shield.

"Yes." She turned her back. Paresi gently rubbed her shoulder. Star closed her eyes, swallowing the bile that suddenly appeared in her throat. She kept herself turned away from the scene until Mitch began the final portion of the autopsy, working on the woman's head.

He made an incision across the top of her shattered head, from ear to ear. Mitch then peeled Charlotte Wilson's scalp down over her face, exposing her skull that had suffered wartime damage. It reminded Star of an egg that had broken, expelling its yolk from one place, while the rest of it remained miraculously whole, covered with hairline cracks.

Paresi chewed furiously on his gum.

"I think I can do this without the saw," Mitch said. Paresi exhaled loudly.

Dr. Grant then deftly removed what was left of the brain, taking the largest piece nearly intact.

The postmortem took a long time, and after it was over, Star and Paresi waited in Mitchell Grant's office while he finished his report.

"Jeez . . ." Dominic sprawled on the couch. "The baby really threw me."

Star sat in Mitch's chair. It was a big, maroon leather chair that made her feel safe somehow, less shaken. "I know, I wasn't ready for that."

Paresi sighed. "My Danish almost made a return visit."

Star turned in the chair, looking out the window. "Sometimes I hate my job."

Paresi got up and walked to her. He massaged her neck and shoulders. "I know, me too, but you're a tough guy, right?"

She clasped his hand. "Right."

Mitch walked in. "You all right, Star?"

"I'm fine." She indicated his chair. "Want your seat back?"

"No, keep it."

He collapsed on the sofa, propping his feet up on the coffee table. He stretched, and locked his fingers behind his head. "The preliminary reports will be ready by tomorrow morning. We'll have to wait out the lab, you know that, but I can tell you that there were no visible signs of chronic drug or alcohol abuse. Her liver was clean, her lungs clear, her heart sound."

He stretched again. "She was in excellent condition, very

well-muscled. I'd say she worked out, took care of herself, and ate right. Her arteries were clear, no fatty deposits, but that's no surprise, she was young."

"Women don't have the potential for cholesterol problems that men have, right?" Star asked.

"As long as they're premenopausal," Mitch said. "The older you get, the more susceptible you are to blocked arteries. Before menopause, hormones more or less protect the arteries from fat deposits, they keep things moving, as it were. However, after menopause, they aren't strong enough to prevent blockage, so the arteries fill up pretty fast."

"Oh swell." Star shook her head. "You mean in addition to hair on my face, mood swings, hot flashes, and Howdy Doody mouth, I can look forward to a heart attack every now and then to brighten up the day."

Mitch and Paresi laughed.

"Howdy Doody mouth?" Mitch grinned. "I'm not familiar with that particular aspect of menopause."

"It's when you get those two lines." Star put her fingers to both sides of her mouth, moving them down toward her chin. "Right here . . . you know, puppet face."

Mitch smiled. "Not to worry, Lieutenant, I don't think you're going to have that problem. I'm sure you'll be fine. I have no doubt you'll age beautifully."

Star looked down at her hands. She felt a grin coming and she didn't want either of them to see it.

Score one for the doc, Paresi thought, but said nothing.

"Anyway," Mitch continued, "she'd eaten very little, not much there in the stomach contents."

"Do you think she knew she was pregnant?" Paresi asked.

"Not necessarily, but she should have missed at least one period."

"Women know when they're pregnant," Star said. "They know from the moment it happens."

"Oh yeah?" Paresi said. "When was the last time you were on the nest?" He leered at her.

"Okay, okay, so I've never been pregnant. But I've got

friends with children, and they all say they knew they had conceived when they got out of bed!"

"They must have been boinking Italians." Paresi grinned, winking at Mitch. The two of them burst out laughing.

Star shook her head in disgust. "You guys are pigs." That made them laugh even harder.

"I'm sorry, Lieutenant." Mitch said, grinning. "I can't speak for your partner, but I'm a true gentleman. Let me prove it to you by taking you to lunch."

Mitch's reputation crossed her mind. She hesitated.

"Hey, I am what I am," Paresi said. "At least I'm honest, and I say let's do lunch. That invite did include me, didn't it, Doc?"

"Of course, Dominic."

"What d'ya say, pard?"

"It's nearly lunchtime, and you've got to eat," Mitch coaxed her.

Star swiveled in the chair like a little girl. "As long as I don't have to listen to any more testicular humor."

Mitch raised three fingers in the Boy Scout salute. "I promise, not another word. I'll have my secre—uh, assistant, make reservations at Leslie's. They have a great continental menu."

"Beats Buster's Burger Pit," Paresi said.

It was nearly lunchtime, and already he'd made his first sale. The skinny broad with the kid liked his smile, so he showed it often. By the time he'd finished grinning, she was the proud owner of the latest top-of-the-line FrigidQueen refrigerator. Sometimes he wondered if they'd named it after his wife, but who gave a shit, there was lots of pussy out there.

He went to the back room and grabbed his sandwich from the fridge. He didn't even have to open it to know what it was. Leftovers from the "cold supper." Here's hoping she hadn't put mayonnaise on his baloney sandwich.

He got a Coke and a bag of corn chips from the machine and sat down at a blue plastic table. He unwrapped the sand-

wich and lifted the top piece of white bread. Mayonnaise . . .
but of course. He mushed the wrapping and the sandwich into
a ball and gracefully lobbed it over his head, hitting the silver
door of the trash can, setting it swinging.

"That's a three pointer," he said, and tore open the bag of
chips. His mind raced back to the day before. The woman had
been so sweet. So sweet, but he couldn't spend the day thinking about her.

He got up, looking for the daily paper. He rummaged
through the stack on the counter next to the coffee machine.
Most of the papers were at least a week old; nobody bothered
to throw them out. He'd just about given up when he picked
up the last paper.

"Bingo!" The morning *Dispatch*, intact. He took it back to
his table. A story on the bottom of page 11 caught his eye.

"A killing in Niggertown, I'm so shocked." Laughing, he
turned the page.

"You say something, Jer?"

He looked up to see Ike Standler, pouring himself a cup of
coffee at the machine.

"What?"

"I thought I heard you talking when I came in."

Jerry Auster looked down. "No. I didn't say anything. I
was just reading the paper."

"Oh." Ike dumped most of a pint carton of half and half
into his oversized coffee mug. Jerry noticed that the man was
whiter than the cream he poured. The rum-headed bastard
must have had another night of serious drinking, Jerry said to
himself. What a loser.

"My mistake." Ike indicated the paper. "You finished?"

"Yeah, you can have it." Jerry held it out.

Ike walked unsteadily across the room and took the paper
from his hand. "You're sure you're finished?"

Jerry could smell the booze seeping from his pores. "Yeah,
I'm due back on the floor." He crushed his bag of chips and
drained the Coke in a couple of gulps. He belched loudly.
"Sorry."

"No prob." Ike settled in at the table.

Jerry lobbed the chips and can into the trash, another overhead toss.

"You've got a great arm there, boy. Graceful, like Michael Jordan."

Jerry faced him, his face blank. "You know, there are some great white players. You ever see the Celtics? White guys, legends playing the game. You ever hear of John Stockton? Utah Jazz? Even the fucking Bulls got Toni Kukoc and Luc Longley. Blacks don't have a lock on the sport."

Jerry's hostility stunned Ike. "You're right. I'm more of a baseball man myself. Don't see too much hoop, you know."

You don't see too much of anything, except the bottom of a bottle, Jerry thought.

"Yeah," he said, and stomped out of the room.

Ike spread the paper on the table and tried to read an article near the bottom of the page. He struggled to focus his eyes, but the lines were smudged, as if rubbed out by a sweaty hand.

He gave up. "I'll pick up the evening paper later, at the liquor store."

7

Paresi and Star, heading up the investigation, were in the middle of third round interviews when the second body was found. They hurried to the scene.

In the parking lot of the Mid-City Mall, a young black woman lay across the bucket seats of her metallic blue Mercedes 380SL. The narrow skirt of her eggplant-purple linen suit was shoved up around her waist. Blood stained her pale lilac silk blouse and the top of her suit. On the ground, next to the open car door, lay a pair of eggplant-colored, snakeskin Maud Frizon high-heeled shoes.

The woman wore amethyst earrings, ringed in gold, and a thick gold bracelet.

She had been strangled. She had lain in her car all night, awaiting daybreak and Penelope Donovan. On her way to fire up her ovens in the small bake shop at the far end if the mall, Penelope had seen the car. It sat with the driver's door open and the stylish shoes lying outside. Against her better judgment, Penelope walked slowly toward the car, calling out. She hadn't really wanted to go, but she was a good Christian woman, and she had to see if anyone needed help. It was her duty.

Penelope's life and faith had not prepared her for this. The sight of the woman in the car made her momentarily lose her voice. When it returned, she screamed loud and long enough to alert several cleaning people and a few early arrivals for their day of work in the mall. Now she stood, visibly trembling, watching a group of police officers swarm around her discovery.

Star waited until the video and still photographers were finished and all the evidence had been tagged. The heat of the morning sun had released the smell of death. She put a Vicks inhaler to her nose and breathed deeply. After pulling on her latex gloves, she opened the passenger door of the Mercedes and crawled in, carefully avoiding a dried puddle of blood near the corpse's head.

The woman's envelope-shaped, under-the-arm snakeskin purse lay on the floor. It matched her shoes perfectly. A lilac, gray, and deep purple geometrically patterned silk scarf lay next to it.

Star called for tongs and two plastic evidence bags. She carefully lifted the purse and dropped it into one bag. She suspected the scarf might be the murder weapon, and it steadfastly refused to be picked up by the tongs, slipping to the floor again and again. Frustrated, she carefully lifted the long piece of fabric with her latex-gloved fingertips and dropped it into the other plastic bag.

Mitchell Grant arrived while she was huddled in the car, on her knees. He liked the view. "Good morning, Lieutenant," he said.

Star backed out of the car. "Morning, Mitchell." She'd expected him to turn up. "This one is pretty bad," she said, pointing to the woman's raised and spread legs. "Do you think we can get something to cover her? I mean, even though she's past caring . . . "

"Of course." Mitch waved one of his crew over. "Get a sheet for her, please."

"Right away, Doctor." The young woman hurried back to the coroner's van.

Mitch put on his latex gloves and leaned on one knee into the space Star had vacated. He manipulated the woman's jaw. It was rigid. He attempted to move her arm. It shifted slightly. He pressed her hand between his thumb and fingers. The skin's grayish pallor did not change.

Paresi leaned into the driver's door. "What's the matter, Mitch, think she's playing possum?"

"Not a chance my friend, she's decomposing as we speak." Mitch took a small penlight from the breast pocket of his dove-gray suit and looked into the woman's eyes. "She's in early rigor. Judging by the cloudy corneas, and the maggot eggs in her eyes, I'd say she's been dead about six to eight hours. We can get a liver temperature in the van, that will help in setting the time."

He unfolded his long frame from the car and stepped back to allow his team to do their work. He glanced over at the still shaken Penelope Donovan. "That the woman who discovered her?"

"Penelope's Pies," Star said. "She came in early to start her ovens. I guess there won't be any pies today."

Excusing herself, Star crossed the parking lot to the now less hysterical pie maker. The woman stepped back as Star approached, her wet eyes widening.

"Ms. Donovan," Star said, keeping her voice low and soft, "I'm Lieutenant Duvall, Homicide. I'd like to talk with you."

Penelope Donovan looked up at the tall, soft-spoken black woman. Her heart was racing and she was nearly crazed with fear. "Oh God, oh God!" She murmured over and over. "Oh God!"

Star took Penelope's hands in her own and spoke to her quietly. The frightened woman calmed down a little as she listened.

"It's going to be all right, Penelope, it's going to be all right." Star slipped an arm around the short, chubby woman in the yellow candy-striped uniform and led her toward a bench. "Let's sit down, you and me. We'll talk, okay? Just us, is that all right with you?" Penelope nodded, her eyes brimming with tears.

Paresi watched them pass. He walked around to the passenger's open door and looked again at the body. The dead woman's head was turned toward him on its broken neck. He studied her face; another pretty one. At least she *had* been pretty.

He looked at the earring on her left ear. The gold surrounding the amethyst appeared to be a nugget that had been flattened. The striations and crevices made the design one of a kind. Definitely a woman with style.

Star held Penelope's hands as she stood up. "Thank you, Penelope, you've been a big help. If you can just stay here for a minute, I'll get an officer to take you home."

Penelope gripped Star's hands as if she were drowning. "God," she said again.

Star patted her shoulder. "I'll get someone to get you some coffee. It'll be all right, you'll be fine."

She gently extricated herself from the woman's grasp and walked back to the car.

"This is not good," she said to Paresi. "Two young black women in this area, in three weeks, tell me this is not developing into a pattern."

"You can't tell about a pattern until you've got a lot of pieces."

"Don't even think that." Star leaned into the car and studied the woman's face. "Foam on the lips, purged blood, ruptured blood vessels in the eyes, black tongue. This one was strangled, the other one was shot, no connection." She looked back at Paresi. "Right?"

He knew what she wanted to hear, but he couldn't give it to her. "Maybe he likes to diversify his work."

"I knew you were going to say that."

Paresi nodded at Penelope, who was sitting on the bench, holding a disposable cup filled with black coffee that one of the uniforms had gotten her. It appeared like the slightest sound or movement would send her over the edge.

"What about the pie lady, what's she got?"

"Not a thing," Star said. "I've never seen a witness so spooked. She rambled a lot, but bottom line is she found her, that's all. Same story for the others who came over after she started screaming. Nobody saw anyone or anything. The uniforms will run her home and we'll go by later, after she's had time to chill."

Mitch walked over to the car and lifted the sheet from the

woman's lower body, staring at her. Star stood next to him. "Has she been raped?" she asked.

He covered the woman and peeled off his gloves. "I can't say just yet. The position says yes, but that's not always the case."

"I think she's been raped," Star said, folding her arms.

"Women's intuition?" Mitch asked.

"No, her underwear's missing."

Mitch and Paresi looked at one another.

"See?" Star lifted the sheet. "Her pantyhose and underpants are gone."

"It's been hot," Paresi said. "Maybe she wasn't wearing any."

"Uh-uh. This was a profiling sister. She obviously had the bucks and the job. You don't go to work carrying a snakeskin bag, wearing Maud Frizon shoes with no panties or stockings. He took them with him."

Paresi shrugged. "You might be on to something. But maybe she was getting it on out here, in the car with some guy."

"Wrong," Star said, a hard edge to her voice. "Women like this do not fuck in cars, even if it is a Mercedes. Whoever did this took her underthings with him, the warped son of a bitch!"

"Could be," Paresi agreed. "But let's say she met somebody, and he did her someplace else and then brought her back to her car."

Star turned to Mitch. "What do you think?"

Mitch shook his head. "Not likely. I say she hasn't been moved. Still, I can't agree about her not having sex in the car. I know she appears to be refined, but when the urge hits, it hits hard."

Star looked at him. "I say the woman was raped and murdered right here in this parking lot," Star insisted, her voice flat and cold, "and the guy did her for fun, otherwise he would have taken the car and her purse. Instead, he copped her underwear, and five will get you ten he's off somewhere in a bathroom exercising his wrist, the sick bastard!"

Disgust and anger clouded her face.

Paresi and Grant exchanged looks.

Star turned her back on the body, as if it were too painful to look at anymore. "Will she post today?"

"Yes," Mitch said. "They were stacked in the hallway when I came out, but I'll make sure she goes today. In fact, I'll do it myself." He put on his aviator shades. "If this one ties in to the other one in any way, I may be able to pick it up. I'll do her this afternoon if you two want to come by."

"We're going to see Penelope later, but we'll come by right after," Star said.

"Why don't you call me when you're finished with the witness. That way I won't start till you're free."

"Thanks, Mitchell, I appreciate that," Star said.

"No problem."

Patrolman Rossi touched her in the center of her back and she turned around.

"Excuse me, Lieutenant, Captain Lewis is on the air."

"Thanks, Steve." She looked at Paresi. "I wonder what he wants."

Paresi turned his palms up. "Two women murdered in our sector in three weeks, and no leads. I'd say our butts on a plate with a side of fries."

"You're probably right. I'll schmooze him while you get some uniforms into the mall. See if you can find out where she went last night. Make sure Impound leaves the car intact until either you or I can get to the search. I don't want anything touched, capeesh?"

"Loud and clear, Lieutenant." Paresi gave a heel-clicking salute and headed for the tow truck that was pulling up.

Star turned to Mitch. "Let's hope Lewis doesn't call me in and bite my ass off. I'll see you later."

He watched her walk to the squad car, an instant picture forming in his mind. The thought of ass-biting and Lieutenant Duvall made him smile.

8

Arthur Charles Lewis looked up to see Starletta Duvall and Dominic Paresi heading for his office.

"Captain Lewis," Star said.

"Lieutenant." He nodded at her.

Paresi barely moved his head in acknowledging Lewis.

"Paresi."

"Sir."

"Sit down, both of you."

They sat.

Star watched Lewis as he stood up and walked around his desk. She could tell by the dark blue color of his eyes behind his wire-rimmed glasses that their asses were definitely headed for some serious chewing. He took a deep breath and stared directly at them. He wasn't a tall man, or even a tough-looking one, but he definitely had an aura of power.

Star had heard a million tales about him when he was on the street. Some of them had come from her dad. Lewis's street name had been "Blackjack." Word was he was a head-banger, a major taker of scalps. Even though he'd mellowed and was doing his time till retirement, she knew it was true, he was not to be messed with. But she still liked him, even if the scalp on his belt was about to be hers.

Lewis had been her father's first partner and lifelong friend. He'd been good to her when she came on the job, the only woman in her unit. He was her first sergeant, and was there for her when some of her fellow officers rode her nearly to the breaking point.

Her mind went back to her first month in the squad; so

much shit had been thrown at her in the Academy and in this unit that she no longer paid any attention to the smirking and giggling going on around her. At the end of her first night, when she went out to the parking lot to go home, she found a used condom stuck to the windshield of her car.

When that didn't keep her from coming back, they brought out the big guns. During that first month, she found a pornographic magazine, a crude, hand-lettered invitation to a "Poke-Her" game, and assorted photos of the male anatomy in a state of arousal either on or near her locker.

She knew she was being watched, so she never reacted to the offensive material. She just threw it into the big green, chrome-topped can in the squad room and held her tears until she got home. This was the department that her father had given his life for. She was so hurt by the hatred that she couldn't even tell Vee about it.

One night she snapped. She'd come in a few minutes early, as usual, already dressed in her uniform. She sat at one of the long tables in the room, her back to the officers waiting for roll call. She tuned out the laughter and the smirking, and pretended to read a *New Yorker* magazine while she argued with herself about continuing in this stupid job. She felt she owed it to her father, but she couldn't take any more, not one more thing. What she didn't know was that Jim Catanya, the rudest and most obnoxious guy in the unit, was pretending to clean his gun, which was still loaded, with the barrel pointing directly at the back her head.

Lewis entered the room for roll call. He took one look at the situation and was across the floor in a heartbeat. She heard the sound of a body being slammed against metal and turned to find Catanya, who was over six feet tall, pinned against the supply cabinet, his feet off the floor. Lewis had Catanya's weapon in one hand and the officer's neck in the other.

She was so dumbstruck, he had to tell her what Catanya was doing behind her back. She couldn't speak. Anger and shame froze her vocal cords; she just stood there, not uttering a sound, her body shaking with fury. Lewis took his hand away from Catanya's throat and made him apologize. When he grudgingly said he was sorry, something inside her tore loose. She didn't even remember the punch, but Lewis later admiringly said she came up from the floor and stepped into it like a power hitter at the plate.

She didn't even feel the crunch of Catanya's nose under her fist. When she came to herself, Catanya's nostrils were gushing blood and Sergeant Lewis and some of the others were laughing their asses off.

Lewis dared Catanya to bring any kind of charges against her. He turned to his troops, saying how unfortunate it was that Officer Catanya tripped, fell and broke his nose. The men, none of them able to look at her, agreed with him that it was a shame.

From then on they left her alone. Lewis had later gone to the emergency room and relieved Catanya of his badge and gun, putting him on sick leave for an "undetermined period of time."

Later that night he hooked up with her on the street, sent her partner for coffee and asked how she was doing. Still mad, she told him her hand hurt but she was okay.

He told her to head down to hospital emergency and get an ice pack. The smile on his face told Star she'd passed her trial by fire. He sat grinning at her.

"You got a mean right cross, you know that?" he said, his eyes twinkling. "Goddamn, Lenny would be proud."

"Thank you, sir." She couldn't help but smile herself.

"A mean right cross, and an iron spine. I'm not gonna have to worry about you."

He had been good to her, over her fifteen years in the department. He was always there, and always honest, even when it meant an ass-chewing. Now she sat staring at him, knowing she was smiling and that she shouldn't be, but she couldn't stop herself. She knew him well, and she knew that she and Paresi were in mucho deep brown.

Lewis sat on the edge of his desk, looking at the two of them over his glasses. "Do you two have something to tell me?"

Star and Paresi glanced at one another. "We're working very hard, Captain," she said.

"I don't doubt that, Lieutenant." He stared at her. "I know you're giving all you can ... still, I don't see any breaks, I don't see any new information, I don't see any indication that this matter is being handled. All I see is a new victim."

"Sir?" Paresi spoke up.

Lewis shot him a look.

"With all respect, Cap'n," Paresi, bold as ever, continued, "what do you want from us? We're in our shoes sixteen hours a day, and this morning we've got another one. We're doing the best we can. Why aren't you reaming out Darcy or Rescovich? They're working on this thing too."

Lewis leveled his gaze at Paresi. "Detective Sergeant Paresi, I have spoken to the officers you mentioned, and I know that they too are working on this case, but you and Lieutenant Duvall are heading up the investigation, and in that position of power, it would seem to me that you two would definitely be privy to all new information before any members of your team."

Paresi glanced at Star as if to say, Why didn't you shut me up? Star smiled at him with her mouth closed, as if to respond, We're toast.

"Yes sir," Paresi said.

"Now, children ..." Lewis got up and went back behind his desk and sat down. "Details?"

"None," Star said.

"Why not?"

"We've just come from the scene. You called us away before we could really get working. The body won't be posted until this afternoon—"

He held up his hand, silencing her. "Witnesses?"

"One, but she really didn't see anything."

"A witness who didn't see anything?"

"Yes sir, I mean she discovered the body but it was very early this morning, there was no one around. Dr. Grant said the woman had been dead about six to eight hours."

"Grant was there?"

"Yes sir."

Lewis pursed his lips. He didn't approve of Mitchell Grant. Although the man was a hell of a pathologist, he couldn't keep his fly zipped. "And the only thing our learned, celebrated Chief Medical Examiner could say was that she'd been dead about six to eight hours?"

Star shrugged.

Lewis's voice growled out of him: "Get out of here, both of you, and bring me something concrete. And I want it today!"

The two of them stood. "We'll report back right after the autopsy," Star said. "Maybe Dr. Grant can tie this murder in to the other one."

"Let's just hope he doesn't tie in a third one, Lieutenant," Lewis said.

"Yes sir."

"Della Robb-Ellison," Mitch read from the file on his desk. "A twenty-seven-year-old African-American female, sixty-five inches long, weighing 110 pounds. Brown eyes; dark brown hair, tinted auburn." He looked at Star. "She died from asphyxiation. The murder weapon is the scarf you found in the car." He closed the file and slid it across the desk to her.

She opened it. The images inside made her gasp. Paresi looked over her shoulder. The close-up, color morgue photos of Della Robb-Ellison were ghastly. Her eyes were open and rolled back in her head, showing the whites. Her black tongue set atop her gaping mouth like some kind of exotic flower; blood caked on her lips and in and around her nose. Her killer had twisted the scarf so tightly around her throat that it broke the skin and left an angry purplish lesion on her neck.

Star touched her own throat. For a moment she couldn't breathe.

"I found silk fibers in the wound," Mitch said. "Tests show

they match the fibers of the scarf you picked up from the car floor. Her trachea was crushed. From the direction of the ligature mark on her neck, my guess is the killer grabbed her from behind and hoisted up. It looks like he tried to use the scarf as some kind of pulley, like he wanted to hang her in the car."

"Was she raped?" Star asked, her voice sounding hoarse.

"That's hard to say. She'd had sex, but there was no sign of force. She'd also been manipulated."

"Manipulated?"

"Yes. I found bite marks on the outer labia and the upper left inner thigh. She had also performed oral sex. There were microscopic traces of seminal fluid in the stomach contents. Natural acidity had rendered it pretty much useless, but there was definitely evidence of semen having been swallowed. However, there was none in the vagina."

He pointed to the photos. "There were no injuries to the lips or tongue, so I would guess she willingly participated in the oral sex."

Star looked at the pictures. "You don't think it was rape?" she asked.

"Rape calls are difficult, even with trauma and lacerations. Some people go in for rough sex."

"Did this appear to be rough sex?"

"Not by my estimation." Mitch leaned back in his chair. "But there were irritations to the vaginal wall, consistent with possible fingernail scraping."

"And you don't think that was rough?" Star said. "Having somebody shove their fingers in you so hard they leave scars?"

"Not if she liked it like that," Mitch said. "Some women do."

"Not any sane ones," Star said.

"One person's pain is another person's passion, Lieutenant." Something in his voice made Star unable to look at him.

"Yeah . . . so, what about the lab work?" She closed the folder.

"Jason couldn't get an impression from the labial bite, but the thigh has a good partial."

"Labial bite?" Star shook her head. "What kind of a wacko bastard is this?"

"Time will tell, Lieutenant." Mitch indicated a bowl filled with silver-wrapped chocolates on his desk. "Kiss?" he asked.

Star slid the bowl of candy to her side of the desk and dipped inside, taking a handful. "Swell," she said, putting two chocolates into her mouth. "Just swell."

It was after one A.M. when she got home. Star headed straight for the bathtub and filled it with hot water and Shalimar-scented bubble bath. She climbed inside and sat, letting the water and glorious scent ease her tensions away. She leaned back, and sipped chardonnay from the crystal, long-stemmed wineglass in her hand. From the bedroom CD player, Gladys Knight gave way to Aretha Franklin.

Star sat the glass on the edge of the tub, singing along with Lady Soul, and doing a pretty good job on "Chain of Fools." She lazily rubbed her loofa along her shoulders and arms, and leaned back again, letting the music take her.

On the stereo, Aretha slid into "Dr. Feelgood." Star turned on the hot water tap with her toes, feeling the fresh water heat up and mingle with the cooling bathwater, soothing her tired body.

"Dr. Feelgood," she said. "Where can I get one of those? In fact, I need two, one for me and one for Vee, because there ain't no reason why two good women like us should be alone."

She closed her eyes. Mitchell Grant entered her thoughts. She wondered if Dr. Grant was a Dr. Feelgood. He sure looked the part even if they didn't see eye-to-eye on what was rough sex. "Hmmm, I wonder just how rough he can get." She shook her head. "Stop that!"

She sank further into the water. "I don't want to think about him." She closed her eyes, relaxing, until Della Robb-Ellison's dead face floated in front of her.

Her eyes snapped open. She sat bolt upright, knocking the glass of wine to the carpeted floor. "Damnit!" She clasped her hands to her chest, breathing hard. "Oh . . ." She tried to catch her breath. "Paresi is right." She ran a hand through her hair. "The only way to deal with this job is to get relentlessly and endlessly laid, which he is no doubt doing at this very moment."

When Dominic left the squad room at midnight, he'd grinningly told her he had a late date with Theresa Borghese, the new clerk in records.

Star splashed at the suds in the tub. "Paresi, you're a pig, but a lucky one. I could use a tension breaker along about now." She leaned back into the water, thinking about her last love, Ron Davis, a detective in Grand Theft. What a disaster!

She preferred to think of it as hormonal overload, brought on by tight buns, muscular thighs, and tremendous biceps. The man looked like a god, with ebony-colored skin and a smile to make you slap your mama. They met at the police impound of all places, and she suffered immediate cessation of brain function. When Vee met him, she pronounced him "a crocodile." Vee was right.

The "relationship" lasted about four months, out of which three and one half were spent in total hell. She'd thought he would understand her job and her need to do it, but he kept pushing her to quit, leave the department. It was "no place for a woman."

He didn't want to know how hard she'd fought for that gold shield. The idea that she outranked him also upset him. So it was hasta la bye-bye to beautiful Ronnie.

Since then she'd been on her own, and it was really getting tired. She missed having a man in her life. Not just for sex, though she really felt that loss, but because she liked men. She liked talking to them, and laughing with them. Her father had been her friend, and so men were easy to relate to. They were always around, but if they were outside the department and found out what she did for a living, they were either intrigued with the idea of kinky sex or scared shitless of her.

Either way, it was slim pickings, and after Ron, she'd had her fill of cops. Still, while she dated him she'd never needed to explain when the job made her want to sit alone in a room all day. That part she liked. Now if she could just find a man who wasn't a cop but who understood cops, she'd be happy. He'd have to be secure with his own thing, so he wouldn't be intimidated by her job.

She moved her legs lazily in the water. "Nice shoulders would be a real plus," she said out loud. She closed her eyes again and smiled to herself. "Mitchell Grant has incredible shoulders."

The open bathroom door creaked. She leaned out from the tub to see. She knew who it was. They were the only two in the house. Softly, he walked into the room and perched on the closed toilet seat. His bright green eyes regarded her coolly.

"Hello, handsome," she said. He tilted his head and a soft sound escaped him. She watched him settle comfortably on the seat, prepared to watch over her while she soaked away the day's tensions.

When she climbed out of the tub, a few drops of water sprayed him, sending his fat gray and white furry body bolting. Star laughed as her cat scampered out of the bathroom, a sharp little sound trailing behind him.

She dried off and wrapped herself in her favorite bright blue and white striped terry-cloth robe. She picked up the wineglass and mopped up the spilled wine with a towel.

Marvin Gaye rocked out from the stereo. She turned her bed down in rhythm to "Got to Give It Up."

Dropping her robe at the foot of the bed, she climbed in. The cool sheets felt wonderful against her bare skin. She turned off the lights and lay staring into the darkness, listening to Marvin and wondering about the killer. What was he doing on this warm, moonlit night? She prayed that the morning wouldn't bring another victim. Jake curled up alongside her, his soft purrs soon turned to snores.

She stroked his head in the darkness. "I *would* get a cat

with a deviated septum!" She smiled at the cat, turned on her side, and was soon asleep.

Maureen Auster knocked on the door of her husband's "studio." It was actually a spare room in the cellar, which he'd taken over for his photography work.

When they were first married, and he was drunk on her body, he shot rolls and rolls of nude snaps of her and himself. He liked to say they were two perfect specimens. Since he didn't trust taking his pictures to photo shops, he learned to do his own developing. In the eight years of their marriage, this little kink had become a major part of his life. Since the birth of their daughter Jenny, five years ago, he no longer took pictures of her. The baby had put fifty-two extra pounds on Maureen's body, and she'd never taken off more than six.

When their daughter was thirteen months old, she was diagnosed as autistic, and Jerry didn't speak to Maureen for nearly two months. After their child was institutionalized, he wouldn't come near her. He blamed her, saying she was inferior, that it was her fault Jenny wasn't perfect. It was nearly a year before he touched her again.

By the time he came back to her bed, she didn't care. Her only feeling was that she desperately did not want to get pregnant again. He'd forbidden her to have her tubes tied, and he refused to even consider a vasectomy. He touched her so infrequently these days that she never thought about pregnancy anymore.

She knew there were other women, and she didn't care. It took the pressure off. Besides, Famous Amos and the Keebler Elves made her feel much better than her own husband had in years. She knocked again. He didn't answer.

"Jerry, breakfast is ready."

"I'm not hungry," he shouted through the door.

"Aren't you going to work today?"

Silence.

"Jerry?" She knocked again.

The door flew open with such force that she jumped back, hitting her elbow against the wall. Pain rocketed up her arm into her hand, making her fingers curl.

"It's my day off, okay? I don't want to be bothered. I'm working, *now leave me the fuck alone!*" He slammed the door in her face.

"I just wanted to know . . . " She rubbed her throbbing elbow, and again raised her hand to knock, but thought better of it. Turning around, she walked slowly back upstairs. A loose pudding of a woman, trapped in a life she didn't understand or want.

Jerry Auster cursed under his breath. Why couldn't she just leave him alone? He went back into the tiny chamber that served as his darkroom.

The pictures were almost ready. With the tongs, he moved the paper back and forth in the fluid. The image began to rise.

There she was. Her dark eyes stared at him. Her skin looked like it was glowing. She was beautiful. The memory started the heat glowing between his thighs.

He took the picture out, dipped it in the stabilizer, rinsed it, and hung it on the line to dry. The next one was almost ready. This one showed her from another angle.

He saw her the day she came into the store. He was immediately attracted. He watched her walk up and down the aisles, checking the merchandise. Even though she was wearing cutoff jeans, sandals, and a white tank top with no bra, he knew she had money. It was in her attitude.

He approached her while she was pushing buttons and fiddling around with the wall display. He could see her eyes light up behind her sunglasses. Piece of cake. She purchased a top-of-the-line CD unit from him and paid with a gold MasterCard.

When he went out to put the merchandise in her car, he knew he'd hit the jackpot. She was driving a metallic-blue Mercedes 380SL.

After he loaded the unit, he stood in the rear doorway of the shop, letting her check him out.

She sat behind the wheel, grinning at him with that mouth. It was big and generous and the thought of what he could do with it made him hot. Her full lips glistened with a deep red color. She must taste like ripe cherries, he thought.

He liked everything about her, especially her eyes. She'd taken off the shades in the store, while he showed her the ins and outs of her new system. Now, she grinned as she looked at him. He could see the hunger. The eyes never lied. He liked her hair too, pulled straight and dangling in one long braid down her back.

Watching her check him out, he returned her smile, slightly thrusting out his pelvis, letting her see that she had his complete attention. She caught his move and laughed.

Oh yeah, he thought to himself, next.

That night, after the store closed, he copied her address from his book. He cruised by the building on his way home.

Gaylord Terrace Apartments, high-rent district, underground garage parking, and a uniformed doorman—it didn't get any better. She'd been easy to follow. She didn't pay much attention to what was going on around her, she always seemed preoccupied, her mind someplace else.

The third photo was ready. This one was definitely his favorite. Everything on view, just for him. He was a take-charge guy. He told her what he wanted and she did it—she liked it, all of it.

The memory of his orgasm made him hard again. Grinning, he pulled another photograph from the developing fluid, stabilized it, and rinsed it.

She had been so easy. He hung the photo on the line. She had a routine, and he knew it after the first few days. He'd decided to make his move at the mall. She worked out three nights a week at the health club there. He followed her for about two weeks, watching her do aerobics through the plate-glass window of the club. He'd damn near come one night, when she was down on all fours with her ass in the air, doing some kind of belly exercise where she swung her pelvis back and forth, in and out. He imagined her doing the same thing on him.

She knew he was watching. She liked having him stare at

her, and would glance at him from time to time while she worked out. She enjoyed yanking his chain, but he would show her who was boss.

The last time he watched her, some bimbo oozed out and asked him if he was interested in joining. After that, he sat in his car in the parking lot, waiting for her to appear. She was usually the last to leave, at about ten o'clock. He'd gotten used to the wait; sometimes he got a coffee and went back to his position in the parking lot.

The night he finally hit, she'd only been in the club about thirty minutes. He decided it was time; he'd gotten tired of following her.

He climbed into the rear of her car just after she'd gotten out. The door was unlocked. Man, she made things easy.

The tiny space behind the driver's seat cramped his body. It was a lot like the Tiger Cages in 'Nam, but he knew how to project his thoughts so that his body wasn't the most important thing. He was able to stay in small places for a long time. He lay on his side, knees tucked to his chest, camera bag wedged against his body, contenting himself with images of what he would do to her when she returned to the car.

She always parked in a deserted section of the mall lot, so her precious doors wouldn't get dinged. He was aware of the fact that no other cars had pulled anywhere around her. In his mind he was shoving his cock down her throat, when she opened the car door.

She slid into the seat and put her key in the ignition.

He rose up from behind. "Surprise!"

The last photo was now hanging on the line. Jerry moved from picture to picture. "Beautiful, just beautiful." He studied each one carefully, deciding which ones to blow up. He made a second check, selecting the shot of her with her legs spread.

"First things first," He said to himself. He plucked it from the line and settled into his old recliner. Slowly, he unzipped his fly.

9

Starletta sat across the table from Mitch in the station lunch-
room. From near the ice machine, Elvis kept his eye on her.
Actually, he was looking somewhere to the left of her head,
but he was watching her. She sipped an iced tea while Mitch
nursed a glass of pineapple juice.

Mitch rolled his head around in circles, trying to free up
the tightness in his neck and shoulders. He had no idea why
he had gone to the precinct at seven that night, but here he
was and here she was.

"You look like you could use a good massage," she said.

"Pardon?"

"Your neck." She pointed at him. "You seem to be having
a problem."

"It's been a long day." He sighed.

"For me too."

"I guess you're wondering why I'm here."

"Actually, yes, I mean I didn't expect to see you this
evening."

Mitch sipped the juice. "I didn't expect to be here, I just
thought maybe you and Dom could use some help. I know I
could. I've been over the reports on both women so many
times, I know where all their birthmarks are. I figured I
needed a fresh perspective, so I thought if we all sat down
together, we might be able to help each other, you know, see
what we're missing."

She stared at him.

He shrugged his shoulders. "You know, when you do a

job, sometimes you miss things, because you're trying so hard to be thorough, so I thought that maybe if you two looked over my reports and pictures, and I looked over yours, we might be able to check one another and maybe come up with something that otherwise would be lost."

"Great idea, except Paresi is out of here. His niece AnnaLisa turned fourteen today, and his sister Rosine gave a party. He's probably knee-deep in adolescent girls swooning over him by now."

"And loving it," Mitch said, grinning.

"Don't you know it!" She laughed. "As for me, I'd love to try your technique, but I'm so tired, I probably wouldn't see a hatchet buried right between somebody's eyes."

"Have you had dinner?"

She pointed at the watery tea. "This is it."

"Doesn't have to be. Why don't we go out and get a bite?"

Star looked wary. "Is this a date?"

"No, it's two tired, hungry people who have to eat, eating together."

That smile was making her tingle.

"Besides," he said, "if it were a date, what would be the problem? I'm not the big bad wolf."

"That's not the way I hear it," she said, enjoying the jousting.

He leaned across the table. "Don't believe everything you hear, Red. Now, I'm starving, so what do you say ... two people, working together, eating together, a great meal, no strings, and one of us is even buying."

"Gee, I hope that's you."

"Me? I thought you were gonna spring." He stood up and took her arm. "I like expensive restaurants, Lieutenant. I'm sort of a snob that way."

"Good. I'm sure you'll enjoy the Colonel, his food is famous all over the world." She turned toward the man busily wiping down the table behind them. "Good night, Elvis."

Elvis gave a wan flapping of his towel and watched them leave. He didn't like this at all, she looked way too happy. He was going to have to make his move soon, or lose her to that tree-topping, pretty-boy morgue jockey.

The elevator arrived. They were alone inside. Mitch stood close to her, and she could feel the fabric of his jacket on her bare arm.

"How about Japanese?"

"What?"

"Japanese. Do you like Japanese food?"

She had to look up at him. Even though she was six feet tall, he towered at least six or seven inches over her. His lankiness dwarfed her. She liked it.

"Not particularly," she replied. "Maybe we can just get a pizza."

"Fine by me."

The elevator door opened and they stepped off in front of the Homicide Bureau. The office was deserted between shifts, except for the cleaning lady and Tim O'Halloran. He was a career cop who had been in Homicide longer than Star had been on the planet. He had not been one of her dad's favorite people, but she'd learned to tolerate him. Tim was an alcoholic, the result of all those years of bodies and mayhem. He looked up when the two of them entered the room.

"Checking out, kid?" His voice sounded like hard shoes walking on broken glass.

"Yep." Star picked up her jacket and put her peg on the assignment board to the out position. "I've got to sleep sometime, Timmy."

O'Halloran looked over his shoulder at Mitch, who was standing in the doorway. "I doubt if you'll get any tonight, kiddo."

A strangled kind of sound rose from his gut. Star realized he was laughing. She looked over at Mitch. He shrugged.

"Night, Timmy," she said.

Mitch helped her on with her jacket, and his hands lingered on her shoulders. She felt warm inside. Her sensible self said, Don't forget who this is, and it's only dinner.

They decided on Gerardi's, a newly opened Italian restaurant that specialized in deep-dish Chicago-style pizza. They polished off a large one and seriously contemplated ordering another.

"I think I love this place." Star popped the last of her pizza into her mouth. "I know Paresi would flip."

She took a sip of her Bordolino.

Mitch gazed at her over his beer. "I'm sure he'd like it." He indicated her empty plate. "You sure you don't want to order another one?"

She laughed. "Am I eating like a cow?"

"On the contrary, I like a woman with an appetite, especially these days. It's good to see somebody enjoying their food."

"I've never been one to eat like a bird." She grinned at him over her glass. "I've also never been one to pretend that I live on salads. I love to eat, especially when I haven't had anything but an orange and some weak tea all day."

"Let's get another one. What you don't finish, you can take home."

"Thanks." She put the glass down. "But I'm full, really. Besides, I've got to save some room for dessert."

Mitch laughed out loud. "You know, I really like your partner, but I'm very glad he's not here now."

She leaned back against the cushioned booth. Oh please, don't let the grapevine be right, she thought. Please. "Why is that, Doctor?" she asked.

He let a slow smile spread across his face. "Because he'd want to talk shop, and frankly, I'm enjoying your company, getting to know you away from him, and the job. I just want to concentrate on you."

Star's face grew warm. She looked down at her hands. He's hitting on me and I'm digging it. Jeez. "I'm glad he's not here, too," she said. "I'm enjoying the break."

Mitch raised his glass in her direction. "The night is still young."

She looked at him. In the soft light of the restaurant, his eyes were deep green and they seemed to be looking right into all those places she kept locked down tight.

"True, but the morning comes quickly."

"Well, then, we'd better see what's tempting for dessert." Mitch put his glass down and signaled the waiter. "Something with chocolate, no doubt?"

"Surprise me," she said.

"I intend to."

Paresi glanced at the clock and across their desks at his partner's empty chair. Star was late. He pulled the chocolate glazed doughnut he'd bought for her out of the bag and took a bite. At that moment, she walked in.

"Little late this morning, pard." He took another bite of the doughnut. "I saved you a piece of cake from AnnaLisa's party, but when you didn't show, I ate it. All I've got left is this." He held up the half-eaten doughnut.

"Having a sugar rush, are you?" She snatched the pastry from his hand. "Thank you."

He grabbed for the doughnut. "Hey, you snooze, you lose."

She held it out of his reach. "Nice to know you're always thinking of me." She sat down, took a bite and unlocked her drawer.

"So, why are we so late this morning?" he asked.

"Did you oversleep too?" she said.

"Nope, but then, I slept in my own little bed."

She fixed him with a steely gaze. "Are you implying that I didn't?"

"No, not at all. I just heard that you left with Mitchell Grant last night."

"I did. We had a great dinner, at a place you would love, by the way, and I returned with the same Mitchell Grant."

"Really?" Paresi rocked back in his chair.

"Yes. He drove me back to my car, and I went home and he went home . . . to separate homes."

"Uh-huh."

"Why are you behaving like a Senate Ethics Committee?"

"Because I know Grant, and as I recall, you didn't want to join the fucked-and-dumped club."

"That's right, and what makes you think I've changed my mind? Besides, all that's just talk. I don't believe there's a club. We had fun last night. He was great, *and* a gentleman. So lighten up, Sherlock, there's no romance happening here. It was just two people working together, taking time out for dinner."

"So what was he doing here last night, anyway?"

"He came to see if he could give us a hand."

"Yeah? And what other part of his anatomy did he offer?"

Star leaned across her desk, whispering, "If I didn't know better, I'd think you're jealous."

"I'm not jealous. Regardless of the face he showed last night, this guy is dangerous. The stories are true, and I don't want him messing with you, got it?"

"If you're right, don't worry. I can take care of myself." She tore the remainder of the doughnut in half and handed it to him. "You're so cute when you're macho."

"I know."

Star swiveled in her chair. "Where's the mail?"

"Downstairs. I think they're on strike or something, nobody's brought it up."

"Oh, I'm sorry, I didn't realize," she said.

"What?" Paresi stared at her.

"That you're paralyzed." She stood up.

"I thought I'd give you something to do." He smiled.

"Thanks."

She'd started across the squad room when a civilian employee burst through the double doors. Kaye Newman's face was red from running up the stairs.

"Sorry, folks." She grinned, holding a white bin full of mail. "We've got a couple of people out on vacation and one who's sick, so it's late . . . sorry."

Richardson tossed a balled up piece of paper at her, and it signaled the others. Star stepped back as the laughing woman was pelted from all sides.

"Your tax dollars at work," she said to Kaye.

"Yeah." The clerk grinned. "Remind me to cheat next time."

"Right." Star smiled and reached for the bin.

"Thanks, Lieutenant," Kaye said.

"You're welcome."

Star took the bin to the long table at the end of the room. She rummaged through and pulled out several pieces of mail. As she walked back to her desk, Gambale called out, "So you're not gonna sort it and pass it out?"

Star stopped and stared at him. "Do I look like I'm gonna sort it and pass it out?"

Gambale laughed. "What day of the month is this?" he said, grinning.

"The day that's gonna be etched on your tombstone if you don't leave me alone," she said.

The squad room erupted in laughter.

Star went to her desk and sat down, tossing three envelopes to Paresi.

The other detectives crowded around the mail bin, digging through.

Paresi picked up a long, white envelope, addressed to him, but with no stamp. "Hmmm."

"What?"

"No postage." He opened the envelope and read the letter inside. "Oh Jeez!"

"What?" Star looked up.

"A letter from Theresa Borghese."

"The girl in Records?"

"Yeah, she's dumping me."

Star laughed. "Sounds like she's got good taste to me."

"Yeah? She thinks I'm in love with you," he said.

"Aren't you?" Star asked, batting her eyelashes at him.

"Sure, but I don't let it stand in the way of my life as a dog." He tossed the letter into his wastebasket.

Richardson approached their desks. "Hey guys, I think this is for you." He handed a large, brown envelope to Star.

"What is it?" Paresi asked.

"Do I look like Kreskin?" Star said.

"Okay, I'm convinced nothing happened last night. If it had, you'd be in a better mood."

"You are working on this case, right?" Richardson said, pointing at the envelope.

"What?" Star reached inside and pulled out the contents.

"Jesus!"

"What?"

She handed the bundle to Paresi.

"Marrone!"

Della Robb-Ellison's strangled face stared up at them from the seat of her Mercedes.

10

Alma Johnson was on cloud nine. She'd had the best day at work ever. Technitronics Computer Corporation had picked up its biggest contract, thanks to her. The bosses had been grateful and generous. They gave her a huge raise.

She felt like dancing. In fact, she had cut a couple of steps in the ladies' room after she got the news. Mama had been right. She could sell Ray Charles albums at a Mississippi Klan meeting, and today had been the proof of the pudding.

Packard-Jewison placed a multimillion dollar order with her company to supply and service their offices coast to coast with the latest Technitronics computer system.

That meant a soon-to-be trip to Los Angeles and a stop at every Packard-Jewison office across the country, where she, a poor little black girl born and raised in the Ida B. Wells housing projects in Brookport, Massachusetts, was gonna teach all those big guns how to get friendly with the new system.

With the raise, she could buy a new car and put a down payment on that two-bedroom condo in Oakwood Hills. On a whim, she'd gone to look at it during an open house a couple of weeks ago, and lost her heart. As she was leaving, she decided that the place was hers, and now . . . she was going to call the agent in the morning. God bless positive thinking!

The condo was hers, but that was at least two months away. She had to buy something now, right this minute, something to seal the deal, bring the luck home. She knew exactly what she wanted.

When she entered Electric City, she felt like Janet Jackson or somebody, because today she was going to buy a big screen television for watching her favorite soaps, and she was going to pay cash. Antonio Vega on "One Life to Live," big as life in her bedroom, now that was an idea she could get into.

Not bad for a skinny, nappy-headed little black girl raised on welfare. She could still hear the white social worker's voice telling her to forget about going to college, because the welfare bureau wasn't going to pay for it.

"I wonder where she is now?" Alma said aloud. "Wherever she is, I could buy and sell the bitch!" She snapped her fingers and laughed again.

He watched her walking down the aisle. A tiny, skinny black woman, with great tits, wearing a very expensive outfit. She happily wandered in a zigzag pattern through the rows of television sets.

He straightened his lucky tie and approached her. "Hi, welcome to Electric City. What can I do for you today?"

She looked up at him. She couldn't have been more than five feet tall, even though her high-heeled shoes tried valiantly to add three inches. Her tits made him think of a chocolate Dolly Parton, not as big, but close, damn close.

"Well, hi yourself. Yes, you can help me. I'm looking for a big screen TV, you know, one of those humongous ones?" She waved her arms around. "I want it as soon as possible, so don't show me anything that isn't in stock. I don't want to wait for an order, okay?" She spoke quickly; even her voice was cute.

"I see." He smiled down at her. Something in her eyes told him he could tease her, have fun. "You're looking for a big one, and you want it now."

She grinned and batted her fake eyelashes at him. "Oh, but definitely. I want it as big as it can get and as soon as I can get it."

"You're such a little girl." He smiled. "You got room for something that big?"

"Honey, I can handle anything you can show me."

They laughed together.

"Well." He offered her his arm. "Let's go see what we can

find that will bring tears of joy to your eyes and a smile to your beautiful lips."

"Ooh, I do love the way you talk, honey," she said, squeezing his bicep. "Shoot me your best shot." She traced her finger over the name on his store pin. "Jerry."

She was a fox. He liked that, and she was damned adorable. Her lips were full and lush, covered with coral lipstick. He bet she tasted like peaches. He breathed in her expensive perfume, and his pants grew tight around the crotch. He patted her hand. "Let's go."

11

It was eight at night, and Star had been home nearly three hours. Lewis had kicked her loose early. After getting those photos, she had to get out. He understood.

She tried tracing the mailing point for the envelope, but the post office was no help at all. The pictures had come through the main post office. Whoever mailed them could have come in and dropped them in the box in the lobby, or mailed them from one of over sixty mailboxes in the area. The post office was located in the business and commerce heart of Brookport. There was no way to even begin tracing where the envelope could have come from. It had not been a good day.

Paresi had called twice, to make sure she was okay. After she talked to him the second time, she called Vee. Star needed to laugh, and she knew Vee wouldn't let her down. They had passed friendship long ago; theirs was a true sisterhood.

The first face she remembered seeing besides her parents belonged to Verenita Gloria Spencer-Martin. They had eaten crayons, mud pies, and paste together, taught each other the newest dance steps, and sat up all night giggling over their first kisses. They were so close, people actually thought they were sisters, and had it not been for Len Duvall, they would probably be living identical lives.

Vee had married Lorenzo Martin two days after their graduation from high school. Star had been the maid of honor. Vee called her on her wedding night, after Lorenzo was sleeping, to let her know how scared she was of being Mrs. Martin. But even though Vee and Lorenzo were both young, their marriage was solid.

Lorenzo was a good man. He'd loved Vee since they met at Cynthia Hollis's eleventh birthday party. He'd been a musician and singer in high school, and had even traveled to Washington, D.C., with the choir to solo in a ceremony honoring the anniversary of Martin Luther King, Jr.'s March on Washington. Even the President himself had commented during his speech on Lorenzo's beautiful voice.

He had a chance to make it in music, but he wanted Vee and a family, and so, at the ages of nineteen and eighteen, respectively, they set up housekeeping. When Star went over to visit, she felt like she and Vee were still playing house, only this time Lorenzo was in the mix. He got a job working at a candy factory while he went to college at night, working toward his degree in Business Management.

After a night of champagne and celebration, when Lorenzo was promoted to manager of his floor, Roland came along. With one child, both Vee and Lorenzo wanted more, and they figured with Lorenzo's job, they could afford them. Cole came next, and finally, Lena.

Three kids put more strain on their finances than they had figured, so Lorenzo put his degree on the back burner and took a second job driving a cab to make extra money.

He wouldn't allow his parents to help support his young family, nor did he want Vee working. "Raising the kids is your job," he used to say to her. Sometimes, she did dressmaking and alterations at home to add to the income, but things were always tight.

Lorenzo worked for the family, but he didn't take good care of himself. He ignored his rising blood pressure, figuring he was young and in good shape, so it was just stress, no big deal.

One afternoon, when he was thirty-one years old, he came home from work early, complaining of a headache and dizziness. He took two aspirin and lay down on the couch for a nap. He never woke up.

Vee, at thirty, was left with three kids, a high school diploma, and a mortgage. It had been a tough road, but she'd managed. She put herself through business college and was now working as an executive secretary in a large real estate company.

Now that the kids were older, she was taking classes at the community college, and planning to go on for a degree in accounting. She'd always loved working with numbers and figures. Vee had done Star's math homework all through high school, while Star wrote her compositions. Vee's goal was to someday have her own accounting business.

The kids, Lena (named for Lena Horne), Roland (named for Roland Kirk), and Cole (named for John Coltrane), were all in school and pulling good grades. Roland was a high school senior, looking forward to graduation.

The kids loved the fact that their Auntie Star was a cop, especially Roland. He told her he was thinking about the department as a career. Star knew Vee would freak, so she was trying to talk him out of it.

Still, they all liked to talk to her for hours on end about her cases, always wanting to know the most gruesome details, which she never divulged. She constantly reminded them that murder was not like in the movies, or on television, that when you're dead, you don't get up when the scene is over.

Though Star hadn't said anything to Vee, she knew that Roland was thinking of joining the department. The prospect of any of her children doing her best friend's job made Vee's blood run cold. She'd worried about Star from the first day on the job. After Star's father died, Vee sat up with her all night trying to talk her out of joining the force. No way was she going to let any of her kids be a cop.

Even though Star had distinguished herself on the job, Vee still worried. Especially when the phone rang in the middle of the night. She'd just about fall apart before she could answer. She'd once told Star that she felt as if she were married to a cop.

Star's response had been, "Times are hard, but not *that* hard!"

They laughed together.

The call they'd shared tonight had been good. Vee sensed that Star's day had been brutal, though she wouldn't go into details. Still, she'd been able to release some of the outrage.

After Star hung up, she showered, washed her hair, and slathered on an herbal facial mask. She was sitting up in bed, watching a video of the Marx Brothers' *Night at the Opera*, when the phone rang.

"'Lo." She could barely move her mouth; the mask was nearly dry.

"Hey, pard, sorry to bother you, but your night off is over. We got another one."

"Pa'si?"

"Yeah, what's wrong, you sound weird."

"I'm we'ing a ma'k."

"A what?"

"Ne'er min', where the bod'?"

"At 7284 Kinney Street, apartment four."

Her mask cracked. "I'm on the way."

She bounced off the bed, jarring the cat, who blinked at her and yawned. "See you later, Jake," she said, and raced toward the bathroom.

Thirty minutes later Star was standing over what was left of Alma Johnson.

Mitchell Grant put his hand on her shoulder. "Can we talk for a minute?"

"Yeah, sure."

"This just might be the same guy."

"You think?"

"Definite possibility. Look at this." He squatted beside the body, his gloved finger outlining a dark bruise mark on Alma Johnson's left shoulder. "See this?"

Star settled beside him. "It's a bite mark."

"Now, look at this." He moved Alma Johnson's thigh, opening her legs wide. He traced a mark just on the inside of her left thigh.

Star looked closer. "Jesus."

The bite mark was deep enough to have left a bloody wound.

"Remember the marks on Della Robb-Ellison."

"Yes."

"Well . . ." Mitch outlined the mark on Alma Johnson's thigh. "I'm betting there will be more of these on her labia. And we know from the small cast Jason was able to get that the bite is irregular. See?"

Star looked closely. Beneath the blood she could see that the wounds were jagged, as if from teeth that were not aligned.

"So it looks like we may have our own Dahmer, huh?"

"It's a possibility, and, for what it's worth, he's right-handed."

"How can you tell?"

"Because all the bites are on the left side of the body, as it was with Della. You tend to go to the opposite of your hand, left wound, right hand, and vice versa."

"Swell." She sighed. "There's only a billion right-handed guys in the world."

"It gets worse," Mitch said.

"What?"

"I don't think this one is going to be the last."

Star looked at him. "Tell me."

"He came into a fairly populated building, I'm guessing maybe two or three hours ago, since she's still warm. He risked being seen. He's getting bolder. He likes it."

She straightened up, looking down at the body. "I don't want to think about it." Mitch stood alongside her. She looked up at him. "I'm not ready for a serial killer taking out sisters."

Mitch wanted to touch her, put his arm around her. Instead he put his hands in his pockets. "Maybe he'll screw up and we'll get him before another woman dies."

"What are the chances?" she asked.

"Slim and none," they said together.

"You're right, he's going to do it again." Her voice sounded sad and faraway.

"We've got to look at this thing like a game he's playing with us," Mitch said, "a mind game, like chess. The next move is ours."

Just then Paresi handed her a slip of paper. Star looked at it and smiled.

"Check."

"What is it?" Mitch asked.

"A receipt." She studied the paper. "It's from Electric City, for a big screen stereo television set, $2,300." She smoothed the wrinkles from the paper. "Looks like she bought it today." She turned to Paresi. "Where did you find this?"

"Hilliker found it in the hallway."

"Where's the set?"

"Not in here. Maybe they haven't delivered it yet."

Star squinted at the creased piece of paper. "It says rush delivery, it should be here. She must have dealt with a salesperson. There's got to be somebody at the store we can talk to." She tried to make out the scrawled signature at the bottom of the page. "This looks like Jer . . . Jerry something."

The three of them leaned in, trying to read the bottom of the yellow slip of paper. A piercing scream from the doorway made Star drop it.

They turned just in time to see a fat, cocoa-colored, gray-haired woman fall to the floor. She was all breasts and belly, and she landed square on her back, hitting the hardwood before any of them could reach her.

Without missing a beat, Paresi dipped into his shirt pocket and produced a "popper," a tiny vial of amyl nitrite, which he broke and held under the woman's nose. Moaning, she started to come around. Star and Mitch looked at him inquiringly. Paresi grinned a silly grin.

"What? I always carry a few of these . . . you never know."

"Sweet Jesus," the woman moaned. "Precious Father, what happened to her, what happened to Alma?"

Star helped her sit up.

"Are you a relative?"

The woman stared at her through dazed eyes. "No . . . no,

I'm her neighbor from downstairs. I just come up to bring her this." She pulled a slip of paper from her apron pocket and handed it to Star.

"Delivery notice from Electric City." Star handed it to Paresi. "Let's get you up, can you stand?" She and Mitch hoisted the heavy woman to her feet.

She wiped tears from her wide, moon face, more falling as rapidly as she wiped them away. "What happened to her?"

"Here, let's get you a seat." Star guided her to the sofa and sat down beside her.

The forensic team finished tying paper bags on Alma Johnson's hands. The coroner's team put her body into the rubber body bag and zipped it efficiently. They put the bag on a gurney and rolled it past Star and the old woman on the couch.

The woman began wailing. "Sweet Lord, help her, please. Jesus, help her, help her."

Star patted the woman's clenched hands. "I'm sorry Mrs. . . . Mrs. . . . "

The woman clasped Star's hand. "Mrs. Bassett. My name is Eliza Bassett. Oh Lord, Alma was a good girl. Who done this? What happened?"

"We're trying to find out," Star said softly. "Can you tell me something about her?"

"Oh Lord, let me see . . ." She drew deep breaths. "She was a good girl, Alma was, a good girl. She was smart, real smart. She worked with them computer thangs, you know. She made good money. She said she thought she was gonna get a big raise soon, 'cause she sold a lotta 'em to one big company. She was gonna tell me tonight what happened, and if she got it, we was gonna go out and celebrate." She sobbed deeply.

Star rubbed the old woman's back. "Take your time, Mrs. Bassett."

"I live downstairs. Ever since Alma come in the building, I been kinda looking out for her. She jus' a baby, you know, jus' a baby."

"Yes ma'am. Tell me about the delivery, you were coming up with a notice?"

"That's right. The mens come this evening, but Alma weren't home and I didn't have her key."

"Do you usually have a key to her place?"

"Yes, I do. When she gonna get somethin' sent, she always give me her key for me to look out for it . . . see, I'm on pension, I don' work, but I keeps busy at home, you know."

"Yes ma'am."

"Alma trust me, she always let me take her key when somethin' be comin', 'cause I don' go messin' in her thangs, you unnerstan'?"

"Yes ma'am."

The woman looked intensely at Star. "Is you a po-leece, baby?"

"Yes ma'am, I'm Detective Lieutenant Duvall."

Mrs. Bassett shook her head. "Lord, colored women today . . . Alma was making more money than I ever even heard of, and here you is, a po-leece, just like them gals on the TV."

"Yes ma'am. Is there anything else you can tell me about the delivery today?"

"No, just that two mens come 'bout six o'clock and they couldn' get in, so they rung my bell. I took the notice so I could tell Alma when she come home, but I went to bingo tonight and I jus' come back. I was 'bout to heat up some red beans and rice, when I heard walkin', so I figured I'd bring it up here now, 'cause I thought she was home. Sweet Jesus, I never 'spected to see nobody puttin' her in a bag." Tears ran down her face. "Lord, she looked so scared, that poor baby died in fear. Lord, God, please rest her soul."

12

His shirt was torn and there was blood on the sleeves and tail.
He stripped it off and pushed it into the garbage can under the
sink. The sound of the cabinet door slamming woke Maureen.
She stumbled sleepily into the kitchen, her hair heading in all
directions and her shabby nightgown hanging from one shoulder.

"It's real late, Jerry, where you been?"

He didn't answer, he just stood there, glaring at her. He
looked drunk.

"Where's your shirt?"

"I got some oil on it." He slurred his words. He was
crocked.

He turned his back, opening the refrigerator. "Any beer in
here?" He shoved food around until he found three cans,
anchored in their plastic collars. He clumsily pulled them
from the refrigerator. "Why don't you go back to bed," he
said without turning around.

"Give me the shirt, I'll put it in to soak tonight and wash it
first thing in the morning." She tried not to sound disgusted.

"Forget it, just go to bed. I'll wash it myself."

"If it's got oil on it, it should soak or it's gonna be ruined.
Give it to me, I'll put it in the sink."

He fixed her with a drunken stare. "I said go to bed, I'll
take care of it myself."

Maureen pulled a lank strap back over her shoulder. "It's
really no trouble, I don't want the stain to set."

Jerry looked at her over the rim of his beer can. For a second he wanted to smash the can into her pig face, but she was

only trying to please him . . . well, tonight she would. He drained the can and belched. "C'mon." He grabbed her fat upper arm.

"Jerry no . . . no, I can't!" She tried to squirm away from him.

"No such word as can't." He shoved her ahead of him, down the hallway, toward their bedroom.

"No!"

He pushed her into the room, down on the bed. He was still hot, fired up from her, the one in the apartment. He could still see her begging, offering him anything to just leave her alone.

He made her strip for him, nice and slow. He played with her tits, nibbling and twisting her nipples until she cried. That really turned him on, so he fucked her, hard, twice, holding his orgasm until he'd forced her head down on him. She started gagging. That pissed him off, so he educated her on the fine art of cocksucking.

The memory made him hard as concrete.

He grabbed Maureen's sweaty hand and pressed it to his crotch. "See what I need?" he whispered in her ear. "I need a woman to take care of this, and since I'm home, you'll have to do."

It was over in minutes. He withdrew and staggered, still exposed, down the hall to the kitchen. On the rumpled and sweaty sheets, his wife cried. He popped another beer and headed for his darkroom.

When Maureen was able, she got up, dragging herself into the bathroom. She ran a warm tub and got into the water. The heat caused her to bolt upright, her body stinging. She bit her lip and eased herself back down.

The combination of the pain and the warmth of the water made her cry loudly, like a child. She sat in the tub, wailing, trying to swallow the sobs so he wouldn't hear. Had she locked the door? If she had, he'd be furious.

She gulped her cries, listening. The hallway was silent. Maybe he was asleep, or down in the basement. She sighed deeply and sat back. After her bath, she'd take his shirt, if she could find it without upsetting him. It had to be soaked, oil was so hard to get out.

In his darkroom, Jerry Auster was too drunk and too turned on to do his work and enjoy it. He put the chemicals back on the shelf and turned out the light. What the hell, tomorrow was another day.

He climbed the stairs and stopped again at the kitchen, taking the last beer. He thought about banging Maureen again, but she was no fun. He walked past the bathroom. The door was closed. He turned the knob; it was locked.

On the other side of the door Maureen jumped when the doorknob rattled. "Jerry, I'm in the tub."

She sat in the water, quaking. She listened, holding her breath, expecting the door to be kicked in. He shook the knob once more and went away. Maureen thanked her saints that Jerry was too drunk to make her pay for that locked door.

13

Star walked slowly down the stairs of Alma Johnson's apart-
ment building and sat on the third step from the bottom.

The blood, the chalk outline on the carpet, all of it, on top
of those sick pictures, was making her crazy. She couldn't
stay in the apartment. Alma Johnson was shoving her right to
the edge. She'd been just a kid; there were dolls on her bed,
and Snoop Doggy Dog CDs in her music cabinet.

Star took a deep breath. The night air was cool, but she
barely felt it. The possibility of these killings being connected
was too much. She blew the air out of her lungs forcefully. It
was an epidemic, a spree, open season on sisters.

In a few months it would be a movie of the week, women
dying because of their skin color. Of course, for TV they
would all be killed for their hair color, all blondes, played by
Pamela Anderson Lee, Heather Locklear, and Christina
Applegate. Jean Stapleton would play Mrs. Bassett.

Star shook her head slowly. That old lady had just about
broken her heart. After seeing her to her apartment, Star had
wanted to keep walking, right off the end of the earth, but she
settled for the front steps. The old woman had hugged her at
the door and told her to be careful. The stoop of her shoulders,
and her tears, had just about torn Star in half.

The night was alive with blue and red lights whirling from
the tops of squad cars. Three of them sat across the street, and
another one was parked a few feet down from the steps. The
coroner's van sat at the curb, with the doors open. She could
see the black bag inside. Alma Johnson was so small, she
barely made a bulge in the rubber.

Star wasn't aware of Mitch until he sat down next to her.

He said softly, "So this is where you disappeared."

She stared off down the street.

He leaned against her, watching the lights dance across her skin. "He's going to slip up, you know."

She felt the pressure of his shoulder against hers. "Yeah, I guess." She felt like crying. "But how many more times before we can nail this son of a bitch?"

"Soon. He's getting sloppy," Mitch said. "That receipt, the bite marks, at least it gives us a place to start."

"Yeah." She put her hand under her chin, and gazed off into the darkness. "He sent pictures to the division, did you know that?"

Mitch stared at her, her long arms and legs, the look in her eyes; he wanted to hold her. "Yes. Dominic told me. Was there any way to trace them?"

"Nope. I spent the better part of the afternoon dealing with the main post office. The postmark was from there, at five-thirty P.M., two days ago. No way to trace, nothing unusual about the envelope, normal nine-by-twelve brown mailer, no markings, no stains, no fingerprints, no nothing."

He took a deep breath, stood up and offered her his hand. "You need a break, let me take you for a nightcap."

"Thanks, but I'm not much of a drinker." She took his hand, and he pulled her up alongside him.

"A misconception, Lieutenant. A nightcap isn't necessarily liquor. You need to talk, and I'm a great listener."

She shook her head. "I'm not dressed to go anywhere. In case you haven't noticed, these jeans have holes in them."

"I noticed, it's a bold fashion statement." He made her smile. "You look fine. C'mon, I promise to have you home early."

Paresi bounded down the stairs, trying to look as if he hadn't overheard their conversation. "Darcy is securing the scene, I'm heading back to the station."

"Maybe I should go with you," she said.

Mitch looked down at the steps, as if hoping she wouldn't.

"No need," Paresi said. "Nothing's going to change between now and tomorrow morning. As for the report, you're officially off duty, so I'll take care of it. I can practically fill in the blanks from the other ones. BCI got everything they need, so all we have to do is put this piece in the puzzle and hope it gives us enough to catch this psychotic bastard."

"Amen." Star looked at Mitch. "You really want to go for a nightcap. You're not going to let me worm out of this, are you?"

Mitch shook his head. "Nope."

"Go out, have a few pops, I got it knocked," Paresi said.

"All right, all right. I know when I'm being jacked." She turned to Mitch. "Can I drive my car? I don't want to leave it here."

Paresi spoke up before Mitch could say anything. "Give me your keys, I'll drive it to the station. I'll have one of the guys take my car in."

"Oh, okay, thanks." She fished in her pocket for her car keys. "I'll pick it up in a little while."

Paresi took the keys. "It'll be in your space."

She touched his arm. "Thanks again."

"Don't do nothing I wouldn't do," he said over his shoulder. "Later, Mitch."

"Night, Dom." Mitch put his arm around Star's shoulder. He hoped he didn't look as much like a teenager as he felt.

"You're sure you don't want to join us?" Star said. "You can, you know, I won't tell."

Paresi read Mitch's eyes. "Nah. I'm just gonna head in. I'll see you in the morning."

"Night," she said, then turned to Mitch. "Let's go."

Paresi watched them walk down the street to Mitch's midnight-blue Porsche Carrera. He watched them until they disappeared.

"Yo, Frankie!" he yelled at a uniformed officer. "Take my car in for me." He tossed his keys.

As he got into Star's Honda and started the engine, the van carrying Alma Johnson's body pulled in front of him.

Mitch and Star sat in a corner booth at Saint Germaine's, one of the oldest of the old money eateries in town. Christian, the maitre d', nearly passed out when he saw Star's outfit, but Dr. Grant was a regular, and he dared not turn him away. He managed his best smile and showed them to the booth. He even took their order himself. Two hot fudge sundaes . . . rich people were crazy!

"I can't believe you brought me to Saint Germaine's for ice cream." Star pointed at the two enormous sundaes sitting in front of them. "I've got to say, Doctor, it certainly takes chutzpah!"

They giggled like children.

"What it takes," Mitch said, "is stones, but who cares? They make the best sundaes here, so where else would I go? Besides, I think it takes a certain amount of style to wear ripped jeans and a Bullwinkle sweatshirt into this haven of blue hair and bluer blood." He toasted her with his spoon.

"Hey, if it doesn't bother you, it doesn't bother me. I wasn't going to pass up a chance to come here. Besides, it was worth it, just to see the faces falling all over the room!"

"Lieutenant Duvall, I do believe you and I share the unpopular trait of being unpredictable."

"I don't know about me, but you are definitely a candidate for the Unpredictable Hall of Fame." She plunged her spoon through the warm ribbon of fudge, into the icy, pristine vanilla ice cream. "Just what I needed." She put it in her mouth and licked the back of the spoon. "Mmmmm."

"I knew you'd be hooked with one taste," he said, digging into his sundae.

"You're so right." She ate a bit more and sat back in the booth, the sadness returning to her eyes. "This thing is working me, Mitchell."

"I know. It's got to be personal for you."

"Personal doesn't begin to cover it. I mean, I can't even imagine . . . " She waved her hands around. "What kind of a guy could do this and send pictures? Christ! This one was just a kid." Star put the spoon down, unable to take another bite. "You know what the worst thing is?"

"What?"

"I'm scared . . . scared to death it's going to happen again before we can get him."

"Not if that receipt turns into something we can run with," Mitch said. "And if the bite marks match the ones from Robb-Ellison, then we've got something.

"*If* is the key word."

"Listen. People don't realize that teeth marks are just as incriminating as fingerprints. If we can match the bites, and run checks on known rapists and sex offenders, then we'll be ahead of him."

"And if he's never been arrested, we're screwed," Star said.

"We'll deal with that when it happens. Enough shop talk, I brought you here to cheer up, now eat your ice cream."

She smiled at him. "Yes, Daddy."

She took another spoonful and looked around the room, chuckling at all the heads suddenly turning away in unison.

"Did you see the old duck on the left, she turned away so fast, she got whiplash!" Star laughed out loud.

Mitch loved the look on her face. "I'm sure the butler will have to run out for Madam's Ben-Gay this evening," he said. They cracked up.

"Well, Dr. Grant, you certainly are full of surprises." She looked around the room. "Saint Germaine's."

"It's been a haunt for some time," Mitch said. "When my daughter was little, I would bring her here on our special days together. We'd usually take in a show, or a movie, and come here for lunch. She loved it, until she became a teenager. Then hanging out with dad wasn't cool."

"What's her name?"

"Robin. Her mother named her. Like most important decisions during our marriage, I had no say so in the matter."

"Where's Robin now?"

"At the university. She's a sophomore."

"Are you close?"

"Not particularly. She never forgave me for the divorce."

"How old was she?"

"Almost fourteen. I thought she was old enough to understand, or that she'd at least understand when she was older, but Carole Ann has pretty much convinced her that I didn't want to be a husband or a father."

"What have you done about that?"

He stirred the fudge sauce in his melting ice cream. "Not a lot, I'm sorry to say. She didn't want to hear anything from me, so in time I stopped trying. Robin and I haven't talked for a long time now."

"That's rough," Star said. "Fathers and daughters should have a special bond. My dad and I did."

"I remember Len. He was an exceptional man. He had a lot of courage and a lot of heart. I don't think there was anybody on the force who didn't love your dad."

"The man who shot him didn't love him." Her face hardened. "Let's not talk about him, okay?"

They ate in silence for a while. Out of the corner of his eye, he watched her. She took the cherry off her sundae and put it on the serving plate, like a child, saving the best for last. When she finished the ice cream, she put the cherry in her mouth, and moments later laid the stem down tied in a knot.

"That's quite a trick."

"What?"

Mitch pointed at the tied cherry stem.

"You mean you can't do that?"

"Nope, but I'm fascinated with any woman who can."

"If you promise to do something else to pull the rug from under the blue hairs, I'll teach you how to do it."

"Deal." He put out his hand, she shook it. "On one condition."

"Name it," she said.

"You have to come with me, be my partner in all ego-deflating missions."

"You're on. Grant and Duvall, A.A. Attitude Adjusters."

"I like it, but I'm old-fashioned. I think Duvall and Grant is better. Ladies first."

"Okay. Duvall and Grant, but I'm thinking alphabetically."

"Either way, it works. To us." Mitch handed her the cherry from his sundae. She put it in her mouth and a second later handed him the stem. Untied.

The morning dawned hot and muggy with the sunrise. When Star and Paresi walked into the coroner's building, the air-conditioning was already on high. The temperature drop made her break out in goose bumps.

Mitch, dressed in scrubs, waited in his outer office. "Morning troops," he said.

"Morning," the two detectives said in unison.

"How's Bullwinkle this morning?" Mitch said to Star.

"Full of hot fudge and expanding, thank you."

"Not that I can see," Mitch said, grinning.

His secretary, Lorraine, looked up from the file in her hand. She took in Star's two-piece orange cotton outfit.

Star could see she wasn't impressed. Well, blondie, she thought to herself, we can't all shop at Bimboland.

Lorraine crossed her legs in her three-inch blue and white spectator pumps and eyeballed Star's flat straw-colored sandals, her big gold earrings, and the dozen or so thin gold bracelets on her left wrist. She glanced down at her own chest, which was at least two cup sizes bigger than Star's. A smug little smile crossed her lips. "Would either of you like some coffee?" she asked.

"No, thanks," Star said.

"Got any Danish?" Paresi asked.

"No time, Dom," Mitch said. "We're ready."

"Right." Paresi turned to Lorraine. "Save me an apple-pecan if you got any."

Lorraine's smile never wavered. "I'll put one aside for you, Detective."

"Two." Paresi held up two fingers.

"Two," Lorraine said.

"C'mon, Paresi." Star nudged him, her bracelets jangling. "You'll have to excuse him," she said to Lorraine. "He's got breakfast mooching down to an art."

Lorraine laughed. "I don't mind . . . anything for you officers, you all work so hard," she drawled in her syrupy southern accent.

Star caught the look in Lorraine's eyes and returned her piranha smile. It looked like Miss Belle don't much care for the doctor's attention to the riffraff, she thought. She pushed Paresi toward the door. "I'll buy you a double chocolate doughnut afterward."

"Two, with sprinkles?" Paresi asked, stopping short.

Star nodded. "Two, with sprinkles."

"Cancel the Danish, Lorraine, my partner still loves me."

"You're a lucky man," Mitch said. "See you in Room D."

"Right." Star nodded at him as he passed.

He looked back over his shoulder at her, and Lorraine caught the look that passed between them before the door closed behind him.

Maureen Auster was up with the sun. The bedroom felt like an oven, and she couldn't stand lying next to him. Him snoring and sweating like a pig, smelling of beer and hatred.

She walked barefoot into the kitchen, feeling the bottoms of her feet stick to the already damp linoleum. An empty beer can sat on the sink. She rinsed it and opened the cupboard door to put it in the recycle bin.

Jerry was always yelling at her about the bins under the sink. He tossed everything into the garbage, and she would have to go in after him and pull out the bottles and cans and put them in the recycle bins. As she reached in to drop the can, she saw a piece of fabric hanging out of the garbage pail. She tugged on it. Jerry's shirt fell onto her hand.

No wonder she couldn't find this with his clothes last

night. Did he think they had so much money that he could just throw away a shirt because it had a little oil on it?

She pulled the shirt clear and searched it, looking for oil. She found one sleeve ripped from the shoulder.

He was like a kid, tearing his clothes. She turned the shirt again, finding nothing. There was no oil on it. All it needed was mending. She'd sew it before she washed it, otherwise the machine would rip it to pieces.

When she folded the shirt to put it in her sewing basket, a dark brown stain on the shirttail caught her eye. She held the material up to the sunlight streaming through the window.

It looked like blood. She peered closer. It was blood.

She held the shirttail under the cold water tap and turned it on. She scrubbed the fabric between her knuckles, and dark brown fluid ran into the sink. She watched it swirl down the drain, then scrubbed until the stain turned a faded rust. As she wrung the material, she saw more blood on the other sleeve.

What did he do, open a vein? She rubbed harder. A fresh torrent of dark brown ran into the sink. She squeezed out the water and turned off the tap. With the stains and the tear, maybe she should just toss the shirt, she thought. It was a goner. She shoved it back into the garbage can under the sink.

She heard him moving around in the bedroom. In a few minutes he'd walk into the kitchen, hollering for his breakfast. She heard him stumbling up the hallway. The bathroom door slammed, and immediately the kitchen was filled with the disgusting sounds of retching.

Oh God, she said to herself. He's hung over. Please Lord, let him get better and go to work. I don't want him here with me all day.

Another sickening gag invaded the kitchen. She turned on the radio, blasting the music to cover the sounds.

As they approached from the parking lot, Star saw the small, fair-haired man through the window. He was pacing in his office. She realized he must have been the one Paresi spoke to, the manager of Electric City.

"What was the manager's name?" she asked as they neared the side door.

"Uh . . . " Paresi looked at his notebook. "Douglas, Howard Douglas."

"Well, I think whatever you said to Mr. Douglas made him a little uneasy." She nodded toward the window.

Paresi grinned. "This is gonna be fun."

Star opened the outer door, and the door facing them which led into the office. She walked in. "Hello, are you Mr. Douglas?"

The small man jumped a foot.

Paresi chuckled.

"Sorry, if we startled you, I'm Detective Lieutenant Duvall, and this is my partner, Detective Sergeant Paresi. We'd like to ask you a few questions."

"Can you tell me what this is about?" His voice was high-pitched and shaky.

"No need to feel nervous," Star said. "We just have a couple of questions." She pulled a sales slip from her purse and handed it to him. "This is a slip for a big-screen TV that was purchased yesterday, here, in your store."

He took the paper and looked at it. "Yes, it's our merchandise . . . what's wrong?"

"The set was purchased by an Alma Johnson, and she paid cash."

"Oh yes." Douglas visibly relaxed. He turned toward Paresi and smiled. "Yes, I remember. It was quite a sale. Usually people opt for terms on big ticket items, but she wanted it right away. I had to approve her check. It was for $2,300 plus tax. The bank gave her excellent references. Is there something wrong with the check?"

"No," Star said. "I believe my partner told you, when he phoned, we're Homicide, Mr. Douglas, not Bunco. We're here because Alma Johnson was murdered last night. We want to talk to the salesperson who handled her purchase."

"Murdered?" Howard Douglas's knees gave out. He fell back into his chair.

"Yeah, murdered," Paresi said. "We're just checking her steps, routine, understand?"

"Yes . . . yes I do. I'm just so shocked. When I okayed her check, she was so nice, so bubbly, friendly. . . . You know, very young and very friendly."

Star sat down in the chair in front of Douglas's desk. "We don't want to take up too much of your time, sir, we just want to talk to the salesperson."

"Of course, anything I can do. I'll be right back." He got up and went out into the showroom. Star noticed his hands were shaking.

"Now that's a case," Paresi said, walking behind Douglas's desk. "You know what we call a guy like that in Italian?"

"What?"

"A fagoot."

"Paresi!"

"Didn't you catch that? I thought he was gonna drop to his knees and honk on my—"

"Don't say it!" Star interrupted. "We're not here because of his sexuality."

"I dunno, he coulda offed her 'cause she was prettier than he is!" He rifled through the papers on top. "I'm telling you, Star, this guy is dangerous. No photos around, not even one of the boyfriend. He was probably in love with the same guy as her and decided to ice the competition."

"These hypotheses are why you get the big money, right?"

"Hey, think about it."

"You're a pig, Paresi."

"And Howard's cravin' bacon." He picked up a paperweight from Douglas's desk. "Speaking of piggy things, what was that Bullwinkle crack this morning? As I recall, the moose was on your chest last night."

"Uh-huh."

"So what did Mitch do, bite him off?"

"We ate a lot of ice cream, most of which went right to my rapidly expanding butt, and then he took me back to the station, to pick up my car."

"Oh, so that's all?"

She pursed her lips primly. "I seem to be developing a larger rear end, but he hasn't noticed."

"Yeah, like he isn't always looking at your ass. Believe me, if it's expanding, he's noticed."

"Paresi!"

"I know, I'm a pig."

Howard Douglas walked back into the office, trailed by a young man who looked even more nervous than he.

"Officers, this is Jerry Beacham. He sold the television to Ms. Johnson."

Jerry Beacham looked at the two cops, terrified. "Is there a problem?" The man's voice cracked.

Paresi rounded Douglas's desk and stood in front of Beacham. Jerry looked as if he was facing a firing squad.

"Ms. Johnson was found murdered last night," Paresi said. "We just want to ask you a couple of questions."

Jerry Beacham looked at his boss, a thin line of sweat visible on his upper lip. "Could I please have some water?"

Douglas drew a cup of water from the cooler and handed it to him. "Should I stay here for this?" he asked the officers.

"Please," Star said. "It won't take long."

Jerry Beacham's hands shook so much that the water danced wildly in the cup. "I'm not a suspect, am I?"

Star smiled at him. "No. We just have a few questions, that's all." She touched him gently. "Why don't you take a sip of your water and relax?"

He gulped. His hands shook less.

Star indicated the chair next to her. "Have a seat. This will be painless, I promise."

When they got back to the squad room, there were two messages from Mitch. Star called him.

"Hi," she said. "Sorry it took so long to call back, Paresi and I just got in."

"It's all right," he said. "Are you sitting down?"

"Why, is this going to knock me out?"

"It just might make you sick."

"Tell me." She eased down in her chair.

"I went back to Alma Johnson's body this afternoon, before the morticians picked her up."

"And?"

"We've discussed the bite marks, but something made me check her throat again. I had to take another look at the wound."

"Yeah?"

"The wound, it . . . uh . . . "

"This morning you said it was made by a serrated blade, wide, like a hunting knife . . . is there something else?"

"Yes . . . " His voice trailed off.

"What is it?" She was gripping the phone so hard her hand hurt.

"I found semen in the wound."

"You mean in her throat, like he made her go down on him?"

"No, in the wound. Deep in the wound."

"Are you saying . . . ?"

"It looks like he penetrated—"

Star put her hand to her mouth. "Don't say anymore." She held the phone away.

"Star?" Mitch's voice came through the receiver. "Star, are you there?"

She moved the phone back to her ear. "Yes, I'm here."

"I was able to collect some semen and pubic hair, which is at the lab. In a couple of days we'll know his race and blood type."

"I gotta go, Mitchell." Star hung up the phone and ran to the ladies' room. In the stall, she hung over the toilet, sick, gagging. Nothing came up. She staggered to the sink, her head pounding. She turned on the cold water and splashed some on her face.

"Dear God." She began to cry. "Dear God." She turned the taps on full in one sink, and then in another.

One by one she opened them, eight faucets, all gushing full force. Water splashed out of the porcelain bowls, onto the cracked marble countertops, out onto her orange shirt and the yellowed tile floor.

She couldn't hold the fear and rage rising in her throat. She clapped her hands over her mouth, but the scream worked through her lips, her fingers, spilling out, filling the room. It was soon followed by another one, louder, longer . . . more loud, wailing screams tore out of her. She screamed until she tasted blood and her throat closed, choking her. Little anguished squeaks were all she could utter. Then she locked herself into a stall and waited for the shaking to stop.

14

Jerry Auster began feeling better late in the afternoon. He showered and left the house, leaving Maureen sitting in front of the TV watching "General Hospital" and shoving Oreos in her mouth. He wanted to take the damn cookies away from her, but she had called in sick for him, so he owed her one.

He went down to the Blue Dog and had a couple of beers. He sat ringside and watched the girls dance. One of them reminded him of his wife before she got fat, but the one that gave him the biggest boner was the spade chick with the braided hair.

She called herself Akira, and she danced in a little feather and fake snakeskin bikini that she took off after about a minute. She liked to tease him, shaking her tits in his face. Today, he'd leaned back in his chair, letting her see just how much he was enjoying the show.

Her big eyes fastened on that stiff piece of meat pressed against his thigh, stretching the fabric of his jeans. She actually licked her lips. He winked at her and squeezed himself, spreading his legs wider. She grinned, moved to the very edge of the small stage, turned around and shook her ass right in his face.

She was so close, he could count the hairs peeking out around the string up her butt. He thought the pencil neck in the suit sitting next to him was gonna blow his wad right there. The fuck's glasses were steamed up. She didn't even notice. She was shaking it just for him. He put a ten in her G-string and left. He didn't really want her. She was a whore. No money, probably no education, shaking her ass in white guys' faces . . . she was no threat. Hell, after what he showed her, he knew she'd jump at the chance to fuck him for free.

He stopped at the market and picked up a couple of steaks and some stuff to make a salad. He wanted a barbecue. That would get Maureen off her fat can and at least out in the yard. While she was out there, he could work in his darkroom without her bothering him. He still had the pictures from yesterday to develop.

Paresi was watching the door. He saw her coming. She looked like she'd been kicked in the stomach. She came back to her seat and sat down heavily.

"You okay?" He asked.

"Yeah."

"I thought maybe you were sick or something."

"No, I'm all right." She picked up a fat brown envelope on the desk. "What's this?"

"From BCI, Davis just brought it down."

She slid the envelope across to him. "You handle it."

He opened it. Color Polaroid photographs of Alma Johnson spilled out. Paresi grouped them on his desk, the scene, the morgue, and the autopsy. Star tried not to look.

"You wanna tell me what's going on?" he asked.

"I can't."

He got up and tacked the pictures in a neat line down the bulletin board, on the wall over their desks, directly under the pink three-by-five card that had the name ALMA JOHNSON lettered in black Magic Marker on it.

He stood back and looked at the lineup. Three pink cards. Next to Alma Johnson were the cards and photos of Della Robb-Ellison and Charlotte Wilson.

"What say we take a break and go down to Floogie's?" Paresi suggested.

She knew what he was doing. "I appreciate it, Dom, I do, but I'm not good company."

"Whenever you call me Dom, I know something's wrong. You don't have to talk, let's just get outta this place."

She knew he wouldn't let up. "All right." She pulled her purse out of the drawer and they headed for the door.

It was late afternoon, and the cop bar, Floogie's, was packed. Daniel Leahy, the ex–Vice Squad sergeant who owned it, made it comfortable for his old buddies—painted windows, dark interior, no bright lights, and no civilians allowed. Nothing but wall-to-wall cops, in uniform and out, chowing down on Floogie's famous burgers and swilling beer. Some of them were even on duty, but who was going to tell?

When they walked in, Leahy waved from behind the bar. He recognized the look on Star's face. Burnout had made him turn in his badge and open this place. He liked her; she was Len Duvall's kid and he'd known her since she was in knee socks. Leahy drew a beer for the Italian and a Pepsi for her, with two slices of lemon and crushed ice. He took the drinks to their table.

"How you doin', kid?" he said to her.

"Fine, Dan, just fine."

He put the drinks down.

"Beer?" Paresi said in mock surprise. "Danny, you know I'm on duty."

"No alcohol in this, Dom, just vitamins to make it fizz." He slapped Paresi on the back. "Enjoy, it's on the house." They watched him go back to the bar.

"Ol' Dan's a good guy," Paresi said, and sipped his beer. "Ah, vitamin B for barley, M for malt, I feel better already." He sipped again. "So, you gonna tell me what Mitch said to you?"

"What's Dr. Grant got to do with this?"

"You took up residence in the john after he talked to you, so what did he say?"

She took a long drink of her soda, squeezed some lemon into it, and told him. Paresi was quiet. Only the working of his jaw muscles let her know he'd heard everything she said.

—

Vee heard the car in her driveway. It was a little after eleven-thirty. Jay Leno was making jokes about the President when she turned off the TV set. She opened the door before Star could knock.

"Come on in."

Star took in Vee's robe and bare feet. "I'm sorry, it's so late, I know you got to go to work in the morning, but I just couldn't go home." She collapsed on the couch and kicked off her sandals.

"You want something to drink?"

"Got any Pepsi?"

"How long have you known me?" Vee smiled at her. "I'll be right back."

Star heard the rattle of ice dropping in the glasses. Vee came back with a tray holding two cans of Pepsi, two glasses of ice, a bowl of fried pork rinds, and a bottle of Crystal Louisiana Red Hot Sauce. She sat the tray on the coffee table.

"I forgot the napkins."

"Don't worry about it."

Vee sat down on the couch and pulled her robe around her.

Star shook up the bottle of hot sauce and poured it on the skins. She picked up the one on top, saturated with the peppery sauce, and ate it in two bites. "Lord, that's good." She licked her fingers and picked up another one.

"So whut up?" Vee said, imitating her son Cole.

"You mean why am I camped on your couch eating skins at this hour?"

"Uh-huh." Vee reached into the bowl.

"The job, girl, that's all, just the job."

"You gonna tell me exactly what?"

Star looked at her friend. How many secrets had they shared? They knew everything about each other. Still, somehow she couldn't share this. She put another pork rind in her mouth and licked her fingers.

"Well, you gonna talk or just eat up all my food?"

Star swallowed the story she wanted to tell about Alma Johnson. "It's been a tough day. I know you heard about the sisters we've been finding dead all over town."

"Not too much, just a little stuff on the news," Vee said.

"Well, it's just us, so I guess it ain't exactly page one material," Star said, "but number three turned up yesterday. A kid, really. She was the worst one yet."

"Tell me." Vee leaned toward her friend.

"It's too sick, I shouldn't even be here." She drank the soda and burped. "I'm just tired . . . I'm going home."

"No you're not, you're staying here tonight."

"Vee, you gotta work tomorrow."

"So do you, and what you got to go home to anyway besides that damn cat?"

"You know Jake loves you," Star said, grinning. The feud between her best friend and her cat was long-standing and very funny.

"I hate that fat thing." Vee made a face. "I never could stand no cats!"

"That's because you ain't never had one," Star said, tossing a soggy skin at her.

"Maybe not, but I sure had my share of dogs since Lorenzo been gone. Speaking of dogs, how's that fine partner of yours?"

"Paresi? He'll never change."

"Good." Vee grinned. "He's always telling me what he's gonna do to me. One day I'm gonna make him prove it, and when I'm finished with him, you can come identify the bones, 'cause that's all that'll be left."

Star giggled. "He would love that!"

Vee widened her eyes. "You laughing, but I am serious as a hungry dog with a pork chop, honey. If I ever get ahold of him, he will be one happy soul. If they dig him up a hundred years from now, his dust will be grinning."

They laughed so loud that Lena, in her sleep-rumpled shorty pj's, walked into the living room.

"Mama, can you keep it down?" She was nearly nine, and

on her way to becoming a real beauty. She rubbed her sleepy eyes. "Hi, Auntie Star, I didn't know you were here."

"She ain't," Vee said. "You dreaming, go back to bed."

"Something going on?" Lena asked.

Star reached out for her, and Lena climbed on her lap. The child smelled of sleep and Cashmere Bouquet soap. Star flashed on when Lena was about four and lived in her lap. It was her favorite place to sit and tell Star all of her little girl secrets. She kissed Lena's forehead. "Go back to bed, baby, me and your mama will quiet down."

"Okay." Lena hugged Star again. "You working on a big case now?"

"Lena, you can talk to Star some other time, go to to bed."

The girl gave her mother the look that every kid who wants to stay up gives.

Vee narrowed her eyes. "Good night, Miss Lena!"

"Night."

Lena kissed Star and climbed off her lap.

"Night, sugar," Star said.

The girl hugged her again, then went to Vee. She kissed her mother on the lips. "Night, Mama."

Vee patted her on the bottom. "Good night, baby." Lena went back to her room.

They waited until they heard the door close.

"She's really gonna be a knockout, Vee."

"Don't I know . . . the boys already sniffing around like hounds. Be glad you don't have a daughter, Star."

"I don't know, sometimes I miss not having a family. It gets lonely."

"You got a family . . . us," Vee said.

"And I love all of you, but even so, sometimes I feel . . . "

Vee leaned back against the cushions. "I know how you feel, Star, but you made your choice when Papa Len died. I know it's been hard for you, but you got to look at what you've done, not what you haven't done. You're a great cop. You couldn't do that *and* be a wife and mother."

"Thanks for reminding me."

"Honey, you know what I'm saying . . . it's still not too late, but you gonna have to make a decision. If you want to be a mother, you got to get on the stick."

Star arched an eyebrow. "It ain't the stick I got to get on, it's the—"

They started laughing.

"That's for sure, that's the only fun part." Vee grinned. "If you want kids and all that, you better get to steppin', you're already thirty-seven. Men can drop babies till they're dead, but time runs out on us. You can still hook up with somebody, you work with a million men."

Star shook her head. "If they're not dead, or married, or drunk, then they're either fucked up, addicted, or gay. Let's face it, girl, the pickings are slim and none."

"I don't like to think about that," Vee said, "especially where brothers are concerned, but you're right. Nowadays a black woman don't have a lot of choices. If our men are not in jail, or into drugs, then they're out there using each other for target practice. I don't know what's wrong with us. We don't have to worry about the Skinheads and the Klan, we're doing their job for them!"

"Amen to that," Star agreed. "I see it every day, and it breaks my heart."

"I know, and the ones that are left . . . that's another story. Brothers with good jobs and education got jungle fever. Hell, even the ones I wouldn't wipe my feet on got white women hanging off of 'em. It don't matter if brotherman looks like Denzel or Death sucking lemons in the summertime, he's still gonna have some pale thing on his arm. And the downer they are, the fatter she will be!"

Star burst out laughing. "Girl, what's wrong with you, dissing people like that?"

"I'm tired," Vee said. "I'm tired of fighting the fight, and I'm tired of sleeping alone. Since Lo died, it's been gruesome. I haven't told you about what's out there."

"No need, I know."

"Uh-huh. Then know this," Vee said. "It's time for black

women to wake up. That means cross that line, running, if you have to. I mean white women got their men and ours too, so what are we supposed to do, take up climbing trees?"

Star lay back on the sofa, laughing.

"Go on, laugh." Vee grinned. "But listen to me. I say, you should cross the line, go into the yard and shake the tree, baby, see if you can't shake out that doctor you work with."

Star lay on her back. "Mitchell Grant?"

"No, Marcus Welby!" Vee leaned forward. "I've seen him in the paper and on TV. He's fine, and you know how I feel about blondes, male and female, but I got to say it like it t-i-is. Dr. Grant is one pretty, white boy."

Star sat up. "I never thought I'd hear that from you."

"Hey, the truth is the light, and desperate times call for desperate measures, now get in there and go for it."

"Hook him?" Star said.

"Why not? He's a man, you're a woman, he's fine, and he's got more money than God, what more do you need? He's gonna end up somewhere, so why not with you? If you don't land him, some pale heifer will."

"I never thought I'd hear this from you."

"Well, keep listening and hear this, why shouldn't you be happy? Why shouldn't you wake up grinning? Believe me, if I had him, people would think I'd lost my mind, I'd be grinning so much. He likes you, didn't he take you out?"

"We've had a few meals, and he took me out for ice cream last night, but back up, you think it's okay for me to date him?"

"If your mama was here, she'd tell you the same thing. Sometimes you got to do what you got to do. The man is fine, and I have never been one for white boys."

Star's mouth dropped. "What about Paresi?"

"Paresi is Italian, that's different."

"What?" Star looked incredulous.

Vee pointed her finger. "Don't try to change the subject, we are not talking about me, we're talking about you. Now, in a perfect world, we'd all have Denzels, and they'd all have nine inches, all right? But real life is real life. I would like to see you settle down, and Dr. Grant would be a major catch. He's fine enough to be in the movies, and he's dripping cash, and you work pretty close with him, don't you?"

"Yeah?"

"Uh-huh, so, I know he turned your head back in the Academy. That's all I heard, Dr. Grant this and Dr. Grant that."

"That was a long time ago. I was young."

"Yeah, and now your ass is old, so get with the program. I know he's not married anymore, I remember reading about his divorce, so what are you waiting for?"

Star grinned. "Actually, he is kind of sweet. I had fun with him last night."

"Where did you go?"

"He took me to Saint Germaine's."

"For real?" Vee's eyes widened.

"Yep, like I said, we just had ice cream. It was after we hooked up at the crime scene last night. I was depressed, and he told me I needed to talk, and he took me there."

"I hope you were looking good."

"As a matter of fact, I had on my raggedy jeans and a sweatshirt."

"Girl . . . no you didn't!"

"Yep."

"You wore those funky, fulla holes jeans to Saint Germaine's? Please tell me your knees wasn't ashy, poking through the holes."

Star laughed. "My knees were fine. I used lotion after my shower. I hadn't planned on going out, it was my night off. Remember? I spent part of it talking to you. I was watching a movie when I got the call . . . another fun evening in front of the TV set."

"You and the cat," Vee said.

Star nodded. "Uh-huh."

"So, he didn't care how you were dressed?"

"No, it didn't faze him. I could've gone home and changed, I guess, but by that time the place would have been closed.

When he told me where we were going, I really wanted to go, so I just went. People were gawking and carrying on, but they would have done that anyway, just because I was with him. He thought it was funny, he just laughed at them."

"How did you feel?"

Star grinned. "I actually got a kick out of it. He was comfortable, so I felt comfortable. Like it was the most natural thing in the world, to shock those old folks."

"Well, when you got his kind of money, you can do what you want. Was he looking around, trying to see who was checking the two of you out?"

"Nope."

"He was perfectly comfortable?"

"He seemed to be . . . in fact, he was watching me most of the time. I was the one watching the people."

Vee clapped her hands together. "Go get him. He don't care about what people are thinking, this man is his own person, he's got balls. I like him, Star."

"You haven't even met him! But you're right. I like him too. He's a free thinker, all right. He's also a major hound, at least that's his rep. According to the grapevine, he's drilled every woman on the city payroll."

"Do you believe it?"

"I don't know, I don't want to. I mean, he's always treated me with respect, but a lot of people say he's a hound, and let's face it, the grapevine usually has a kernel of truth. I mean sure, things get blown out of proportion, but they usually start from a truth, somewhere."

"To hell with the grapevine." Vee swished the last soggy skin around the bowl. "Unless they screwed him and got pictures, it ain't nothing but jealous folks flapping their gums. The man has got it going on, and if you let talk stop you from getting with him, then black belt or no black belt, I'm gonna kick your butt myself!" She sucked her fingers. "Remember, don't believe half of what you see, and none at all of what you hear." Vee put the bowl back on the coffee table. "Didn't you say he came down to the station to see you, to help out?"

"Yeah, he's really into these cases, that's the night we went out for pizza. He would have taken Paresi too, if he'd been there."

"I'm ashamed of you. The man obviously wants to get to know you better, so stop bitching and moaning and look at what's knocking on your door. He's fine, let him in!"

"I don't know, Vee . . . that's asking for trouble."

"Why?"

"You said it yourself, he's white, and rich, and every woman on the planet who sees him wants him."

"So?"

"So, do I really need that?"

Vee folded her arms. "Do you want to spend the rest of your life alone?"

Star shuddered. "Scary thought."

"Yeah, so face facts."

"You're right." Star nodded.

"I know I am," Vee said. "It's time to look somewhere else, or spend the rest of your life with some batteries and a friendly piece of plastic."

Star looked shocked. "What do you know about friendly pieces of plastic?"

Vee laughed. "I wish you'd stop thinking of me as innocent. Just because I married Lo right out of high school don't mean I've spent my life in a box!"

They laughed.

"Seriously," Vee said. "Think about giving the doctor a chance, I think he'd be good for you."

"Thank you, Ann Landers, for that sage advice." Star stood up. "I'm going home."

"Hello? Clean out your ears. Didn't you hear me say you ain't going nowhere? Now I'm gonna put this mess in the kitchen, and you are gonna go in my room, get one of my nightgowns, and get in the bed."

"I don't want to sleep with you," Star said, laughing. "You snore!"

"Well, you ain't exactly my idea of paradise either." Vee

grinned. "But I ain't got no guest room, and I don't want to hear your mouth for the rest of my life about how my couch wrecked your back!"

"Okay, okay, I'm going to the bathroom first."

"Please." Vee said. "'Cause I don't want to wake up in no Pepsi puddle, and pull them damn bracelets off, you sound like James Brown's rhythm section!"

Star got up with the family and fell into their morning routine. She waited her turn in the bathroom, and ate Kix cereal with the kids while Vee got dressed for work.

Roland showed her the newest hip-hop move. He kept her current with the latest dance steps, teaching her each one that came out. One night, in their living room, he taught her the freshest, new gyrations to go along with his latest Coolio CD. They performed the steps in unison. He slapped her a high five and said she could have been a dancer on "Soul Train."

Vee, who'd been studying in the dining room, yelled out, "Roland, did you say 'Soul Train' or 'Old Train'?"

"That's cold, Mama," Roland had yelled back, laughing.

"Don't sweat it, sugar," Star said, raising her voice to be heard in the dining room. "At least I'm not still doing the Hustle!"

Vee had joined in with the laughter. God love them, they kept her sane.

Now, they all tumbled out of the house together, the kids heading to their all-day summer activities, and Vee to work.

Star went home to change. When she opened the door, Jake came running, but then remembered she'd left him alone all night. It took half a can of StarKist albacore tuna to entice him to come near her again.

After she was dressed, she picked up the mail from the basket under the slot on the door.

"Bills, bills, bills." She shuffled the envelopes. A flyer from her favorite clothing store caught her eye. They were having their semiannual sale. She turned the flyer over, looking at the label with her name and address.

A light went on. After the first time she'd shopped at Bowman and Baker's, a few months later, she'd gotten a notice about their sale. Evidently, her purchase automatically put her name on their mailing lists. She put the flyer in her purse and ran out the door. She could hardly wait to get to the station.

Paresi had all three files spread out on his desk when she arrived. "How you doin' this morning?" he asked.

"Better." She pulled the flyer out of her purse. "Look at this." She handed it to him.

"What? You wanna buy some new clothes and you want my opinion? Short, tight, and low-cut."

"Thank you, Calvin Klein, I mean the flyer, look at the mailing label."

He turned it over. "So, it's addressed to you."

"Exactly. Don't you get it? When you shop at some stores, and you pay by check or credit card, they automatically put you on a mailing list, you know, to alert you to sales and stuff."

"Yeah?"

"So, maybe if we get a list from Electric City, we might find somebody else on it—"

"Besides Alma Johnson."

"Right, can't hurt. All we got now is a sales slip and a very nervous salesman. What's the harm, if we dig a little deeper?"

"Okay," Paresi said, "I'm game. I'll even put my butt on the line for you, literally. I'll call Howard and get a copy of the mailing list." He picked up the receiver. "I know he's gonna ask me out."

"If he does, just remember, no sex on the first date, and when you do, make him wear a condom," Star said, grinning.

Two hours later a messenger delivered a stuffed brown packet to the detectives. They split the computer printout sheets and began looking for names.

"Got anything under E?" Paresi asked.

"Nothing. No Della Ellison." Star ran her finger down the list. "How 'bout you?"

"Still checking the Wilsons . . . hello!"

Star looked up. "Got something?"

"No, I thought I had, but it's Charlotte Wilton, not Charlotte Wilson."

"All right, let's look again." She started with the E's.

"Wait a minute, Della had a hyphenated name, Robb-Ellison, give me the R's."

Paresi went through his half of the pages. "I'll check." He ran his finger down the page. "Robal, Robalaird, Robb, Robb, bingo! Robb-Ellison, Della." They whooped and high-fived across their desks.

"Does all this yelling mean you got something, or are you just letting off steam?" Captain Lewis stood over them.

"We've definitely got something, Captain." Star stood up. "I thing we should talk."

"My office."

She and Paresi grabbed the sheets and files and followed him.

Jerry Auster had enjoyed his steak dinner last night. At least Maureen could still cook.

He stood by the bank of television sets and wondered if he should take another steak home tonight. She had grilled the meat perfectly. Charred on the outside, on the hoof on the inside, just the way he liked it. He enjoyed the taste of blood in his mouth.

He was getting very hungry. Maybe a good dinner would help curb his appetite.

15

Star and Paresi sat staring at the telephone, waiting for a call from the District Attorney's office. Two weeks had passed since they put together what they thought was enough evidence to get a search-and-seizure warrant for the employee files at Electric City.

Sean Mallory, their attorney, didn't agree. He told them the evidence was flimsy, nothing tangible enough to hang a warrant on, but he agreed to try. He also pointed out that the squad's many calls to Electric City and the persistent questioning of Howard Douglas could very well translate into harassment charges, if Mr. Douglas chose to make trouble for them.

For his part, Howard Douglas had been more than patient with the calls, mainly because he really had a yen for Detective Paresi. He knew Paresi was straight and there was no chance, but he enjoyed the contact. So he cooperated, giving Paresi the mailing list and answering more questions than he had to. But he drew the line at turning over his files. The corporate office had already warned him about giving out so much information. Jobs were scarce, and he wanted to keep his.

Star sat winding a rubber band around her already gigantic rubber band ball. "The weakest thing I can think of is the physical evidence," she said. "The lab says we're looking for a white male, between the ages of thirty-five and fifty, with dark hair and Type A positive blood, which effectively narrows the field down to about two billion guys."

She hunted through her desk drawer for more rubber bands. "Still, that's got to fit some of the staff at Electric City.

If I were the judge, that, added to two victims connected with the store, would be enough. I'd issue a warrant."

The phone rang. She grabbed it. "Hi Sean, yeah . . . uh-huh . . . okay." She hung up.

Paresi looked at her. "What?"

"I guess the only black robe I'll be wearing will come from Victoria's Secret, and you're gonna have to go out with Howard."

"I wonder if he likes to eat Italian?" Paresi said. They both laughed.

Darcy passed their desks and tossed a nine and a half by twelve-inch brown envelope to Star. "This is for you," he said.

Star looked across the desk at Paresi. The envelope was identical to the one she'd been given a couple of weeks before. She picked up her letter opener.

"Let me open it," he said.

"No, I got it." She shook the contents of the envelope out on her desk. "Dominic. . . "

Her voice was so soft; he only knew she was speaking because her mouth was moving.

Star looked at him, tears in her eyes, then jumped up, gagging, and ran from the squad room.

Paresi picked up the pictures. Alma Johnson's gaping throat wound had been artistically photographed. It took him a second to realize what had been jammed in it.

Paresi turned the photos over and went after Star. He heard her in the ladies' room. He knocked on the door.

"Star? You all right . . . ? Star?"

He opened the door and went in. She stood in a stall with the door open, trembling, hunched over the toilet.

"You all right?"

"No . . . no, I'm not." She retched.

Paresi moved to the sink and ran cold water over a handful of paper towels. He went back to her and pressed the cool towels to her forehead.

"Go on, let go."

She leaned back against him. "Jesus." Her stomach pitched. She doubled over.

Paresi held her. "That's it . . . that's it." He rubbed her back. "I got you, baby, go on, get rid of it."

She straightened up and wiped her mouth.

"Finished?"

"Yeah, I think so." She wiped her mouth again. "I'm okay."

Paresi held the towels against her forehead. She put her hand over his.

"Dom . . . " She started to cry.

She collapsed against him. He held her, rocking her gently. "He's not going to get away with it. All right? We're gonna get him." He wiped her tears with his hand. "You and me, we're gonna get him."

Still holding her, he leaned over and flushed the toilet.

"Let's get cleaned up."

He walked her to the sink and turned on the tap. She leaned over, rinsed her mouth, and splashed cold water on her face. Paresi handed her a paper towel. She dried her face and hands. Her eyes broke his heart. He reached out for her. The two of them clung to each other.

The door to the ladies' room opened. Barbara Davies, a civilian clerk, walked in and saw them. She stepped back, looked at the outside of the door, then at Star and Paresi standing by the sinks. "When did we go coed?"

"We're outta here," Paresi said. He walked Star toward the door.

Barbara watched them. "I didn't see this, right?"

"Right," Paresi said, closing the door.

16

Jerry took his lunch break late. He liked having the lunch-room all to himself. He ate slowly, enjoying the meatball sandwich he'd ordered from Squire's Sandwich Shop.

The delivery girl was a young blonde, all eyes and legs. The meatball sandwich had been her last delivery before her own lunch. When she got a look at the customer, she nearly told him it was on the house. What a hunk. The guy made her sweat. He had the coolest steel-gray eyes. When she took the money, he held her hand. She wanted to throw him down on the floor and jump on him. He had jet-black hair, and he was wearing all black, a combination that made his gray eyes out-standing. He even tipped her three bucks. When she got back in the car, she was trembling.

Jerry picked up the paper from the empty table next to him. The front page of the second section carried an editorial about the murders of black women in the city. The reporter's picture and byline appeared at the top of the column. Nancy Dawn Davis, *From Where I Sit.* She was an angry-looking black woman with dreadlocks.

"Sit on this, Nancy Dawn," he muttered. "On second thought, forget it, you ain't my type. Shit happens." He shrugged and turned the page.

Who cared about a bunch of bitches getting theirs? If you made it through the day in this world where niggers, spics, and gooks were calling the shots, you were ahead of the game. It was crazy, not the natural order of things.

Today, a white man didn't stand a chance. All of a sudden

everything was upside down and he was on the bottom of the heap.

He'd fought for his country, been on the front lines in Vietnam. The little gook motherfuckers even captured him. They did everything they could to reduce him to shit. He was just a kid, eighteen years old, but he was strong. He had already walked through hell. There wasn't a goddamn thing they could do to him. He took all they had to give, and he survived.

"For what?" he muttered.

His America was gone. Destroyed. The streets were crazy. There were niggers roaming around in packs like wild dogs, shooting everything that moved. The only blessing in that was they were annihilating each other. You had drugs, bums, freaks, the whole fucking pathetic show. You weren't even safe in your own house.

And everybody was yelling about their stinking rights. Broads, spics, homos . . . what about his rights? Who said he had to support all the fucking garbage that washed up on our shores, and the other ones, the bastards running across the borders?

Even if they shipped them back, his tax dollars were footing the bills, and it was a waste of time. For every one that went back, a hundred stayed.

They had all the perks of living in America, including welfare and food stamps. They even had access to free medical and dental. When his daughter was first diagnosed, her medical bills nearly broke him, even with the insurance. Now, most of his income went to pay her hospital bills, and she was going to be locked up for the rest of her life. If he was a fucking deadbeat, it would be free.

Sometimes it was all he could do to stop himself from grabbing a gun and hitting the streets.

It wasn't right. Here he was, a decorated veteran, fucking war hero, working some crummy job in a glorified appliance store and glad to have it.

What happened to his piece of the pie? When he made a sale, he had to write on a slip that had the store's policy in

Spanish, Japanese, Vietnamese, Chinese, and English. What kinda fucking idiot moves to a country and refuses to learn the language? Even worse, we coddle the bastards by printing everything in their language. If they can't speak English, send them back to wherever the fuck they came from.

When he was overseas, he had to learn some gook, just to know what the assholes were talking about. Nobody handed him a pamphlet with their insults printed in English.

Just last week, he'd lost a sale to a spic, because he couldn't speak Spanish. Where was the justice?

His appetite was gone. He tossed the half-eaten sandwich in the garbage and sent the Coke sailing right behind it. He tried to calm himself by thinking of the pictures he'd developed. He closed his eyes and tried to envision his photographs of Alma Johnson. His breathing grew relaxed and even.

In his mind's eye he saw every picture, including the one that made him smile the most. The angle wasn't great, but it was a dynamite picture.

His photos were his salvation, his badge of honor. He felt the tension leaving his body. He could hardly wait to get home and look at them. There was only one thing that made him happier than looking at his pictures . . . getting new ones.

Jerry had been rattling around in his studio for hours. He'd passed on dinner. Maureen prayed he'd stay in the basement. It had been pleasant for her to have dinner alone, eating what she wanted, not having to know he watched every bite she took. She knew he hated her body, and sometimes she did too, but it kept him away from her and that was just fine.

She took another bite of the frozen chocolate eclair in her hand. She had bought a package at the market and hidden it in the back of the freezer. After dinner she pulled one out and headed for the TV in the living room. She hadn't even waited for it to thaw. She didn't care, she liked the icy crystals mixing with the cream and pastry. If he stayed downstairs, she'd have another one.

She was watching reruns of "The Cosby Show" when she heard him running up the steps. She grabbed the remote and changed the channel. Jerry hated when she watched TV shows that featured colored people. He wasn't really a racist, she told herself, he was just jealous that all these people were making more money than him. She covered the half-eaten eclair with her robe and quickly wiped her mouth.

She needn't have bothered. He went right through the living room and out the front door. She heaved herself out of the chair and hurried as fast as she could to the window. She stood behind the drape, peeping at him. He was carrying his camera bag. Where was he going? It was late. She let the drape fall back into place and went back to her chair. Another woman. It had to be, that's why he had the camera, he was gonna take pictures, like the ones he used to take of her.

When they were first married, he took pictures constantly. A lot of nudes of both of them. He even rigged the camera so that he could take pictures of them making love . . . at least for her it had been making love. For him it was a game, to see how far she was willing to go. He'd get her in the most degrading positions and take pictures. It bothered her at first, but she loved him, and she got used to it. He liked to look at the shots. Sometimes he'd make her go down on him while he looked.

That was hard for her. He was too big, and it always made her jaws ache. It seemed like she'd have to suck him for hours and still the only way he'd come was if she used her hand on him while he looked at the pictures. Now he was playing "the game" with somebody else.

She picked up the last part of the slightly squashed eclair and bit into it. She didn't care, it was good he had somebody, it saved her. She chewed the half-frozen dessert. One day she was gonna go in that studio of his and see exactly what he was up to. She'd have to wait until she was sure he wouldn't come in on her. She'd have to be patient, but soon, real soon.

She licked some melting chocolate off her fingers. He thought he was so smart, locking her out. He didn't know she had a key. Once when he was drunk and hung over, she went to the drugstore to get him some Mylanta. She drove his car, and took his keys. While she was in the shopping center she went over to the hardware store and had the entire set copied. Yeah, he was smart, but she was smarter.

She shoved the last of the dessert into her mouth and clicked back to "The Cosby Show." Good, they were running a commercial. She could go to the kitchen without missing more of the show. He was out having his fun, so she'd have hers. Now that he was gone, she could have all the eclairs she wanted. She could eat the whole damn box if she chose.

He drove four blocks past his house and pulled into an all-night gas station. He filled his tank, paid the bill, and asked the attendant for the key to the toilet. The kid inside the booth, with a brush haircut, Smashing Pumpkins T-shirt, and tattoos, never even looked at him. He took the money, tossed the key into the service drawer and went back to his *X-Men* comic.

Jerry pulled his car alongside the rest rooms and parked. He opened the trunk and pulled out an overnight bag, then locked it and took the case inside with him.

The toilet was surprisingly clean. He removed his clothes, folded them neatly and put them on the closed toilet lid. When he was naked, he shaved and then washed himself at the sink with a hand towel from the case. He put the wet towel into a plastic bag and dried himself with another larger towel. This too he stuffed in the plastic bag. He put deodorant under his arms and splashed Balenciaga men's cologne on his neck and chest. He took out his hair products and wet-combed his dark hair back from his face. When his hair was perfect, he sprayed it lightly to keep it in place and took his fresh outfit from the case.

He finished dressing, and put his old clothes in the overnighter. He moved as far back from the mirror as the wall would allow, to see himself. He looked fabulous.

"You're one good-looking son of a bitch!" he whispered to

his reflection. He ran his fingers down the soft, pearl-gray silk shirt. He'd bought it at Barnaby's and was almost out the door when he spotted the perfect black silk trousers to go with it. He reached down and adjusted himself.

"And a lucky one too!" The face in the mirror wore a radiant smile. He leaned in closer. "Now that's a for-real killer smile." His laughter echoed off the white tile walls. He checked to make sure he'd returned all of his things to the bag. Still smiling, he tossed the key in the sink, turned off the light, and opened the door. He walked out, letting it lock behind him.

The attendant never looked up as his car sped away from the station.

He found a parking space right in front of Arabella's. The best place in town for action. He checked himself one more time in the rearview mirror and got out. He walked past the line of losers trying to get in, approached the door and was waved right through. It's not what you got, he thought, it's what you look like you got.

The club was packed. The music was pulsing and the dance floor was alive with gyrating bodies. Michael Jackson's "Smooth Criminal" blasted from the speakers. The perfect song for his entrance. He went to the bar and ordered a J&B on the rocks. The bartender tried to hold his hand when he paid for the drink. He smiled at her and moved on.

All around him men and women played the game. Smiling too much, laughing too loud, trying to impress each other, struggling to hide the desperation in their eyes. He felt sorry for the guys trying to score before the end of the night. AIDS hadn't changed anything. The measure of a man was still how many phone numbers he collected and who he left with at the end of the evening.

They're working hard. Poor fucks, he never had to try for pussy, they threw it at him, but he wouldn't take just anything. It had to be special. He walked to the top of the stairs leading

down to the dance floor and looked out over the crowd.
Bingo! Across the room, on the opposite landing, bouncing to
the music, drink in her hand, eyeballing, just like him.

Denise Miles was drunk. She'd been in the club for about
an hour, and had taken every drink offered her. She was in
pain. Wardell just up and walked out on her, saying he didn't
need her anymore. She found out the reason; a gap-toothed,
blue-eyed, freckle-faced redhead in his dentist's office. Denise
hoped his dick would fall off.

Jerry sipped his J&B and watched her. Steve Winwood's
"Roll With It" blared out over the crowd. She moved her hips
in time to the music. He liked what he saw. She was tall and
lean; a black plum-colored woman in a butter-yellow leather
suit. Her legs were thin, but long and shapely. She wore high
heels, yellow to match the suit, with ankle straps, the kind he
called fuck me shoes.

He felt tingles in his crotch as she moved her shoulders
with the music. He watched her sway, taking the beat and letting it crawl through her, down her spine, into her hips. She
tossed her hair and let the rhythm settle in her round, bouncing, rotating behind.

She danced with her eyes closed. Her long wavy hair flared
out from her shoulders and, as she turned, down her back. He
watched her swing that high, round butt as he began his slow
walk down the stairs. By the time he started across the room,
he was very hard.

Denise opened her eyes to sip her drink and saw him. A
white boy, about six feet tall, with slick, raven-black hair, and
he was watching her. He was handsome . . . hell, he was more
than that, he was fine! High cheekbones and big lips, full juicy
ones, like Wardell's. You never used to see lips like that on
white people, unless they had some "blood" hanging somewhere on the family tree. But nowadays, with all those colla-
gen injections and shit, who could tell? She looked at him
again. He was dark, maybe he was mixed, or passing.

He walked along the outer rim of the floor, still watching
her. She stared back at him. She liked the way he moved,

slow, like a big cat. As he got closer, she drew her breath in sharply. He was definitely white, and those lips were the real deal, he was gorgeous. He walked up on the steps to the landing. She stopped dancing.

"Don't stop," he said, and smiled. He had beautiful teeth, straight and even, pure white, like some dude in a magazine. He even had dimples. He was prettier than she was.

"Don't stop what?" she managed to say.

"Dancing. I like watching you." His voice was soft and sexy. Was God grinning right down on her head or what? Who the fuck needed that sad-assed Wardell? If he could play white meat, so could she.

"I don't really like to dance alone," she said, running her tongue over her suddenly dry lips.

"Then by all means." He put his drink down on the railing and took hers, setting it alongside. As she moved into his arms, Earth, Wind and Fire's "The Way of the World" poured from the speakers. Her absolute favorite humping song; her nipples got hard.

He pulled her to him. He smelled like heaven, and for a white boy, he surely had a large bulge behind his fly. He moved himself right up against her. She should have been mad, but he felt so damned good, and it had been a long time . . . near the end, Wardell wouldn't even sleep with her.

She put both arms around his neck and leaned back, gazing into his gray eyes, letting Maurice White and the boys wrap them up in a web of silky, sexy music.

"I've never seen you here before," she said, smiling in his face. What a lame fucking line, she thought.

He pressed closer and let his hands slide from her waist to her ass, while he slowly rotated his pelvis against her.

Ordinarily, she would have slapped him into the middle of next week, but she wanted what he was doing, she needed it. After what Wardell said to her, she really needed somebody to want her. Thank God she'd come to Arabella's. She had started to stay home, but she just couldn't face another night of crying.

She decided she was going to take herself out, no girl-friends, nobody to tell her she was drinking too much, and now she was so glad she'd done it. God had sent this perfect angel to help her over. She laid her cheek against his and closed her eyes.

His hands were all over her, squeezing and rubbing, while he slowly moved against her. He was so hard she felt like he could lift her with it. His lips touched her throat in a barely there kiss and he moaned softly.

They were on display, everybody in the club could see them, and she didn't care. He was the finest man in the place, and he was hers. She wanted them to see, especially the white girls. She tightened her grip around him, running her hands up his back, loving the muscular feel of him.

He squeezed her again, and put his lips against her ear, snaking just the tip of his tongue inside. Her panties went past moist all the way to wet. Wardell on his best day couldn't make her feel like this.

"I don't come," he whispered, pausing, "here very often, but I'm glad I dropped in tonight." He licked her ear again, this time running his tongue deep inside.

Denise almost fainted. Her breath hissed from between her teeth. He sighed in her ear. The music changed, and for a second the spell was broken. She stepped back, looking at him. He still held her, his pretty mouth curved in a smile.

"My name's Jerry."

She wanted to take her arms from around his neck, but she couldn't. She was tied and bound, as surely as if ropes had suddenly appeared around her.

"I'm Denise," she said.

"Tell me, Denise," he pulled her back into his arms as the voice of Al Green, before he got saved, filled the room, "do you believe in lust at first sight?"

"I do now." She grinned, swaying to the pulsing drumbeat of "Let's Stay Together."

They danced silently, wrapped around one another. When the song was over, he took her hand and ran it down his body.

"See what you do to me?" he whispered.

She giggled. She'd never felt a dick like that on anybody, and she'd been around the block a few times. "Let's sit down," she managed to say.

"Why? You don't want to stay here, do you?" His voice hypnotized her. She couldn't stop looking in those pale gray eyes.

"No . . . I mean yes . . . I mean, I'd like to talk for a while, you know, get to know you a little."

He held her hand against him. "This is all you need to know."

Denise felt someone positively staring her down. She turned, and looked up on the landing across the room. A young white girl with long dark hair stood staring. She was positively purple with rage and jealousy, and she didn't try to hide it. Denise met her gaze. Wardell crossed her mind. She squeezed the hardness he pressed in her palm.

"Let's go," she said. "We can talk at my place."

Outside, she led him to her car, a jet-black Corvette convertible with red upholstery. His dream car. He was glad she wasn't looking in his eyes.

"Great car," he said.

She dangled the keys at him. "You can drive if you want to."

He didn't want to ride with her and be stranded. He took the keys and held them in front of his crotch. "You drive, if you want some of this."

Giggling, she grabbed the keys from him. He caught her in his arms and kissed her neck.

"You got anything to drink at your place?"

"I've got champagne."

"No beer?"

"I don't drink beer," she said, teasing.

"I do, so I'll pick some up. Give me your address, and I'll meet you there."

A million warning bells went off, but Denise was too drunk and too horny to care.

"Don't you want to ride with me?" She pouted.

He kissed her, licking her mouth, sucking her tongue, biting her bottom lip gently. "I want to fuck you, that's what I want, so tell me where you live so I can meet you there."

Denise stumbled back against the car. "Oh Jesus, who taught you to kiss like that?"

"My mother. What's your address?"

She took a deep breath. "It's 2702 Becker Place, in the condos."

Becker Place Condominiums, where a one bedroom went for about two hundred thousand dollars.

"Okay, 2702 Becker . . . I'll meet you there."

He kissed her again and left her standing in the parking lot. All of a sudden she really had to pee. She tiptoed back to the side door, walking with her thighs squeezed together, trying to hold it. Luckily, Ramon on the door recognized her. He let her in and she just made it to the toilet. When she went back to thank him, he told her she was too drunk to drive and took her car keys. He called a cab while she waited in his chair, praying that the taxi would hurry.

Star met Vee at the China Garden. She slid into the booth and poured herself a cup of tea. "I hope you don't mind, but Paresi will be joining us."

"Mind?" Vee grinned. "Girl, I owe you one, you know how I feel about him. As far as I'm concerned, you can leave right now."

"I love you, too." Star picked up her menu. "We're still working."

Vee looked at her watch. "It's nearly eight-thirty, and you get off at six."

"Until we get something on these murders, I may never be off again." She sipped the tea. "This stuff is cold." She turned, looking for a waitress.

"I thought you had a break on the case."

"So did we, but we celebrated too soon, the break didn't pan out, so we're back up against the wall."

"Against the wall, that's where I'd like to get you, Mama." Paresi slid into the booth next to Vee and rubbed her thigh.

"Hello, Dominic," Vee said, all smiles. "If I'm against the wall, would I have to assume the position?"

Paresi winked at her. "Baby, I would make you assume many positions."

Vee wriggled her plump shoulders. "It's a good thing I'm so flexible!"

"And it's a good thing I've got a strong stomach," Star deadpanned. She handed Paresi her menu. "Leave it to you to make this an adventure in dining." She looked around. "Have all the waitresses died?"

"Whaddya need?" Paresi looked at her over the menu.

She pointed to the cold teapot. He raised his hand and a waitress hurried to the table. "Hi, could we get another pot of tea?"

Star shook her head. "I was thinking of setting my hair on fire to see if anyone would notice, and you come in and it's bang!" She snapped her fingers. "How do you do that?"

"What can I say, women just love to take care of me." He turned to Vee. "And then there's the kind of woman I'd really love to take care of." He took her hand. "I'm telling you, Miss Vee, you looking so fine it's criminal. I can see I'm going to have to search you thoroughly *and* often."

Vee giggled like a sixteen-year-old.

Paresi gazed at her. "Mmmmm, I'm telling you, girl, you keep looking this good, I'm gonna have to take a bite out of you."

Vee put her hand over his. "You can start nibbling anywhere you want, sugar."

Paresi grinned. "Oooh." He turned Vee's hand over and kissed her palm. "That means I got to get under the table." The two of them roared with laughter.

"Dominic, you are so bad," Vee said, beaming.

"Wrong baby, I'm so-o-o good. When are you going to let me prove it to you?"

"It's a good thing I've got an empty stomach, or I'd need a

barf bag," Star said. "Can you two control yourselves, so we can order here?"

"Don't pay any attention to her," Paresi said. "She's jealous."

"In your hat, Paresi, I'm starving. I'm having the garlic chicken," Star said, looking around for the waitress.

She appeared and set down a fresh pot of tea and clean cups. She took out her pad and smiled at Dominic. "You ready to order, please?"

"Give us a minute, sweetheart." He smiled at her.

"I'll have the garlic chicken," Star said.

The woman smilingly ignored her. "I'll be back in a few minutes."

"It's nice to be invisible." Star watched the waitress walk away.

Paresi moved closer to Vee. "Tell me, Miss Vee, do you have any Italian in you?"

Vee looked quizzical, "No, I don't think so."

"You sure?"

"Yeah, I'm sure." Vee was blushing.

Paresi pressed his thigh against hers. "Would you like some?" They burst out laughing again.

Star put her head down in her arms. "What did I do to deserve this? Starved and in hell!"

Maureen threw the empty frozen eclair package in the garbage. She washed her hands and turned off the lights in the kitchen. It was late, and Jerry was still out. She was almost worried about him. He had to work in the morning. She thought about the key she had to his studio, but it was too late. He'd probably be coming in anytime. She didn't want to take the chance of getting caught.

She walked up the hall to the bedroom. The house was eerie and quiet. She turned on the television. A rerun of "Cheers" appeared on the screen. One of the early shows from when the coach was still alive. She took off her robe and crawled up on the bed. It was so odd watching a man she knew was dead. She wondered what he looked like now, lying under the earth.

Paresi drove Vee home from the restaurant and headed back to the station. When he reached the squad room, he found his partner staring out the window into the darkness.

"Something tells me I should have stayed at Vee's," he said, pulling out his chair.

"I was wondering when you'd be back," Star said, not turning around.

"She introduced me to her kids." Paresi sat down at his desk.

"They're great kids," Star said, still looking out the window.

"Yeah. That Lena, she's gonna be a heartbreaker," Paresi said.

"So, you gonna start dating my friend?" Star swiveled in her chair to face him.

"I'm thinking about asking her if she'd like to spend some time with me. Whaddya think she'll say?"

"Don't dick around with Vee, Dominic."

Paresi raised his hands. "No way, she's a great girl. I've always liked her, you know that, and I think she likes me. In fact, I thought about going back tonight, after we're off."

"You don't want to do that," Star said, "'cause then I'd have to kill you in the morning."

They both laughed.

"Don't worry, I know she's not a bimbo, okay?" Paresi said. "I respect her, and I'd like to take her out, if that's cool with you."

"You two are adults. Just keep in mind that she's like my sister, and I don't want her hurt."

"Got it." He leaned forward, lacing his fingers together. "So you wanna tell me why you're sitting here, staring off into space."

"I've been going over and over this thing."

"And?"

"And the answer is in that store, or at least part of it is. We're missing it."

Paresi pulled the mailing list from his desk drawer. "Let's say I agree with you. We got three victims, two customers, and one very spooked salesman, who I know couldn't be that good an actor, so he's not a suspect. We got a fruitcake manager who wants to introduce me to an alternate lifestyle, some sick pictures, and this list."

"One more time." She got up and stood behind him, reading over his shoulder. "Let's see." She pointed to Della Robb-Ellison's name, highlighted in pale yellow marker. "Okay, name, address, item purchased, date of purchase, amount of purchase . . . initials." She looked at Paresi. "Initials."

Paresi smiled. "Of the salesperson."

"Correctamondo. J. A. And we know poor little Alma Johnson bought her TV from Jerry Beacham," she said.

"Here it is." Paresi pointed. "J. B."

She sat on the edge of his desk. "Seems to me you should call Howard again." She smiled.

"You heard what Mallory said, we could end up facing harassment charges."

"Howard wouldn't blow the whistle if you asked him nicely just who this J. A. is."

Paresi ran a hand through his hair. "It ain't the whistle I'm worried about."

She fluttered her eyelashes at him. "Ple-e-ease?"

He looked at his watch. "In the morning, and you owe me, big-time!

It was nearly four A.M. when Jerry picked up his camera bag, the brown bag holding both his empty beer cans, and his extra beer. He'd had a good time. She'd been waiting when he got to her place, with her eyes full of anticipation, and he didn't let her down.

She had been awesome too. A woman who matched him,

she wore him out. "Denise," he whispered, unable to keep the smile from his lips. "A man could fall in love."

He moved quietly down the hall. At the front door he turned off the air-conditioning. She said having it on all the time gave her colds. (Mo would be proud, he was conserving energy.) He reached into his pocket for his keys; they weren't there. He turned, trying to see in the darkened living room. He knew he'd had them when he came in. He checked his pockets again.

"What the fuck?" he muttered.

He put the bags down on the rug and walked back again to the couch. He searched the crevices, nothing. He hadn't taken them into the bedroom.

"Goddamnit!" He paced through the living room back to the door and dropped on one knee, digging through the camera bag. He felt a hard lump under the canvas. He pulled his hand out and opened the front pocket of the bag. There they were. He yanked them out, zipped the bag and stood up, wiping sweat from his face with his forearm.

Opening the door slowly, he looked out into the night. No sign of the security patrol. He stepped out on the mat and quietly closed the door behind him. He walked to his car, humming, "Just the Two of Us."

Inside, the three inch long, six inch round plastic film case that had fallen out of his camera bag rolled on the two-thousand-dollar, hand-tied Oriental area rug that Denise Miles had purchased as a housewarming present for herself.

The rug was pale blue and ivory, with highlights of pink and apple-green, framing a lotus design. Denise loved the thickness under her bare feet. It was, she often said, the best two thousand dollars she'd ever spent.

In the silent house the film case rolled over the pink blossoms, over the lotus, over the pale green band, and finally came to rest behind the brass planter that held the ficus tree Wardell Washington had given her when he moved in.

17

Star lay on the bed, staring at the ceiling. It had been a very rough night. Charlotte Wilson, Della Robb-Ellison, and Alma Johnson had all come to visit.

The women walked in her dreams, calling her, beckoning her. She saw them, arms outstretched, wounds on display, motioning for her to come join them. She had been unable to stop herself from going toward them.

The closer she moved, the farther away they floated, until she suddenly found herself surrounded by the three of them. They moved closer, and she could smell death. As they became clear in her vision, she started screaming.

All three of them had her face.

Star woke up sweating, her sheets drenched. She jumped out of bed, and Jake rolled over, staring at her.

She stumbled into the bathroom and turned on the overhead light. The bright glare made her eyes hurt. She washed her face with cold water and sponged off her body as Jake sat in the doorway, his feline eyes blinking.

"I'm all right," she said to the cat, and herself. "I'm all right."

By the time she stripped the bed and changed the sheets, the sun was coming up. She lay down, her body so tired it wouldn't support her, but she couldn't close her eyes again. Turning over on her side, she stared at the clock. The alarm wouldn't go off for another fifteen minutes.

Her mind wandered to Paresi. He'd been calling Howard Douglas for four days, and they still had no ID on the salesperson with the initials J. A. Maybe Douglas wasn't going to cooperate, maybe he'd finally had enough.

Jake jumped up on the bed, padded alongside her body and rubbed his head on her hip. She turned over on her back and the cat climbed up on her, perching on her chest and looking down into her face.

"I can always count on you," she said, tickling him under his double chins. "Let me guess, this blast of morning kitty breath means you want breakfast."

Jake responded by gently trapping her finger between his upper and lower teeth.

"All right, I get the message." She sat up and deposited him on the floor. "I'm glad one of us has an appetite."

Jake yowled at her feet.

"Okay, okay."

It was just after eight A.M., and Grace Lamont was walking her dog Binky, when she passed Denise Miles's unit. She'd been reticent to have colored people in the complex at first, but she really liked Denise. She was different, so bright and well-spoken.

Her late husband Roger had often said Denise was the most intelligent woman he'd ever met, colored or white, and Grace agreed. When he died, Denise was there for her, calling on her to see if she was all right, taking her out to movies and dinner, getting her out of the house.

She'd been more of a help than some of Grace's oldest neighbors and friends, especially the ones who still had husbands and who, since Roger's death, had begun to view her as some kind of competition. As if she'd be interested in that gang of old coots they were married to!

Binky was pulling at the leash, trying to go up the walkway.

"No, Binky." Grace tugged the other way. "Even though we haven't seen Denise in a few days, we'll call first, it's not nice to just drop in on people."

The Saint Bernard outweighed Grace by about seventy pounds. He ignored her and continued his way along the walk, dragging Grace, gritting her teeth, behind him.

"Oh!" Grace panted. "Only Roger could control this damned dog! All right, Binky, all right!" The dog drooled and tugged her as he trotted to the door.

Grace knocked, and it opened just a crack; it had not been securely closed. Binky pushed with his nose and the door swung back. The odor that hit the older woman in the face made her gag. Her instinct told her to leave, but Binky and something else moved her forward.

"Denise? Denise, it's Grace, are you home?"

The house was hot and silent, darkened by the closed drapes in the living room.

"Denise?"

Grace's voice seemed to echo back at her like some soon-to-be victim in an old horror movie. A lock of hair that had been pinned to the top of her head in a sedate bun unraveled and fell across her neck, making her gasp in surprise and fear.

"Come, Binky, we shouldn't be in here." She tugged on the leash, trying to make the dog turn around. "Denise is obviously not home."

The dog stood still, his nose twitching at the scent in the air. A whine escaped him. Grace wrinkled her nose.

"Oh, the odor in here is foul." She turned toward the kitchen. "She must have forgotten and left some meat out or something and its gone bad. Come, Binky."

She tugged again at the dog's leash. Binky's whine became a bark. He jumped. Grace couldn't hold him. The Saint Bernard went running into the bedroom, the hand-tooled Spanish leather leash trailing after him.

"Binky!" Grace hurried after him. "You're a bad dog, come here, come here this instant! . . . Binky!"

The dog sat on his haunches, howling at the closed bathroom door.

Grace grabbed the leash. "Bad dog, bad, bad dog!" She tugged on the leather strap.

Binky scratched at the bottom of the door, yelping and sniffing furiously. Grace put her hand over her nose. The odor here was especially bad, and she was getting nauseous.

Binky jumped at the door, standing on his hind legs. He threw his weight on it, and the bathroom door popped open, freeing a blast of hot, stinking, fly-filled air.

Grace Lamont caught a glimpse of the thing in the tub and ran screaming from the house. Her dog went inside the bathroom and sniffed at it. He licked a bit of dried blood on its arm and went trotting outside after his mistress, who was committing the unforgivable faux pas of being violently ill on Denise Miles's front lawn.

Jerry Auster woke at fifteen past eight in the morning. He lay there staring at the ceiling, trying not to feel the muggy heat or Maureen sleeping next to him. It had been four days since his last "photo shoot," and he couldn't stop thinking about her. Denise Miles. She was a great fuck. She took all of him without once complaining that he was hurting her.

He scratched himself and turned on his side, away from his snoring wife. Denise, he thought. She really liked him. She'd curled up in his arms afterward and snuggled. Her body felt right against him, they fit. He enjoyed her warmth, and inhaling the sweet scent of her.

She told him he was the best man she'd ever been with, and he believed her. He had her hollering so loud, the entire complex must have heard.

But she'd done right by him, too. He smiled at the memory. He'd never come that hard in his life. It rolled up and shot out of him like it was being ripped from his soul. It had actually hurt. But that could have been because he held back, he didn't drop his first load until he'd brought her off three times, and she couldn't believe it.

She'd been obsessed with paying him back; getting him off was like a mission for her. He closed his eyes, remembering the things she did, the way she perched on top of him, holding him inside her, squeezing and releasing him, all the while staring into his eyes, her body barely moving. It was like a contest between them.

When he'd closed his eyes and thrust so far inside her that he lifted both of them from the bed, she laughed. It was wild. And that mouth, she must have been a sword swallower in another life. It had been so good that when he finally popped, he actually lost consciousness for a moment.

Denise, he said to himself. She really made him happy, and she had the sweetest cunt he'd ever tasted. He stayed down until she begged him to stop.

He licked his dry lips, conjuring the taste of her in his mouth. "Like peach nectar," he whispered.

He liked her, she was beautiful, and she made him happy. He liked her eyes, so dark and full of passion. She made him want to see her again, to get to know her, but that was impossible.

When she snuggled against him and he felt her body mold itself into his, fitting so perfectly, he knew then that she'd touched him, made him want to be with her, to see her again, to get to know her. That made him weak.

"It's a war, Denise," he whispered, seeing her in his mind, "and you were the worst kind of enemy."

"Did you say something, Jerry?" Maureen struggled to sit up.

"No." He wiped his mouth. "I was just looking at the clock. I overslept." He jumped out of bed. "I've got to hustle."

Maureen rubbed her eyes. "I'll get up and get your breakfast."

He could smell her in the morning heat.

"No, I don't have time, I'll grab something later." He headed for the bathroom.

She watched him walk away. He was such a dog. He didn't even have the decency to cover up. Didn't he know she could see the scratches on his back?

As soon as Star walked into the squad room, Paresi turned her around.

"Becker Place Condos, a ripe one, the call just came in."

"Do you think it's our guy?"

"Don't know. A neighbor called, some old lady found the body, she didn't give too many details, she was too busy spewing."

"Swell." Star's earring dropped off. She stooped to pick it up. "I can see this is going to be a great day." She clamped it back on her ear. "A heaving old lady, and brand new, mucho expensive earrings that I had to have, one of which refuses to stay on my ear. This sucker fell off three times in the car."

She went to her desk and pulled out a brand new Vicks inhaler from the center drawer. "You got one?"

Paresi felt in his pocket. "Yeah, let's go."

The coroner's van was at the curb, with Mitch's city-issued car in front of it, when they pulled up. The odor from the open condo door hit Star when she stepped out of the car. She pulled out the inhaler and took two deep blasts up each nostril. Paresi drew the fumes from his inhaler in short, quick breaths.

Star watched him. "You do that like a man with experience."

Paresi winked at her. "Sinus problems."

Inside the house, she could feel the stench all around her. She walked into the bedroom just as Mitch came out. He closed the door.

"What have we got?" she asked him.

"A mess."

"I'm going in."

He grabbed her arm. "Wait, let me talk to you first." He took a small pad from his inside breast pocket. "Her name's Denise Miles. She was an attorney."

"Her?" Star asked. "Is she black?"

"Yes."

"This another one?"

"Looks like it." He took Star by the arm and walked her back into the living room. "I want to warn you before you go in there. She's in water, and she's been dead about four days."

"I've seen decomposed bodies before, Mitchell."

"She's not just decomposed." He stood blocking her way. "She's been disemboweled."

"What?"

"Disemboweled. He cut her throat and then opened her up. It's like a slaughterhouse in there. She's all over the bathroom."

"Jesus." Paresi walked up behind Mitch. "Star, you don't have to go in, I got it."

She pushed past him. "Thanks, but I don't need protecting." She walked back into the bedroom, the two men close behind her. She opened the bathroom door and stepped inside.

For her, it was like stepping into another dimension, where the only sound was the buzzing of flies. In all her years in Homicide she'd never seen anything like it.

She stood there, her eyes taking in every tiny detail. She felt like a robot camera, turning her head, click, the walls, click, the floor, click, Denise Miles.

The pale lavender carpet directly beside the tub had stiffened from the blood. The wall and tiles beside and behind the body reminded Star of a Jackson Pollock canvas.

Through the stink, the flies, and the heat, Star could see the bites on Denise Miles's bloated, blistered, left breast. She turned without a word and walked back into the bedroom, past Paresi and Mitch, and through the living room to the outside, where she stood on the front step, her eyes closed, taking deep breaths of air. Inside, she was screaming.

Jerry Auster was having a great day. He had two major sales before lunch: a home entertainment center and a bookshelf remote CD system.

He sat at a table in the back room, having a corned beef sandwich on rye bread from Squire's. The little blonde who delivered had forgotten his dill pickles, so she gave him somebody else's coleslaw. It didn't really matter, he was in too good a mood to be angry. He pulled out his calculator and began figuring up his commissions.

Howard Douglas fluttered into the room, clapping his hands, calling for everyone's attention. Jerry looked up.

"I have an announcement," Douglas said, smiling at the workers in the room. He turned to the slight, mustachioed, black man standing next to him. "This is Leander Poteet. He's going to be filling in here for Jerry Beacham."

"What happened to Beacham?" Ike Standler asked. "Did he quit?"

Douglas looked embarrassed. "No, he broke his shoulder this morning being a nice guy, helping Stan load a combo on the truck. Leander works in the Victor Street store, but his supervisor has graciously allowed us to borrow him until Jerry comes back."

He turned to the smiling but nervous man. "Leander, this is everybody." He swept the room with his hand. "I'm not going to give you names, they'll introduce themselves. They're all nice people, and they'll make your stay here very pleasant." He shook the man's hand and left the room.

Leander Poteet looked out at a solid wall of white faces. He straightened his tie and picked out the friendliest one. He smiled. "Everybody calls me Lee."

Jerry Auster smiled back.

BCI finished their work on Denise Miles's condo. The last member of the unit carried his case up the walkway to his waiting car. Star stood in the doorway, where she'd spent most of the time. Mitch came up behind her.

"We need to talk," he said.

"All right."

She walked out to his car with him.

"I'm worried about you."

She hugged herself, leaning against the car. "I'm fine."

Mitch stood facing her. "No, you're not. We've got a genuine, crazy bastard here, and you've got to get some help with this. It's tearing you apart."

Star looked down at the sidewalk.

Mitch, aware that they were being watched, leaned down, his mouth at her ear. "If you want to talk later, I'm here for you."

"Thank you, but I'm all right."

He made her look at him. "You don't have to hang tough for me, Star." He said. "You're not all right." He pressed a piece of paper into her hand. "This is my private number. If you need anything, anything at all, use it. Even if it's the middle of the night, call me."

She put her hand in his. "Thanks, I appreciate it."

"Anytime." He straightened up.

Paresi stood in the living room window, watching. Star waited until Mitch got into his car and pulled away before she went back into the house.

"Are you ready?" she asked Paresi.

"Yeah." He pulled the car keys out of his pocket. "You gonna be all right? Mitch seemed really concerned."

"Looks like we've got a sure-enough-for-real serial killer here, and he thinks I'm going to fall apart. He was offering to watch over the pieces tonight."

"You know, if you need somebody—"

"I know, I know." She shook her head. "You guys seem to forget that I"m the senior officer here, it's my unit, I've seen death before."

"Yeah, but never like looking in a mirror, and never from some wacko just out to waste women like this."

She met his eyes. "Does it show?"

"Like Spike Lee at a Klan meeting. We've got a serial killer taking women out, and you're in charge. You've got to be on top of this, so you can handle it. You need to talk to somebody. If you won't tell me, then talk to the department shrink. Trying to tough it out could get you killed."

"You sound like Mitchell. I'll be fine once we get this bastard." She looked around the room. "Did they lock all the windows in here?"

"It's secure. 'Course, they're gonna have to burn it down to get the smell out."

Star ran her fingers over a Waterford crystal biscuit jar filled with jellybeans on the table next to the sofa. "She had good taste, nice things, and a sweet tooth."

Paresi took her arm. "Let's go."

They walked to the door.

"Damnit!" Star stepped back.

"What?"

"My earring, it just fell off again." She backed up, looking down at the rug. "That's the last time I buy clip-ons, I don't care how pretty they are!"

She looked alongside the wall. "Here it is." As she bent to pick it up, she saw the bottom of a black, plastic cylinder wedged between the planter and the wall.

She searched her purse, pulling out her latex gloves. "Damn!" She turned to Paresi. "Do you have any evidence bags?"

He checked his pockets. "No."

"Gloves?"

"Yeah."

She reached into her purse. "I know BCI is finished, but let's not take chances." She pulled on her gloves. "Check the kitchen, find a Baggie or something, and a pair of tongs if you can."

Paresi pulled on his gloves and leaned down. "What've you got?"

"I don't know."

He went into the kitchen and found a plastic vegetable bag in a drawer under the counter. There were no tongs, so he grabbed a meat fork from the pitcher of utensils near the stove and hurried back to Star.

"Here." He handed her the bag, trying to see over her shoulder.

Star was on her knees. "Whatever it is, it's wedged. You got the tongs?"

"I couldn't find any, use this."

He gave her the long-handled fork. She maneuvered it so she could push the top of the cylinder, sliding it backward. It came out from behind the plant with a little scraping sound, and a poof of dust that made Star sneeze. She turned her head, and sneezed again.

"God bless you," said Paresi.

"Thanks." She held her head back, waiting for the next sneeze. When it didn't come, she cleared her throat and carefully lifted the cylinder. Using two fingers, holding the top and bottom, she dropped it in the vegetable bag.

"It's a film canister," Paresi said.

"Yep." Star got up on her feet. "It's very light, there's probably nothing in it, but let's just take it to BCI and see what we get."

18

Loman Rayford was a big man. He stood six feet five and a half inches and he weighed close to three hundred pounds. He liked to eat, and after his shot at pro football went up in a knee injury, eating became a full-time job. He'd been a hell of an athlete all through high school and college.

In his junior year at the university he was courted by the NFL, but being the son of a Pullman porter and a day worker, he knew what the real world was like for black athletes when the cheering stopped and they had limited or no education. He wanted to finish school first. He was so good, they were willing to wait.

It all ended one chilly, wet afternoon. He was out on the field, cutting the fool, showboating for his girlfriend, Regina Battle, who was in the stands. He slipped on the grass and came down with his right knee on a steel measuring rod that some doofus had forgotten about. It just about busted his kneecap in two.

That was the end of the dream, but not Regina. They'd been married nearly seventeen years, and had two great kids. His thirteen-year-old son, Andre, wanted to be a writer, spent all of his time in books and couldn't care less about sports. His daughter, Shavon, loved sports, because, as she told him, with fifteen-year-old logic, "That's where the guys are."

When his football career literally snapped in two, Loman decided to go into insurance. It bored him stupid. His only joy was hanging out with his buddies from school. Two of them had joined the police department. When they suggested he try out for the force, he laughed so hard that the beer he was drinking shot out of his nose.

But the guys wouldn't let up. The force needed more black faces, and Loman's was famous all over town. Strings were pulled, certain requirements were deleted from physical tests and substituted with logic and reasoning, and he was in.

From the beginning, he wanted Forensics. He trained as hard for the Bureau of Criminal Identification as he had for the bowl games in school.

It paid off. After twelve years he was the best forensics man the department had to offer. He was so good, other departments called him in to consult.

He liked being the Big Kahuna. So much fame, and without having to break your neck on a football field. He looked out over the unit, and all the white folks working for him. Life was good, he thought. He looked up to see Starletta Duvall headed toward his office. And it just got better. He stood when she walked in. He was a happily married man, but goddamn!

"Hi, Loman."

"Hey, pretty, what can I do for you?"

She held out the plastic vegetable bag. "You can tell me about this."

He took the bag and held it up. "It's a film canister."

"Thank you so much."

They laughed.

"I know that. I found it at Denise Miles's condo, can you check it for prints or anything else you can get?"

He opened the bag and turned it upside down, letting the container tumble out on his desk. He carefully lifted it.

"Just what I thought."

"What?"

He opened the can. "No worthwhile prints on this thing. It's dusty, it's plastic, and it's empty."

"Plastics hold prints," she said.

"Usually." He turned it over. "But this thing has dust on it."

"Yeah, no cleaning lady I guess," she said.

Loman held the container under his desk light. "Ordinarily, we still might be able to get something, but it also looks like it's been in a hot place. It's a little soft. Anything that might have been on it is gone."

"Isn't there some way you can lift prints from dust?" she asked.

"Oh yeah. There's an electrostatic process that does it, and maybe if we were the NYPD, we'd have it, but it's out of our budgetary reach."

"So's my raise," Star said.

"Mine, too." Loman smiled. "Sorry I can't help you, baby."

"You sure?"

He grinned at her. "As sure as I am that if you said the word, I'd leave home."

"Yeah, right." She smiled. "Let's call Regina and tell her where you'll be."

"I wish I could help you, sweetnin', but . . ."

"Swell, I'm back at zero."

"You found this at the Miles scene?"

"Yep."

"Why didn't some of my people find it? Where was it?"

"In her entryway, wedged between a potted plant and the wall. If it hadn't been for a defective earring, *I* wouldn't have found it. Why weren't you there, where were you?" she asked.

"Over at Greenfield Projects. Some young kid got himself dead sometime last night, but they didn't find him till this morning, in the stairwell. The Miles call came in after I'd left."

"I saw that on the board," she said, "but Paresi hustled me out on the Miles case as soon as I came in. I haven't had time to check the reports." She shrugged. "Don't sweat it, it really isn't anybody's fault, it just rolled out of sight."

"We get paid to find things." Loman put the canister on his desk. "Fine-tooth comb is our speciality." A look of indignation crossed his face. "Sometimes I feel like when it's us, they slack off, because it's not important, understand?"

She nodded. "I hear you."

"See, I can't kneel anymore, but I got a lot of hotshots in here with two healthy knees. Somebody is going to tell me why they missed it."

'Being a leader is hell," she said and smiled at him. "If anything turns up, like some usable prints . . . "

Loman raised an eyebrow.

"Yeah, right. I must have thought this was the movies for a minute. Thanks anyway." She turned to leave.

"Wait. I can tell you something that might help."

"I'm all ears," she said.

"No baby, you all legs, but you got yourself a can from Neopan 1000."

"And?"

"It's a new film, black and white, shoots clear and non-grainy in any kind of light. It's used by pros mainly, and it's hard to find."

She gave him her prettiest smile. "Thank you, big man, you just gave me a present."

"Along with my heart," he said.

She left the department laughing.

"Anything on the film can?" Paresi asked when she sat down.

"Nope, too much dust, and it was empty. But Loman did say it was a new kind of film, Neopan 1000. Evidently, it's pretty hard to come by, so . . . " She pulled out the phone book. "All photo supply places, let's see who carries it."

Paresi reached for his book just as the phone rang.

Star picked it up. "Homicide, Lieutenant Duvall." She looked at Paresi. "Yes, he's right here, hold on." She put her hand over the mouthpiece.

"Who?"

"Your secret love, How-weird Douglas."

Paresi shot her a look.

"Line two," she said.

He picked up the phone.

"Yo, Howie, what's going on?" He tossed his pen across the desk at Star. She ducked, laughing.

"Really? Well, I'm sorry to hear that . . . what?" He motioned to Star, whispering, "Gimme back the pen." She pitched it to him, he grabbed a pad and began writing.

"Slow down, slow down . . . yeah . . . yeah, no problem, no, don't sweat it . . . uh-huh. I'm sorry to hear that. I understand, yeah." He wrote faster. "Right, yeah . . . got it. I got it. Thanks, Howie, I appreciate it, and I know things will work out. Take care." He hung up the phone.

"That was certainly friendly. Have we had a change of heart?" Star asked.

"I've spent a lot of time talking to him. He's not a bad guy, he can't help it if he's light in the loafers. He's been a big help, and he apologized for taking so long to call me back, but the big brass didn't want him involved in our investigation, he had to wait till he could safely leak the info, and on top of that, he's had a really bad day."

"What happened?"

"Our old pal Jerry Beacham got hurt, so he's out, and Howard's mom was just taken to the hospital with heart problems, so he's gonna be out of town for a while, looking after her and unjangling his nerves. That's his word, 'unjangling.'"

He picked up the pad. "Anyway, he gave me the name. J.A. is Jerry Auster."

"Two Jerrys. That's interesting." Star leaned back in her chair. "I wonder if Denise Miles was a customer? She wasn't on the mailing list, but she sure had a lot of expensive electronic equipment. Do you think she could have bought something after the most recent update?"

"Too late to find out from Howard, but I'm sure we can find a way to get the info without having the store come at us."

"I'll leave that up to you," Star said. "Right now, let's get on the photo shops."

Paresi stood up and stretched, rested his hands on his hips and stared into space.

"Paresi . . . Paresi!"

"What?"

"Where are you? What are you thinking?"

"Photo shops, there's a photo shop in the mall near Electric City."

She snapped her fingers. "Right, what's the name of it?"

Paresi rubbed his jaw. "I can't think . . . Klein's or Kling's . . . I can see it but I can't get it."

Darcy walked by their desks.

"Glenn's."

"Glenn's what?" Star asked.

"The photo shop by Electric City, it's called Glenn's," Darcy said. "My wife takes our stuff there to get it printed. Then she goes over to the warehouse store across the street and spends a couple of hundred bucks saving me money."

He pulled a fresh pack of bubble gum from the pocket of his shirt. "I got twenty-four packs of this stuff. You guys want some gum? It's grape."

"No thanks." Star opened the phone book and looked up the number. "Glenn's Camera and Photo Shop." She dialed.

"Hello. I'd like some information please . . . yes, I'm looking for a film called Neopan 1000, and I'm having a terrible time finding it. Do you carry it by any chance?"

She made a thumbs up signal to Paresi and Darcy.

"You do? Is it in stock? . . . But you can order it for me? How long would it take? Great, thank you . . . my name? Oh, I see, it's Janine Bohannon. I'll call you back when I know how much I need. Thank you." She put the phone down and jumped up, doing a little dance.

"Janine Bohannon?" Paresi smiled at her.

"A girl Vee and I were in grammar school with. I always thought she had a cool name."

"Well, Janine, what did he say?"

"He said he doesn't keep it in stock, but he special-orders it. Get this, he wanted my name because he said he keeps a list of the people who buy it because it's constantly being changed, so he keeps the list to keep his customers up-to-date."

She threw her arms around Paresi. "Let's go get that list."

"You're on." He grabbed his keys.

At that moment, Captain Lewis appeared in the door of his office. "Just a minute. I need you two."

"We're headed out on a lead, Captain," Star said.

"Let Darcy handle it. I just got a call from the tenant's committee at Becker Condos. They want to talk about the murder, seems a few of the residents have information to share."

Darcy parked his gum in his cheek. "No sweat, Star, me and Rescovich will go talk to Glenn. He knows me anyway, 'cause of the wife, leave it to me."

"Okay. You guys take it." She turned to Paresi. "Captain's office, after you."

19

Maureen wiped the sweat from her face with the hem of her apron. She had dragged both the trash and recycle cans out to the curb for pickup. It was her job to get them out. If she waited for Jerry to do it, they'd be buried in garbage. It was so hot that she stood out there for a few minutes, looking up and down the street, wondering where she'd go if she left him.

Her neighbor drove past, waving and grinning. Maureen knew the grin; the woman thought she was too fat. She'd overheard her in the supermarket, commenting to another woman that she looked like a whale and yet was buying ice cream and sweets.

Maureen had gone back to the snack aisle and added two boxes of Hostess cupcakes to her cart, right in front of the women. She'd hidden them from Jerry when she got home, but she had to get them.

At the checkout, she'd stood in front of them and deliberately dropped her wallet on the conveyer belt, so that the old picture of Jerry and her, taken when they were first sweethearts, was in plain view. She knew she looked slim and shapely in the picture. She wanted them to see what she could look like and that he'd stayed with her despite all the weight she'd gained.

They got the idea, the skinny, ugly bitches! Both of them looked so whipped and jealous that she almost burst out laughing. They were married to scrawny, stupid-looking lugs in baseball caps, and her husband was so good-looking he stopped traffic. They could say what they wanted, but she had Jerry. At least to the outside world.

She fanned herself with the apron and went back into the kitchen. The clock was fast, but she knew he'd be home in a couple of hours, so she had to get dinner started and put a new bag in the garbage can under the sink.

She opened the cabinet and felt underneath for her paper bag stash. She liked to think she was adding to her save-the-planet activities by reusing the paper grocery bags for garbage.

Jerry never even noticed the money she saved by not buying plastic garbage liners. She used plastic bags from the market and put her paper bags inside them. At least she was doing something. He just always said, "The world's already fucked anyway, so who gives a shit?"

She moved her hand around under the sink; nothing. She couldn't be out, she had a ton of them stashed in there. She kneeled down, her weight driving her knees into the linoleum, and stuck her head into the darkness under the sink.

There they were, way in the back. As she stretched to reach the bags, something fell on her hand. She jerked it out. Jerry's shirt, the one she'd thrown away. It must have fallen out of the can and lodged back with the extra bags.

"Well, I guess you're going to be a dust rag," she said to the shirt. "I'm not going back out on that curb." She dropped it on the floor and pulled out a bag. After she'd set the garbage can up, she took the shirt and tossed it in the rag bag she kept hanging on the pantry door.

Paresi and Star sat on folding chairs in the social center at the Becker Place Condominiums. They were surrounded by residents; some older couples, but mostly aging or elderly widows with blue hair. In spite of the weather, they each balanced a cup of steaming Earl Grey tea in Royal Worcester china cups, and several Pepperidge Farm Party Collection cookies on matching dessert plates.

They'd been listening patiently for over an hour as, one by one, residents stood up and told a story of what they thought happened the night Denise Miles died.

"It's not that we think she did anything wrong, detectives," Alice Silverman said, "but we think whoever did this must have been a friend of hers."

"Why, ma'am?" Star asked the somber, birdlike woman.

"Well, we just didn't have this sort of thing happening here until she moved in. Not to say that she wasn't a good tenant, she was excellent. We voted whether or not to have her here, and no one dissented. But shortly after she moved in, she had a man living with her."

"That's right." Betty Chaput brushed cookie crumbs from her bosom. "He was a colored man, quite nice-looking, but we haven't seen him lately."

"Denise Miles was no whore!" Grace Lamont stood up. Star had been surprised to see her slip in and take a seat after the meeting began. Earlier, she'd been too distraught to talk to the officers.

"She was a good person, a decent young woman, who understood loneliness." Grace leveled her icy gaze on her neighbors. "She helped me when Roger died. Where were all of you? None of you has the right to demean her. She was in love with that man. They just broke up and she was devastated. If any of you had taken the time to get to know her, you would have found that out." She wiped her eyes. "Denise was a lovely young woman."

"Do you know who the man was, Mrs. Lamont?" Star asked.

"Yes. His name was Wardell. I don't know his last name, she never told me, but she talked about him constantly. He worked in her office, and she loved him, but he's not your killer, he couldn't have done anything so terrible." Grace's eyes flooded.

"I only came to this meeting because I knew somebody would try to put the blame on poor Denise."

"If she was so good, then what about all those sex sounds coming from her place the other night?" Frances Herbert stood up, her plump face red and angry-looking. "They kept at it nearly all night."

She pointed to her husband, who looked like he would

rather have been anywhere else, and said, "My poor Edgar needs at least ten hours of sleep, and that night, he never closed his eyes."

"I'll bet he didn't!" Paresi whispered to Star. She put a whole cookie in her mouth to keep from laughing.

"I didn't get to sleep until after four in the morning." Frances was practically shaking with righteous indignation. "It was disgraceful!"

"You say the noise stopped after four?" Paresi asked.

Frances Herbert sniffed. "I assume they finally went to sleep, but it was awful, both of them, her and the man, grunting and groaning like animals!"

Star put the cup of tea down, opened her purse and pulled out a notebook. As she leaned forward, she adjusted her jacket and heard Ella Rubenstein, sitting next to her, gasp at the sight of her gleaming, stainless steel 9mm Beretta. Star realized it was visible in her shoulder holster. She straightened up, pulling the garment over the weapon. "Did anyone else hear the noises?"

A heavyset woman near the door raised her hand.

"Yes, ma'am?" Star said.

"My name is Constance Harper. I heard some noise, but it didn't keep me awake. The thing that woke me was someone slamming a car door a few feet away from my bedroom window."

"About what time was that?" Star asked.

"Sometime after four. I'm not sure."

"Did you get up and take a look?"

Constance Harper's face was stern. "I am not a busybody. I don't make a habit of spying on my neighbors!"

"No, ma'am, I didn't mean that," Star said. "I just wondered if you might have taken a look, it's a very late hour to hear car doors slamming, some people would have looked."

"Not me. I don't like to be involved with other people's lives."

"Thank you, ma'am." Star turned toward Grace Lamont. "Mrs. Lamont, you're about three units down, did you hear anything?"

"No, officer. Since my husband died, I take a pill so I can sleep. It pretty much puts me out."

"Well, I don't see how anyone could have slept through that ruckus!" Frances Herbert pulled her green sweater tightly around her plump body. "It was disgusting. She had no respect for her neighbors at all."

It was nearly three hours before they got back to the squad room. Their shift was over, and Star found the list Darcy had left from Glenn's Photo Shop on her desk, along with a large brown envelope addressed to Homicide.

"Mail's in," she said.

"Let me." Paresi picked up the envelope and opened it.

Denise Miles lay in her bathtub.

"I can guess," Star said, looking at his face.

"Denise in the tub, fresh," Paresi said. "Wanna see?"

Star shook her head. "No thanks. Get copies made for Mitchell. Seeing her before decomposition will help him."

Paresi shoved the pictures back into the envelope and looked at the postmark on the outside. "Mitch said she'd been dead about four days, right?"

"Yeah."

"Then he dropped these in the mail the next day. Nice of him to want us to have a souvenir."

"Same postal station?" she asked.

"Yep, Royal Street, the central post office, no return address. Same as the others, and no way to trace it." He put the envelope in his desk. "What about the list?"

As she read the names, a slow smile spread across her face. She handed the page to Paresi. "Check out number six."

They looked at one another.

"Jerry Auster," they said in unison.

"Now why would a salesman at Electric City buy professional-quality, high-grade film?" Paresi asked.

"Maybe to send us his vacation snaps. What say we find out?"

"Tomorrow." Paresi picked up his jacket. "Tonight, you need to forget all about this stuff. Why don't you come with me over to my uncle Ange's? The special is lasagna."

"Thanks, but I'm gonna head over to Vee's. After today, I feel a real need to hug her kids."

"So when are you gonna have some kids of your own to hug?"

"Don't remind me."

"Hey, you mind if I come with?" he asked. "I could use a few hugs too."

She raised one eyebrow. "Something tells me it ain't the kids you want to hug."

"Why do you say that? I like kids. Besides, hugging's contagious, start with the kids and end up cuddling Mama." He wiggled his eyebrows like Groucho Marx.

"Dominic." She shook her finger at him.

"I know, I know. Don't worry, I haven't forgotten our talk."

Star's eyes narrowed.

"What's that face? We made a deal, right? You got nothing to worry about."

Star was silent.

"I got an idea. Vee's coming home from work, she's tired, right? She don't want to cook, so why don't you call her and tell her not to make dinner. You and I can swing by my uncle's place and pick up antipasto, lasagna, and gelato for everybody. We'll all have dinner together."

Star picked up the phone and punched in Vee's number. "Good move, Paresi. Consideration, I like that."

Captain Lewis's morning pickup of black coffee laced with ground cinnamon and nutmeg sat cooling on his desk. He listened quietly to Star and Paresi.

After their report, he looked through the three sets of photographs they gave him. Star saw his hand tremble as he turned the last one over.

"What's your next move?"

They looked at each another.

"We're not sure yet, sir," Star said. "We wanted to let you see everything before we proceed. We're working on a plan."

Lewis indicated his office door. "Don't let me keep you."

They almost ran over each other getting out.

"Jeez, he's a cantankerous son of a bitch!" Paresi said from the safety of his desk.

"It got to him. He just wants this thing over. Imagine what he has to swallow when the chief comes down on him. I can understand where he's coming from. I told him we're working on a plan. So we'd better get one."

Darcy stood at Star's desk. "Since this Auster guy is on the list, why don't you let me talk to Glenn some more, try to find out what kinda pictures he takes, see if he uses a lot of that film. Maybe we can turn him up as the one sending those goddamn pictures."

"Okay," Star agreed. "But talk in general terms about the film, what it can do, who would use it, and don't mention anybody by name, especially Auster. If he's our guy, we don't want Glenn hipping him that we're curious."

"No sweat, Glenn's a good egg. I'll just talk about the film, you know, it's being so new and all the quality, blah-blah, and ask him real innocent-like what kind of customers buy the stuff."

"Right. Kid gloves, Darcy," she said.

He gave her an okay sign with his fingers. "Piece of cake." He was out of the door.

She looked across the desk at Paresi. "I've got an idea."

"Like what?"

"Like I go undercover. I fit the profile, don't you think?"

"You know I do, and I don't like it."

"C'mon, Paresi, I can get in close, check this guy out, see what he's like."

"Then what?"

"Then we cross that bridge when we hit it."

Paresi stared at her, his arms folded across his chest. "If he's our guy, I can tell you what he's like. He's a freakin' wacko bastard who'll make you dead, and I really wouldn't like that."

She tried to laugh. "Will you lighten up? He's a salesman in an electronic-appliance store. I really don't think he could be the guy, but it can't hurt to check him out."

Paresi leaned forward. "Listen to yourself. Did you see that woman yesterday at Becker? Wanna look at the pictures and refresh your memory? Whoever this bachaguloop is, he's a lunatic. You're not playing a game, Star."

"Why are you on my case?"

"I saw you yesterday. I'm the guy who watched you standing outside trying not to come apart. I'm also the one who held your head while you lost your lunch, after you saw an up-close and personal sample of his handiwork. Remember? You're in deep on this case, and your judgment may not be sound."

"You think I'm burnt?"

"Crispy Critter comes to mind. Listen, you got fifteen years on the department, ten of them here in Homicide. You got commendations up the whazoo, but you're a woman, a human being, who is seeing women who could be her turning up dead, everywhere. I watched you when we were at Vee's, having dinner. Everybody was laughing and talking, and you had this look in your eyes. I knew you were seeing that woman in the tub."

She looked down at her desk, not wanting him to know that he was right.

"This is tough for you, admit it, there's no shame in being scared. You won't talk to me, you won't talk to Mitch or Vee, you gotta tell somebody, see the department shrink, deal with it. You wanna play undercover . . . what if this guy is the one? I tell you, pard, you better have it together, because I don't wanna ever bring you flowers you can't smell, capeesh?"

Her anger died at the look in his eyes. "I know I haven't

been handling it well, and I know I'm probably basing my ideas about the guy on the men we saw at the store. They were a bunch of jimokes, salesmen, none of them is a killer."

"You don't know that."

"You're right. I mean, after all, how did the film canister turn up at her place?"

"Exactly."

"But there's no way to prove it belongs to Auster," she said.

"No, but as long as his name is on a list of users, and he works at the store, and two out of four victims purchased items there, including one he sold to, he's a suspect, sight unseen, and you can't generalize about him."

She stood up. "You're right. I'm losing it."

"You're just tired and scared. That means you turn over the case or—"

"I'll never turn over the case," she interrupted.

"Then toughen up, deal with your feelings and go it like the pro you are. Let's go scope this guy out, and move from there."

She sat back down. "Before we go, I think maybe we should split up, you know, go separately."

"Is it my breath?"

"No. I told you, I want to go in like a customer, you know, sharp-looking, like I got money."

"So you can't have a husband?"

"He's not going to come after me if he thinks I have a man."

Paresi nodded. "You're right."

"I know I can do this," she said.

"Okay, then let's talk to the cap'n." He stood up. "After you."

"No, you stay here," she said. "You know how you irritate him. I want this assignment."

Paresi sat back down. "Fine, you talk to him, but don't expect to leave me out, I'm in on this thing, I'm not letting you go alone."

"All right, but remember who's the senior here."

"Yeah, and you remember who loves you."

Richie Bamberger walked across the squad room. His motor-cycle boots scuffed along the floor. Richie refused to pick up his feet, a childhood rebellion carried into adulthood. He slid along and stopped at Star's desk.

"Children, children, no fighting," he said, grinning, a wad of gum visible in the corner of his mouth.

"Yo, Richie." Paresi looked up at him.

"How you doing, Rich? How's your brother?" Star said.

"Philly's cool, but he's gonna feel better when I tell him the lovebirds are fighting. What's up?"

"Nothing, you know how it is," Star said.

Richie looked at the two of them, his grin widening. "Hey, if you two break up, we could use you in Vice, Star. Man, I bet you'd be smokin' in a red leather miniskirt."

Star smiled. "Funny, I was just thinking the same thing about you."

The Bamberger brothers had been in Vice as long as she'd been in Homicide. They were identical twins, and thrived on undercover work. Star couldn't remember the last time she'd seen either of them clean-shaven or in decent clothes. Richie wore his hair long, and Phil sported a military brush cut, for identification purposes.

"Bought you a present," Richie said. "If you don't kiss and make up, I'm gonna take it back."

He tossed a brown envelope on Star's desk. She stared at it. Paresi picked it up. He opened the flap and spilled the pho-tographs out on his desk. Star leaned over to see. Charlotte Wilson's body lay on the lawn at 6021 Blackstone. Her shat-tered head lay away from the camera, but two other photos taken with a telephoto lens concentrated on her shocked eyes and ruined skull.

"The missing puzzle pieces." Star sighed. "Where'd you get these?"

Paresi pulled out the other photos. "They round out our set."

Richie looked at the pictures on Paresi's desk. "Mmmmph, I don't know about these, but mine came from the shooter."

The two detectives looked at each other.

"Yeah, the shooter." Richie grinned. "He's downstairs in interrogation, wanna see him?"

They were out of their chairs instantly, practically carrying Bamberger with them.

Star and Paresi couldn't believe what they were seeing. Behind the one-way glass, Phil Bamberger was interrogating the hit man.

"This can't be," Star said.

"He's the guy, all right." Richie leaned close to Star. "We took the pictures off him. He was carrying them around like family photos. He was proud. He took them to show his homies, you know, to prove he did it."

Paresi shook his head. "A gang initiation. How old is he?"

Richie laughed. "He looks twelve, don't he? That's the beauty of the thing. The little puke is nineteen! Puny, skinny, no hair on his face, but he's sho' nuff nineteen. They picked him as the trigger because they thought he was a baby. He wanted in, so he didn't say different. They figured if he got caught, he'd walk with a reprimand. He never thought he'd slip up, but being a gang-banger don't take much brains. He bragged a lot."

Richie hooked his fingers in his belt and nodded toward the boy. "Looks like he's gonna roll over on the other ones too. Who said there ain't no Santa Claus?"

Star leaned in close, shaking her head. "I can't believe this. Look at him."

Behind the glass, under the bright light of the interrogation room, the young man's eyes watched Phil Bamberger intently.

He was a spindly kid, with light brown skin and tight, dark curly hair. Star could see the freckles across the bridge of his nose. He looked afraid.

"His name's Hector Sanchez," Richie said. "He's only been in the neighborhood a little while. He lives behind the Frederick Street Projects, you know, on that dead-end street there." He snapped his fingers. "Uh . . . uh . . . whatchamacallit"

"Faraday Court," Star said.

"Yeah." Richie nodded. "He iced the broad to teach her boyfriend a lesson."

"Darnell Pope?" Star said.

"Darnell Pope." Richie nodded.

"We checked him," Paresi said. "He was clean."

"You didn't dig deep enough." Richie popped his gum. "He was working for a big ad agency downtown."

"Yeah, we got that," Star said.

"Uh-huh, but what you didn't get is that the whole place was full of young executive types, all running for the big prize. The whole joint lived on cocaine. Darnell was the candy man."

"A drug dealer?" Star folded her arms. "We went over him like white on rice, we got nothing."

"He was good at it," Richie said. "Hell, we might not have got him if he hadn't got greedy. The Conquistadors, Hector's gang, was his supply. He tried to cut them out after a while, so they sent baby brother around to teach him a lesson.

"Hector, being a smart guy, figured what could the skeezer learn if he was dead? Besides, he was a potential money maker for the gang. Dead, they got squat. Lesson learned, they would own him, so he figured the best lesson he could give was to cut down Pope's old lady, so . . . " He put his finger to the side of his head and mimed pulling a trigger.

"Badda boom, badda bing," Paresi muttered.

"Exactly."

Star shook her head. "Well, Hector Sanchez, you closed one case, but we're still at ground zero."

"Yep." Paresi agreed. "He's not ours."

They turned to Bamberger.

"Thanks, Richie B.," Paresi said.

"Yeah, thanks a lot." Star turned to her partner. "I'm gonna talk to the captain, let's go."

"Hey, Star?" Bamberger grinned at her.

"Yeah?"

"My brother told me to ask you if you've ever dated a good-looking vice cop?"

Star smiled. "Tell him I've never seen one!"

Star watched Lewis's face as she unfolded her plan. He was less than enthusiastic.

"It could be a dead end," he said.

She counted off her reasons on her fingers.

"Even though the Bambergers have cleared Charlotte Wilson, we've still got three dead women, two of whom were customers at that store. We've got a film can that turns up at the scene of another homicide, which can maybe be tied to a salesman in that store, and that same salesman sold appliances to one of the victims. Captain, it doesn't get any better than that."

"You know what the D.A.'s office said." Lewis looked her in the eye. "All the contact with that store from this unit was bordering on harassment. We don't need any charges like that."

"Yes sir, I agree," Star said. "But the manager was a willing participant in our investigation. It was only after the main office heard about it that we were shut out. We didn't intimidate Howard Douglas at all. It was strictly by the book and aboveboard, Captain."

"I'm not saying it wasn't, but the corporate headquarters came down personally on the chief about our requesting so much information from that store. It doesn't make a good image for them."

"Captain, if they've got a homicidal maniac working for them, do you think that's gonna be a good image? We're just trying to do our jobs here, before another woman dies. All I want is to be a decoy."

"They've already seen you," Lewis countered. "If we're going to decoy, we should use somebody else."

"No, sir," Star said. "I was only there once. Paresi and Darcy made the calls, and Darcy did two in-person visits, after our initial contact. The only ones who've seen me are Howard Douglas and one salesman. Both of those guys are now out of the picture. Douglas is out of town seeing to his sick mother, and the salesman is out with a broken shoulder. Nobody else noticed me, and if they did, they saw a cop, not a wealthy, upper-class customer. With some makeup and different clothes, nobody would put two and two together."

"Makeup, a different look." Lewis shook his head. "This isn't a Halloween party, Star, this is serious business."

"I know that, sir, and you know this is my case, I'm the only one who can do this."

"It's too personal for you. I heard about yesterday, at the Miles scene. I also know you and Paresi spent some time together in the ladies' john. You're losing your edge."

"Bullshit!" She was on her feet. "I'm tired of hearing that. Don't you understand what's happening here? Black women are being slaughtered. If I don't find out what's going on and who's behind it, another one of my sisters is going to die simply because of the color of her skin. Have you forgotten about my father? How many of us have to die because we happen to be black? It's my case. Turn it over to me, or I'll do it on my own!"

"Sit down, Lieutenant Duvall." Lewis's blue eyes blazed from behind his glasses. "Sit!"

Star sat down, her teeth grating in her jaw, her pulse racing.

"First of all, don't you *ever* throw your father in my face! I worked side by side with Lenny Duvall for over sixteen years. I loved him like he was my own brother. I put my knees under his table, just like he put his knees under mine, you know that. I'm on record about the way he died, and goddammit, you have no right to try and beat me up with it!

"I grieved over that man and I miss him still, do you understand me? I think about him every day of my life. I look at you and see him in your eyes. He loved you. That's why I'm trying to protect you.

"I've bent so far over backward for you, I can see up my own ass. Let me remind you that I'm the one who let you continue to go out on cases after you got your bars, simply because you wanted to stay on the street. Your job is supervisor to this unit, answering to me, but do you sit at a desk all day? Would you even take an office, like you're supposed to? No, you're out there in the squadroom, and on the street, behaving like you never got a promotion."

"I'm a good cop," she said, glaring at him. "What am I supposed to do? Sit on my brains all day, and get my information secondhand? How am I gonna know what's happening with my unit, what they're up against, unless I'm out there!"

The look on his face made her want to take back the words even as they tumbled out of her mouth.

He stared at her for a long time.

"Nobody disagrees with that. We value you and your dedication. A lot of us even love you, but frankly, I don't like what I'm seeing here. You're on some kind of vindictive trip. That's the kind of shit that gets cops dead. You're too involved. Rule number one, just like the mob: it's business, not personal. With your temperament being what you're displaying here, you could get yourself killed. You say you're a good cop, then goddammit, think like one, not like a woman on the rag. If you want this assignment, Lieutenant, get ahold of yourself."

"I'm sorry, sir."

"Sorry don't feed the bulldog if you're waist deep in shit!" He leaned forward in his chair. "Don't you get it? I don't want anything to happen to you. I want this bastard as bad as you do, but I'm not gonna sacrifice you to get him."

"Again, sir, I apologize." She took a deep breath. "You're right, I'm behaving irrationally. Paresi even says it's getting to me, but I can't take the risk of letting somebody else carry the ball. It's my case."

"Wrong, Lieutenant. It's *a* case. Look at the board out

there. We got new ones everyday. This department is inundated, overextended. *You* just happened to draw this one."

"Yes, sir."

Lewis sat back and took a deep breath. He couldn't stand the hurt look on her face. They sat opposite one another, both of them barely breathing for a long time.

"Star?"

"Yes sir?" She didn't look up.

"Let me talk to the chief about this."

"About me taking some R and R?" Her voice shook.

"No," Lewis said. "About you going under. If you do it, you're gonna have to go deep. That means we're going to have to set you up, it's going to have to be real, a luxury car and address to match. It's going to take money because you'll also have to buy something expensive."

"And pay cash," she said.

"Right. We can get some gold cards for you to flash, but the deal will have to be cash."

She wanted to hug him. "Thank you, Captain."

"Don't thank me, just do the job. I'm warning you, if I find myself at your funeral, I'm gonna be so pissed I'm liable to pump a few rounds in the box."

"My friends would be horrified, and I can't let that happen. Count on me, Captain, I won't let you down."

"Get outta here and let me work on my shit-eating voice, so I can call the chief."

Paresi was waiting when she got back to her desk. "Well?"

"It took some persuasion, but I'm going under."

"Okay, then we need to get together, but first . . . " He showed her a blue sheet of paper.

"Impound?"

"Yep. They got a 'Vette towed in today from the parking lot at Arabella's, and it's registered to Denise Miles, 2702 Becker Place."

"How long had it been there?"

"I just called the club, and according to security, almost a week."

"That means she was in there the night she died."

"Uh-huh, and she left in a cab, so nobody saw if there was a guy around. One of the security guys remembers her having to go to the bathroom. She went in a side door, used the john, and when she came out, he took her keys. He said she was too drunk to drive."

"So she was alone at that point. The guy drove himself to her house."

"I'll go for that," Paresi said. "The question is, was it somebody she already knew or somebody she picked up in the club?"

"Let's get over there, talk to a few people, see what we turn up," she said.

"Let me handle that, you work on your sting."

Paresi pulled a tattered piece of paper from his breast pocket. "I've also got the goods on her ex, his last name is Washington, Wardell Washington. He didn't go in to work today, but I got hold of him at home. He sounded really shook, but he agreed to see me this afternoon. After I leave there, I'll hit Arabella's."

She looked around the squad room. "Darcy's out, take Couchure with you."

"Right." He stood and pulled his jacket off the back of his chair. "Give Mitch a call, he wants to talk to you."

She dialed the Medical Examiner's office.

Mitch got on the line immediately. "I missed you at the post."

"I couldn't."

"I understand. She was in really bad shape, but I found some evidence that she'd had sex shortly before she died, and there was skin under her nails. It's being analyzed."

"We know she didn't spend her last night alone. Paresi and I were at Becker Condos last evening, at a tenants' meeting. Seems the whole joint heard her and some guy knocking boots till the wee hours."

"That explains the smile," Mitch said. "Official cause of death was the wound in her throat—she bled to death. All other injuries were postmortem."

"Thank God for that," she said. There was a pause. "What about the bite marks?" Star asked.

Mitch cleared his throat. "The decomposition was advanced, as you know, but the breast bite was visible. By the way, thanks for the pictures, they were helpful. The marks were clearer on the blow-ups we did. In addition to the marks on her breast, there was a deep one near her left wrist, which had been submerged. They matched what we had. It's the same guy."

She was quiet.

"Star, you there?"

"Yeah." She tried to sound detached. "The Wilson case is closed. The Bamberger brothers pulled in the shooter, and we think we've got a lead that could pan out."

"So Charlotte isn't part of the package?"

"No."

"Well then, even small successes call for celebration. Why don't you tell me about your lead over dinner tonight?"

"Dinner?"

"Yes. I think it's about time for another appearance of Duvall and Grant, Attitude Adjusters."

She grinned. "Should I wear Bullwinkle?"

"It's up to you. How about the Oakwood Room at the Park View Hotel?"

"I can smell the old money. I'll trot out Rocket J. Squirrel for this one."

They both laughed.

"I think I'll wear an old B-ball jersey," he said. "How's seven for you?"

"*You've* got an old basketball jersey? I'd pay money to see that."

He laughed with her. "Lieutenant, I wasn't born wearing Armani, there are a lot of sides to me."

"Basketball?"

"One day I'll show you my slam dunk. I'm fierce!"

I'll just bet you are, she thought. "I'll look forward to it. Do you mind picking me up here?"

"See you at seven."

"Seven," she said, and hung up. "Mitchell Grant playing basketball . . . right."

Paresi came back as she was getting ready to leave.

"Get anything?" she asked.

"Nothing."

"What did the boyfriend say?"

He plopped down in his chair and put his feet up on the desk. "Ex-boyfriend. He confirmed that they'd just broken up. He said she didn't take it well."

"Did he tell you why they split?"

"He didn't have to. Her name is Vicki. She's about twenty-two, with flaming red hair and blue eyes. She was all over him, trying to"—he held up his fingers, forming quotation marks—"make him feel better."

"Great. What did he say?"

"Nothing much, just that she was real upset with the breakup and she started hanging out and drinking too much. He said she was kind of a straight arrow, until she got upset, then she'd hit the bottle."

"Dumped and drinking, dangerous combo. What did the club people say?"

"It was early, not too many folks there, but a couple of the security people recognized her picture. They said she used to come in with this Washington jimoke from time to time. The guy who let her in to use the bathroom said she was a pretty nice woman, you know, friendly and all that. He said he'd never seen her get that loaded before."

"He's the one who took her keys?"

Paresi looked at his notes. "Yeah, Ramon Alvarez."

"So he's certain she left alone."

"He put her in the cab."

"Great, another brick in the wall." She leaned back in her chair. "Did you get the cab company name? We've got to reach the cabbie."

"Done. I talked to him. He said she was singing to herself all the way home. He remembered her because she was a knockout, and very high. He said he helped her to her door, and she tipped him twenty dollars."

"So she was alone when she got home. The killer arrived after she did."

"Yeah." Paresi looked at his notes. "The cabbie's name is Mohammed Hamid El Albazz."

"Middle Eastern?"

"Black."

They both laughed.

"He said she seemed in good spirits. He helped her inside and left."

"You got proof of that?"

"He was on another call seven minutes after he dropped her off, and he worked steadily through till five the next morning."

"Good job, Paresi." She stood up and picked up her jacket.

"Thanks. I need to get back to the club during party hours, when the place is packed. I wanna talk to some customers, maybe find some regulars who know the joint, who might have seen her, you know, maybe somebody who could say if she spent time that night with anyone in particular. They tell me the party don't start till after eleven, so, you wanna go dancing?"

"You dancing? The second shock of the night, first Mitchell Grant and basketball, and now, you dancing."

"I'm a great dancer, I'm Italian, didn't you see Travolta do his thing in that *Fever* flick?"

"That was twenty years ago, times have changed."

"Yeah, but he can still dance, and so can I."

Star giggled. "I'll put it on my list of things I have to see."

"What's the rush, you got a date?"

Mitch walked into the squad room. "As a matter of fact, she does." He extended his hand. "How's it going, Dominic?"

Paresi shook it. "It's crawling, Doc, it's crawling." He looked at Star. "What did you say about the doc and basketball?"

"Only that next to you dancing, it's something I've got to see."

Mitch smiled. "I'm not sure I want to know what this is about."

"The woman don't know Italians got rhythm, or that tall white guys can make good B-ballers." Paresi winked at Mitch. "You'll learn baby girl," he said to Star. "Go, have fun."

"Thank you, Sergeant. I intend to have a wonderful dinner and a good time." She leaned over and tickled Paresi under the chin. "I suggest that you, my handsome Sicilian darling, go out and have some fun as well."

Paresi grinned at Mitch. "She can't keep her hands off me." He pulled the phone to the edge of his desk. "I think I'll give Vee a call, maybe she'd like to go dancing."

Star picked up her purse. "Just don't do anything I'll have to kill you for."

Paresi leaned back in his chair. "Hey, it would be worth it."

Mitch offered Star his arm. "Have a good evening, Dominic."

She took it and turned to Paresi. "Mañana," she said.

"Later," said Paresi.

He watched them leave.

After two weeks of head-butting with the stiffs upstairs, Lewis got his way. The sting was ready. Star had a luxury address and a car to match. Lewis sat with the duplicate house and car keys in his hand. Grant had been able to prove that the bite marks pointed to a single killer, and Lewis, like his officers, had the fever to get the bastard. He would retire in style and go out in a hell of a blaze of glory. If anybody could drag in this creep, it would be Lenny's kid. She had the stuff, and he had faith in her.

Jerry Auster was getting antsy. It had been a couple of weeks and he needed some action. Work was beginning to really annoy him. He'd been chosen to help Leander Poteet get comfortable at the store.

The bastard worked at the Victor Street outlet, so what did he have to learn? Jerry had asked himself. Then he remembered the Victor Street store was in a predominantly black neighborhood. He actually laughed when he imagined that "Lee" would have to learn how to speak English and not sell by jive-talking and high-fiving.

The weird thing was that the shine actually liked him, wanted to hang with him after work and all that. Jerry was keeping him at bay by telling him he had a sickly wife and so he had to leave directly after work every evening.

Truth was, he was spending a lot of time at home, working in his darkroom. Every minute he spent away from the fat bitch he was married to was gold, but she'd started whining about him never hanging around with her, so tonight he'd had dinner at home and was sitting on the couch, watching the news with her.

He couldn't believe his ears when he heard the newscaster talking about the rash of murders of black women in the past few weeks. Who cared? He didn't read the crap about niggers getting wasted in the papers, and he didn't want to see it on his television. Why give airtime to this? He got up to take a piss. The photographs of the victims appeared on the screen. He froze. This couldn't be.

The last picture was of Denise Miles. He bit his lip to keep from making a sound when he saw her. She was so damned beautiful. He closed his eyes.

Maureen spoiled it all by clucking her fat tongue and talking out loud.

"It's so awful," she said. "How could anyone just go out and kill people for no reason?"

He didn't answer, he just stood, staring, listening to the newscaster say the police had no leads but were working around the clock to prevent another murder.

They better work fast, he said to himself.

20

Star pulled the white Mercedes into her parking space and went inside the building through the side door. When she walked into the squad room, she was stopped at the door by the whistles, cheers, and catcalls, everything from "Hubba-hubba" to "Oh baby!" She'd expected it.

She posed in the doorway, one hand on her hip, the other waving royally to the crowd. She tilted the tip of her white wide-brimmed straw hat, removed her Pierre Cardin shades, and smiled at the detectives.

"It's so gratifying to be loved by the little people." She walked regally to her desk.

Paresi stood up. "Money becomes you."

"Don't it, though?" She burst out laughing. "Check out the threads." She performed a model's turn, showing off her flowing, hand-painted peacock-blue, gold, and green abstract print silk jacket.

"Very nice," Paresi said.

She took off the hat and jacket, garnering another volley of wolf whistles and catcalls. She did another slow turn, showing her matching peacock-blue silk halter top and short, sarong-style white silk skirt.

"Now that I like." Paresi said. "If I pull that little bow on your hip, does the whole thing fall off?"

"I chose it with you in mind," she said, laughing. She sat down and crossed her bare legs, displaying bright red-painted toenails peeking though Joan and David strappy white sandals.

"Mmmmmph." Paresi shook his head. "You look really hot. In fact, I think Rescovich is gonna pop any second."

Star wouldn't look across the room. "To hell with him. I don't want to look hot, I want to look rich!"

"You do. You look classy, like a country club broad. Must be all those dinners with Mitch."

"I feel a question coming," she said.

Paresi leaned forward. "Right as usual. You two have been having quite a few after-hour get-togethers, and we haven't gone out for pizza for a while."

"And?"

"And it's been noticed. You're on the grapevine. The buzz is, the doctor is in. They say he's drilling you like Chevron."

She laughed. "I've been on the grapevine for one thing or another since day one. I don't really care about that. But you should know better."

"Yeah, I guess I should, but what am I supposed to think? Lately you two have been practically joined at the hip."

"Nothing's changed. Mitchell is just a really nice guy. We haven't even kissed if you want the truth."

Paresi shook his head. "The legend lives. This guy is some operator. You know what he's gonna do, don't you? He's gonna get you all misty and trusting, and boom! Home run."

"Is that how you do it?"

"Sometimes, depends on how horny I am."

"I'll pass that on to Vee."

"She knows." He gave her a devilish grin.

"Oh yeah? She hasn't said anything to me."

"I mean, she knows how I am. She's your friend, you should know. Ain't no sneaking up on her. I have to lay it out on the table."

"Yeah, so what've you been 'laying' on the table?" Star asked. "I told you from jump, this is my sister, and I don't want you screwing around. I remember your last grand passion, Theresa in Records. What happened?"

"She's a kid, she don't understand cops."

"Uh-huh, and Vee does?"

"Vee's a woman, a real woman. She knows what the job is like."

"And she hates it," Star said.

"I'll work on that." Paresi winked.

Captain Lewis walked into the squad room. "Morning." He stopped at Star's desk. "Both of you, in my office." He signaled across the room. "Cooch, you too."

Detective Donald Couchure, the newest addition to Homicide, ran his hand over his brush haircut and followed them in.

"Okay, here's today's drill." Lewis sat on the edge of his desk. "Star, you go in and just meander, stay as long as it takes you to get a feel, but don't buy anything. If you think you got something, then we'll discuss it here."

He turned to Paresi. "You stay outside, but keep an eye on her, understand, no fooling around."

He pointed to the young-looking man. "Cooch, I want you in the store, just for backup if we need it."

"Yes, sir." Detective Couchure nodded.

Lewis turned to Star. "Remember, all of you, no matter what goes down, no superhero stuff, you're out there to feel it out, not play *Lethal Weapon*. Got it?"

"Yes, Captain," Star said.

"All right, now go on."

They headed for the door.

"Star!" Lewis called out.

"Yes, sir?" She turned around.

"You look great."

"Thank you, sir."

21

Jerry Auster had just taken a customer to the service desk when he saw her. She walked past him without looking his way, leaving the scent of expensive perfume in the air. He fell in step behind her, unable to see her face. The big picture hat she wore only allowed him a glimpse of her profile as she turned her head, looking from aisle to aisle. She was tall, long-legged, and the color of polished mahogany.

He watched her short skirt. He could just get a glimpse of it beneath the silk jacket that fluttered and floated behind her. With each step, the skirt rose and fell on the backs of her thighs. He watched her hips sway from side to side as she moved along the floor. He paced himself, so that he wouldn't get too close. She stopped at the stereo wall, looking over the selection.

Star stood in front of a wall that seemed to cover the entire side of the showroom. She had never seen so much electronic equipment in her life. She hadn't even known there were this many brands of stereo receivers, speakers, CD and tape players. She was so busy reading the lists of features attached to each item that she didn't hear the man come up to her.

"Hi, may I help you?"

She looked at the dark-haired, pale, hollow-eyed salesman in front of her. He reminded her of a character from a Stephen King novel. His name tag read DENNIS.

She held her breath for a moment, wishing she was wearing a necklace of garlic and carrying a stake in her purse.

"Oh, thank you . . . no. I'm just looking."

"My name's Dennis." He pointed to his tag. "If you need anything."

"Thank you." She smiled and moved quickly away, turning a corner, moving down another aisle. She was looking back to see if he was watching her when she collided with someone.

"Oh! I'm sorry." She stepped back. The man in front of her was so handsome her mouth dropped open.

"No problem."

"I was just looking around," she said, taking off her shades. "I had no idea there were so many items on the market, just to play music."

He licked his lips. She had great eyes, golden-colored, with long lashes that were real.

Her light eyes against her dark skin excited him. The wide-brimmed hat framed her face. He couldn't really tell since the hat covered her head, but she appeared to have curly hair.

Jerry Auster felt his heart beating faster. His gaze moved slowly over her body. She was lovely. Her mouth really turned him on—she had full, sweet-looking lips and gorgeous white teeth. Even in flat shoes she was a shade taller than he, and that added to his desire. Getting her down was going to be real fun.

"Yes, it can be confusing," he said.

"I'll say."

"If I can help you . . . " He looked straight into her eyes.

"Maybe you can show me a few things so I won't sound so stupid when I talk to a salesman."

"You could never sound stupid, and I *am* a salesman."

Her hand flew to her mouth. "Oh, I'm sorry . . . "

"No problem. I forgot my name tag this morning." He held out his hand. She took it. "I'm Jerry."

"Jerry?" she repeated. Her hand in his began to tremble.

"Yes, Jerry Auster."

Her whole body went numb. "Jerry Auster." Her heart dropped in her chest. She was standing only by sheer force of will. Her legs had turned to jelly. This can't be happening, she thought, not this guy, this gorgeous gray-eyed hunk. No, this was not acceptable. He couldn't be Jerry Auster.

He reached into his breast pocket. "Here's my card." He smiled.

She took it and stared at it, unseeing. She didn't want to look at him, but she did. He had a smile that could melt stone, even though his bottom teeth were slightly crooked. God, she thought. She palmed the card. "Thank you."

"Can you tell me what you're looking for?" he asked.

"I'm not really sure. I just bought a brownstone in Regency Estates, and it's a three-story place, so I wanted a kind of whole-house sound, you know?" She could feel the perspiration rolling down her spine.

"What you need is a setup, with a master control, so that the music can be programmed and then turned on from any part of the house."

"Yes, that's what I was thinking about."

His eyes held hers. "That can be very expensive. We're talking about rewiring, from either the attic or under the house, depending on where you want the master control. Then we'd have to do some notching."

"Notching?" She looked confused.

"Yeah. I'm sorry, I'm talking like a contractor. Notching means drilling small holes in the walls, to pull the wires through, then, of course, we'd patch that up. It could get really expensive."

"Money's no problem. I can afford it."

"In that case, let me take you into the listening room, so you can hear what some of these units sound like." He put his hand on her upper arm and she jumped.

"I'm sorry," she said. "I just got a little shock. It must be the carpet."

He began walking her toward the back of the store. She glimpsed Couchure over by the portable CD players. He had a headset on and was listening to music. He didn't look up as she passed.

Star felt like she was going to faint. This couldn't possibly be the man they were looking for. Killers didn't look like this.

Her mind screamed: TED BUNDY! She stopped.

"Oh, I just remembered."

"What?"

She moved away from him. "I've got an appointment. I only stopped in here to browse for a minute. Would you mind if I listened to the units some other time?"

Disappointment showed in his eyes, but he smiled. "No, whatever you want, just call me. Pick a time that's good for you and I'll take care of it. Tell me your favorite kind of music, and I'll make sure we have it for you to hear."

"Thank you." She backed away from him. "I'll call you probably by tomorrow. I really have to go now." She hoped she was smiling; she couldn't tell.

"I'll look forward to it, Ms. . . . ?"

"Bohannon, Janine Bohannon. I won't forget. Good-bye."

She turned around and walked swiftly up the aisle, trying not to run. Couchure saw her go by, but he knew Paresi was in the parking lot.

He picked up the portable CD player on the counter in front of him and smiled at the salesman. "Great sound, how much did you say this thing was?"

Outside, Star hurried down the sidewalk and almost sprinted to her car. Paresi sat watching her. She was totally spooked. He started his engine when she backed out of her space.

A big Lincoln Town Car pulled in behind, blocking him. He leaned on the horn. The old couple in the car sat staring straight ahead. He honked again.

"Hey, get out of the way."

The old man driving turned his head in Paresi's direction, with a blank expression. The old woman was saying something and pointing across the street. The man turned to look in that direction. Star paused at entrance of the parking lot. She turned right, roaring into traffic.

"Goddammit, move that thing!" Paresi yelled out the window.

The old lady looked at him and tapped her husband. He

seemed to see Paresi for the first time. He smiled, nodded, and backed up, just enough for Paresi to squeak by. As he pulled out, the old lady waved at him.

"Thanks for the space, son."

Paresi sped to the front of the parking lot and turned right. There was no sign of Star.

Jerry Auster crouched in a stall in the men's room, trying to be quiet as he reached orgasm. He leaned against the wall and waited for his breathing to return to normal. He had never wanted a woman so much. She was like an oasis in the desert. There hadn't been anyone since Denise, and he couldn't get drunk enough to fuck Maureen. He'd been dating Madam Hand and her Five Daughters since his night at Becker, and he was ready.

He heard the door open and waited for whoever it was to go into a stall. He tossed the soiled tissues in his hand into the toilet, adjusted his clothing, flushed and walked out to the sink. He washed his hands and leaned over, splashing cold water on his face. He heard the toilet flush, and Leander Poteet joined him at the sink.

"Hey, Jer!" Leander ran hot water onto his hands and squeezed the last drops of liquid soap into his palm. "You okay, bro? You sick or something?"

Jerry straightened up, grabbed a paper towel and wiped his face and hands. "Naw, just hot, my man, just hot."

Paresi drove down Sherman Street, looking to both sides, trying to spot the Mercedes, when it hit him.

Collette's. He'd bet she went to Collette's. It was on Garfield, and Garfield ran off this street. He took a left turn at Garfield and Sherman. Collette's French Pastry Shop was the second shop in on Garfield. He saw the car.

"Bingo!" He pulled up behind it and parked, hurrying into the shop.

Star sat at one of the small tables in the rear. He walked up and sat down across from her. She couldn't talk, her mouth was full of chocolate pastry.

"What the hell happened? You flew out of there."

She swallowed. "God, Paresi, I'm sorry, but I had to get to chocolate, quick."

"I figured you'd come here. What is it?"

Her hands were shaking. "Jerry Auster."

"What about him?"

"He's beautiful, really beautiful."

"So?"

She didn't mention Auster's teeth. She didn't want to think about that. Almost nobody had perfect teeth. She ate more cake, to avoid looking at Paresi. "He's scary . . . you know?" she said, looking down at her plate. She licked her fingers. "He's like a snake, he charms you, he charmed me. When I first saw him, I couldn't believe it. He's the kind of guy women fantasize about, you know, the kind that can make a woman do anything."

"The kind that could make Denise Miles give him her address?"

"And her mama." She took another bite of the pastry. "I'm telling you, the guy is . . . " Her voice trailed off.

"I don't get it, you've seen good-looking guys before. You work with me every day."

"It's not like that . . . it's more than just good-looking. He's got some kind of . . . " She waved her hands. ". . . some kind of power over women, some kind of pull. This guy is like a Svengali."

"Sven who?"

"Never mind. I've got an idea."

"What?"

"Let's get a copy of his driver's license from Motor Vehicles and blow up the picture. You can take it to Arabella's and see if anybody recognizes him."

"Okay." He pointed at the partially eaten pastry in front her. "That looks good."

"Dark chocolate cake and frosting, white chocolate mousse filling, layered with brandy-soaked cherries. It's heaven. Order another one for me."

He raised his hand and the waitress stood at the table before he could put it down.

22

Maureen ate silently, watching him across the table. He hadn't said one word to her, and now he was eating like it was just something to fill him up. He didn't even seem to be tasting it, just shoveling one forkful after another into his mouth.

"Would you like some more salad?" she asked.

"No."

He didn't look at her. He got up from the table and went downstairs. Maureen took her time, chewing slowly and wondering just what he was up to. She had to get into that place, and soon. She had thought about it while he was working, but sometimes he showed up in the middle of the day, saying he wanted a break from the job. She couldn't take a chance of him catching her. She had to be sure he was gone and not coming back for a long time.

It was after ten P.M. and she was still at the station. Paresi called her from the manager's office at Arabella's. Even with the door closed, he could barely hear her. The club was packed, and the loud music had set his brain throbbing.

"Your idea did the trick." He rubbed his temple.

"Somebody recognize him?"

"Oh yeah, it's been worth the headache I got. A couple of the security people said he's been in a few times."

"Great."

"It gets better. There's a girl who hangs out here, practically every night. Her name's Sue Harrold. When I showed her the pictures of Auster and Denise, she identified both of them. She said they were all over each other, practically balling on the dance floor, and they left together."

"The night of the murder?"

"She's not sure of the exact night. She said a week or so ago. That's close enough. She'd get chewed up on the stand, but she could definitely put him here, getting it on with the victim."

"Great job, Paresi, come on in, I'll wait for you."

"On the way."

Star hung up and sat with her hands folded across the top of her desk. "So, Jerry Auster, you're really beginning to scare me."

She leaned back in her chair, trying to picture him hiding in the backseat of the Mercedes, surprising and strangling Della Robb-Ellison with her own scarf.

The pictures came fast in her mind, one victim after another, and Denise Miles, poor Denise Miles. They were all as clear as daylight, but she couldn't see him. She could see the murders, but not him, not his face. All she could see was the pale gray eyes, the handsome, poised man who had taken her breath away at Electric City.

Get past his looks, she heard a voice inside her head say. *It's a cover, get past it.*

It was nearly eleven when Paresi walked through the door. "I got caught up, I didn't think you'd wait."

"I couldn't go anywhere, we have to talk."

"You got something for a headache? My brains are about to run out of my nose."

She opened her bottom desk drawer and handed him a bottle of aspirin. He shook three into his hand and swallowed them without water.

He reached into his jacket pocket. "Take a look at this, tell me what you think." He pulled out a multicolored fluorescent bracelet and handed it to her.

"What's this?"

"A badge thing, you know, so if you leave the joint you can get back in. I thought I'd give it to Lena." He turned the bracelet in his hands. "It's kinda pretty. It glows in the dark, something a young girl would like, right?"

"Yeah, she'll think it's dope." She smiled at him.

"As long as she don't think I'm a dope."

"Honey, you got to get hip, dope means cool, and don't look now, but you're acting like a daddy."

"Oh no, I just thought she'd like it."

Star took the bracelet and turned it in her hand. "She'll love it." She handed it back to him and he dropped it in his pocket. "So, tell me about the place," she said.

"It's jumping, women by the yard, it's like an orchard full of ripe apples."

"It must be your night, good time, and positive IDs."

"Nah, I'm past the club scene, too much jailbait. I like my women more experienced." He winked at her, and pulled out Auster's blown-up driver's license photo. "Merry Christmas." He handed it to her.

"God, he's even gorgeous on his driver's license. Nobody looks good on these things."

"We got to get closer to this guy," Paresi said.

"Right. I'm going to call him in the morning and make an appointment to listen to some equipment."

"I think I'll check out his house," Paresi said. "I'll wait till I'm sure he's gone, and I'll take a ride over."

"I'll call you tomorrow and let you know when the appointment is, then you can check it out safely, no possibility of him being there or showing up."

"Great." He stood up. "Let's go by Uncle Ange's for a nightcap, cappuccino or something."

"Okay, I could use a cannoli. You think he'll have any left?"

"If not, Aunt Rosa will improvise, c'mon."

It had been a seriously hot morning, and the afternoon showed no sighs of change. Maureen wondered if the heat wave would ever break. She'd been working since she got up. She looked at the clock on the mantel. It was one-thirty, and she still had the polishing to do in the living room. But first she was going to take a break and have a glass of lemonade. She put the cleaning rag and the can of lemon wax on the end table; she was just about to get her drink when the young man knocked at the door. She saw him through the screen.

"Yes?" She didn't move from the center of the room.

"Hi, Mrs. Auster?" The man smiled and nodded at her.

"Yes?"

"Hello, ma'am, I'd like to talk to you if you don't mind."

She walked to the door. The man was young, and very handsome, but Jerry didn't allow strangers in the house.

Paresi looked at the overweight, damp blond woman facing him and decided she probably had been a looker about a hundred pounds ago.

"My name is Ron DelSignore, I'm with Federal Insurance, and I'd like to talk to you about your coverage. May I come in?" His smile was sincere.

Maureen didn't know what to say, she never handled these things. Jerry was in charge of the insurance and all the bill paying. She didn't even know if they were with Federal.

She peered at the man through the screen. He was very good-looking. He reminded her of the actor on one of her favorite TV shows. It was off the air now, except for late night reruns, and she always stayed up to watch, especially when she was alone. On the nights that she had to go to bed, she taped the show. It was a guilty pleasure for the next day. The man on her step looked like his twin; he couldn't possibly hurt her. She unlocked the door.

"Come in," she said, and stood to one side. "I don't know anything about our insurance, my husband handles all that."

Paresi looked around. The house looked as if she was in the process of a major cleaning.

Maureen caught the look in his eyes. "Forgive the clutter. I'm real late with my spring cleaning, but summer cleaning is good too." She giggled like a child.

Paresi laughed with her. "Yes, ma'am, cleaning is cleaning, a pain in the butt no matter when it's done."

She smiled and nodded her head. He thought she could actually be pretty even now if she fixed herself up a little.

"That's exactly right." She indicated the sofa. "Won't you sit down? I was just about to have some lemonade. Would you like some, or some iced tea? I've got both."

"Actually, I'd love a beer, but I'm working, so lemonade sounds good."

"All right, I'll be right back." She shuffled down the hall and around the corner, toward the back of the house.

Paresi sat down and looked around. A major cleanup during a heat wave. This was a babe with all her burners on low, or she was seriously frustrated.

He took in the lemon wax can, and the cloth lying beside it. It had a stripe, gray and blue; a shirt. He picked it up. It looked fairly new, too new for a dust cloth. He turned it briefly, saw the torn sleeve and dropped it back on the end table. As it fell, the fabric flopped. What had been the tail of the shirt landed on top, showing a large, rusty brown stain. Paresi looked closer.

In the kitchen, Maureen pulled out her loveliest crystal iced tea glasses. She never had visitors, and he was so cute, he deserved the treatment. She stood on a step stool to reach her wedding china, which was stored on the top shelf. She only used it for holidays and special occasions, and he was very special. She slid a dessert plate from the stack and climbed down. She wiped sweat from her upper lip with her apron, and opened a fresh box of her favorite ginger cookies. She arranged them prettily on the plate.

Paresi leaned forward on the couch and looked down the hall. There was no sign of her, and he could hear the clatter of dishes in the kitchen. Quickly, he picked up the shirt and attempted to tear a portion of the fabric. It wouldn't tear. From the kitchen he heard the sound of a cabinet door closing. He looked around the room. Across from the sofa, next to a chair, he spotted a canvas bag, the kind his sisters kept their needlework in. He moved quietly across the room and grabbed it.

He heard the refrigerator door opening and closing, and the sound of ice being popped from a tray. He plunged his hand into the bag and rummaged through it.

She was doing some kind of embroidery project. Paresi poked his hand through the yarns until his fingers hit metal. He pulled out a small pair of scissors. Back across the room, he grabbed the shirt and cut a patch from the stained end. He heard her in the hallway, stuffed the fabric in his jacket pocket and bunched the shirt so that the cut wouldn't show.

She was coming down the hall when he sailed the scissors back across the room, watching them land in the canvas bag and sink from sight. He sat down just as she rounded the corner.

"Here we go, some nice fresh lemonade." She set the tray down on the coffee table. "I hope you like ginger cookies, I've loved them since I was a child. My husband hates them, so take as many as you want, because I'll just end up eating the whole box, and Lord knows, I don't need to have even one."

"Thank you, ma'am, this is very nice of you."

She reached beside him, picked up the can of lemon wax and the shirt and put them on the floor, beneath the end table.

"There, now you won't have to smell lemon wax while you're eating. I didn't expect company." She sat down on the sofa, next to him, her watery blue eyes searching his face while she smiled. "Do you know who you look like?"

"My father." Paresi grinned.

"No, you look like that actor on TV."

"What actor is that, ma'am?" Paresi took a long drink of the lemonade and a bite of a ginger cookie. It was delicious.

"You know, that show about the guy who was working for the government, but the mob thought he was one of theirs."

"Oh yeah, that was a good show. It's not on anymore."

"They show reruns late at night. I watch all the time. You look just like that guy."

"Thank you, ma'am, he's pretty good-looking."

She giggled and blushed. "Both of you are, and please, don't call me ma'am, my name's Maureen."

Paresi stuck out his hand. "Glad to meet you, Maureen, I'm Ron." He held her hand gently, watching the blush spread across her face. She really was a sweet woman, he could tell. He felt sorry for her.

She took her hand away and reached for a cookie. "I just love these things." She shoved the entire sweet into her mouth and prodded Paresi to take another. "Eat some more. If you don't, I'll end up eating them all." She subconsciously ran her hand over her belly.

"Nothing wrong with a full-figured woman in my book," he said. "I can't think of anything softer to cuddle with."

She turned bright red. "Oh." She put both hands to her face, like a child. "Stop it, you're making me blush."

They both laughed.

"Seriously," Paresi said, grinning. "I'm not trying to be forward, but a pretty woman is a pretty woman."

She looked down at her hands. "Thank you." She couldn't look at him, so she reached for another cookie.

Paresi opened the briefcase he carried, turning it toward him so she couldn't see inside. He rattled a few papers, old reports he'd stuffed the case with. "I'd really like to talk to you about increasing your life insurance, but your husband should be here, if he handles those things."

"Yes, that's what I was going to say. Maybe you can come back when he gets home."

"He works at Electric City, right?" Paresi asked. "Jerry Auster."

"That's right."

Paresi stood up, putting his hand in his pocket, making sure the material was still there. "Why don't I call him and set up a time when it would be convenient for both of you?"

Maureen got to her feet. "That's a good idea, he's the one who knows all about this stuff, anyway. I'm sure he'd like to talk to you. Do you have a card?"

Paresi made a show of patting his breast and jacket pockets. "Oh shoot!" He smiled at her. "Looks like I'm out. I forget sometimes to put a supply in my pocket."

She pointed to the case. "Maybe you have some in there."

"Oh no, I never carry them there, it's too awkward to get them out. I usually have them in my pockets." He patted his body again. "Yep, I'm out, but don't worry, I'll call the store and get an appointment."

He reached down and picked up another cookie. "One for the road."

They smiled at each other.

"Thank you for your hospitality, it certainly made my day easier," he said.

"Oh, my pleasure, I enjoyed the visit."

He took her sweaty hand and kissed it. Maureen flushed. Nobody ever paid any attention to her anymore, and here was this gorgeous man . . . yes, Jerry was beautiful, but he was her husband, and she was used to him, but this one . . . he was real, from the outside.

"Good-bye, Ron." She walked him to the door.

Paresi turned on the steps and waved. "Bye, Maureen." Poor cow, he thought as he walked down the stairs.

She watched him, waving until he was out of sight.

"Back to work." She sighed, and took the shirt and the lemon wax can from under the table. She stuffed the remaining cookies in her mouth, put everything on the tray, picked it up and headed for the kitchen.

Mitch looked at the piece of fabric between his fingers. "It's definitely blood," he said to Paresi. "Old blood, but I think there's enough to test and type."

"What about DNA?"

"Nope, the fabric's been washed, and it's got cleaning gunk on it. We'll be lucky to get a blood type." He stood up. "I can run the test, why don't you just have a seat?"

23

Star walked down the center aisle of Electric City. She was on her own; Paresi was checking out Auster's house. She knew Captain Lewis would stroke out if he knew, but she couldn't wait for backup and let the trail get cold. She'd called Jerry Auster and made an appointment to listen to some equipment. As she walked down the aisle, she looked up at the big clock at the end of the store. It was one-thirty P.M.

Jerry Auster saw Star heading his way. He was with a customer. He looked at his watch: one-thirty on the dot. She was right on time. He'd expected her to be late—it was a habit with "them"—but here she was.

He smiled at the couple standing in front of the freezers, and told them he would be right back. He hurried down the aisle to intercept her.

"Hi." He was slightly out of breath.

"Oh, hi." She smiled at him. She was wearing a bright yellow pants outfit that set off her skin. She was hatless, and he liked her hair. It was short and curly, just as he'd suspected, with a coarseness that fired him up. "Am I early?"

"No, you're right on time. I just have to finish up with a couple of people. Why don't you wait for me in the listening room?"

"Fine."

"There are some catalogs and booklets showing different setups. Why don't you browse through them?"

"I will." She smiled and headed for the back of the store.

He watched her, feeling himself getting hard.

Leander Poteet saw the woman coming up the aisle. Star

smiled at him as she walked past. He walked after her, but she went into the listening room and closed the door. He knew only serious customers were allowed in there, so obviously she had a salesman. It wouldn't do for him to try to move in, especially in this "Mighty Whitey" territory. Just as well. Hell! She was so fine he'd give her the merchandise.

He walked a few steps toward the room, watching her through the plate glass. She sat down and opened one of the catalogs. She looked familiar. A man didn't forget a face like that. He was sure he'd seen her before. But where?

Jerry Auster basically blew off the customers looking at the freezers. They weren't serious anyway, he told himself as he hurried to the listening room.

She looked up as he walked in. Her eyes knocked him out. They were so golden, so light. They reminded him of a TV show he saw once where these aliens from another planet had golden eyes.

"Sorry I took so long." He sat down next to her, breathing in her perfume. "You smell good, what's that you're wearing?"

"Boucheron," she said.

"Very nice."

"It should be." Star looked right at him. "It cost enough." It's a good thing I didn't have to pay for it, she thought. She'd convinced Lewis that she needed the expensive fragrance to add realism to her rich bitch persona. He frowned a lot, but signed the reimbursement slip.

Jerry Auster's expression didn't change when his stomach tightened. "Guess when money's no object, it doesn't matter. Must be nice . . . "

"Very," she said, watching his eyes. She put the catalog on her lap and opened it up. "This is kind of along the idea of what I want."

He leaned in close, his shoulder touching hers. Star willed her body not to shake.

"Let me see." He picked up the catalog, his hand brushing

her thigh as he did. He moved closer, his knee resting against hers, and he looked in her eyes. She wanted him. He could smell her need, right through that goddamn, expensive perfume.

"Do you think you need something this big?"

Star shifted, moving her knee away from his. "Yes, it's a big house."

He moved closer to her, again bringing his knee in contact with hers. She looked at him and saw Denise Miles in his eyes. She swallowed hard.

"Something wrong?" he asked.

"No, just thirsty, I guess."

"I'll get you something to drink. Would you like coffee, tea, or a soda?"

"Water, please."

"Just water?"

"Yes, please."

"I'll be right back."

When he left the room, Star pulled a tissue from her purse and blotted the sweat from her face. Maybe they were right, she thought. Maybe she was in over her head. If this guy was their killer, she couldn't be weak. He was messing with her mind, getting to her. Killer or not, she couldn't let that happen, she had to get it together.

He walked back in the room and closed the door, handing her a paper cup full of ice cold water.

She drank it in two gulps. "Thank you."

He took the cup from her. "You *were* thirsty. Would you like some more?"

"No." She stood up. "I think the best way to choose something is for you to come to my place and see what it's like. That way, you know what you're dealing with, and we can cut out a lot of this stuff."

"Come to your house?" he said.

She couldn't look at him. "Yes, that's the only way, don't you think? If you see the space, then you'll know better what I need."

"Okay, that's fair." He moved close to her. "I have to know what you need, in order to give it to you."

She felt like she was going to suffocate. She backed up. "Why don't I call you later and give you a time?"

"I'll have to get permission from the manager before I can make a house call."

"Do you think that will be a problem?"

"No, because I'll do it no matter what he says. Regency Estates, right?"

"Yes."

"Tonight, after work?"

"No, I'll have to work out a time. I'm very busy and I'm rarely there, but I'll call you."

He licked his lips. "I'll be waiting."

Paresi, Star, and Lewis sat in his office. Lewis read the report on the bloodstain Mitch had analyzed from the cloth.

"It's not conclusive enough," he said. "There's no real evidence, no DNA, nothing's strong enough." He handed the paper to Star.

"But it's the same type as two of the victims," she said. "Both Alma Johnson and Denise Miles were A positive."

"Along with just about everybody else in the world," Lewis said. "It isn't enough. Look, I'd like to be able to stop all this stuff and just get a warrant, but the evidence isn't that strong."

"Then we go on to the next step," Star said. "I want to make an appointment with him to come to the house, maybe he'll move on me. I've already said something to him about it."

"That's pushing all his buttons," Lewis said. "And we don't want some sharp-assed lawyer yelling entrapment."

"I say we've got enough probable cause to go forward, and if it gets that far, we can get our own sharp-assed lawyer," Star said. "Besides, it's the only way." She leaned forward in her chair. "He's got to come to the house, and see how I live."

Lewis looked at Paresi. "You're being very quiet."

"I agree with Star, Cap'n."

"You do?"

"Yes sir, I think we can put somebody in the house, like a maintenance man or something. We can rig her with a mike and set up a unit outside in the street, enough guys to storm if that becomes necessary."

Lewis rubbed his chin. "The chief is going to shit a brick if I present him with a bill for surveillance on that level."

"You mean he'd rather spring for a funeral?" Paresi asked.

They glared at one another.

"Let's work on an alternate plan." Lewis pulled a piece of paper from the pad in front of him. "Now, Star, what time would you have him over?"

"Afternoon, say about two."

He wrote that down. "All right, let's say we have one man in the house, and Paresi and another officer outside."

"That will be enough," she said. "If I'm wired, they'll be able to hear everything, I won't be in any danger."

"She's right, Cap'n, first sign of trouble and I'm in there," Paresi said.

"We'll get someone to be with you, Paresi, probably Couchure. The two of you have been seen at the store, so look different, you know what I mean?"

"Yes, sir, but I don't think you have to worry, that place is so big, nobody could remember anybody there unless they were on fire."

"Better safe than sorry, I don't want any slipups." Lewis laid his pen on the desk.

"Fine, sir."

"All right, then make the appointment, Star, and we'll go from there . . . and watch your ass."

She called him the next day. "Hello, Jerry, this is Janine Bohannon, how are you this afternoon?"

"Now that I've heard from you, my day has improved a hundred percent," he said. "What can I do for you?"

Star looked across the squad room at Paresi, who listened to her conversation on an extension.

"Remember I told you that I thought we could get a better idea for my sound system if you saw my place?"

"Yes."

"I'd like you to come over tomorrow afternoon, would that be possible?"

"What time?"

"About two?"

"I don't think that will be a problem. Let me get your address." He reached for a pad. "Go ahead."

"It's Regency Estates, and I'm number 4519 on the Hudson side."

"Okay, 4519 Hudson, I'll see you at two."

She let concern show in her voice. "Are you sure this will be okay with your boss? I remember you said you'd have to get permission."

"No problem, we have an interim manager, our regular is out of town, and the replacement believes in whatever it takes to make the sale. When I tell him what you want, he'll probably drive me over himself."

She tried to laugh. "I guess it's true what the say, money talks."

"Loud and clear. I'll see you tomorrow at two."

"I'm looking forward to it. I can't wait to get my sound system in. I miss my music. It just doesn't sound the same on a bookshelf unit."

"Well, we'll work as quickly as we can. I promise to make sure you're happy and satisfied. See you tomorrow."

He hung up the phone and looked around the showroom. He hoped he didn't look too much like fucking Sylvester with a mouth full of Tweety Bird feathers.

Vee sat on one of the twin champagne-colored sofas in the living room. Star brought out a tray of take-out Chinese from the China Garden. She put the food on the pecan wood, glass-topped coffee table.

"Just think . . ." Vee looked around the room. "People

actually live like this. It looks like a room out of a magazine."

"It's nice all right." Star dished up the food and handed her a plate. "It belongs to the chief's nephew."

"The chief's nephew? Who is he, Bill Gates?"

Star laughed. "No. He's an entrepreneur who opened a bunch of wine bars, back in the late eighties, when yuppiedom was in bloom. He made a lot of money, and he travels."

"I see, so it was okay with him that you move in here?"

"Chief Delaney volunteered the place. Seems he's not too found of his nephew, T. J. , because T. J. likes the boys."

Vee grinned. "I see, so T. J. 's off having fun, and Uncle decided he'd rather see you in here than some guy with a flair."

"Something like that. I don't know the details, but Lewis got the place for as long as we need it." She looked around. "It looks like a movie set or something, but believe me, I've gotten used to it."

"On a cop's salary, I suggest you get unused to it." Vee laughed.

"I heard that! I'm gonna miss it when this is over." Star handed her friend a set of chopsticks.

"Honey, please!" Vee waved them away. "Give me a fork, unless you want Kung Pao chicken flying every which a-way."

"I forgot, I'll get one from the kitchen."

"And bring me some more soy sauce, these little packets ain't gettin' it."

Star came back with a knife and fork. "There isn't any more, they only put three in the bag, you can use them all."

"You sure?"

"Um-hmm." She handed Vee the silverware and sat down on the other sofa, facing her across the coffee table. She folded her legs beneath her, yoga-style, and put her napkin in her lap. "I really love this chicken." She picked up her plate and chopsticks and dug in.

They ate in silence for a while.

"So, are you nervous about tomorrow?" Vee asked.

"No. I'm used to having a guy who could be a homicidal maniac in my house . . . of course I'm nervous!"

"Then why are you doing it?"

Star put her napkin and chopsticks on the table. She sat her plate down beside them. Her appetite had disappeared.

"You know why. Too many of us are turning up dead. It's the only way to get him."

Vee took another bite of chicken. "What about all the evidence you got, doesn't that mean you can just get a warrant and go get the guy?"

"It's not strong enough. It wouldn't hold up in court."

"I can't believe that all the stuff you turned up isn't good enough. You got a positive ID on him from somebody who saw him at the club, you got a piece of bloody shirt from his house, what else do you need?"

"Believe it or not, it's still circumstantial. Just because he was with her at the club and left with her doesn't prove anything. Nobody saw him at her house, and the cabbie who drove her home said she was alone. As for the blood, it's a common type. It matched a couple of the victims, but it also matches a million others, including him. A judge would bounce us out the door with that."

"I think it's time to change the legal system," Vee said.

"Welcome to the club."

Vee looked down at her plate. "I don't want you to do this."

"I'll be all right, I'm protected. There's going to be somebody here inside the house, and Paresi and Couchure will be outside. I'll be wired, so they can hear everything going on. If he gets cute, they'll be all over him, like you on Paresi."

Vee didn't smile. "I still don't like it, and don't try to change the subject."

"It's my job, Vee."

"It doesn't have to be."

"I don't have a choice."

Vee set her plate down. "You had plenty of choices, Star, and Papa Len wouldn't like what you're doing."

"My father has nothing to do with this."

"Tell that to somebody who don't know you. The only reason you're even on the department is because of him, and believe me, he wouldn't want you to do it for that reason."

"You don't know what he would want." Star's voice rose.

"I knew him all my life, and I know he loved you, and you don't have to prove anything to him."

"This is not about Pop." She clasped her hands together. "This has nothing to do with him. Women are being murdered because they're black and for no other reason. I just want to put an end to it."

"Uh-huh, and that's why you're willing to give your life to a police department that killed your daddy. You've got to prove you're not scared, you're a brave little soldier."

"It's not about that!" Star was on her feet, her voice rising. "It's about saving someone else who could die because of the color of their skin. It's not about proving anything!"

Tears stood in her eyes.

"Star." Vee got up, facing her. "I love you. I've been your friend since we were babies. I loved Papa Len, and I loved your mother. I was with you when you lost her when you were twelve years old, and I was with you when they took your daddy seven years later. I know he wouldn't want this, you putting your life on the line for the department.

"He didn't even want you to be a cop. Remember? He wanted you to study music and dance. That's what you loved. He used to say one day he was gonna watch you dance on Broadway."

"After he died, there was nobody else to carry his name." Star wiped her eyes. "I owe it to him."

Vee sighed, exasperated. "Who told you you got to be Hogan *and* all his heroes, huh? Girl, you are a lieutenant, you got a gold shield, you're already higher-ranked than anybody that came on with you, isn't that enough? Let somebody else do this."

"I can't. My father gave up his life for this department. There's a tradition here."

"What tradition? Getting killed for nothing? He didn't lay down his life, *they took it!*" Vee yelled. "It was his day off, he was minding his own business and happened to walk into a bad situation."

"If he hadn't gone to the cleaners that day—"

"But he did, he did go to the cleaners to get that goddamn uniform, and a white man chose that moment to rob the place. Your daddy did what he was supposed to do, he went after the thief, he chased the man, but the very same department that he worked for pulled up, saw two men running, both of them with guns, and they shot him to death!"

Star burst into tears.

"Don't you see?" Vee was crying with her. "They didn't care that he was a cop. That didn't even cross their minds. All they saw was a black man running with a gun in his hand, and they blew him away before he even had a chance to identify himself. The robber had a gun too, in plain sight, but did they shoot him? No, they ran him down like a dog, but they killed Papa Len, because all they saw was a nigger with a gun. And you're willing to risk your life for them? Baby, don't. I say you've given enough. Let them set somebody else up, not you. You've paid your dues and then some. Papa Len wouldn't let you do this."

"He would want me to try and save somebody's life." Star said, regaining her composure.

"Nobody saved his." Vee took her hand. "Remember that. Nobody saved his."

24

Star stood in the hallway of the brownstone, trying not to think of the conversation with her best friend the night before.

There had been justice of a sort, for her dad. Joe Carroll, the officer who killed him, had been relieved of active duty and assigned to a desk. He lasted nearly three years, but alcohol and drugs became his way of coping. He finally shot himself in the head one early morning on a bus stop bench near his house.

Even though he was found not guilty by the department committee, and retained his job, with modification, he never got over the guilt.

Star could still see him at the graveside, sobbing his heart out while she watched him, dry-eyed. He tried to explain to her what happened, and she never said a word, she just sat there, staring at him. After he died, she was sorry she hadn't been more forgiving, but in all honesty, even now, years later, forgiveness wouldn't come.

She loved Vee, but she had a job to do. She knew her friend was worried and her words came from that fear, as well as love, and her own pain. She'd call Vee later and make up. For now, she had to get "up." She had a show to do.

Star stood in the entry hall, fingering the whimsical-looking imitation diamond musical note pin on her shirt. She began singing softly.

In the bathroom, Detective Sam Rainey, dressed in a maintenance man's uniform, listened to her croon "Stop in the Name of Love."

"Keep singing, baby," he said, fiddling with the controls on his Walkman. "You comin' in loud and clear. The diva got nothing on you, sho' nuff stone Supreme!"

Outside, Paresi was bare-chested, dressed like a jogger in shorts and running shoes. He also wore a Walkman attached to the waist of his shorts, a headband, earphones, and shades. He stood a few doors down, stretching and bending, like a runner preparing for a jog.

Star moved to the window and caught sight of him. "Whoa baby!" she said into the mike. "That chest, those legs, those pecs, Paresi, I've got to have a talk with Vee. You're a hunk!"

Paresi turned toward the window and smiled.

"What I want to know," she said, "is where is your gun?"

Paresi pointed to his crotch. She laughed. He was picking her up loud and clear.

Jerry Auster's silver Toyota pulled up at exactly two P.M. He'd told his boss he wasn't feeling well and had to leave early. Paresi stood jogging in place as Auster got out of the car. Auster smiled at him.

"Good day for a run, huh?" he said amiably.

"Yeah." Paresi grinned, stretching, bending, showing more of his back than his face. "Not as hot as it's been."

He continued to stretch as he watched Auster walk up the stairs.

Star opened the door just as Auster rang the bell. "Hi, glad to see you're right on time."

"I wouldn't keep a pretty lady like you waiting."

She let him in. Paresi jogged by, heading down the block. He ran to the corner and crossed the street, where he could observe the brownstone, yet not be seen. Couchure, wearing a navy-blue sleeveless T-shirt, red visor, shades, and white shorts, waited at the end of the block on a racing bike.

Inside the house, Star was the perfect hostess. "Would you like something to drink?" she asked Jerry Auster.

"A soda would be nice."

"Make yourself at home." She indicated the living room. "I'll be right back."

She went into the kitchen and pulled two colas out of the fridge. She filled two glasses with crushed ice from the refrigerator door and put the drinks on a tray. When she turned around, she almost dropped them. He was standing in the doorway, watching.

"Oh!"

"I'm sorry, I didn't mean to frighten you. Let me take that." He took the tray. "I just thought I'd get a look at the kitchen."

"It's okay, I just didn't expect to see you. Let's go into the living room."

"All right."

He let her lead, as he followed, checking her behind in the crisp white trousers she wore. Her shirt was black silk, and she wore it open and tied at the waist, with a white cotton tank top beneath. He especially liked the diamond musical note pin she wore as an accent. She had good taste.

"I like your pin," he said as he set the tray down on the coffee table.

"Oh, thank you, I picked it up in Paris last year," she said. "I was at a jazz festival, and I couldn't resist it."

"Very nice." He sat down on the sofa, and she sat on the other sofa facing him.

He looked around. "This is a beautiful house. May I ask what you do for a living?"

She laughed. "Nothing really. I inherited a very large estate from my father. He was a businessman, African-American cosmetics. He made a fortune."

Auster tried to swallow the lump in his throat. "So you don't work."

"Not unless you call traveling, partying, and nonstop hell-raising, work." She crossed her legs. "I like to enjoy my money. Of course, I give some away for worthy causes, and for thrills I dabble a little in the stock market. It's a lot like a roller coaster, and I do like thrills."

She poured the sodas, feeling his gaze, trying not to let her hands tremble.

"Thrills," he said out loud. I'm going to give you plenty, he thought.

"That's right. I like to live every day to the fullest, and thanks to dear, departed Daddy, I can." She sat back, holding her glass with both hands.

"You're lucky. Working for somebody else can be a drag."

"I'm surprised at the work you do, Jerry," she said.

"Why?"

She gestured in his direction. "Look at you, you're a very handsome man, you should be in the pages of magazines and on the runways in Milan, not in Electric City."

"Thank you, but it takes luck—being discovered, that is—and besides, I'm not really the model type."

"I think you'd be perfect. Too bad you're not darker. I'd insist they use you in some of our men's products ads."

He was about to burst; too bad he wasn't a nigger? She was going to pay, big-time. "Well, we are what we are." He set the drink down. "Why don't we talk about your needs."

"My needs." She ran her hand through her hair. "That covers a lot of territory, as you can see."

He looked her in the eye. "I can handle it."

"I'm sure you can." She put her glass down on the tray. "I guess you'll need the tour. Follow me."

He got up.

She walked down the hallway. "First, you see how this is laid out. It's three stories. There's the top floor, which I use as sort of a catchall area—it's got three really big rooms—and the second floor has my two guests suites and the combination library and study. Down here is the real living part of the house. The kitchen, dining, and living rooms, as well as the master bedroom suite. There's also two full baths and one half bath, and there's lots of alcoves and slanted ceilings.

"It's going to be a big job, all right," he said. "Why don't you tell me where you spend most of your time?"

"Down here, follow me." She led him to the master bedroom. Jake lay sleeping on the bed. "I hope you're not allergic to cats," she said.

"No, I love them." He reached out and stroked the sleeping animal. Jake opened his eyes and stared, but didn't move.

"He likes you," she said.

"Most animals like me." He looked around the large room. "Would you like a control panel near the bed?"

"Near the bed?"

"Sure, that way, when you're in here and you want music, you can do it all without having to leave the comfort of your bed."

He spoke in a soft voice and moved closer to her, putting his hand on her back. She felt the warmth.

"See, if we put the panel in here"—he indicated a space near the left side of the bed—"you can have the panel built as low as you'd like so that you wouldn't even have to sit up to program your music."

He was standing too close. She felt him against her. He was aroused. Part of her wanted to lean back, press against him, let him touch her, and the other part wanted to drop kick him out of the window.

His hand slowly, hypnotically, moved up and down her back, soothing her, arousing her, alarming her.

She felt herself relax under his touch, wanting more.

Her eyes closed. The women came. One by one, breaking the spell, silent witnesses to his madness. She moved away from him.

"This is where I spend most of my time, and I do like to be comfortable." She tried to sound detached.

"Perhaps a wall unit, near the side of the bed."

She reached down. His hand covered hers, his mouth close to her ear, his erection pushed against her.

"It might not be good to put it that low, maybe you'd want it higher up."

He ran his hand up her arm. She jumped.

"Am I making you nervous?" His lips were at her ear. He continued stroking her arm while he wrapped his other arm around her waist, pulling her back against him. He swayed with her, his hips slowly pressing, his hand at her waist and inching down. "You feel good, Janine, you smell good, you look good."

He turned her toward him. "You're very pretty, you know that?"

He kissed her neck and moved his mouth to her ear, the tip of his tongue barely touching inside. He drew his breath between his teeth, making a soft, whispery sound that made her skin burn. He spoke, his voice soft, low, yet husky with passion.

"You're so pretty."

Denise Miles floated behind her closed eyes. She could feel a sense of panic rising. She knew she had to take this further, but this was too close. He was touching her as if he knew she wouldn't object, and as prepared as she thought she was, he was getting to her. She was aroused, her body responding to this man. Logic pressed forward.

Her mind screamed, THE HANDS THAT ARE TOUCHING ME KILLED ALL THOSE WOMEN!

Jerry knew she wanted him. He ran his hands down her back, grabbing her behind, squeezing. He pushed her against the wall and pressed himself against her. He could feel her heat through their clothes.

His hands were everywhere. He untied her shirt, kneading her breasts, stroking her nipples until they stood up, hard, against her T-shirt. One hand slid down to her waist; his fingers opened the top button of her slacks.

She felt the zipper inching slowly down. She tried to move away, yet a part of her was enjoying this, his mouth on hers, his eager hands, the hardness pressed against her responding flesh. She raised her arms to push him away and found herself embracing him. He was kissing her, his tongue in her mouth, moving with a life of its own, sliding, sucking, teasing, drawing her. She couldn't breathe.

"I want you," he sighed into her mouth. "I want you."

Star twisted away, feeling his fingertips just below her navel, moving down, inching along her skin to the lacy border of her panties. "No . . . Jerry." She pushed against him. "No!"

His fingers slid beneath the lace.

"They all . . . mmmm, yeah, sing, ooh yeah, why I love the blues." Sam Rainey's voice startled them. They jumped apart.

Star quickly zipped her pants and tied up her shirt.

Sam came out of the bathroom, singing loudly, his Walkman on his belt and earphones on his head, over his turned-backward Chicago Cubs baseball cap. He popped his fingers to the sound only he could hear. He looked surprised when he saw them.

"Oh, hey Miz Bohannon." He took off the earphones. "I din't know you was home. I'm jes' listenin' to some B. B. King. He the real thang, sho' nuff blues man." He grinned. "Cain't nothin' beat de blues. Ain't dat right?"

She moved away from Jerry. Sam could see the gratitude in her eyes.

"I'm a Motown woman myself." She sounded breathless, her voice throaty. "Sam, what are you doing here?"

He shook his head. "Don' be scoldin' at me. I knows I was s'pose ta be heah yestiddy, but I got tied up. Yo' housekeepah done let me in before she leff out. I been workin' on that there showa in there, jus' tryin' to make up for missin' you."

"It's okay, Sam, I'm glad you're here. There are a couple of other problems in one of the bathrooms upstairs, and I really think you should look at all the sinks, including the one in the kitchen."

"Well, now, you got me, an I owes you, since I couldn' git c'here yestiddy. Jus' point me where you needs me." He grinned.

Jerry Auster was unable to hide the loathing in his eyes. He regarded the chocolate-colored handyman as a chicken-choking, watermelon-eating fool, who was probably making more an hour than he did in a week, without commissions. He didn't know that behind that big smile stood a former Green Beret who could break his neck before he could blink.

"The garbage disposal is really acting up. The other night it spit the garbage right back out at me." She started walking Sam toward the hall.

Jerry stood his ground, his anger in his eyes.

"Now why would it do sumpin' like dat? You mus' not be treatin' it right. 'Member, I done tol' you, Miz B., machines, dey got souls too. You gotta be nice to 'em."

I didn't come here for no coon show, Jerry Auster thought.

Star looked back at him. "Why don't we go out into the living room, Jerry." She walked up the hallway. He had no choice but to follow. On the bed, Jake regarded him with emerald eyes.

Star showed Sam to the kitchen and walked back into the living room, to Jerry. She felt flushed, and she couldn't look at him.

"I'm sorry about the interruption, but you know how it is, when you get the handyman, you make sure he fixes everything that needs to be fixed, because who knows when you'll get him again. These are old buildings and they need a lot of maintenance." She was rambling, talking too fast and too much, yet she managed to move him through the hallway, toward the door.

"You've got an idea of what I want, so why don't I call you later to make an appointment at the store to come in and see what you think will work in here." She opened the door. He found himself on the steps.

"Thanks again for coming, Jerry, I'll call you tomorrow." She closed the door in his face.

Jerry Auster looked at his watch. It was ten minutes till three. This entire thing had taken fifty minutes.

Inside, Star waited until her heart stopped thundering and Auster had walked down the stairs before she went into the kitchen and put her arms around Sam.

"About that dialect!" They laughed together.

"It works with white people. They think when you're as black as I am, you got to be stupid." He looked in her eyes. "How are you doing, baby?"

"Fine, just thank you for being here."

"I heard him hitting on you, I figured it was time to come out."

"I'm glad you did, I was losing it. He's almost magical. If you hadn't been in there . . . "

"You would have nailed him anyway, because you're Lenny Duvall's little girl, and you ain't no coward, you did just fine. I was only there for a little backup, and we both know if you had to take him, you could."

"He's so smooth." She could still feel Jerry's warm tongue in her mouth.

Sam took off his cap. "Yeah, he is that, he's a smooth, pretty, slick motherfucker. But you're tougher than he is, don't worry about being spooked. You do what you gotta do, you go as far as it takes. Hell, ain't nothing wrong with a little fear, it keeps you on your toes."

"Yeah?" She suddenly felt cold. A chill ran the length of her body. "Well, just call me Baryshnikov."

25

Maureen wiped the sink and looked at the clock over the counter. It was twenty minutes after three. She shook out the dishcloth and hung it on the rim of the sink. The door to the basement was slightly open. She stared at it. Her hands twitched. She looked again at the clock. If he was going to come home, it would have been at lunch or shortly after. Late afternoons were usually their busiest time.

She went into the bedroom and picked up her purse. She unzipped the top compartment and felt under the ripped cloth lining. It was there, where she'd hidden it, the key to Jerry's studio. She pulled it out and put it in her apron pocket. She put the purse on the floor by the bed and went back into the kitchen.

The door to the basement seemed to have opened itself wider. Inviting her in, making her welcome.

"The time is now," she said.

She took a step. "Now."

She looked at the clock again and opened the door all the way, pushing it against the wall. She stood on the top step for a full minute before slowly walking down.

At the bottom of the stairs, she faced the locked door. She put her hand in her apron pocket and pulled out the key. Her palm was drenched in sweat. As she put the key to the lock, it slid out of her hand and skidded under a cabinet that sat to the left of the door. She got down on her hands and knees, scrabbling for it. The key, as if alive, moved farther back under the cabinet.

She lay nearly flat on the floor, stretching as far as her arm would reach, trying to get it. Sweat ran into her eyes as she grunted and forced her arm farther, scraping her skin. She pushed harder, groaning, the key just beyond her reach. From somewhere, she summoned the strength and pushed farther, inching her nearly wedged arm along. Her fingers came within millimeters of the gleaming, silver key. It was then she heard footsteps on the back stairs.

"Oh God!" She tore her arm free, ignoring the long scratch and the welt rising on it. As quickly as she could, Maureen got to her feet and grabbed the old wicker laundry basket. Wiping sweat from her face, she nearly ran to the dryer and pulled out a load of dry clothes. Thank God she hadn't gotten around to taking the laundry upstairs earlier.

The key would have to wait. She had to get upstairs. Large circles of perspiration wet her dress beneath her armpits. She wiped her face again on one of the towels in the basket and hurried upstairs.

He was standing at the refrigerator with the door open, searching for beer.

"Hi honey." She tried to smile. "You're home early, I didn't expect you, I haven't even started dinner."

He barely looked at her. "Have I got a clean shirt in there?" He pointed at the basket.

She set it on the table and prayed. A short-sleeved blue denim shirt appeared in the mix of towels, underwear, and her big summer tent dresses. "Here you go, hon."

He took it from her hand and headed toward the bathroom. He wanted to shower and get changed; he had work to do.

Paresi and Couchure changed clothes in the police locker room after Star's meeting with Jerry Auster. The whole incident had left Dominic rattled. Couchure put his wallet badge in his pants pocket and slammed the locker door. He turned to Paresi.

"So, you got plans for tonight?"

Paresi barely heard him. "No. In fact, I think I'm gonna go back to Star's."

"What for?" Couchure said. "The guy's long gone, our shift is over."

"I don't like the idea of her being there alone." He picked up the keys to his unmarked car. "Come with me."

"Our shift is over, we're off duty," Couchure said.,

Paresi closed his locker door. "A cop is on duty 24-7. I'm your senior officer, detective, and I said, come with me."

Star was in the tub, with the Jacuzzi jets on full power, attempting to wind down from her encounter with Jerry Auster earlier in the afternoon.

She couldn't believe she'd let it go so far, that she'd actually been turned on by him. Had it been that long? Was she so needy that she'd risk her life? She lay back, letting the water circulate around her, massaging her back and shoulders. Still, she was tense. What if Sam hadn't been there, if she hadn't been wired, how far would she have gone? Would he have killed her?

Her mind replayed the afternoon encounter. He was so smooth, so damn gorgeous. What could have happened to make him so sick?

She wasn't his psychiatrist, she admonished herself. Her job was not to analyze him. Her job was to stop him.

Outside the brownstone, parked about a block down the street, Paresi was sipping a monster-sized plastic cup of cola. He looked at his watch. It was just past six-thirty. Couchure was sulking in the driver's seat when the silver Toyota passed and came to a stop in front of Star's house. He recognized it from earlier in the day. Jerry Auster.

"Cooch." He elbowed his partner. "Can you get a number on the plates on that silver Toyota?"

Couchure put down his meatball and provolone sandwich and picked up the binoculars. "I can't see the last two numbers, wait till he pulls out."

Paresi took a bite of the sandwich. "How can you eat this? It's cold."

Couchure turned to him. "You don't like it, leave it alone. I'm workin' here when I should be home having a hot meal, a real dinner, got it?"

Paresi looked at him. "So this hot meal, do you eat it, fuck it, or both?"

Couchure hung his head, a tight smile on his face. "Shows, huh?"

"Yeah." Paresi nodded. "Hey, we all get horns, but the work comes first. If she's a stand-up chick, she'll understand that."

"I know, she does . . . sometimes, but she's been away for a while."

"Be patient. The longer the wait, the better it'll be." Paresi shifted his weight. "He's pulling out."

Couchure picked up the binoculars. "772 S-Sam, X-X ray, E-Easy."

Paresi repeated it aloud as he wrote on the paper bag from the sandwich. "772SXE." He punched the license number onto the keyboard of the car terminal, requesting a license check. The screen flashed:

UNABLE TO COMPLETE REQUEST AT THIS TIME, PLEASE REENTER LATER.

"Goddamn!" He grabbed the microphone. "Dispatch, this is car 81, get me a license check, 772 S-Sam, X-X ray, E-Easy."

The dispatcher's voice filled the car. "No can do, Detective, the computer's down."

"You got phones? It's urgent!"

"Sorry, no computer, no information." The dispatcher sounded bored. "Try again in a little while, it shouldn't be much longer."

"*Fuck!*" Paresi hurled the microphone at the dashboard. It bounced off and clattered to the floor of the car.

"Take it easy." Couchure picked it up by the cord. "It'll be up in a minute. Why are you so pissed?"

Couchure hadn't heard the exchange between Star and Auster that afternoon. He wasn't miked. Paresi didn't want to tell him. Instead he gazed down the street in the direction the Toyota had disappeared.

"Because I know Jerry Auster was driving that car, and I know he's our man, and I know if he gets the chance, he's going to kill my partner."

Couchure shook his head. "Lighten up, you don't know shit! All you have is a suspect, the guy could be innocent."

Paresi turned to him. "How long you been on the squad, Cooch?"

"Almost a year, why?"

"Then you must have been here long enough to have some kind of instinct, right?"

"I s'pose, I mean I can tell sometimes. After a while, yeah, you get feelings, but I don't get that about this guy."

He turned in his seat to face Paresi. "Like when I watched him in the store with Star, I didn't feel like she was in any danger. Shit, I think she was enjoying herself. You see this guy? Have you looked at him? He's better-lookin' than that fuckin' Kennedy guy. She's alive, right? As for him, hey, he wants to pork her, and frankly, I can understand that."

Paresi shook his head and laughed, a long, low chuckle. "Cooch, I'm gonna give you some advice."

"Okay."

"Get your mind off your dick and start thinking like a cop. This guy is a serial killer. I don't know if you noticed all the black women that have been getting dead lately. I know you've been at a couple of scenes, but while you were there, did you happen to notice the bodies?"

"Very funny." Couchure was almost pouting. "I know what's happening, but that don't mean this is the guy."

Paresi held up his hand. "Let me finish. See, if you wasn't concentrating on your gonads, you might have heard some of the things the cap'n and Star and I have been talking about in the briefings. See, all the victims have been young, pretty—

and pay attention now—black. See where I'm going with this?"

Couchure opened his mouth. Paresi shook his head.

"Uh-uh, just listen. I know you think you know what I'm gonna say, but hear me out. See Cooch, us old-timers, we look at this as a game, the object of which is to nail the bastard that's going around wasting women."

"We"—he pointed first to Couchure and then himself— "are the good guys. We're the ones who are supposed to win, but we can't, unless everybody involved stays on their toes, watches every little thing, lets nothing slip by, capeesh?"

Couchure didn't like the look in Paresi's eyes.

"Now," Paresi said, "I need to know if you ever really took a good look at the lieutenant? Remember now, the dead women were young, pretty, and black."

Couchure started to speak. Paresi shushed him.

"Listen up, just listen. Now our fellow officer, she fits all those categories, and since she gives you a hard-on, I'm sure you've noticed the lady is fine.

"Now that crazy bastard that just drove up here and checked out her house, he has taken out three women so far. So that makes me think she's in danger, and sooner or later he's gonna try and kill her."

"It's theory, man," Couchure said. "*Your* fuckin' theory. We got no hard evidence, everything is circumstantial."

Paresi laced his fingers together. His large hands trembled as he stared out the window and prayed for the control not to punch this guy right in the face.

The video screen beeped and a message flashed across it: ONLINE, PLEASE REENTER REQUEST.

Paresi typed in the license check code and entered the plate number. In seconds the information scrolled down the screen:

Vehicle License Number: Massachusetts 772SXE
Vehicle Make: Toyota Sedan–1992
Vehicle Color: Silver
VIN: JP1LB1520FG280387

Registered Owner: Jerome Auster
Address: 1187 Palmer Street
        Brookport, Massachusetts
        01792

"Gotcha, you son of a bitch!" Paresi grinned.

"Could be a coincidence," Couchure said.

Paresi got out of the car and sprinted up the street. If he hadn't, he was gonna beat the punk to dust. He rang Star's bell. She didn't answer. He rang again. He was just about to try the back when she cracked the door.

"Paresi?" She pulled her bath towel tighter around her body.

"Let me in."

She stood back.

He walked in, eyeing the towel. "I like the outfit."

"I was in the tub. What are you doing here?"

"I just felt like checking you out before I went off duty, so I grabbed Cooch and we've been piking you for a while."

"Let me get a robe."

He sat on one of the sofas while she went into the bedroom.

"So, whatcha got?" She came out in her blue and white terry-cloth robe, leaving wet footprints on the rug behind her.

"He was just here, scoping out your place. It's time we move on this bastard, and up the security. He's watching you."

Star sat down next to him. Inside, her stomach was pitching. She struggled to keep her face immobile. The concern in Paresi's eyes was more than she could take. If he felt she was coming apart, he'd tell Lewis and she'd be off the case.

"Swell." Her voice sounded weak. She stared at the wall. "At least now we know he's really it."

"All of us except Cooch. You know what that shithead was thinking when he was watching you in the store?"

"What?"

"He was thinking the guy just looked like he wanted to nail you; not dangerous, just horny. In fact, popping you has been on his mind too!"

Star shook her head. "He's young, he's only got a year or so, he's still green."

"Yeah, well, I'm requesting a new backup. I'd rather sit around with Darcy and his goddamn shirt than deal with this jimoke. The thing could be going down, and he'd probably think the fuck was dancing with you!"

She laughed.

"It ain't funny."

"I know." She leaned against him.

"Believe me, this afternoon really hammered it home for me. It's definitely not a joke."

Paresi put his arm around her. "I heard it, I kept wondering when you were gonna stop him. I figured you knew what you were doing, but it was too close for me. If Sam hadn't come out when he did, I was coming through the fucking door. He put his hands on you."

"I let him," she said. "I think I even wanted him to."

"No, no, you didn't. You don't want him, you were scared, but that's okay, because from now on I'm gonna be with you, no matter what it takes.

"We all get scared sometimes, we get weak, and that's what happened this afternoon. It won't happen again, because believe me, if you fell because any of us was jerking off somewhere, not paying attention, then they'd better dig two graves, 'cause I couldn't live with it."

"Dominic." She rested her head on his shoulder.

"I know," he said, holding her. "I know."

Jerry Auster lay on a lawn chaise in his backyard, drinking beer and gazing up at the night sky. He'd been out there for hours. He didn't even go in for dinner. She was all he could think of. The way she responded to him, the way she felt in his arms. He had to get inside that place. He knew there was a silent alarm setup, even though he hadn't gotten out to check because there was too much activity on the street. But he was going back, he had to. He couldn't take any more teasing. It was time for her to pay up.

26

The dawn was cool, in spite of the sunlight that followed it. A sharp, white light jabbed Paresi's closed eyes, making him squint.

The sound of Couchure's snoring brought him completely awake. He rubbed the beard stubble on his chin and looked at his watch. It was just after seven A.M. The last time he'd checked the time, it was five. He'd been out for a little over two hours. He turned his head, trying to pop the stiffness out of his neck. His back was aching. He stretched and turned his head again, just in time to see the silver Toyota cruising down the street.

Paresi watched as Jerry Auster got out of his car and ran quickly up the stairs. He checked the locks on Star's door.

"Cooch, wake up!" He shook his partner.

"What?"

"He's checking her doors, wake up!"

Couchure rubbed his eyes. "So what, he ain't doing nothing, he's not trying to break in. Look at him, he looks like he's checking to see if anybody's up, maybe she asked him to come back today."

"At seven in the morning?"

Couchure shrugged and closed his eyes.

Jerry finished his examination and moved to the front windows. He appeared to be measuring something, without actually touching the glass. After that, he rushed back to his car.

"Follow him." Paresi shook Couchure awake again.

"What?"

The Toyota sped down the nearly deserted street. Paresi got

out of the car and ran around to the driver's side. He shoved Couchure into the passenger seat, gunned the motor and roared out after the Toyota. Couchure rubbed his eyes and yawned.

"You really got this Rambo thing down, don't you? The guy didn't do anything. What are you gonna do, bust him for trying to see if she's home?"

"You know, Cooch, you really oughta try a different line of work, like maybe undertaker, 'cause sooner or later you're gonna get somebody killed, but it ain't gonna be me and it ain't gonna be Star."

He caught sight of the car and dropped back in early morning traffic, following from two car lengths behind.

"What's that supposed to be mean?" Couchure sat up in his seat.

"It means that as soon as I find out where this bastard's headed, we're going in and I'm telling Lewis to take your ass off the case."

"You're overreacting, man. Star can take care of herself, as far as I see—"

"Shut up, if I want shit from you, I'll squeeze your head." Paresi turned the corner, keeping the Toyota in view.

Couchure was angry. "Dig yourself, man, look at how you're acting here. What? Is Star your pussy or something? You're way over the top!"

Paresi turned his head and looked at Couchure. The set of Paresi's jaw and the look in his eyes let the young detective know he'd gone too far. Couchure leaned back against the seat and decided to do as he was told.

They followed Jerry Auster to Electric City, and parked across the street as he opened a side door with a key.

"He's probably looking for something he can use to break into her house," Paresi said.

Couchure was silent.

Auster was in the store for about twenty minutes. He came out, locked the door, and got back into his car. They followed him to a chain restaurant and parked a half block from the door, waiting.

"How do you like this fuck, he's gonna have breakfast," Paresi said, shaking his head.

Couchure sat looking at him. He liked Paresi, and maybe he had said some wrong things, he wanted to make it right. But he really didn't think anybody had to worry about this guy. With his looks, he didn't have to murder anybody to get laid, that was just a fact.

"Dom?"

"Shut up, Cooch."

Couchure sighed. "Look, I'm sorry. I didn't mean what I said about Star. You're right, I haven't been taking this thing seriously, and I know I'm wrong."

"You're out, Cooch."

Couchure shook his head. "Okay, if that's the way you want it." He reached for the door handle.

Paresi grabbed him. "Where are you going?"

"I gotta take a leak."

"So you're going in the restaurant to use the john?"

"Yeah, he won't see me."

"I don't care if your goddamn back teeth are floating, you ain't leaving the car."

"I got to take a leak."

Paresi picked up the large plastic cup from his soda the night before. "Use this. You're not leaving the car."

Couchure looked at him like he was crazy. "What's wrong with you, I got to piss. He just went in for breakfast, he won't be back for a while. I won't go inside, I'll go through the parking lot, around back, in the bushes."

Paresi's blue eyes turned a stormy shade. "Listen, you brainless bastard, I don't give a fuck if he stays in there till Christmas, you're not leaving the car. If he comes out and I lose him because of you, I'll shoot you myself! You either hold it, piss in the cup or in your pants, cause you ain't getting outta the car!"

Couchure knew he meant it. "Jesus H. Christ." He unzipped his fly. "You're a fucking maniac, you know, a maniac."

Jerry Auster came out of the restaurant carrying a white bag and a cup of coffee, just as Couchure finished. He zipped his fly with one hand, holding the cup away from him like it was radioactive.

"What do I do with this?"

"Drink it!"

Paresi pulled out into traffic, following the Toyota. Couchure's hand wobbled, spilling some of the liquid onto his pants.

"Christ, Dominic!"

Paresi picked up speed, keeping pace with the Toyota. He followed Jerry Auster back to Electric City. He parked across the street and watched Auster let himself in through a side door.

"Now what?" Couchure said angrily. "He went to fuckin' work."

"He's early." Paresi stared unblinking at the closed door. "He wants to be alone to plan how he's gonna do Star. He's gonna sit there, drink his coffee, have his breakfast, and plot just how he's gonna waste my partner."

The look on Paresi's face actually scared Couchure. He started to speak, but thought better of it.

"We're going in." Paresi started the engine.

"You gonna talk to the captain?" Couchure's voice was small.

Paresi smiled at him, a smile that gave him cold chills. "No more jacking off, little man." He looked at the plastic cup that Couchure held carefully.

Couchure read his mind, and snatched the cup quickly. More of the warm liquid spilled, running over his hand and thigh. Paresi laughed and pulled out into traffic.

Star checked her reflection in the mirror and picked up her purse. The phone rang just as she headed for the front door.

"Hello."

"Star, get in here right away," Captain Lewis said.

"What's up?"

"Change in plans, come directly here."

"I'm on the way." She hung up, wondering what could have happened. She hoped he hadn't heard about her freaking out. If he knew, this sting was history.

Maureen lay in bed, dreading the morning. It was already hot, and she had no energy. Jerry had gotten up and left very early, without saying a word. There had to be another woman.

She sat up, swinging her heavy legs over the edge of the bed. Well, that was just fine, but she was going to find out once and for all. She had no idea what she'd do with the information, but today she was going to find out. Right after she got that stupid key from under the cabinet in the basement.

Star sat listening to Couchure trying to explain his behavior to Captain Lewis. It was all she could do not to punch his lights out.

Who does he think he is? she asked herself. Sitting there with that damned lawn-mower haircut and those white socks. Why in the world do they think they know all about us? Because I'm black and female, I'm supposed to be a brainless machine just programmed to screw and drop babies. What planet do these people come from?

"Is it true you thought the suspect was just after sex with Lieutenant Duvall?" Captain Lewis asked.

Couchure looked at Star. She stared at him, unblinking.

"Well sir, it appeared that he was interested in her like a man who wants to . . . you know."

"No, Detective Couchure, I don't know, enlighten me." Lewis folded his arms across his chest and leaned back in his chair.

Couchure wanted to drop into another dimension. The three of them stared at him. His ears turned bright red. When he tried to speak, his throat closed. He coughed twice.

"He looked at her and behaved like a man who wants to know her intimately."

"And that's all you saw, a man who wanted to know her better."

"Yes sir."

Lewis looked at Star. "How do you feel about Lieutenant Duvall, Detective Couchure, do you want to know her better?"

"Yes sir . . . I mean, no sir, I mean not in that way, sir."

"Why not?"

Couchure looked like he wanted to die. Star didn't have any idea where Lewis was going with this, but she was enjoying the ride.

"She's my superior officer, sir, she's my boss."

Lewis smiled. "Exactly, and how do you think she got to be your boss, Detective Couchure?"

"Hard work, sir?"

"Against odds and obstacles you can't even imagine." Lewis's eyes were cold behind his glasses. "Apologize, detective, and mean it!"

Couchure turned to Star. "I'm sorry, Lieutenant. I really am, I realize now that your life could be in danger and that I was not viewing the situation realistically or professionally."

Star said nothing. She looked away from him. She'd been fighting this battle since the first day she put on a uniform. She had gotten used to it. Over the years, it had become routine, but it never got easier.

It was part of the territory. Men hit on women, that was a fact, even in these politically correct days of sexual harassment. Cops were cops, it came with the job. You knew who was kidding and who wasn't. You also knew how far a guy could go with his remarks, and you knew when he crossed the line. When Paresi told her about Couchure's feelings, she'd been able to laugh it off, but to actually sit, listening to him, made her want to tear him apart.

She had worked with men for fifteen years. She had feelings about the things they said, but she'd heard all the lines and seen all the moves. She had laughed at some, and called them out on others. She made them respect her, but she'd never felt as angry or as vile as she did listening to Couchure.

She wished she'd been in uniform with her bars and shield visible. That gold shield was her talisman, it said it all. She had earned it with pride and hard work.

Most of the men she commanded regarded her highly, and she had no problems with them. Oh sure there were a few, like Rescovich, but that didn't bother her. All her officers knew that with her, the work came first. They had to be a team. Your life depended on who had your back. She faced him again.

Couchure looked down at the floor, unable to meet her gaze.

"I accept your apology, Detective Couchure," she said calmly. "This is not about personal feelings, it's about trying to stop a killer. I'm sure you understand that."

"Yes, ma'am." Couchure kept looking at the floor.

"Good, then you'll also understand that I agree with Detective Sergeant Paresi. I think you should be removed from this investigation."

Couchure didn't raise his head or say anything.

"Detective Couchure, please wait in the squad room while we discuss strategy on this case," she said coldly.

"Yes, ma'am." Couchure stood, looking at her. "I'm really sorry, Lieutenant."

You don't know how sorry you're going to be, she said to herself. "Apology accepted," she said out loud.

She waited until Couchure closed the office door before she spoke to Captain Lewis.

"Do you want to pull me off?" she asked him.

"I don't think that would be wise. He'd know something was up if you stopped dealing with him."

"I agree," she said.

"What was your plan for today?" Lewis asked.

"I was just going to go in and talk to him some more about the system and maybe invite him over again."

"You think he'd come back, after the interference yesterday?" Lewis asked.

"Yes sir, I do. I flirted with him. I tried to make him think it was more than just a house call."

"I don't know if that's a good idea," Lewis said.

"It's the only way. He's got to think I want him. He'll come back."

"I'm not sure I like the idea of waving steak in front of a starving dog. What do you think, Paresi?"

"I think she's right, but I'd like to wait till tomorrow for the invite."

"Okay," she said, and turned to the captain. "That gives Dom a chance to get some rest, and for me to get ready. I'll call him today and tell him that I want him over tomorrow afternoon."

Lewis nodded in agreement. "It's settled then, tomorrow we move. You get him to come after you, and we'll take him, and I don't give a shit about the cost. So those fat bastards upstairs will have to pay for their own vacations."

She laughed. "Thanks, Captain."

"Paresi, you take off, go home. Star, make your call."

"Yes sir, I will, after I have a talk with Detective Couchure," she said. "Do you mind if I use your office?"

Lewis knew what was coming. He wanted to stick around. A little smile crossed his lips. "No, go ahead, take all the time you need." He turned to Paresi. "Why don't I buy you a cup of coffee before you leave."

Paresi looked at Star. For a moment he felt sorry for Couchure, but he wouldn't miss this for gold.

"Yeah, thanks, Cap'n." He indicated the door. "After you." He turned to Star and grinned. "I'll send Detective Couchure right in."

"Thank you," she said.

"The lieutenant wants to see you," Paresi said to Couchure as they passed his desk. "God be with you." He made the sign of the cross.

Lewis snickered.

The young man looked terrified. He walked slowly toward Lewis's office.

Captain Lewis poured two mugs of coffee and handed one to Paresi. "I'd give my left nut to hear what she's telling him."

Paresi took a sip of the coffee and put the mug on his desk. He sat down, running his hands through his hair and over his unshaven face. "Well, you can bet it ain't 'Have a nice day.'"

The two men laughed.

"You know, if I keep drinking coffee, I could probably last all day," Paresi said.

Lewis shook his head. "Naw, go on home, get some sleep."

"You sure?"

"Yeah."

"Tell Star I'm just gonna grab a shower and take a nap. I'll be back, maybe I'll crash on her couch tonight."

Lewis drained his mug. "I'll tell her."

Just then Star walked out of the office, leaving Couchure slumped in a chair in front of Lewis's desk.

"Hey," Paresi yawned. He stretched and popped his knuckles. "I was just telling the cap'n to tell you, I'll be back."

"No need," she said. "Get some rest."

"I'm gonna just grab a shower and sleep for a couple of hours." He rubbed his eyes and yawned again.

She sat down. "Not necessary, I'll be fine."

"We can discuss that when I get back." He stood, picked up his jacket and patted the pockets. "I can't find my keys."

"On your desk." She pointed at them.

"Oh yeah." He picked up his car keys. "So, you do your do?"

"Yes, Lieutenant, may I have my office now?" Lewis grinned.

Star looked over her shoulder. "You might want to give Detective Couchure a few minutes. He just found out he's being transferred to patrol duty, on the midnight-to-eight shift."

Lewis's eyes twinkled. "Any route in particular?"

"I thought he'd be very effective in the Remington Street area," she said.

Lewis and Paresi exchanged grins. Lewis ran a hand around his jaw. "Remington Street, huh, the area behind the dump?"

"That's the one."

"He's gonna ride that beat?" Paresi asked.

"Not exactly. We've been talking about reviving the foot patrol, and Detective Couchure has graciously volunteered to be an example for the department."

Paresi laughed and high-fived her.

Lewis struggled to keep a straight face. "Very good, Lieutenant."

"Thank you, sir." Star picked up the phone and dialed Electric City.

Jerry Auster was on a break when he heard the page. He was in the back room, trying to figure out how to get past that silent alarm setup in the brownstone.

He knew that morning, when he checked the door and windows, that there was a system, which is why he didn't touch anything. He'd fiddled with some motion detectors and electric eye systems in the store, before it opened, to see if he could rig something that would disable the alarm. So far, he hadn't been able to come up with anything.

"Jerry Auster, telephone, Jerry Auster, telephone."

He hated the sound of Louisa Morales's voice over the page system. Why did they let a spic do the paging? It didn't sound good to hear that chu-chu frito accent all over the store. He went to the phone on the counter.

"Jerry Auster."

"Hi, Jerry, it's Janine."

"Hello." He said, his voice cool.

Star picked up on his tone. "Sorry to bother you if you're busy, but I was wondering if maybe you could come back to my place tomorrow so that we can finish checking it out. You know, for speaker locations and all that."

He'd known she would call, because she wanted him, but

he had to play cagey, yet let her know he wouldn't be shoved around again.

"I don't know, Janine. I mean, I had to take time off yesterday to go out there, and even though he wants the sale, my boss may not let me do it again, since I didn't come back with an order."

She tightened her grip on the receiver. "I'm really sorry about that. I didn't expect the handyman to be here, and you know how those things are. If I was rude, I apologize."

She waited. He said nothing.

"I'd really like to get this settled, it's terrible being here without music. Would you like me to talk to your supervisor and explain what happened?"

"No, that won't be necessary." He tried to sound like his feelings were hurt. "I guess I can get him to let me come back." Inside, he was turning cartwheels.

"I tell you what," she said impulsively, "to make up for yesterday, why don't you let me take you to lunch?"

"What?" He couldn't believe this. She was really hot for him.

"Lunch, today, my treat, what do you say?"

"Uh, okay, if you want."

"Perfect. I'll pick you up at noon, and maybe if you have time, I'll come back and listen to some of the units you showed me the other day."

"Great, I'll see you at noon." He hung up.

Star stood holding the receiver, listening to the hum of the line. She had done the right thing, she was losing him, she had to make him trust her again. She looked at her watch. She didn't dare wake Paresi. She hung up the phone.

I can handle this, she said to herself. He's not going to try anything in public. She looked around the squad room. Rescovich was the only detective in sight. "I'm safer on my own," she muttered. "I don't need backup, I can do this, just go somewhere with lots of people, I'll be fine." She reached for the phone book.

—

Jerry Auster stood near the customer service desk. He had a clear view of the lot outside the store. He saw her behind the wheel of a white Mercedes as she drove in. He quickly walked to the back of the store.

Star parked the car and got out. She was nervous. She was violating a sacred rule, *never* move without backup. She knew Lewis would have her scalp if he knew, but she was losing Auster, she had to do this. She took several deep breaths as she walked toward the front door. Once inside, she stood for a few moments looking around.

The place was so vast, she'd never find him. She decided to head to the service desk and have him paged.

Leander Poteet watched her walk by. She was wearing a white, shirtwaist dress with epaulets. The dress was thin and semitransparent. It was long, almost to her ankles. He could see the delicate shoulder straps and lacy outline of her white, full-length undergarment. As he watched, Jerry Auster came out from one of the aisles and intercepted her.

"Hey, Lee, I'm out to lunch," he said as they walked past Poteet. She looked at him, nodded and smiled.

"Yeah, Jer, no problem. Have a good one."

Jerry Auster put his arm around Star's waist. "I will."

27

Maureen had taken a broom and swept the key from under the cabinet. After much effort it was in her hand. She put it in the lock and turned the key, entering Jerry's studio.

She hit the light switch in the corner, and was amazed. The place was so neat. He was like a pig upstairs. Down here you could eat off the floor. She stood in the center of the room, looking at the shelves stacked with boxes of paper, film, and about a million years worth of photography magazines and books.

She looked closer. The magazines were arranged in chronological order. Did something magical happen to Jerry when he came into this room, something that changed him from Oscar Madison to Felix Unger when he crossed the threshold?

She looked at some of the books he had on the shelves. All names she didn't recognize. She pulled down one book called *Harry Callahan: Color.* She expected to see pictures of Clint Eastwood in the movie *Dirty Harry*, but soon realized that Harry Callahan was the real name of a very talented photographer.

The book was in a slipcase. It must have cost a fortune, and she didn't even know he had it. She put it back and wandered around, not touching anything, just looking.

It was like some kind of alternate world down here. He had a draftsman's table, with a high stool, and right next to it another long table, which was bare except for a strange-looking box with a fluorescent top. She remembered that was called a light box, and next to it was a circular domed piece of glass with a lens encased in a black plastic top. Jerry called that a loupe. It was really just a magnifying glass. He used to let her use one to look at the sheets of photos he'd developed from their sessions.

He thought he was giving her some kind of honor when he let her look through the glass and choose which proofs he would print.

She hated looking at those pictures. She walked around the room in a tight circle. The door to her left must be his darkroom, she thought. She put her hand on the knob and turned. It was unlocked, but she decided not to go in, just in case he was working on something. She couldn't take the chance of ruining anything.

He even had that old hunk of junk reclining chair in here.

The chair made her smile. It had belonged to Jerry's uncle Will, and Jerry had it in his first apartment, before they were married.

She stroked the worn leather and let it bring back memories. They used to make love in that chair. She smiled, remembering how they couldn't keep their hands off each other in the beginning.

A tall, four-drawer file cabinet stood next to the chair. She pulled open the top drawer. There were rows and rows of neat manila folders. She opened one, and saw the pictures.

The folders were full of photos of her from their early years together. She sat down in the chair, looking through them.

She looked at the young, slim blonde who smiled up at her from another lifetime. She picked up another picture, a nude, taken before she got pregnant. Tears filled her eyes.

The woman in the photographs sat proudly, showing high, firm breasts, slim hips, and long, pretty legs. She closed the file and put it back; she couldn't look anymore. She shoved the drawer shut and sat back in the chair, letting the memories pour over her as she cried.

Star pulled up in front of Electric City and turned to Jerry Auster. "I'm glad you came for lunch, I had a good time."

"So did I," he said. "I've never been to Leslie's before. It's a great place."

She smiled. "I like the garden room, it's so pretty. It makes lunch a festive occasion." She touched his hand. "Of course, the company really made the day." She had him back. She congratulated herself on her decision to go it alone.

He stared into her eyes. Yesterday had been just a warm-up. He bet she could wring out her panties along about now. All through lunch she'd avoided looking at him. He knew why. She couldn't hide anything from him, she would've jumped him at the table if he'd said the word.

He covered her hand with his, slowly stroking her skin with one finger. "We haven't talked about yesterday," he said softly. He turned her hand over and laced her fingers with his own. She could feel the heat of his palm pressed against hers.

"I know. I don't know what came over me," Star said. "I don't usually behave like that." He brought her hand to his lips and kissed it. Star felt chills racing through her.

"Neither do I, but I couldn't help myself." He stared into her eyes. "I want you, Janine, you're all I think about."

Star looked around the parking lot. "I think about you too, but this isn't the place to discuss it. Maybe we can talk when you come over."

He kissed her palm. "Just talk?"

She didn't answer. She smiled at him. "Listen, you've got to get back to work, I've kept you far too long as it is."

"You're right." He squeezed her hand. "We'll work this out privately." He opened the car door. "Are you in a rush?" he asked.

At the thought of spending more time with him, Star felt a flush creeping through her body. "I really didn't expect to take so long for lunch, and I've got somewhere to go, but I can take a few minutes." She let concern show in her face. "You're not in any trouble, are you? I haven't kept you too long?"

"No, as long as I'm with a customer, it's okay. I just

thought maybe you might want to take some of the catalogs with you, so you can kind of visualize what you want. You know, look at them against your furniture and all that."

"Good idea."

She turned off the engine. They got out of the car and headed into the store. She walked with him into the listening room and he handed her a bunch of catalogs and booklets. "Thanks." She squeezed his hand. "I'll see you tomorrow."

He walked her to the front of the store and watched her as she got into her car and drove off. On his way back down the aisle, he ran into Leander.

"So how was lunch, killer?" Leander grinned at him.

"Delicious." Jerry licked his lips and winked. "Very tasty."

"You a lucky dude, man. That's a fine-looking woman."

"That she is," someone said from behind them.

They turned to see Jerry Beacham standing there.

"Hey J.B., what are you doing here?" Jerry slapped him on the shoulder.

"Careful, I'm still in pain here."

Jerry Auster looked at the canvas sling wrapped around Beacham's shoulder. "I'm sorry." He turned to Leander Poteet. "Lee, this is Jerry Beacham, you're taking his place."

Leander stuck out his hand. Jerry Beacham shook with his left. "Hey man, nice to meet you."

"Nice to meet you." Beacham adjusted his shoulder sling.

"So, you coming back, or what?" Auster asked.

"Not for a while." He turned to Leander Poteet. "I hope you like it here. The doctor says I'm gonna be off for at least another two months."

"I'm sorry to hear that," Leander said, "but I am enjoying it here, it's different from Victor Street."

"We borrowed him from the Victor Street store," Jerry Auster said. "So, tell me, if you're not coming back, what are you doing here?"

"I came to pick up my check. Somebody upstairs screwed up and didn't mail it. I had to see the doctor, and he's just a few blocks down, so I decided to come in."

"Well, it's good to see you, man."

"Thanks. I saw you in the listening room a few minutes ago with that pretty lady. Still up to your old tricks?"

"What tricks, she's a customer. She's doing a central stereo unit for her place."

"Yeah? Well, I guess the police department pays better than I thought!"

"What?"

"The police department. Treat that lady right, man, or she'll lock you up. She's a cop."

Leander Poteet hooted with laughter. "Man, that honey dip can lock me up anytime. The thought of her with handcuffs makes my shorts stand. That is one fine woman!"

He and Jerry Beacham laughed heartily. Jerry Auster stood frozen, all the color drained from his face.

"How do you know she's a cop?" he asked.

"Because she interviewed me."

"For what?"

"A while back, one of my customers got killed. Turns out that customer was one of a bunch of black women that have been turning up dead lately."

"Yeah, I remember hearing about those killings," Leander said. "They just found somebody else a couple of weeks ago, a lawyer or something, she had a fancy address over in Becker Condos. I remember that one, because they showed her picture on TV. She was beautiful."

"Right," Jerry Beacham continued. "About two, maybe three months ago, this really cute little black girl bought a TV from me. She was cute as a button, with great tits. I tell you, man, I almost asked her out." He looked at Leander. "No offense, bro."

"None taken, my brother," Leander said. "A fine woman is a fine woman."

"Right," Jerry Beacham agreed. "Anyway, I guess it was the same night she bought the TV, somebody killed her. The cops came to talk to me because I sold her the set."

"Why did they come here, how did they find you?" Jerry Auster asked.

"They found her sales slip or something and traced it here. They talked to me and Howard. I remember I was really nervous, and that lady's eyes just calmed me right down. She's got dynamite eyes."

"We never heard anything about any investigation," Auster said.

"Right, since they only wanted to talk to me, Howard said to keep it quiet, and frankly, it's not the kind of thing you want to tell your fellow workers, you know? That somebody thought you could've killed a woman." Jerry Beacham rubbed his shoulder. "It's not a good thing."

"No, I guess not. Do you remember her name?" Jerry Auster's voice was cold.

"Yeah, Alma Johnson. She bought a twenty-three-hundred-dollar big-screen TV and paid cash."

"Not the customer, the cop."

"Don't you know?" Jerry Beacham teased. "It looks to me like you're out to sell her a lot of equipment, and you don't know her name? You're slipping, Jerry boy."

Auster's eyes narrowed. "I want to be sure you've got the right woman. You could be mistaken."

"No mistake, she's got a great name." Beacham's mouth split into a wide, oafish grin. "She gave me her card, and I keep it by my bed, just in case I have an emergency in the middle of the night, you know?" He elbowed Auster.

"What's her name?"

"Duvall, Starletta Duvall. Star, you know, Star, like in star bright."

"Starletta Duvall," Leander crowed. "Star light, Star bright, make my wish come true tonight." He made a pumping motion with his arm. "For real!"

The two of them laughed.

"Knowing this guy," Jerry Beacham pointed to Auster, "she better have a fat wallet, because when he turns on the charm, it's gonna cost her."

Jerry Auster stared straight ahead. "Count on it."

28

Jerry Auster left Leander Poteet and Jerry Beacham heehawing over Star and went directly to the men's room. He splashed cold water on his face and stood with a death grip on the sink, his body rocking with the waves of rage washing over him.

"I don't fucking believe this! A goddamned cop." He glared at his reflection.

"They wanna play with me? Fucking assholes!" He smiled at himself. "I got moves they can't even imagine. Surprise, cunt, the joke is going to be on you."

Star heard the phone ringing when she got out of the car. She ran up the stairs, opened the door, and caught it on the last ring.

"Hello."

"Hi, Janine."

"Jerry?"

"Yeah, you sound out of breath, did I interrupt something?"

"No, I was outside. I ran in to catch the phone."

He could picture her looking so clean and pure in that white dress. A little blood would add just the right touch.

"I wanted to thank you again for lunch today, and to tell you that I'm sorry, but I'm going to have to cancel tomorrow."

"Oh, that's too bad, is something wrong?"

"Yes, it's my wife."

"I didn't know you were married," she lied.

"Don't let it bother you, it's not made in heaven or anything. In fact, we're probably going to separate." He gripped the phone. "Anyway, she's not feeling well, so I'm going to have to look after her for a few days, you understand?"

"Yes, I do, I hope she's going to be all right."

"I'm sure she'll be fine, it's probably just a virus." He lowered his voice, and spoke in a soft whisper. "I hope this doesn't change things, I still want to be with you. I think about it all the time."

His voice was seductive and frightening to her.

"I'm a big girl, nothing's changed. I want to be with you too." She closed her eyes, alarmed at the truth in her words.

Jerry gritted his teeth so hard a pain shot through his jaw. "Good. It makes me feel better knowing we want the same thing." He drew a deep breath, his voice soft in her ear. "I'm touching you, can you feel me?"

"Yes." Star's mind was screaming. God help her, she could.

Jerry Auster smiled. "I'll call you in a few days."

"I'll be waiting."

She hung up and sat down on the sofa, wrapping her arms around her body, trying to stop the shaking. He got to her. She could still hear that voice, soft, whispery, sending flames through her.

"You're doing stupid things, get a grip," she said out loud. She stood up. He had changed since lunch. Something was wrong. Maybe he *was* telling her the truth. If his wife was really ill, he'd be concerned, wouldn't he? She paced in front of the sofa. It was logical he'd be distracted, distant. Still, the things he'd said. . .

Jake wound himself around her ankles. She picked him up and hugged him.

"Oh Jake, I've got a feeling, a really bad feeling."

He stood in the office holding the phone receiver tightly in his hand, listening to the buzz of the disconnected line. He put the receiver in the cradle and leaned on the phone, stopping himself from tearing the fucking thing out of the wall.

Louisa Morales hadn't liked the way he looked when he came upstairs and asked her to do a credit check, and she liked it even less now. She walked up to him and handed him the computer printout. His eyes made her blood run cold.

"Thanks." He took the paper and turned his back to her.

She couldn't see why every woman in the place was turned on by him. True, he was great-looking, but he had El Diablo in him. She saw it in his eyes. They were evil, cold and dead as a snake.

"Do you need anything else?" she asked him.

"No." He waved her way. "Thanks."

She went back to her desk.

Jerry sat down and read Starletta Duvall's credit report. He took a pen and paper from the desk and wrote down her phone number and address. He could hardly wait for quitting time.

Paresi answered the phone on the tenth ring. "Yeah?"

"Hi, it's me."

He sat up in bed. "Star, what time is it?" His mouth felt like somebody had been storing cotton in it.

"It's after four."

He looked at the clock on his nightstand. "Jeez, I slept the day away."

"It's okay, you needed it."

"What's up, did something happen?"

"I set him up to come by tomorrow, and he just called and canceled."

"Did he give a good reason?"

"He said his wife is sick."

"She probably ate Nebraska."

"What?"

"Never mind. Are you at the brownstone?"

"Yeah."

"I'm coming over."

"It's okay, you don't have to, I just wanted to let you know what happened. I'm just gonna take a shower and watch some television."

"You sure you don't need me?"

"Positive, go back to sleep, you're tired. I'll see you tomorrow."

"If you're sure."

"I'm fine, get some rest."

"I can sleep on your couch."

"You're too tall for both my couches."

"Then I'll bunk with you."

"Maybe in your next life." She grinned. "Go back to sleep."

"All right, but call me if you need me."

"Promise." She hung up the phone and picked up her cat. "Well, sweetie pie, it's just us."

She carried Jake into the kitchen and set him on the floor. He made figure eights between her ankles as she pulled a can of cat food from the cupboard, opened it, and spooned some into his dish. She ran fresh water into the other dish, and opened the freezer. She plucked an ice cube out of the ice bin and plopped it into the water.

"I spoil you silly," she said, putting the dishes on the floor. She watched him lick the ice and then eat.

29

The sun had gone down and a pink and purple twilight hung over the city as Jerry Auster drove down Salisbury Road. He looked at the piece of paper in his hand.

He said out loud, "Right side of the street, 3065."

Star's house sat at the end of the block, a piece of corner property. He pulled up in front of it and parked his car.

"Nice place." He looked at the neat, two-story red brick house with white shutters. He got out and walked up the flagstone walkway, whistling as he took the three steps onto the porch.

In the fading light, he could just make out the name Duvall on a brass plaque on the front door. He tried looking through one of the two slim glass panels on either side of the door, but it was too dark to see anything but the lacy pattern of the custom-made curtains.

He went back down the walkway and around to the side of the house. Near the back was an eight-foot wooden fence. Between the fence and the side of the house there was about a four-inch opening. He bent over and squinted, making it possible for him to dimly see a group of plants and some flowers.

"Nice garden, a good place for burying things."

There were no neighbors on this side of the house. Beyond the wooden fence there was a tree-filled lot, but no house. Jerry walked, whistling, around the fence. It joined with another fence, which was smaller and lower. He looked over it and saw the trash can area. By stretching his upper body, he could also see more of the garden and her patio.

With no effort, he jumped the smaller fence and found

himself face-to-face with a latticework wood door that closed off her private yard from the trash can area.

He looked at the lock.

"Cops. Wouldn't you think she'd spring for a good one?"

He opened his wallet and pulled out a credit card. He inserted the card between the latch and the plate and wiggled it. The door opened with a soft click.

Auster walked around her yard, taking in the neat rows of flowers and the potted plants. She probably had a gardener to tend the place, he thought. It looked too big for somebody with her schedule to take care of alone.

He walked up to the sliding glass door facing the patio. He didn't touch it, but knew there was a lock on the inside bottom ledge. No problem. He knew he could pop that with his eyes closed.

He knew all about sliding glass doors. When he and Maureen were first married, they had one, and she was forever losing the key.

"Piece of cake." He backed up, looking up at her windows.

"All locked down tight, but I know the magic word." He walked around the side of the house, shielded by the fence. He looked through a window, and could dimly see into the dining room and beyond that a little of the kitchen.

"Very nice." When he finished his tour, he let himself out through the latticed door, which he again locked behind him.

She was going to have to come home soon. Once the pigs figured out he wasn't going to play, they'd regroup, and she'd more than likely come back here, because after all, there's no place like home.

He walked back to his car, looking up and down the street. No sign of life, nobody looking out the window. Great, a neighborhood where people actually minded their own business.

He started the engine, and laughed all the way home.

30

Jerry Auster didn't call Star, and every attempt she made to contact him was met by a stone wall. Whenever she phoned, she'd be put on hold for a few minutes, only to hear the voice of a stranger asking who was calling. When she said "Janine Bohannon," she found herself holding again, only to be told by the same unfamiliar voice that Jerry Auster was unavailable. After over a week of this treatment, Star decided it was time to call off the sting.

She and Paresi sat in Lewis's office as Lewis explained to the chief why they were backing off. He finally hung up the phone.

"He's less than thrilled," Lewis said.

"I understand." Star looked down at the floor.

"It's not her fault, Cap'n, if he's cooled off," Paresi said.

"I know." Captain Lewis leaned back in his chair. "Any idea of where to go next?" he asked Star.

"I don't know. I can't even figure out why he went cold. He was ripe, ready to fall, I know it, and boom, he's frozen!"

"Do you think he's on to you?" Lewis asked.

"Not a chance." Star shook her head. "Something else got to him. Maybe he really is looking after a sick wife."

"But he's been at work," Lewis said.

"I know, still, maybe he's worried, preoccupied about her."

Paresi spoke up. "I think we oughtta just fall back and regroup."

"I agree," Star said. "Let's come at it from another angle. Maybe I should actually buy something, so that I can go in and talk with him. You know, give him the feeling that I'm on the level."

Lewis rocked back in his chair. "When a sting goes cold like this, it usually means the mark is on to us."

"But how could he know? Anybody who could identify me is out of the picture," Star said.

"I know." Lewis sighed. "But we have to take that possibility into consideration before planning our next move."

"Captain, would you mind if while we're planning I took some time at home?" Star asked. "I like the brownstone, but I miss sleeping in my own bed."

Lewis waved his hand. "It's okay, in fact, why don't you two get out of here early today. I need some time to figure out which way we're going, and both of you've earned time off."

"Thanks, Captain." She got up. Paresi stood next to her. "C'mon, Paresi, help me take some of my things home."

31

Jerry liked the look of her house in the daylight. He'd been coming over at night, getting the feel of it. Today he was going to draw the final plan. He had to see what he was doing. He drove his Toyota down to the end of the street, in front of the vacant lot, and got out.

He was wearing his navy-blue jumpsuit, a souvenir of a summer's work at the power plant years ago. It made him look like a city worker or a garbage collector, he didn't much care which. He carried a bright orange metal tool case and whistled as he walked around to the rear of her property. Once he jumped the fence and popped the lock of the latticed door, he was in.

The house didn't appear the same. It was still locked up tight, but it seemed different. He hadn't seen any cars in the driveway or any sign of life when he cruised by, but the lawn looked recently mowed, and there was some moisture around several of the potted plants, so the gardener must have come. It didn't worry him.

He walked onto the patio and squatted down beside the plate-glass door. He couldn't see inside. He figured the door opened up into the dining room, because if the curtains were open, you'd have a direct view of the patio and garden. Maybe she liked to open the doors and let the sun in on her days off. She probably liked sitting out here eating or reading. She looked like a reader.

As he squatted there, a movement of the curtains caught his eye. He leaned closer to the glass. The curtain stirred again, and in the left corner of the window he saw the bright green inquisitive eyes set in the gray and white feline face. He smiled at the cat.

"Hello boy, good to see you again. That must mean your mommy is back."

Jake pressed his nose against the window glass. He couldn't smell the being outside, but the hairs on his back stood up.

"Kitty, kitty." Jerry grinned, bringing his finger close to the glass but not touching it. "What a big bruiser you are. She must love you to take such good care of you."

The cat sniffed at the glass.

"Yeah, you want to come to old Jerry, don't you? Don't worry, kitty, you and I are gonna be real good friends. I've got special plans for you."

Inside the house, Jake tired of the game, yawned, and turned away. The curtain once again fell into place.

Jerry walked around to the side of the house, still shielded by the fence, and peered into the ground floor windows. He could see a brown cardboard box sitting on a counter in the kitchen. Yeah, she was back.

He went around to the rear again and stepped back to gauge which room might be her bedroom on the second floor. It didn't matter which room she slept in. He knew the layout of the house. Most of these places built in the sixties were the same. He could get in and find her with no problem. He went back to the sliding glass door and kneeled down, opening his toolbox.

The sound of someone coming down the back walkway stopped him cold. He froze, even though he couldn't possibly be seen from the street.

The footsteps came closer. It sounded like they were headed for the yard. He jumped up, grabbed his toolbox and plastered himself against the far side of the fence, where he couldn't be seen even from the latticed door. He held his breath.

"I'm sure I left them here." He heard a man's voice.

"Ms. Duvall would have put them out here if you did,"

another man's voice chimed in. There was the sound of the cans being moved.

"You're right, I don't see them." The latticed door rattled.

"I forgot my keys," the man said. There was a pause and he spoke again. "I don't see them anywhere. How could I lose my shears, what kind of a gardener leaves his shears laying around?"

"Your kind," the second man said. "First you forget the shears, then you forget the keys, you got CRS syndrome."

"What's that?"

"Can't Remember Shit!"

The two men burst out laughing.

"You got Alzheimer's and don't you forget it! C'mon, I got an extra pair of shears in the truck, you can use them until we find yours."

Jerry stood listening as the two men went back up the walkway. He closed his eyes, his heart racing. The sound of the truck engine starting allowed him to breathe again. He'd been so into his work, he hadn't heard them arrive.

"You're getting old, Jer," he said to himself. "Nobody is supposed to sneak up on you like that." He went back to the window and again opened his toolbox.

Maureen put the dinner leftovers away. Jerry had been acting so strangely. He ran out as soon as he came home. She didn't mind, because she wanted to go back downstairs. Even though the pictures she found made her sad, they also took her back to a time when she felt good, when things were right between them.

She wiped the table, shook out the dishcloth and hung it up. He was more than likely gone for the night, so why not? She fished the key out of her pocket and went downstairs.

She was sitting in his chair, looking at the photographs, when she heard his car in the driveway.

"Oh Jesus!"

She jumped up and stuffed the file folder back into the

cabinet. She looked around, making sure nothing was disturbed, and ran out, slamming the door. She was halfway up the stairs when he walked into the kitchen.

"Hi, sweetie." She tried to sound cheerful. She'd been running. She was sweating.

"What were you doing downstairs?"

Maureen had been cursed with what her mother called an open face. The kind of face that couldn't lie. She looked over Jerry's head, her eyes darting back and forth like the eyes in one of those silly cat clocks.

"I just put something in the dryer."

He tilted his head toward the basement. "I don't hear it running."

Rivulets of sweat inched down her waist.

"I'm out of fabric softener sheets. I came up to get some."

He stood in front of her, his eyes boring into hers.

She wanted to disappear. She stood there, silently praying. "I know I've got some up here." She tried to squirm past him.

He stood solid, letting her rub against him as she tried to get around him. She opened the cabinet beneath the sink.

"Here, I knew I had some." She pulled a box of softener sheets out. "I always keep one up here, just in case I run out downstairs."

He didn't speak. He just looked at her.

"If you want something, this can wait, I mean I can get whatever you need, honey."

"I need some fresh clothes." His eyes never left hers. "I'm going out."

"Right away."

When he disappeared into the bathroom, she sank into a kitchen chair, tears pouring down her face. She clapped her hand over her mouth and tried not to make a sound.

Vee and Star drove up in the Mercedes and parked in her driveway. "How long are they going to let you keep this car?" Vee asked as she got out.

"As long as it takes, I guess." Star pushed the button on the remote door lock in her hand, causing all the locks to click in place.

"I could really get used to this," Vee said.

"I noticed . . ." Star laughed. ". . . when you were profilin' to the brothers at the light."

Vee laughed. "Hey, they was peepin' the Benz. I just thought I should look like I belonged in it."

"Well, you carried it off. I was beginning to feel like I was drivin' Miss Vee!"

"Next time, wear your cap."

"Yezzum." Star bowed her head. "Lawsy me, I sho' will."

Laughing, they went inside the house. Jake came running up to Vee.

"Get him away from me." She backed up, trying to keep the cat away from her feet.

"Now, you know he's only saying hello. He's just trying to be friendly to his auntie Vee." Star picked up the cat, cuddling him. "He's just trying to say 'I wuv you Auntie Vee.'"

Jake purred and sniffed in Vee's direction.

"If he don't get out of my face, I'm gonna snatch at least two of his lives!"

Star laughed and put Jake down. "Don't worry, sweetie, she loves you, she just doesn't want me to know."

Jake meowed and ran off into the kitchen.

"He's hungry."

"He's not the only one," Vee said. "But I know from experience, there is no food in this house."

"Some folks just think they know everything. You're wrong."

Star beckoned her to follow. "Dr. Grant came over last night, and he, my dear, is quite a chef."

"From the way he looks, I bet he's quite 'A' everything!" Vee said, raising an eyebrow.

"I don't know about that," Star grinned, "but he certainly makes a marvelous chicken curry, and I have some left." She pulled a dish out of the refrigerator and set it on the counter. "And," she leaned in again, "I even have rice, basmati rice."

"What kind of rice?" Vee asked.

"Basmati."

"What in the world is basmati rice?

"You're asking me? He made it. You know the only rice I use is Uncle Ben's, and I only buy it because it's got an old black man on the box."

Vee burst out laughing. "If Uncle Ben knew how you murdered his rice, he'd change his name and put the back of his head on the box."

"All right, all right, so I can't make rice. This will be easy, all I have to do is put it in the microwave."

"Here." Vee took the dishes. "Let me heat it up, I'm too hungry to hear you say oops!"

"Then I'll fix the salad."

"Don't tell me he taught you to make salad!" Vee took the glass cover off the curried chicken and sniffed it. "Lord this smells good." She put the cover back and set the dish in the microwave, programming it for five minutes at half power.

Star looked over her shoulder. "How do you do that? I can't figure out for the life of me how to make it cook on half power."

"Honey, you can't figure out how to get the door open, so why am I not surprised?"

Star stuck out her tongue and opened the refrigerator. She pulled two mesh plastic bags from the crisper; one filled with salad greens and the other with chopped vegetables.

Vee took the bags. "Is this the way you make a salad?"

"Well, actually, he made it last night. All I have to do is put it in a bowl, pour some dressing on it, and toss it."

"Lord, honey, please. Did he tuck you in too?"

"No, but I seriously thought about tucking him in."

They cracked up.

By the time the food was ready, Star had fed Jake, opened a bottle of white zinfandel and filled their glasses. They sat at the kitchen table, barefoot, eating, drinking, and laughing.

The cat curled up under Star's chair, licking his paws.

"Mmmmph, the boy can cook." Vee spooned more chicken and rice on her plate.

"Didn't I tell you?"

"Mmmm-hmm," Vee said. She poured herself more wine. "So, he's been over here making curry, what *else* is he making?"

"My acquaintance." Star grinned. "All he's getting is the pleasure of my company."

He stood outside the window, looking in. The kitchen curtains were open, just a bit. He couldn't hear what they were saying, but they were certainly having a good time. He watched her sitting with her friend, the two of them laughing.

"Enjoy yourself," he whispered. "Have a good time. I know I will."

32

Another week passed. There had been nothing from Auster. In an effort to keep the lines open, Star had called him several times. He refused to speak to her, and never responded to the messages. She felt like something had gone out of her. Finally she conceded the sting was dead.

Even then she couldn't let go. She'd driven past the store several times, trying to catch a glimpse of him. She told herself that it was because of the job, but her heart knew better.

After a week of sleepless nights, she and Paresi sat in Lewis's office.

"We've hit the wall on this one," Lewis said. "I can't think of a single way to get him back."

"You're right," Star agreed. "He's cold as ice, totally shut down."

"What happened?"

"I don't have a clue. I can't figure out how he made me, but either I've done something to really turn him off or I'm made."

"No leaks?" Paresi asked.

"Not from this office," Lewis said. "These guys know how a sting works, none of them would slip."

"How about Couchure?" Paresi asked.

"He's green, not stupid," Lewis said. "Besides, where he's walking, there's nobody to talk to but the rats." He pulled off his glasses and rubbed his eyes. "He's on to us, there's nothing we can do. The only good thing is that we've still got all the marbles on our side."

"I don't know, Cap'n," Paresi said. "Looks to me like he's got some marbles we don't even know about."

"Then we'll find them." Lewis turned to Star. "You and Paresi take it easy for a couple of days. We'll meet again at the end of the week, after everybody's had a chance to think."

"We've already sat on this for nearly two weeks," Star said. "Suppose while we're thinking, he kills somebody else?"

"Not hardly. If he knows we're on to him, he's not gonna take that chance." Lewis pointed to the door. "Go home, both of you."

33

Jerry stood in his basement sanctuary, filling his camera bag for another shoot. He reached up on the shelf to take down a couple of boxes of Neopan. As he dropped the film into the bag he saw the tip of a plastic folder sticking out under the bottom shelf of the wall unit. He picked it up. It was from his box of transparent covers. He always kept a few stuck in the folders with his pictures, so when he got ready to add them to his notebook, he wouldn't have to search for them.

He turned and looked at the file cabinet. He opened the top drawer. Everything seemed fine, but something wasn't right. He stood looking down at the drawer.

One file folder stuck out slightly from the others. He pulled it out and opened it. An old shot of Maureen, nude, lay on top. He looked through them. It had been a long time since he'd looked at these, and he couldn't be sure, but they seemed out of order. He had arranged them by semi-nude, full nude, and some with spread legs. They weren't the way he'd left them.

He closed the file and put it back in the drawer. As he shut it, he looked around the room. His photography books looked different, and one, *Harry Callahan: Color,* had been put on the shelf with the open end of the slipcover facing out. He never stored slipcased books like that. He always put them in title side out.

Maureen.

She'd covered her tracks pretty well, but still his things had been moved. Nobody came in this room; it was his place, and she'd been snooping in it.

In the darkroom, everything seemed to be in place. It

looked as if she didn't have the guts to go in there, but she had been in here, touching his private things.

The rage returned. He shook the top drawer of the file cabinet in the dark room. It was firmly locked. He reached in the small space between the cabinet and the wall. The key was still there, on the hook. By the time he walked upstairs, he could literally see blood.

Vee called about seven and tried to coax her out for pizza and a trip to a new blues club. She begged off, saying she was tired, but the truth was she just needed to be alone. Her mind felt like an egg in a blender. Jerry Auster's coldness hurt her on some level she didn't even want to think about.

She thought about calling Mitchell, then remembered he was out of town, at a Forensic Sciences Conference.

"Pull yourself together, Scarlett, deal with this," she said out loud.

Jake lay on the foot of the bed watching her.

"All right, so I'm talking to myself," she said to the cat. "Maybe I should have gone for a pizza. I obviously need some companionship about now."

The cat meowed.

She smiled. "Another country heard from." She rubbed his ears and chin. "Listen to you purr. At least *you're* happy."

Star reached for the remote control and turned on the TV. She stumbled onto the last few episodes of an "I Love Lucy" marathon on the nostalgia channel. When it was over, she still felt keyed up.

She put a videotape of *Mildred Pierce* in the VCR and watched Joan Crawford barging through the tearjerker, chewing both scenery and actors equally. By the end, she felt like she'd been in a fight.

She looked at the clock. It was nearly one in the morning. Still unable to sleep, she went downstairs, trailed by Jake, and found the latest issue of *Vanity Fair* magazine; there was a story she wanted to read. She went to the kitchen, grabbed a handful of chocolate chip cookies, wrapped them in a napkin and went back upstairs.

The article didn't hold her interest. She ate the last cookie, brushed the crumbs off her nightshirt, and dropped the magazine on the night table near her bed, next to the CD player. She reached for her earphones.

There were several CDs on the bookcase headboard. She picked up a couple, loaded the player, then fiddled with the remote until she had the lineup she wanted. She put on the earphones and turned off the lamp, lying back with the sound of Luther Vandross filling her head, crowding out the dark thoughts of Jerry Auster.

Closing her eyes, she tried to picture Mitchell Grant, but he kept turning into Jerry Auster.

She still hadn't told Vee about what happened the day Auster came to the brownstone, and she'd sworn Paresi to secrecy.

She was ashamed and frightened of what the man unleashed in her. It wasn't just the hunger of a woman a long time without a man, it was something else, something deeper and darker. She shook her head; she didn't want to think about it, or him.

The cat moved close to her, rolled himself into a ball and settled in, falling asleep instantly. She stroked his head, saying, "I wish I could do that."

This house, which she'd lived in most of her life, seemed almost alien to her. Though she'd been home awhile, she was still having trouble getting to sleep.

Even Mitchell Grant and his famous hot cocoa with brandy and whipped cream couldn't cure her insomnia. He had teased her, before he left, saying he'd gladly send her tapes of the speeches from the conference, calling them sure-fire cures for insomnia.

Mitchell. She smiled to herself. She concentrated, bringing his face into focus in her mind. Who would have ever thought he'd be so sweet and so funny?

She thought of her conversation with Vee over dinner a

couple of weeks before. He'd probably laugh if he knew how they'd talked about him.

She stretched, her eyes still closed. Luther's voice had her floating. She turned over, opened her eyes and looked at the clock. It was nearly half past two. Over an hour had passed, and she was no closer to sleep than before. She sat up, took off the headphones and turned on the lamp.

"God, I wish I could sleep," she said out loud.

"I know a good way to tire you out."

He was sitting across the room on the antique love seat she'd bought at a flea market, naked to the waist, barefoot, and smiling, a .357 Magnum in his right hand. Jerry Auster stood up and walked to the foot of her bed.

"Would you like me to help you get to sleep?"

The television set in the Auster living room played to an empty couch. Maureen Auster was downstairs, in Jerry's studio. He had dragged her down there and shown her exactly what she wanted to see.

Maureen had screamed and fought her husband for the first time in her life. He hit her in the jaw, and she fell, stunned, but still conscious. He lifted her as if she weighed less than a hundred pounds and threw her into his favorite old chair.

"Jerry . . ." She tried to talk. Her mouth was bleeding and her jaw hurt.

He wasn't listening. He pulled a length of rope from a box near the chair and reached for her. She twisted away, scrambling, and fell to the floor. He grabbed her by the hair, hauled her up and threw her back into the seat.

Maureen didn't know where her strength came from, but she fought. She bit him and kicked at him, landing a powerful blow to his stomach.

"You fat bitch!" All control left him. He backhanded her, slapping her so hard the blow echoed upstairs, in the empty kitchen.

She tried again to get out of the chair. He threw himself on her and planted his knee in her soft belly.

"You fucking cow!"

Saliva sprayed her face. She sobbed and struggled.

He grabbed her face, squeezing her cheeks, the look in his eyes cold. "If you make one more sound," he said, his voice level and soft, "I'll slit your throat."

Maureen swallowed her sobs. Her eyes bulged in her head. Jerry twisted her jaw. She tasted blood.

"Do you understand me? One more sound."

She nodded. Her belly was on fire. He pressed his knee into her.

"Now . . ." He moved off her and stood back, again picking up the rope. "You only came down here because you wanted to see what I do in here, right?"

Maureen's eyes rolled in her head like an animal caught in a slaughter pen.

"I'm talking to you." He leaned down, his face inches from hers. "You were curious, right?"

She nodded, tears streaming down her face.

"I can't hear you."

"Y-Ye-Yes," she stammered. Her nose ran.

"That'a girl." He plucked a few tissues from the box near the chair and tenderly wiped her face. "Nothing wrong with that. All you had to do was tell me you wanted in, and I would have brought you down here myself." He tossed the tissues in the basket near the chair. "I got nothing to hide," he said as he wound the rope around his hand. "How did you get in?"

"I had an extra key made." She spoke softly, her voice full of tears.

He laughed. "Very clever, very clever. I never would have thought you had the guts to do that." He kissed her loudly on the cheek. "Now, since you've shown me what a smart girl you are, I'm gonna give you a present."

He popped the rope like a whip, snapping it around her body, tying her to the chair, pulling the knot so tight that the rough hemp cut into her arms and breasts.

"No." She struggled.

"Don't jerk around, Mo, it won't hurt if you just stop moving around."

"I'm sorry, Jerry. I didn't do anything wrong. I wanted to see this place, yes, but I've never been in here before." Tears dripped off her chin.

"You're lying to me." He pulled the rope tighter. "You know how I can always tell—you ain't got a poker face, baby, you can't carry it off."

Her arms ached, a fine line of blood appeared just beneath the rough fiber. "Please, I'm sorry." She sobbed. "Jerry, I'm sorry."

"Yeah." He tied the last knot and pulled her head back, making her look into his face. "You got that right, you are sorry, you're about the sorriest bitch I've ever seen!" He tugged on her hair, making her scream.

"Jerry!"

Sobs racked her and she struggled in the chair. The ropes cut deeper.

"You wanna see my work? You're always yapping about how I don't share with you. Let's share."

He walked around in front of Maureen, looking down at her gasping for breath. "I just got an idea. Not only am I gonna share my work with you, I'm gonna make you part of it."

Maureen swallowed tears.

"Remember how it used to be, in the good old days?" He leaned down very close. "I'm gonna take your picture."

He walked across the room and opened his camera bag.

"You're gonna like this, babe, just like old times."

He took out the camera. "Now, these are just the prelims, don't be nervous."

He rolled off a series of snaps. "Smile for me, baby."

He moved in closer and clicked the shutter in her face. "This is great film I'm using. It's new. You get dynamite prints with just natural light. Isn't that something?"

Maureen closed her eyes and prayed.

He kept snapping away. "Very good." He put the camera down. "You did real fine, baby. I think the ones with the closed eyes and tears on the cheeks will be primo." He pulled her head back, making her look at him.

"You're just such a good girl, that calls for another treat." He kissed her wet mouth. "I'll be right back."

He went into the darkroom. She heard the opening and closing of a file drawer. He came out smiling, several manila folders in his hands.

"I should have done this sooner, but you know how slow I can be," he said, grinning. "You're always saying we should be closer, and sweetheart, you're right. Let me show you my work."

He held a photograph of Della Robb-Ellison in front of her. Maureen shut her eyes at the sight.

"Oh God, oh God . . . please, Jerry, please . . . " She struggled, choking on her tears.

"Now, baby, you wanted to see, so go on, look . . . look!" He yanked on her hair until she opened her eyes.

He shuffled the photos. "Now this one, this is one of my favorites. This little girl disappointed me. She lived in a dump, but she paid twenty-three hundred big ones for a TV . . . cash. I saw her when she came in, but that horse's ass, Beacham, got to her first." He grinned at Maureen. "I really liked her tits."

Maureen tried not to see Alma Johnson's terrified face.

"She didn't want to play at first, but she soon came around." He shuffled the pictures again. "Now this one . . . oh man." He laughed. "This one really gets me, look at it." Maureen closed her eyes. He pulled her hair again. "I said look at it, goddammit!"

She opened her eyes. When she realized what she was looking at, she screamed and gagged.

"Aw, sugar, don't tell me you're going to be sick. You used to like blowing me. This is nothing but a little cocksucking . . . good technique, don't you think? She didn't even ruin her lipstick."

Maureen prayed, mumbling the words, begging for help.

"You want help . . . asking God?" He laughed. "Go on, ask away, because tonight, I'm God . . . and I'm feeling benevolent. I'm going to help you." He yanked her hair again, pulling a handful of dirty blond strands from her scalp. "But first, you've got to witness my power. Look at this one, it's the cream of the crop. Look at it."

"No!" She kept her eyes tightly closed.

"I said look at it!"

He hit her so hard she saw lightning.

"No!" She shook her head like a child.

"All right, if you don't want to be my witness." She heard the click as he pushed the button on the knife.

"You're really hurting my feelings, Mo." He touched the tip of the blade lightly to her cheek. "Open your eyes."

She squeezed her eyes shut, shaking her head.

"Come on, Mo, open your eyes." He raised the knife. "If you don't, I'm gonna pop 'em, like grapes."

"Jerry!" she screamed as she felt the tip of the blade press on her closed eyelid. *"God!"* She opened her eyes and found herself staring at a photograph of Denise Miles in the bathtub.

"Now that. . . that, you porky bitch, is what a real woman looks like. Sweet . . . she was so fucking sweet. I get hard just thinking about her."

He pressed himself against Maureen's shoulder. "Feel that. Makes you want some, huh?" He laughed, shaking the photo in his wife's face. "Look at her. She took it all, every inch, all the way."

Maureen swallowed. She recognized the woman from the pictures on television, the pictures of those murdered black women. Dear God, could he have done that? The others, what about the others? She couldn't look again. Her stomach twisted.

"I'm gonna be sick . . . please, let me go."

"C'mon, babe, don't start that."

"Really, please." She gagged. "I'm gonna be sick."

He grabbed her hair, pulling her head back, making her

look in his eyes. "You don't want to do that, Mo, you know how I hate it when you puke."

"Jerry," she muttered weakly.

"Remember how you were when you were carrying Jenny? Disgusting, barfing all the time. What was that medicine you took? You said the doctor gave it to you . . . yeah, you took it and you fucked her up, you scrambled her brain, taking shit because you were *uncomfortable*!"

She tried to speak. Another wave of nausea hit and she swallowed it back.

He stood over her. "You fucking fried my kid's brain because you couldn't hold your breakfast, a perfectly natural thing *when you're pregnant!*"

"Jerry," she said softly, "I was sick. Dr. Peterson said it would only get worse. I had to take something." Tears poured down her face. "It wasn't the drug, I didn't hurt her with the medicine."

"You didn't hurt her with the medicine." He slapped her. "You short-circuited my kid, you fat, shit-brained cow!" His eyes were wild. "You made her a fucking, screaming animal!"

"Don't blame me," she moaned.

He paced around her. "Don't blame you. Oh, right, like I shouldn't blame you for blowing up like goddamn Shamu, huh? Like I shouldn't blame you for being so fucking disgusting that I'd rather stick my dick in dogshit then you!"

She was sobbing, her stomach pitching. "I'm sorry, I'm sorry," she cried. She had to get away from him, she didn't want to think about what he was going to do to her . . . what he had done to those women.

"Please, let me go, I won't ever come in here again, I won't tell anybody. I promise. Please, Jerry. Please, let me go."

He stood in front of her, his body still, his rage suddenly gone. "You surprised me, you know, kicking me, all that. You hurt me, Mo, but that's all right, because I understand, you didn't mean it, you were scared, right?"

She nodded, her eyes closed.

"Yeah, I know." He stroked her face. "I'm gonna be fair, I'm gonna do what you asked."

He walked around behind her and grabbed her hair, pulling her head back, making her look directly into his eyes.

"I understand. You really want to go." He gazed tenderly at her. "You really want out, right?"

"Yes." She sighed, her voice nearly gone. She couldn't fight or beg any more.

"Well, okay." He leaned down and gently kissed her forehead. "Sayonara, bitch!"

Maureen saw his fist headed toward her face. She closed her eyes.

"How did you find me, how did you get in here?" Star sat still, staring at him.

"Some things should remain secret. But I will say this, Detective Duvall—little girls playing cops shouldn't be so pretty." He wrapped an arm around the bed post and leaned toward her. "See, when you're pretty, even a cretin like Jerry Beacham remembers you. Your eyes, and even your name."

She was stunned. "Jerry Beacham?"

"Yep. He came by to pick up a paycheck the front office forgot to mail, and just happened to see you in the listening room. Tough break, huh?" He shook his head. "By the way, your TRW says you're an excellent credit risk. Top rated, very good."

She looked quickly toward the door.

"Don't even think about running." He pointed the gun at her.

"Get that gun out of my face!" she said.

The strength in her voice surprised her.

He raised it higher. "Be rough with me, honeychile, I like it like that." He leaned close to her. "Do you know I could blow your head off, but you're too pretty to shoot in the face. I want you to have an open casket, so everybody can cluck and sob about how young and pretty you were, and what a shame for you to be so goddamn dead." He smiled, then pouted like a child. "Besides, you didn't even save me any cookies."

Star's breath caught in her throat.

"Yeah, I've been here for a while." He ran a hand over his

naked chest. "I hope you don't mind, but I made myself comfortable." He smiled. "You know, in your own place, you're a terrible hostess. At the brownstone, you at least gave me something to drink. What happened, officer, did you leave your class across town? Looks like I'm going to have to teach you some manners."

He moved to the other side of the bed, the gun pointed at her. He liked making her turn her head to watch him.

"Hey!" He snapped his fingers. "I've got a better idea. Why don't we try something new? I'll bet you've never been fucked with a gun before."

He licked his lips. "What if I shove this in your cunt and pull the trigger when you come? Guess you'd really get off, huh?" He laughed. "We could say you came and went."

"I want you to put the gun down," she said.

He laughed. "Oh yeah, right, like in the movies." He aimed again at her face. "Like my uncle used to say, folks in hell want ice water."

She lay very still, praying he couldn't hear her heart pounding. "So, if I don't put the gun down, you're gonna have to hurt me, right? Maybe even kill me?" He laughed again.

"So, sistuh, whatcha planning to do, fuck me to death? The way I see it, little girl, you're laying there in a nightshirt. I don't see no weapon, unless it's that sweet little pussy under there. If you want to kill me with that"—he rubbed his crotch—"I'm ready."

He winked at her and wiggled his hips, letting her see the bulge in his jeans.

Star inched her feet closer to the edge of the bed.

"Uh-uh." He pointed the gun directly at her. "One more move and you're gone."

She lay still. "What do you want me to do?"

"What do you want me to do?" he parroted, rubbing his chin. "Let me see." He clicked his tongue against the roof of his mouth.

The sound went through her like fingernails on a blackboard.

"Golly, Detective Duvall—that is a mighty fine name, by the way—what do I want you to do?"

Star felt her limbs fluttering, trembling, and prayed to be still. The voice inside her head whispered, *I will not show fear. I will not allow myself to be humiliated. I will not break.*

He watched her. "Whatcha doing, baby, praying? Looks like I get to be God again tonight."

She hadn't known her lips were moving. She breathed deeply and held it, then slowly let the breath escape, her eyes on him.

"Oh, deep breathing, that's good, steadies you, calms you down. I know all about that. I used to do a lot of it when I was in 'Nam."

He stretched. "Once, I was locked in a tiger cage for two weeks, no place to go, nothing to do but get pissed on by those little yellow fuckers, and you know how I handled it? I breathed. Yeah, I took long, deep breaths, and when they were pissing on me with those tiny, little pricks, I flew away, just fluttered overhead and watched it all. Deep breathing, it's a miracle. Do some more, honeychile, it raises your shirt, maybe I'll get a glimpse of heaven."

"What do you want from me, Jerry?" she asked. "What do you want me to do?"

"What can you do for me?" He walked around the bed. "Well, first, you can lay back down, the way you were when I came in, all comfortable, not stiff and tense like you are now. I liked the way you looked, all long and pretty, laying there with your eyes closed. What were you listening to?"

"Luther Vandross," she said.

"Oh, that's good. From what I hear, that's regulation spade fucking music." He grinned at her. "Wanna fuck? I know you did when I came to your house before . . . oh, excuse me, the setup house.

"How far were you gonna take it? You were wet, and ready. I know, I felt you. If that black bastard hadn't been there, you would still be riding my cock, wouldn't you?"

Star turned away from him, shamed by his words and the truth in them.

He grinned. "It's all right, you don't have to say anything. I could smell you then, and I can smell you now. You've been thinking about it, haven't you?" He squeezed himself. "Well, tonight's the night, nobody gonna come outta the can to stop you, right?"

Star felt tears coming to her eyes. She put her head down so he wouldn't see.

"Better late than never, I always say." He held up his hand. "It'll be fantastic, just like you've been dreaming about. Relax, lie back like before. I promise you, I'll make you feel good."

She tried to let her body fall into a more natural position. It wasn't working.

"Do it!" He pointed the gun at her. She lay back.

The cat rose up, looking at Jerry. "Hey kitty, pretty boy," he cooed at Jake.

Star moved her leg, trying to ease away from him.

"Don't do that. Don't try anything. I'll blow your fuckin' face off." He aimed the gun right at her forehead. "Now, you're gonna do as I say, and you're not gonna try anything cute, got that?"

She nodded.

"Answer me. Say, yes Jerry."

"Yes, Jerry." The words came softly, wrapped in an anger so strong it literally blinded her for an instant.

"Good." He moved to the center of the foot of the bed. "Raise the shirt."

"No."

He shook his head. "That's not the right answer. Didn't you just agree to do what I tell you?"

She watched his hand on the gun, his finger on the trigger. He wasn't playing. Star closed her eyes and raised her shirt. She stopped midway up her thighs.

"Nice. Let me see more. I want you to pull it all the way up and spread your legs. I want to see cunt."

"No!" She pulled the shirt back down.

"What's this? Are you shy?" The hand holding the gun trembled slightly. "You're not going to show me your pussy? You wanted to before, when the fucking house was bugged. Now, we're all alone, you say no? What is it baby? Do you need an audience? Is it better for you when you know your cop buddies are listening, beatin' off in the crapper?"

He motioned with the gun. "C'mon, show me, I know you've spread it around. Isn't that how you got your gold shield, Detective?"

"Detective Lieutenant," she said evenly.

"Oh, so sorry, Deteckative Lieutenant! What did you do, blow the chief?"

"Your mother did it for me." Her gaze locked with his.

"Oh, that's funny, that's really funny." He raised the gun again. "Why don't I just pop you another funny hole right between your eyes . . . snapping, isn't that what you coons call it? Talking about the other guy's mama. Well, it don't make me mad, Detective Lieutenant, because you're right. My old lady would have sucked off the whole goddamn police department to get a stick of gum. That's the kind of whore she was. Hell, she might have even made me watch."

"Boo-hoo," Star said.

He was around the bed in a heartbeat, shoving the barrel of the gun right to her forehead.

"Go ahead, kill me!" she screamed. *"Do it! I'm not afraid of you!"*

He backed up, the gun leveled at her face. "You think I won't?"

She felt the last of the fear leave her body, replaced by a cold, hard rage.

Jerry shook his head, rolling his tongue around inside his mouth. "All right, Detective, let's play this game another way."

He unzipped his jeans with his free hand.

"See, I'm a fair guy." He reached inside. "I'll show you mine, then you can show me yours." He pulled himself out of the jeans and stood in front of her, stroking and squeezing himself. "Look at that. Isn't that a prime piece of meat? You ever have anything like that?"

"Bigger and better," she said.

"That's funny." He walked again to the side of the bed.

Star's head turned, following his movement.

"Is that supposed to mean some nigger you rolled around with, or are you talking about that big, blond, faggot doctor son of a bitch that's been sniffing around here?"

He got a kick out of the look of surprise on her face.

"Oh yeah, I know all about him. You haven't given it to him, I can tell. He's probably riding some whore right now, thinking about you, but you can't give it to him, because it's mine. It's my pussy, it's got my name on it. It's me you want. Even if you spread it for him, it won't be any good, because you want me."

Star bit back her tears.

Jerry laughed and stroked himself. "Truth hurts, don't it? This is what you want." He squeezed himself. "Your pretty doctor ain't got nothing like this, I don't give a fuck how tall he is. You've never seen a cock like this on any man, black or white, admit it."

She looked away. The thought that he'd been watching, spying on her and Mitchell, made her sick.

He put the gun to her temple. "Don't make me blow your brains out and ruin that pretty face, bitch."

He pressed the gun hard against her flesh. *"Look at me!"*

Star kept looking at the far right wall. A framed photograph of her father and herself, when she was about eight years old, looked back at her. She felt her body grow cold; sweat rolled down her chest.

"Scared yet? Maybe I should show you some pictures. I brought some with me. He pointed to two cases on the floor near the love seat, a brown canvas camera bag and a zippered black leather case.

"Tonight, you get the main event. I've already taken some good shots of my wife, but yours are gonna be better, right?" He grinned.

Star didn't move.

"I told you our marriage wasn't made in heaven, that we were most likely gonna separate." He smiled at her. "And we have, so you don't have to be jealous. It's just you and me now."

Star flinched.

"Uh-huh, I knew you were scared."

"You're right, I'm scared," she said softly.

"What?" He backed up.

She turned her head and looked into his eyes. "I said, I'm scared. I don't want this, but if you have to do it, then go on because I'm not giving you the satisfaction of begging."

He wiped his forehead with his free hand.

"That's good, real, real good. What a brave trouper you are." He walked around to the foot of the bed, stroking himself. "Brave, brave, brave. Don't worry, honeychile, we're gonna get to it in a little while." He closed his eyes. "I can almost feel you sucking. Mmmm, I'm gonna fuck you so hard, it's gonna leave a hole in your heart. Then I'm gonna crawl down your throat and come." He opened his eyes. "It's gonna feel real good."

An image came into her mind. She saw her body on a stainless steel table, with Mitchell sobbing over her. She started to tremble. She turned her face away from Jerry Auster.

"Look at me," he said.

"I'm not going to watch you masturbate."

She focused again on the picture on the far wall. It was her favorite photo of her and her father. They were on one of their famous park outings. A man had been taking pictures for a dollar. Her father gave him five, and he snapped the two of them, so full of orange and lime sherbet that neither one of them could eat a bite at dinner. They were so happy that day. They'd spent the whole day with their favorite people, each other.

Help me, Daddy, she said silently.

"What are you looking at?" Jerry Auster moved into her line of vision.

"You." She turned, facing him.

"That's better. I like that."

"Please cover up," she said.

He shook himself at her. "See how stiff that is . . . driving you crazy, right? You want some, I can see it." He stroked himself. "I want you too. I'll make you happy, promise."

"All right," she said.

"All right? You giving in?"

"Yes." She backed up against the pillows. "Do what you want, I don't care."

His laughter ripped through her brain, making her body shiver. She closed her eyes and tried to stop her teeth from chattering.

"In that case . . ." He stuffed himself back into his jeans and zipped up. "I'm gonna make you wait. Pretty soon, you'll be begging for it."

This was his game, humiliation, degradation, and death. Is that what he'd done to the others? Star wondered. Did he make all of them go through this? Della, Alma, and Denise, poor ruined Denise. The vision of the woman in the tub drifted past her unseeing eyes. She wasn't going to die like that. Not like that.

"You don't care what I do?" he asked.

"No."

He aimed the gun at Jake. "Well, then, why don't I just start by blowing this furry little fuck to kingdom come."

She grabbed the cat and pulled him to her chest. "Don't hurt him."

"At last, something you care about, something you love."

Tears came to her eyes and she willed them back. Hold on, she said to herself. Hold on. Jake lay still in her arms, sensing the danger and mewing softly.

"Put the gun down, please. We can talk. Let's just stop this."

"Is that your way of saying I need help? You want this to be over?" He leveled the gun at her again. "Well, it is over, for you."

"Please put the gun down."

"I will, when I'm fucking you."

She held the cat closer. "Why do you want me? You obviously hate what I am, why do you want me?"

"Good question." He looked at her. "You're right, I fucking loathe you, but I want you. It's in the genes." He grabbed himself and laughed harshly. "In the jeans, get it?"

"I don't understand."

He moved around the bed. "I come from a good family, you know, not rich, but well-off."

She shook her head. "I didn't know."

"When I was a kid, we had it all. Nice house, cars, vacations on the shore. My dad owned car dealerships. He had three lots by the time I was five years old."

"What happened?" she asked softly.

Jerry Auster laughed. A deep, chilling laugh that made her bones ache under her skin.

"What happened?" He rubbed his eyes. "You—you happened."

"Me?"

"Yeah, at least a black woman, like you. From what I recall, she worked for my dad in his main office and he fell in love with her. I mean really in love, out of his fucking mind in love.

"Blacks were the people who cleaned our toilets and scrubbed our floors. They weren't the people you crawl into bed with, but my dad did. It would have been okay if he'd just fucked her and come home. But he did the unforgivable, he fell in love.

"I was about nine. I remember the arguments, and my mom screaming at him to give her up, to just give the nigger up. My dad said he'd rather cut his throat than leave Cora Mae. That was her name, Cora Mae."

Star stroked the cat in her arms. "What did he do?"

"He left us. He divorced my mother and married the shine. It was a big deal, and my mom kinda went 'round the bend after it was all over. He provided for us, but not like before.

My mom couldn't handle it. She started drinking, pissing the money away. Before long we moved out of our house, and things went downhill from there."

"I'm sorry," she said.

He laughed again. "You're sorry? Man . . . "

His haggard eyes gazed off into a past she couldn't see.

"I had to grow up fast. I had to take care of Mom and myself. I became the man of the house . . . in every way."

She shuddered inside. Her eyes gave her away.

"That's right," he said. "When I was fourteen, she took me into her bed. She said I looked like 'that bastard,' and I do, I'm the spitting image of my dad, right down to his dick. Hung, just like him. She couldn't do without, and the thought of him pounding it to that black bitch made her crazy.

"She picked up guys in bars for a while, but none of them made her feel like he did. None of them had the cock for it. I think she was so stretched out from years of taking him that she couldn't even feel a normal man, so . . . "

He looked directly at Star.

"She turned to me, and she taught me." He looked down at the gun in his hand. "She taught me about women, how to touch them, how to kiss them. She was insatiable, the bitch."

The softness of his voice made the ugliness of his words ring loudly in the quiet house.

"She wanted it all the time. She never got enough. Even though she was in the bag most of the time, she still wanted it. She would curse me and cry the whole time I did her, calling me by his name, screaming about his nigger whore."

Tears spilled from his eyes.

"I never even had a girlfriend. She wouldn't allow it. Any girl who liked me, she scared them off. She wanted me all to herself. In time, I stopped thinking about girls, she was my whole world."

A deep sob escaped him.

"My senior year in high school, when I was eighteen, I came home from my part-time job at the camera store. She was on the couch." He wiped his eyes with the back of his hand. "Her brains were on the floor."

Star stroked the cat in her arms, silently.

"My old man came back for the funeral." Jerry's voice grew softer. "He had the good sense to leave his whore at home, but he told me I had a brother, two years old." He shook his head. "The same day she was buried, I went out and signed up for a tour in 'Nam. That's why I hate you."

"Jerry . . ." she said softly.

He looked up. "You're no different than all the other ones. Don't try to act like you care . . . taking, fucking white men, screwing over their minds, making them leave their families, fucking your way up the ladder." He ran a hand over his mouth.

"Women like you . . . " He turned to her. "Walking around, shaking those high, round asses, laughing with those big, cock-sucking lips. . . My dad didn't stand a chance. She took him, just fucking yanked him away from his family. He turned over everything for pussy, black, fucking pussy. I hate you for it, and I hate you for being in my head, messing up my thinking, making me do this."

Star was quiet, still stroking Jake. Keep him talking, her mind said. Keep him talking, get him tired, that's a heavy gun, make him drop it.

"I don't know what's happening anymore," he said. "My whole country is falling down around me. Overcome by niggers and foreign bastards, taking, taking, taking."

He wiped sweat from his face with his free hand. "I'm shit in my own land, you know that? What the fucking Japs don't own, the niggers and the outsiders are either taking or ruining. I got no home anymore."

"I understand," she said softly. "You must be so tired of all of it."

He looked at her for a moment, as if he wanted to stop, to end the nightmare. He walked two steps toward her.

"I'm tired of talking." He pointed the gun at the cat in her arms. "I think I'll kill your fucking cat instead."

Star didn't think, she just reacted. She flung the cat at his bare chest. Jake landed and dug his claws into Jerry Auster's chest and stomach. The gun fired, and slipped from his sweaty hand. The bullet penetrated the wall just above the picture of Star and her father. She rolled off the bed and hit the hard-wood floor.

Jerry struggled and wrestled with the cat, trying to tear the animal from his body. His flesh ripped and bled. He tried to grab Jake's neck, but the animal's sharp fangs sank deep into his hand, his claws gouging farther into Jerry's bare chest. He cursed and flung Jake against the wall. The cat screamed and hit the ground running. Jerry's chest and stomach bore deep tears and scratches, and blood ran down his body.

On the floor, Star rolled on her stomach and reached under the bed. Her fingers wrapped around the butt of her Beretta. She scrambled backward and came up on her knees, her gun pointed at Jerry Auster.

"Freeze motherfucker!"

She got to her feet.

He glared at her, hate and madness showing in his eyes. He stared at her for a full minute and then started to laugh.

"Oh Jeez." He laughed hysterically. "What now? Hey, I saw your pussy, little girl, looked mighty tasty." He licked his lips and howled again with laughter. "Motherfucker! See how you are?" He laughed again. "I can't tell you anything. A few minutes later you're throwing it in my face." He chuckled. "It don't matter, I didn't want to do it." He pouted like a child. "She made me."

Star faced him, the gun pointed directly at him. "Drop to your knees and put your hands behind your head." Her voice was so deep, she didn't recognize it. "I said, on your knees, hands behind your head."

Auster grinned at her, inching his bare foot toward the gun a few feet away.

"Don't do it." She tightened her grip on the gun. "I want you on your knees, *now!*"

"Only if you'll let me eat your pussy." He grinned at her. "I'm real good. Mom was a great teacher."

"On your knees."

"You know what they say about the blacker the berry." He licked his lips. "I'll bet you're like honey. C'mon, give me a taste."

"On your knees!"

"No," he said, with a silly grin. "Make me. I got a gun too." He pointed and moved a fraction of an inch.

She spread her feet farther apart, balancing her weight, bending her knees, taking the stance. Her arms were straight out in front of her, the gun in her right hand, supported by her left. Her finger dead on the trigger; sweat puddled in her left palm, and the wooden grip slid a little in her hand.

"Don't make me kill you," she said.

"You won't hurt me. You want me too much."

"I'm through playing with you." She slid the bolt back, releasing a round into the chamber. "Hands behind your head and on your knees, *now!*"

Jerry Auster's foot moved again. She fired. The bullet tore a hole in the floor between his legs.

He whistled. "Good shooting, honeychile."

"Your balls are next," she said.

"Not a good idea. You wouldn't get fucked." He lunged for her.

Star sidestepped him. He lost his balance. She power-kicked him square in the kidney, using the outer edge of her bare foot. He went sprawling. She stomped him, slamming her heel again into his kidney as he lay on the floor.

Jerry Auster tried to turn, to get hold of her ankle, but she was too fast. Again a kick, this time to the side of the head. The blade edge of her foot felt like a concrete block. His head snapped back. He tried to sit up.

"You bastard!" She kicked him again, this time in the stomach, the rush of his breath on her skin making her madder.

"Sonofabitch!" she screamed.

Jerry Auster fell back against the foot of her bed, the wind knocked out of him. His head rolled back against the bed-spread.

"This is my house, you fuck, you came into my house!"

With her free hand, she slammed her fist hard into his throat, punching his windpipe. Auster gasped. Blood poured from his mouth. His glazed eyes looked at her. He reached out. She backed up, drawing down on him with both hands, pointing the gun at his bleeding face.

"I should kill you. I should blow your fucking head off!"

Tears ran down her face. "This is my house, you hear me, motherfucker? I *live* here. It's *my* house!"

Auster struggled to stand. She knew he wouldn't make it. He looked at her, his eyes glazing over.

"Bastard!" She aimed another kick at him, catching him in the chest. She heard his ribs crack. He spewed blood and fell over sideways, his head at an odd angle.

She made a tentative, small step toward him. Sweat ran in her eyes. She wiped it away with the back of her hand.

"Don't get up," she muttered. "Just don't get up."

She moved two more steps toward him and waited, her gun pointed at him, her body aching with tension. He was still, no sound came from him. She watched him. He was breathing, he was still alive.

With the gun trained on him, she backed around the bed to the night table and opened the top drawer. A pair of gleaming silver handcuffs lay atop her copy of the latest Stephen King novel. She grabbed them and went back to the unconscious Jerry Auster.

Holding her weapon straight up, she kneeled next to him, the cuffs dangling from her free hand. She pushed him over on his face. She put the gun behind her, on the bed, and pulled his left arm to the center of his back, slapping the steel cuff painfully against his wrist bone. She fastened it.

Jerry Auster sighed, more blood running from his mouth.

"Don't die on me," she said, and wrestled his right arm behind him. He coughed and gagged.

"Don't. Don't choke. I'm not going to let you die that easy.

You're gonna live, asshole, you're gonna live and spend the rest of your life locked away like the fucking animal you are." She yanked his arm, hard; there was a popping sound. She smiled.

"Guess what?" She leaned close, speaking softly into his ear. "I'm gonna make sure you hear from me on every birthday and every holiday. You're gonna get greetings from me and all my sisters you killed. You wanna rape and kill black women? Well, get ready for prison, and Bubba, pretty boy, I guarantee you, with that face you'll be everybody's bitch, and I hope your cherry buster is the biggest, blackest, meanest motherfucker in the joint."

She yanked his arm again, bringing his sweaty hands together behind his back. She clicked the handcuffs tightly over his wrist and pulled him back, leaning him against the foot of the bed.

Jerry Auster's head dropped, blood spattering on his chest.

"There. If you vomit you won't choke." She picked up her gun and retrieved his from the floor. She put both guns on the chair by the closet.

"I need something else," she said.

She opened the closet door. On the wall, hanging from a hook was a thick, brown leather belt. She pulled it down and went back to Auster, shoved him facedown on the floor and wrapped the belt around his ankles. She pulled his legs backward, bending them at the knees, then wove the remaining length of belt through his cuffed hands, securing it with the buckle down near his ankles.

"Just in case you wanna play Houdini."

She rolled him on his side. He lay still, his legs bent back, his heels nearly touching the small of his back. She checked the belt and cuffs. They were tight.

She stood, looking down on him. His pale gray eyes opened, and closed again. Star wiped her face with her hand. Her legs shook, suddenly refusing to support her any longer. She collapsed onto the floor.

She began shaking, cold chills running through her. She

was oblivious to the blood oozing from her torn left knee. Jake crawled out from under a chair, moved alongside her and licked her arm.

She picked him up. "I'm sorry, sweetie." She rocked the cat in her arms. "I'm sorry, but I had to do it, I had to."

Jake meowed.

"You were so good." She kissed his head and held him against her trembling body.

She looked down at the animal, overwhelmed by the emotion she felt. Tears flooded her eyes, then sobs racked her as he gazed up into her wet face.

"I could have lost you. He didn't hurt you, did he?" She rubbed his back and pudgy belly. "You're okay, you're all right . . . we're both all right."

The cat licked her sweaty fingers. She sat holding him, listening to him purr.

Finally, she could move. She put the cat down on the floor, and he crept up to Auster and sniffed.

"He can't hurt us," Star said. She got up and walked around Jerry Auster. "He won't be hurting anybody else, ever." She looked at the two cases near the love seat.

"New pictures," she said, a tear rolling down her face. "New pictures." She wiped her eyes and looked back at Auster. "It's evidence now, evidence to bury you with."

He was still. His face pale. For a moment she thought of the ending of every bad horror movie she'd ever seen, where the out-of-commission bad guy gets up and comes after the victim.

"Not a chance." She picked up her cat, crossed to the chair and picked up the guns. With one look back, she walked out of the room.

Downstairs, she went into the kitchen and turned on the light. She laid both guns on the counter and reached for the phone.

No, she'd call from the hall, just in case. She picked up her gun. "You stay here," she said to the cat, and closed the kitchen door, keeping Jake inside.

Star picked up the cordless phone from the hall table and sat cross-legged on the floor, facing the stairs. She left the lights off, just in case he somehow got loose. She would see him before he could see her.

She lay the gun in her lap and put the phone to her ear.

"Put it down."

Star felt the hard gun barrel at the back of her head.

"I said, put the phone down."

She looked up. The mirror next to the staircase reflected someone, partially concealed in the darkness, standing directly behind her. She could see the silver glint of the weapon at the back of her head. The gun pressed deeply into her scalp.

"Are you hard of hearing? Put the phone down."

She put the phone down on the carpet beside her.

"Good girl, now, give me your gun . . . slowly, don't try anything 'cause I'll blow your brains out."

She reached into her lap.

"Don't get cute." The gun pressed harder.

"No . . . no, here." She handed back the weapon. Her hand touched his, a thin latex glove rubbing against her skin.

"Get up."

She stood, her legs shaking.

"Don't turn around."

Jake's high, shrill yowl echoed in the hall.

"Where's the cat?"

"In the kitchen. Please, don't hurt him."

The laugh startled her. "The cat's the least of your worries." The gun barrel slid against her skin. "In the living room." He shoved her. *"Now!"*

"Please," she said.

"Please what?" The voice was mocking, slightly high-pitched.

She moved on rubbery legs. He pushed her again. In the darkness, her living room was like a strange planet. She stumbled, and bumped into an end table. He laughed.

"What's the matter, Lieutenant, scared?"

"Yes," she said clearly. "Very scared."

"Well, you should be. Sit down, bitch!"

He shoved her. She tumbled into the big overstuffed chair near the bookcase.

"And I always thought you were so graceful, dancer that you are."

Star heard a gun drop to the coffee table. She stared into the darkness. She couldn't see his face, but his weapon still gleamed in his hand.

"Where are my manners? You must be wondering who I am," he said. She heard the smile in his voice. "Go ahead, turn on the light."

She reached up to the tall lamp next to the chair and pushed the button. Light flooded the room.

"How you been, Detective?"

She stared at the man in front of her.

"I don't know you."

He threw back his head and laughed. She caught a glimpse of his amazingly white but crooked teeth.

"Sure you do. All this time, I thought I was unforgettable. Look again." He leaned toward her.

The pale, vampiric face grinned.

"Dennis Glover."

"Very good, see, you know me. Only it's not really Glover. Glover's my stepfather's name, he adopted me after my dad died. My given name is Carroll, Joseph Dennis Carroll, Jr. I'm named after my father, Joe Carroll."

"Jesus," she said.

"You shouldn't take the Lord's name like that." He shook a gloved finger at her. "It's sacrilegious, but then, so is suicide. You know all about that, don't you? Suicide, like my dad. He's burning in hell because he blew his brains out on a bus stop bench. He couldn't forgive himself for killing your old man."

Star moved back against the cushion, pressing her back into the soft chair.

"Dennis . . . "

He brought the gun up. "Don't . . . don't try talking to me, just listen, because I want you to know why you're going to die."

She sat still.

"You thought it was Auster, didn't you? I really had you guys going. I got to hand it to you, great detective work, Lieutenant, really great work. I knew you the minute you walked in the store, but Auster, pussy hound that he is, it never dawned on him you could be the law."

He grinned at her. She could see those teeth, biting, gnawing.

"I could have blown your cover all to hell, but I loved watching the game between you two. Auster couldn't kill anybody, he's just a pretty boy led around by his dick. He likes it rough, and if the lady doesn't agree, he usually beats the fuck out of her and takes what he wants, but he doesn't have the guts to kill anybody. Not even his fat wife. He hammered her good, though, just before he came over here."

"How do you know?"

"I've been his shadow for months. I know everything about him. He's no killer."

"And you are?"

He nodded vigorously.

"Yep, I did all of them. The little one with the tits, she tried to fight. After Auster got through with her, she didn't have a lot of strength, but she tried. She pissed me off, so I cut her throat . . . then I made her blow me . . . the hard way." He laughed.

"The one in the car, she was something else. She fucked him you know. She fucked him right there in the parking lot up against his car, right out in the open. No class, like a bitch in heat. I saw the whole thing. I was in the bushes, off to the side. They thought they were alone.

"She came out of the mall, and he was waiting, hiding in her car. I think he scared her shitless at first, then she started laughing. They started kissing and pawing each other, and I don't know, I guess it's because her car was small, they moved to his.

"It was ugly, you should have seen them. She took off her underthings right there and let him put it to her. Cheap bitch. She even let him pull out and come in her mouth. I nearly puked. When they were finished, he talked her into posing for his stupid pictures. He shot her in the car, on the car, with her skirt up and legs open, from behind, showing all her business. They never figured anybody was watching.

"The pictures got them hot again, so they started up one more time. That's when I got the idea. If he could do it, I could too. I snuck around and got into the backseat of her car. They were so into each other, they didn't even realize it. When they finished, he walked her back to the car.

"I was wedged down behind the front seat. It was so small, I don't know how he stayed there. It was dark, they couldn't see me. I found a scarf back there. It came in handy for giving her another big surprise that night." He laughed.

"She was a pig. She didn't even put her underthings back on. To think I was so sure she had class when she came in the store. Auster was on her before I had a chance to get to her. Even if I got there first, he would have taken her . . . obviously.

"But I won. I even took her underthings to remember her by." He looked directly at Star. "They smelled great."

Star realized that Mitchell and Paresi had been right about Della Robb-Ellison. But she struggled not to show any emotion.

"She was a pig, but you know something? I tasted her. I don't know what made me do it. I mean, Auster had been there, you know? Still, I couldn't help myself. I even took a few bites out of her. Imagine that. I liked the taste of her, so I tasted the other ones too. Different parts of the body taste different, did you know that?" He giggled. "I left the pig in her favorite pose, for you folks. Did you like it?" He stared at her with empty eyes.

"Yeah. That was good, but she wasn't the best. My very favorite was the one in the bathtub. She was gorgeous, and Auster, well, I think he fell in love with her. That's what made it so special. He really liked her." A smile spread across his face.

"I don't blame him. She was beautiful. D'ya know I had to wait till four in the morning for him to come out of her house? I thought he was gonna stay all night. He didn't want to leave. I think it was the smile on his face when he walked out that made me so mad.

"I went through a side window. She was in the tub, candles all around, with her eyes closed, and that same kind of smile. It was romantic. I got a little jealous, and I guess I went crazy on her. I wanted to see what was inside her, what was it that made a woman like her be such a whore for a bastard like him.

"You know something? When the stories started about the murders, he didn't give a shit. He knew each one of them, and he never said a word.

"He's got no respect for anything. Especially when it comes to me. No respect at all. He makes fun of me all the time. He steals my customers. He's such a fucking waste of breath, and the women still go for him.

"I thought about that the whole time I was with Denise. He liked her, I know, even though he never said anything after the news broke about her death. I know he liked her."

He sat on the edge of the coffee table, facing Star.

"I finally took something from him, after everything he took from me. You know, if I had a woman on the hook, he'd watch me, and when I thought I had her, he'd just swoop down like a fucking bird of prey and steal her away. He'd smile and wink, and boom, I'd be talking to air. He cost me a lot of commissions."

He looked in her eyes. "Why are women so stupid? Anything for a good-looking face and a hard body."

"Dennis—"

"Shut up!" He leaned closer to her. "Whores, that's what they are, whores. They let him touch them, meet them later, fuck them, and they would buy anything from him. He could sell 'em shit in a blender and they'd buy it, gladly."

"The pictures," Star said.

"I sent them," he said laughingly. "You cops really cracked me up on that. Nothing about them in the papers, nothing on the news. Good move, something only the killer would know, right? Limited information, let the killer expose himself, and that prick Auster walked right in.

"I knew you'd find out he was a shutterbug. He used to bring pictures of his conquests to the store and show them off. He'd get women in the filthiest positions and brag to us how he got them to do it. Lucky me, I got a chance to watch him operate."

Star kept staring at him.

"You traced him through the film, didn't you?"

"Yes."

"I knew you would. Glenn turned me on to Neopan, and I made sure he told Auster about it."

"The film is unique."

"Yeah, yeah. I knew Glenn kept a list of customers, but I wasn't on it. I'm his pal, he never even charges me for stuff. We trade, he likes electronic gadgets. It evens out, good for both of us."

"We found a sales slip at Alma Johnson's."

"I know, I left it. I wondered how long it would take you to pick up on it. You were in the store the next day. Excellent work."

"How did you know I'd be assigned to the case?"

His knee bounced up and down. Star could see the sweat rings in his latex gloves. The gun was getting heavy and hard to hold.

"That's why I picked niggers. I knew you'd take it personal. Auster, he fucked anything, it didn't matter to him, but he really came on to the colored girls. He seemed to prefer them. That's when it hit me—the perfect way to get that bastard *and* bring the illustrious Lieutenant Duvall right to my door. Good plan, don't you think?"

"Brilliant," she said quietly.

He raised the gun. "I know you, Duvall. I've studied you

since I was a kid. My father died because of your old man. He was just doing his job."

"So was my father," she said evenly.

"He should have identified himself."

"He didn't have a chance. Joe Carroll fired on him while he was running. He shot him in the back."

"It was an honest mistake."

"He killed my father, while the white gunman Dad was chasing ran right by him. He chased that guy down and disarmed him. He took him alive, while he left my father dying on a dirty sidewalk."

"My father was doing his job. He saw a man running with a gun in his hand."

"Two men!" Star's eyes blazed. "He saw *two* men running, both armed, one black, one white. He shot the black one."

"Justifiably," Dennis said, smiling.

She clenched her fists. The same blinding rage she felt upstairs was back, and she had to keep her head.

"Niggers commit more crimes, you know that. Be honest, my father made the right decision. My mom and I tried to tell him that. He wouldn't listen. He crawled into the bottle and the needle. When that didn't keep the pain away, he took that walk to the bus stop."

"Gee, that's rough," Star said.

She didn't see it coming. Dennis slapped her so hard, her teeth rattled.

"Don't make me kill you, not yet, not yet." He was on his feet. "I got plans for you."

Not as big as the ones I got for you, asshole, she said to herself. She closed her eyes, shutting out his gaunt frame, his pale white skin, the saggy black Levi's he wore and that washed-out green jacket with a white shirt.

"Open your eyes," he said.

She looked at him.

"I'm going to do to you what Auster came to do."

"He's upstairs," she said.

"I heard. He should be unconscious for a month. It doesn't

matter, though, if he comes to or not. When they find you, you're gonna be dead and so is he. It was a very tragic thing. He broke in, raped you and shot you, but you were brave to the end, firing one bullet, right between his eyes, killing him dead and ruining that pretty face. A closed casket, for sure. You're going out a hero. The feminists will make you a saint."

"Good plan," she said.

"Thank you." He beamed at her. His hand went to his belt. "I know you couldn't tell in the picture I sent of me and the late Miss Johnson, but I'm not built like Auster." He registered the surprise in her face. "Oh, we all know about his legendary sword. Some of the guys even measured him once. Let's see, it was about ten inches long and five inches around . . . very impressive. I'm nothing like that, but it'll be enough. When they find you, it'll be obvious you've had some very rough sex."

"You don't want to do this," she said.

"But I do." He laughed. "I really do."

Star pressed herself farther back in the chair. She had to think. Her hand slipped between the side of the chair and the cushion. She felt something hard just under her fingertip.

Dennis moved his gun to his other hand, slipping one arm out of his jacket.

Star watched him, her hand sinking farther in the chair. She slowly moved her finger over the hard, round object, caught it in her fingertips and moved them slowly down the length of it. It was long. She grasped it in her palm. Her mother's old steel knitting needle.

Star had been passing on her only domestic skill to Lena, teaching the girl to knit, as her own mother had taught her. The two of them always sat in this chair. Star used her mother's needles because they were the ones she'd learned on. Now, she realized that the last time Vee came to pick her daughter up, Lena must have accidentally left the needle in the chair, and the chair swallowed it, like it did everything else left on its surface.

"Why don't you come over here, on the couch?" Dennis said.

Star looked up. He had opened his shirt to his waist. His pale white chest reminded her of a sickly chicken. She moved her hand farther under the cushion.

"Why don't you come to me?"

"What?" Dennis looked surprised.

"If you're going to do this, we might as well both enjoy it, right? Isn't that what they say, when rape is inevitable . . . "

He licked his lips, his eyes were wary.

"It'll be my last time, Dennis, don't you want it to be good?"

"I guess."

"Come over here, let me unzip you."

He walked toward her, the gun stretched out in front of him.

"Are you gonna hold that thing the whole time?" She smiled at him.

"Yeah," he said. "I'm not putting it down."

"Too bad. You won't be able to do much with one hand."

"We'll see." He stood over her, the gun pointed at her face.

"At least kiss me, Dennis. I need something."

He smirked and leaned over, the gun pointing down toward the floor.

Star stretched her body upward, licking her lips, her mouth open. Dennis moved closer.

Her hand shot up from the bowels of the chair, the nine-inch steel knitting needle in her grip. She shoved it into his ear, ramming it through the eardrum.

Dennis Glover screamed in agony. The gun slipped from his hand, bounced off his foot and skidded across the carpet toward the wall. It veered off the baseboard and slid toward the hall, coming to rest near the door.

Star shoved him backward and dove for the weapon, banging her hip against the edge of the coffee table as she hit the floor.

Dennis Glover roared and pulled the needle from his ear.

He grabbed for Star and she scrambled past him, the pain in her hip making her cry out.

She got to the gun a second before Dennis threw himself on top of her. Rolling onto her back, she brought both knees up sharply, ramming his testicles against his body.

Dennis screamed and lashed out, punching her in the face. She tasted blood, but still she held the gun. With her free hand she cupped her fingers and slammed her palm against his injured ear, causing a suction that made him bellow with pain.

"Get off me you sonofabitch!" She slapped his ear again.

Dennis tried to pin her with his body.

"No! Get off me!" She slammed the heel of her hand into his chin, crunching his lower jaw against his upper one. His teeth sank into his tongue. He screamed but held on. Blood ran down his chin. His hand was over hers, fighting her for the gun.

"You bastard!" she screamed directly in his face, holding his hand with her free hand, attempting to wrestle him off her. She tried to pry his fingers loose, to pull one back and break it, but her sweaty skin kept slipping on the latex gloves.

"Go on, fight me, *fight me!*" he yelled, his eyes hard and cold. "I like it. You're not gonna stop me, I'm still gonna kill you."

She felt the barrel of the gun being jammed into her stomach. He was trying to fit his finger over hers, to force her to pull the trigger.

Her wrist was near breaking. She couldn't hold him much longer.

Dennis Glover's bloody mouth curved into a hideous grin, raining laughter down on her sweaty face.

"Laugh at this, asshole!" She slammed the heel of her hand under the tip of his nose, ramming the cartilage backward, breaking it. A fragment tunneled into his brain, short-circuiting his movements, making him jerk in convulsions.

His grip on the gun loosened. Star turned the weapon and pulled the trigger.

The bullet tore into Dennis Glover's abdomen, whirling like a drill through his liver. It hit bone and veered off through his kidney and out his left buttock. The flattened slug buried itself in the cream-colored wall next to a framed Varnette Honeywood print depicting colorful black churchgoers on a Sunday morning.

Star scrambled backward on the rug until her shoulders touched the wall. She pressed her back against it, holding the gun stiffly out in front of her with both hands.

Tears ran down her face, and her nose ran, but still she held the weapon, watching Dennis Glover flopping around the floor.

His body jumped as if he were being controlled by invisible strings. He tried to sit up.

"Don't," she said, releasing another bullet into the chamber. "Don't."

His head turned toward her, his eyes blind. He fell back on the carpet, vomited blood,0 and was still.

She sat rooted, waiting. She could hear Jake's loud wailing from the kitchen. The only other sound was the old wooden schoolhouse clock in the hall, ticking off the seconds.

Dennis Glover was silent.

Finally, she got up. Her hip was on fire and pain shot down her stiff legs. Blood ran from her skinned knee. A nasty bruise had already appeared on her left calf. She wiped her nose on the back of her hand.

"Jesus," she whispered.

She walked over to Dennis Glover. His eyes were open, fixated on the ceiling.

Holding the weapon straight up, she crouched and touched his carotid artery; nothing, no pulse.

Still watching him, she backed out into the hall and pulled the phone from the carpet there. She used her thumb to punch the talk button and 911.

"Police Emergency." The clerk's voice came through the earpiece.

"This is Detective Lieutenant Duvall, Precinct Seventeen, Homicide." Her voice sounded calm and detached. Inside, she wondered who was speaking.

"I need assistance at 3065 Salisbury Road. There's been a break-in and a shooting. It's my home."

"Are you all right, Lieutenant?"

"Yes. Please notify Captain Lewis and Detective Paresi of the Homicide unit, and also Internal Affairs. I've fired my weapon in self-defense."

"Someone's on the way, Lieutenant. Do you need an E.A.?"

"Yes, send the ambulance and notify the coroner's office. Thank you."

She hung up the phone.

Jake was scratching at the door, his cries loud and insistent. She pushed it open and picked him up. She carried the cat and the phone to the front door and opened it.

The first rays of the sun were just breaking through the night sky. When she was a rookie, working graveyard, this had been her favorite time of day.

She walked out onto the porch and put the cat down. The bright red impatiens in terra-cotta pots on both sides of her door caught her eye.

"My God." She started to sob. "My God." Tears dripped off her chin. She stood there clutching the phone. "Oh, Pop." Her legs gave way. She sat heavily on the top step. "It's over, Daddy, it's over."

She put her head in her lap and cried.

Jake rubbed against her lacerated legs. She wiped her eyes and nose with her hand.

"It's over." She reached for the cat and pulled him into her lap.

In the distance she heard the sound of sirens.